MOTHER TONGUE

A LOST LANGUAGE HOLDS UNSPEAKABLE POWER

ALSO BY DAN CRAY

The Reality Meltdown

Piercing Maybe

Friends From 4 A.M.
(Short Stories)

Soaring Stones:
A Kite-Powered Approach To
Building Egypt's Pyramids
(Nonfiction)

MOTHER

TONGUE

DAN CRAY

Published by Third Quandary Books
An imprint of Delcominy Creations, LLC
531 Main St., Ste. 231
El Segundo, CA 90245

Edited by Betsy Mitchell
Cover Design by Jeroen Ten Berge

Mother Tongue/ Dan Cray
Library of Congress Control Number: 2018911470
ISBN 978-1-940317-08-3 (hardcover)
ISBN 978-1-940317-09-0 (paperback)
ISBN 978-1-940317-10-6 (ebook)

For Jane
Autumnal Spark and island-spotter.

And, for Mom
Always the remedy.

MOTHER TONGUE

A LOST LANGUAGE HOLDS UNSPEAKABLE POWER

ONE

The moment Jon Wanamaker's dizziness lifted, he saw words. Not handwriting, not electronic characters, but actual printed text, his thoughts and actions suddenly written out before his eyes in heartless, cosmos-black lettering that jabbed into, and across, his field of vision.

He couldn't see his arms, or his legs, though he did see words indicating he couldn't see his arms or legs. The wildfire roaring toward him, the acrid smoke stench, the boulder-strewn Sirretta River Trail... all of it had transformed into words, streaming in front of a muted, frozen, wallpaper-like version of normal. Even Ernie Renssalear, his hiking buddy, was reduced to two-dimensional text.

What the hell?

Panicked, Jon took a breath—or was it just the text saying he did?—and force-fed himself some calming thoughts. *It's a hallucination,* he reassured himself. *Just my messed-up head giving me a crazy, analog view of the world... like taking a picture using infrared instead of visible light. It'll shift back in a few minutes.*

Which didn't explain why it had happened now, some two years since the last time his vision had suddenly flickered from normal to text. Drenched in sooty sweat, he knew he needed to focus on escaping the wildfire... but how could he? He watched the words closely, hoping they might simply scatter and be gone. Moments later they did, his vision flickering back to normal. Only a few words remained, ethereal and soundless, careening in haphazard patterns.

He felt a smack to his face, and heard Ernie shouting.

"Yeah... I'm okay," Jon managed. "The heat got me, but I'm good."

He wasn't, but the raging wildfire urged otherwise. The blaze raced along the ridges adjacent to the trail, incinerating the September-yellow brush blanketing California's Sierra Nevada mountains. Fire breaks—the clear-cut bands carved into hillsides—looked like zebra stripes across the otherwise charred mountains. Even the sky seemed aflame, scarred by sickening orange streaks.

Jon shook off what was left of the streaming words then lurched after Ernie, who was already scampering up the trail. Sweat dripped into his eyes from the matted tips of his dark bangs, a minor inconvenience compared to the billowing, cough-inducing ash. The medium complexion which kept people from guessing his ancestry had turned dark, and gritty, from the soot.

Thirty minutes earlier, during their casual Sunday hike, the ridges bordering the Sirretta River Trail had been a breathtaking blend of granite boulders and autumn grass. Now... Jon didn't know how, or where, the wildfire had started, but a bomb blast couldn't have sent it roaring through the hills any faster. If he was half the trail master that people assumed when they found out he was Native American, he'd have led Ernie out alongside the first bounding, fleeing mule deer. Instead, they had waited several precious minutes, until billowing, bruised smoke transformed the gorgeous, azure sky into a hellish-hued dome.

He glanced at Ernie, who had hiked the area since childhood. Day-old growth powdered his friend's chin, decades-old engine grease underscored his fingernails. His T-shirt and hiking shorts were as sweat-soaked as Jon's.

"Never seen a fire move so fast," Ernie said, slowing so they could catch their breath. "One more ridge, we reach Blackmule Gulch. That's our way out. Problem is, as fast as this thing's moving..."

He didn't need to finish. They both knew there was no outrunning a wildfire, especially the drought and wind-driven variety. Jumping into the nearby Sirretta river wouldn't help; temperatures at the heart of a wildfire reached 1,500 degrees Fahrenheit, and the river, though crazy fast, wasn't very deep.

Flames reflected in Ernie's eyes and ash speckles dotted his shaved, white hair... *the same ash I'm feeling in my lungs*, Jon knew. Though slender and athletic, Jon wasn't in the same shape as he was a few years back, when he spent his mornings jogging.

They heard a crack; something ricocheted off the nearby granite outcroppings.

"That sounded like gunfire!" Jon said.

Was someone shooting at *them?* A teacher and a bus driver? In the middle of a wildfire? They shouted at the unburned pine stands, thinking maybe someone was trying to signal for help... but the answer was more gunfire. A bullet struck the ground near Jon, kicking up dirt.

Ernie's eyes went wide. "Move!"

They sprinted behind a trailside boulder, their only cover. Jon's mind flashed to his fifth-grade students, who knew he was thirty-six but liked to tease him that he was pushing forty. Right now, the sniper seemed to be pushing back. He shuddered. Sure, the elders of his *Kaagwaantaan* clan insisted he was ageless, a continuance of an ongoing Tlingit heritage... *but he was only thirty-six.*

His vision flickered; the text reappeared, this time superimposed over normal life, like augmented reality software run amok. Heart pounding, he watched the streaming words grow in size and clarity, until it was clear they were becoming exactly what he feared most.

Ribbons.

He said it like someone coming down with a cold, denying the miserable week in store. *Ribbons...* because they reminded him of the sentences that streamed across digital ribbon boards, but also because the name made them sound benign, and he was determined to consider them benign. They gushed out of the ether from who-knows-where, written in what seemed like thousands of languages... including a few from Jon's native, endangered tongue. Some swarmed but most streamed past, Doppler style, describing what he was doing, and seeing, even what he was feeling. He watched them assemble into looming sentences that scrolled across his eyesight. Touching them did nothing; his fingers passed through each spectral letter.

He shook his head vigorously, imagining he could toss the ribbons the way a dog sprayed bath water. *What a time to be hallucinating*, he thought. What was he going to tell Ernie? His friend wasn't going to want to hear about crazy, floating words in the middle of a life-and-death situation.

"Sorry, I was..." he started.

"Yeah, whatever, just go!" Ernie said, pushing him.

The ribbons faded... mostly. A few persisted.

"What about the gunman?" Jon said.

"He gets us, the cremation's free."

They leaped out from behind the boulder and took off toward the ridge. Flames lashed across the trail, their heat smacking Jon like a devil's shove, but he managed to stagger forward. More gunfire rang out, pinging left, right, and behind them. "Like it's intentional," Jon muttered between coughs. "Like we're being herded."

As they approached the ridge, searing heat boiled what little sap remained in the drought-parched pine groves, exploding their bark into blazing cinder. Jon glanced trailside and stopped short. A smoke-shrouded figure was crossing the river chasm, walking tightrope fashion over a withered rope bridge that looked like something Tom Sawyer might have built... and the guy was carrying a rifle. *The sniper*, Jon knew. Whoever it was looked prizefighter-large and just as beefy, with shredded clothes and wild hair, but Jon couldn't make out much more. Terrified, he tugged Ernie toward the ridge line.

"*Onatay!*" the sniper shouted, his voice strangulated.

Jon gasped. His dead grandmother was the only person who knew his Tlingit name.

"I'll blast the words right out of your head!" the sniper shouted over the roar of water and flame. "I'll steal your final shot at The Race!"

Jon backed away, startled. The sniper seemed to know about the ribbons... and that his career objective was to win The Race, a term he only used around friends and family.

So many things happened in the second that followed, Jon wasn't certain about the order of events. The sniper aimed his rifle; the rope snapped; wildfire roared to the far edge of the chasm, its searing heat transforming the rope crossing into a line of flame. The sniper plummeted toward the river, legs down, chin up, rifle raised. His body sliced into the rapids and disappeared.

"Holy shit," Ernie said.

———————

More than three thousand miles away, in Boston's Fenway Park, Razor Castillo signaled the umpire for time. The sold-out crowd went silent as the lanky pitcher walked to the back of the mound, dropped to his knees, and put his head in his glove. Teammates jogged in from their infield positions to see what was wrong, but Razor's catcher, a mailbox in a mask, motioned them back.

Razor looked up at him with a vacant stare. "I just saw someone fall, bro... I saw someone drop into a river."

TWO

Even as the wildfire and the phantom text raged, Jon couldn't keep from staring at the spot where the sniper had plunged into the Sirretta river. Trivia sprang to mind: third fastest river in North America, more than 100 drowning deaths in forty years. *No way the guy survived... right?* He heard an engine roar, saw a fire-fighting bomber dumping pink retardant onto a nearby pine stand. When his eyes darted back, he saw the sniper's beefy figure emerging from the water, looking up in their direction.

Jon gave Ernie a push and they scrambled away, headlong through dense smoke, trying to distinguish trail from terrain. Cresting the ridge, they saw their way out: Lake Isadora, a cobalt comma strung between the upper and lower Sirretta River canyons, spanning some fifteen Sierra Nevada miles. The shoreline had boulders, brush, and a dock lined with aluminum fishing boats right where their trail ended, in Blackmule Gulch. Ernie had one of the boats hot-wired in less than two minutes.

"Pretty smooth for a bus driver," Jon called, climbing aboard.

Ernie flashed his middle finger. "Shut up and steer us out of here."

Jon squeezed the throttle, just as a gunshot struck the bow. *Already?* They ducked as the boat surged away, two more shots pinging off the dock as they left. A shadowy figure matching the sniper's size and shape stood between smoke plumes on the ridge, looking wet, hairy and disheveled, his glowing green eyes reflecting the fire. Then the smoke enveloped him. By the time the next smoke pocket formed, he was gone.

"Burned?" Ernie said.

A sickening yet satisfying thought, but Jon wasn't so sure. The boat's engine groaned and ash particles rained upon them as they sped across the gulch, a watery wrecking yard for truck-sized boulders that foolish water skiers used as an obstacle course.

"Finally got cell service so—what the hell is that?" Ernie said, pointing.

A massive red buoy bobbed nearby... with stripes, struts, and hooks that reminded Jon of a buoy he had seen before moving to the Sirretta Valley... a buoy forever engrained in his memory. *What if the sniper knows about the buoy, same as he knew everything else about me?* He lifted his binoculars. Sure enough, a wolf's head logo no bigger than a child's hand was painted below the hook.

"Like the one in Rowock," he mumbled, shaken... then zoomed the binoculars. "Except there's a bottle floating next to it, tethered to a strut."

"So?"

Jon hadn't realized Ernie could hear him. "So... long story, but we should grab it. I think it's connected to the sniper."

Ernie looked at him with an irritated, questioning expression. "Someone's got a gun aimed at our heads and you want to fish a bottle from the lake?"

"We leave trash, I lose my Indian card."

"I've tasted your dried salmon," Ernie said, grabbing the binoculars. "You should've lost the card years ago."

Jon cut the engine, allowing them to coast toward the buoy, then leaned over the bow. His distorted doppelganger peered back from the lake, watery ripples contorting his dark eyebrows into mushrooms. The tethered bottle soon pierced the reflection, looking like a wine jug without the narrow spout. Only an inch of its transparent glass floated above the surface; something heavy was inside.

"Got it," he said, using an oar to pull the bottle close. "Look, you can read what's on the interior paper, right through the glass."

The words were printed in faded, dappled ink.

Sidney, Upsweep, Amelynd. Because Bonnicksen lies.

Startled, Jon nearly dropped the oar. He recognized those words.

"So, what's inside?" Ernie said, grabbing the bottle.

He turned it over so they could see the contents. Jon gasped.

"*Ku'cta-qa*," he said.

Ernie let out a yell then flung the bottle overboard. Jaw trembling, he turned away. Jon wanted to turn away too, but he couldn't. He had to look again, to make sure he hadn't imagined what he'd seen. The bottle floated a few feet away from the boat, bobbing and rolling with the whitecaps. Jon stared. The next swell hit.

The bottle lifted and spun, revealing a mutilated brain.

Ernie was still on the phone with the 911 operator when the Lake Patrol roared up to Blackmule Gulch. Their thirty-foot boat was overkill at sleepy Isadora, as were the two armed officers on board, but after everything that had happened Jon was grateful to see them.

He didn't see them for long. Reality flickered to ribbons; the officers, their boat, and the lake transformed to words. Jon scowled, hoping the scrolling sentences were just stragglers—smaller ribbons that looked like gnat lines flying across a summertime yard. They weren't. These were the rare variety... the looming, throbbing ribbons that had cost him his marriage.

Another flicker; "normal" returned. He shook off the dizziness, then joined Ernie with the Lake Patrol officers, who escorted them to their pontooned headquarters once they realized the two had stolen a boat. More questions followed... this time by a sheriff's deputy.

Carl Sharp looked like every mountain cop Jon had ever seen: short hair, mustache, arms held away from his body to keep his elbows from scraping his holstered gun. Allergies kept him sniffling as he seated Jon and Ernie inside the Lake Patrol's HQ, which had a sweeping view of the valley's two lakeside communities: Quail Point, with its looming ski resort at the lake's northern end, and the more pedestrian Wofford Notch, Jon's current hometown, seated along the western shore. An aging laptop computer sat on Sharp's desk, its screen wiggling each time a lake swell made the dock rise and fall.

They waited for the deputy to say something but it didn't happen right away... and when it did, it wasn't what they were expecting.

"I hear you're gonna propose to Virginia Hanafin," Sharp said, to Ernie.

Jon and Ernie exchanged glances. Neither had said any such thing to the Lake Patrol officers, but people always knew other people's business in the Sirretta Valley. Sharp and Ernie traded pleasantries about Virginia, a postal clerk who doubled as Sirretta Valley royalty, the daughter of the grandson of one of the valley's pioneers... or something like that, Jon wasn't entirely sure. All he knew was that the Hanafins built the ski resort, and their name was on street signs, ranches, businesses, and smoky back rooms throughout the valley.

"I don't know what the boat owner is going to say," Sharp continued, still looking at Ernie, "but since it turns out he's one of Virginia's cousins, I'm guessing you're clear. So, you're free to go."

That was fast, Jon thought as they stood up.

"Uh-uh. Not you," Sharp said, to Jon.

Ernie hesitated, but Jon told him he'd call him later.

Sharp waited until Ernie was gone. "I understand you teach a controversial class up at the grade school," he said.

Oh, for crying out loud, Jon thought.

"It's just a language class," he said.

"I hear you," Sharp said. "But I also hear people tell me this is an English-only kind of place."

"You must mean the Sirretta Valley is English-only, right?" Jon said. "Because America sure isn't."

Sharp didn't react. Glancing above the deputy's shoulder, Jon saw the erect, droid-like barbeques of an evacuated lakeside campground through the Lake Patrol's rear window.

"Look, my program teaches endangered Native American languages to elementary students, mostly Tlingit and Paiute," Jon said, feeling obligated to offer details. "Until tomorrow, anyway. It's on the budget bubble."

There were no other Tlingits in the Sierras, but that was a detail the local Paiutes hadn't seemed to mind when they recruited him to teach the program. The rest of the community... well, that was a different story, especially in Wofford Notch. Where Quail Point was fast becoming the Sierra Nevada's answer to Park City, the

Notch lobbied for English-only curriculums and anything anti-cosmopolitan.

Sharp nodded. "You'll have another week on the job. Virginia tells me the school district plans to postpone layoffs until then."

Jon sat back in his chair, incredulous. *Only in this valley would a sheriff hear about school budgeting decisions before a teacher*, he thought.

"Here's what I don't get," Sharp said. "You're running from a sniper yet you veer toward a buoy rather than getting as far away as you can. Why?"

Jon knew the question would come up eventually. "We saw our cell service pop up and figured we needed to throttle down to hear the 911 operator," he said. "It was stupid, but in the heat of the moment it seemed like a good idea."

Sharp nodded and scribbled into his incident log. Jon was pretty sure he wasn't buying the answer.

"What about that 'Sidney' note? Make any sense to you?

Yes, he thought. "No," he said.

Sharp nodded again. "I ran your name while the officers questioned you at the lake. Seems you had some trouble with the law in Alaska," Sharp said.

Now the real mess begins. The image of a lifeless, nine-year-old girl floating in an icy pond surfaced in his mind. He wanted to tell Sharp the details, to make sure the sheriff understood he had nothing to do with her death... but he could already tell that wasn't going to satisfy things.

"I was cleared of all charges," he said, sticking with the simple truth.

Sharp nodded. "Yes, you were."

From the sound of his voice, it didn't matter. Sharp studied his notes for a moment before continuing. "Lake Patrol tells me you started speaking in a foreign language after you told them about the brain," he said.

Jon couldn't stifle a small laugh. "Just one word," he said. "*Ku'cta-qa.*"

"Hold up. Koosh—what?"

Jon spelled it for him.

"Huh... Kóosh-daa-kaa," Sharp said, slowly parroting Jon's pronunciation. "And that's, what, a Middle Eastern word?"

Jon released a strained breath. This wasn't the first time someone in the Sirretta Valley equated him with the Middle East... a not-so-subtle way of suggesting he might be tied to a terrorist group. "It's a Tlingit word," he said. "I'm originally from a Tlingit clan on Prince of Hollis island."

"Prince of...?" Sharp said, jotting notes.

"Prince of Hollis, about twenty-five miles off the Alaskan coast. Lived in Rowock, one of the little towns there."

"And you say you're a Klansman."

Jon wasn't sure whether to laugh or cry. "I'm Jon Wanamaker of the *Kaagwaantaan*—the wolf clan. That's 'clan' with a C, not a K."

"So... Tlingit, wolf clan, from Alaska. Meaning you're what, an Eskimo?"

"An Indian. There's a difference," Jon said.

"I'll put Native American," Sharp said.

"Whatever. The Tlingits I know call themselves American Indians."

Sharp looked uncomfortable writing 'Indian' on his tablet. "I thought Indians had red skin. Even half-covered in soot, you're as white as I am."

No one's as white as you are, Jon thought.

"What's 'koosh-daa-kaa' mean?" Sharp said.

Jon sat a little taller. "*Ku'cta-qa* is a shape-shifting land otter from my grandmother's Tlingit stories, a creature that saves you in a moment of need."

Sharp looked up from his notes, leaned back in his chair. "And saying its name in reference to the floating brain...?"

Jon shrugged. "What you might call a prayer," he said. "My way of hoping *Ku'cta-qa* will help."

As Sharp rolled his eyes, a knock at the open door interrupted. An Asian doctor Jon knew far too well stood in the doorway, brushing lint fibers off her cream-colored lab coat. The dock's sway seemed to bother her, and maybe the dock itself.

"Excuse me, Doctor," Sharp said, "but I'm in the middle of questioning—"

"In the middle?" she said. "I was in the middle of treating a firefighter for smoke inhalation."

Sharp stood up. "Sarah, someone dumped a brain in the lake," he said. "With the roads temporarily closed from the fire, whoever did it might be just as trapped up on this mountain as the rest of us. Meaning any information I can get before everything reopens would be a big help. That okay with you?"

She didn't look like it was okay. "What's *he* doing here?" she said, casting a stink eye at Jon.

Seeing Sharp register the recognition in Sarah's voice and eyes, Jon figured he'd head off the obvious question. "Sarah... I mean, Dr. Ushida... she's a good friend of my ex-wife," he said.

Sharp's eyebrows hoisted into the "oooh, awkward" expression. He removed the bottled brain from a leather bag and handed it to Sarah. Inside, Jon could see the note, which appeared laminated, and the deteriorated brain's spongy tissues. Everything flickered; the ribbons slammed Jon yet again, but this time he fought them off by focusing on the ghastly brain.

"Wanamaker here pulled this out of Blackmule Gulch," Sharp said to Sarah, then turned to Jon. "I'll be in touch. Meantime you're free to go."

"Wait," Sarah said. She tilted her head to look inside the bottle before glancing at Jon. "Pretend I like you for a minute and tell me: did you find it just like this? No liquid inside, just brain and note?"

He nodded, thinking it was an odd question.

"Because this isn't a bottle," she continued, turning to Sharp. "It's a specimen jar. An old one too; it has a metal cap. That might mean a vacuum-seal, but even so, this tissue's too pliant to survive without chemicals."

"You're suggesting it wasn't in the lake for very long," Sharp said.

"Correct, but I don't think it's a fresh brain, either," she said, holding the jar up to the light for a better look. "Each lobe has slits from angular incisions, and pits where the tissues oozed together after being drilled for core samples—all telltale signs of lab study. Look: the meninges have been shaved, too."

She turned the jar, angling it to the light. Her dark hair fell to the side, exposing a polished roadrunner earring that clinked against the glass. Sharp studied the earring for just a moment too long and was rewarded with the same stink eye Sarah had given Jon.

"If I were to guess," she said, "I'd say someone took it from a laboratory or university, drained the preservatives so they could add the note, then tossed it in the lake."

"So, not a homicide," Sharp said, giving Jon a long look. "Though we might still press charges when we find out who dumped the thing... and why."

Sarah pointed a thumb at Jon. "I hope he's more open with you than he was with his wife," she said, passing the jar back to Sharp. "If you need to waterboard him, let me know."

Jon let it pass.

"The only torture here is the bad wireless on this dock," Sharp said. "One simple word-search for 'Amelynd,' it won't connect."

Sarah did a double-take. "Did you say 'Amelynd?'"

Jon shifted, uneasy, as Sharp nodded. He hoped Sarah didn't make the connection, or if she did, that she didn't know many details.

"How do you spell that?" she said.

Sharp raised the bottle and turned it so she could see the note. Sarah nodded right away, then gave Jon a vindictive smile.

"It's your lucky day, Deputy," Sarah said. "I know someone who can tell you about Amelynd... and it just so happens Jon knows her too."

THREE

Shifting to ease the pins and needles in her shoulders, Remedy Conover watched a sand rivulet cascade from a ceramic palisade into a miniature vacuum pump, which began the cycle again. The so-called sand mobius was the latest Pet Rock, but Remedy couldn't help but imagine it as an hourglass, its sands counting the time she had left before George Klase ended their interview.

"I've never heard of Amelynd Island," Klase said while typing on his smartphone, "and I've never seen it listed on an atlas. Guess I shouldn't be surprised, a reporter coming in here trying to fabricate a news story. Are you the reason I have some cop leaving me messages about the same place?"

Remedy scribbled his response into her notebook. "No," she said, "but if it makes you feel better that same cop's been leaving me messages too, for three days now." She didn't say what she was really thinking: that her friend had a big mouth. *Sarah should know better than to tip a sheriff about a story I haven't finished reporting yet,* she thought, irritated.

Klase, a senior project coordinator for the U.S. Department of Defense, was in his late 50s with green eyes, a dark flattop, and a jaw so square it could have been the model for the original Superman cartoons. He wore a dark suit with several pins on the lapel, and fielded her questions as if they were no more important than a single grain of the sand mobius displayed on his desk.

"Let me get this straight," Remedy said, tugging her blouse so it wouldn't touch her aching torso. "You're saying Amelynd doesn't exist because it can't be found on any world atlas?"

"That's right. Every inch of surface land on this planet is atlased. Been that way since the 1800s."

Klase didn't bother to look at Remedy. Most people didn't, in her experience; disability was an uncomfortable sight. She gave him credit for braving the occasional glance at her atrophied shoulders. Between that, her cherubic face, and a dime-store shoulder bag, Remedy knew she looked harmless—a real hindrance when questioning guys like Klase. The fact she'd walked into the DOD's Porterfield office using a kitchen broom as an improvised cane probably didn't help much either.

"Actually, that's not true," she said. "Ever since the second world war, the U.S. has admitted to using small islands for training and refueling, and the locations of those islands were classified, meaning they didn't appear on any standard atlas."

Klase lowered his phone. "Who are you with again?"

"The *Sirretta Valley Mountaineer*. But you and your staff know me from six years ago, when I was with the *Dallas Morning News*."

"Ah... the woman who wrote the ordnance overpayment story. Buddy of mine got a reprimand because of that one."

"Your buddy was one of the lucky ones," she said.

He placed the phone atop a paperwork pile. "Look, Ms. Conover, I get that you pulled a few favors to get in here, but let's get down to it," he said. "You're a long way from your newspaper's little mountain town, and I see you're dealing with other... challenges... so I'm going to clarify what I said, in case the elevation change from there down to Porterfield is confusing you a bit.

"No, every island in the Pacific isn't listed on Google Maps, but they're certainly on the maritime charts. At some point every university with a geography department began charting the seas, and that, my dear, marked the end of uncharted islands."

Remedy could overlook him mentioning her "challenges." People often equated physical disability with mental deficiency, and besides, her broom reinforced the image. Calling her "dear," on the other hand, was unforgivable.

"Most of those mapping projects were funded by the DOD," she said, a statement rather than a question.

Klase sat back and sighed. "Yes, but if you're implying we could somehow hide the presence of an entire island, that's just not the case, not in this day and age. Even if we wanted to, the technology in every spy satellite can zero in on an amoeba swimming in the Pacific. So whether you put an island on the charts or not, these days it's a known commodity. Quite simply, you can't hide a land mass anymore."

"But the Navy can still restrict access to islands, right?"

"That's right, they restrict access to U.S. government-owned islands where they conduct Naval training exercises. Same thing with islands where we have use agreements thanks to a treaty with the local government."

"So, if an island isn't in any standard atlas, and there's no access even if people get there... then from a public standpoint, that's an unknown island."

Klase issued the kind of scowl worn by a plumber just splattered with sewage. "Give it up, Ms. Conover. There's no story here, no matter how hard you try to slant things."

Remedy decided it was her turn to sit back. The "s-word"—slant—always came up at some point in an uncomfortable interview, usually used by someone with something to hide.

"How many of these islands are there?" she said, twirling a finger through her short, ginger hair. "How many that the public has never heard of, being used by the Navy for undisclosed operations?"

"I really don't know," Klase said.

"You must have some idea," she said. "Ten? A hundred? Thousands?"

He eyed her for a moment, his eyes unblinking. "It depends on what you want to define as an island," he said.

"Anything big enough to get off your boat and walk on."

"Then you're probably talking about a thousand. But a lot of them are literally 50 feet by 100 feet, visible only in low tides. The Navy sites off of them."

"Sites?"

"Takes markings, for navigation purposes."

She nodded. "And how many of those islands are large enough to carry their own ecosystems, support their own plant and animal life, but small enough to ensure they don't appear on any but the most detailed oceanographic charts?"

"Again, I have no idea."

"Well, I do, Mr. Klase. Land use treaties and U.S. government property gives the DOD access to more than thirteen thousand islands worldwide, more than one-quarter of which do not appear on standard atlases and are restricted from public access. Amelynd is one of those islands."

Klase shifted, and for the first time his face let a hint of discomfort slip through the confident façade.

"It's a three-quarter-mile chunk of rock in the Pacific," Remedy continued, "about sixteen hundred miles southeast of Hawaii and roughly eighteen hundred miles east of Palmyra Atoll. I'm surprised you don't know about it. I'm told the Navy sometimes warns ocean vessels and aircraft that the region is off limits. Care to explain why?"

Klase shuffled paperwork without looking up. "Ms. Conover, I'm about done here. Yes, we have classified island operations as you've suggested, but Amelynd, if there is such a place, is not one of them. You have no story."

"Funny thing is," Remedy continued, ignoring his response, "Amelynd Island is not listed on any atlas, and I've yet to see it on any of the major maritime charts."

"Then perhaps it exists only in your mind," Klase said.

"I'm afraid not," she said. "You see, I've managed to obtain satellite images proving its existence."

For a split second Klase's eyes widened and his chin dropped by a fraction of an inch, but he was too seasoned in his job to allow more than that. Remedy straightened, as if ready to get up and leave. Then she dealt her ace.

"What can you tell me about Project Upsweep?" she said.

"Never heard of it."

"Oh, I think you have," she said. "Just like I think you're familiar with the name Erich Bonnicksen."

This time Klase stood up. "This meeting's over. There's nothing more I can comment on."

"Mr. Klase, please... if you don't talk, it only makes you look worse when the story's published."

He folded his arms. "From the sound of it, I'll be looking pretty bad no matter what."

She slapped her notebook shut, frustrated. "Look, I'm sorry about your buddy, the one you said got the reprimand, but I wasn't after him and I'm not after you. I'm after the truth. That's it."

"Never said you weren't. Doesn't mean I can help you."

Remedy studied him, waiting, hoping. Klase pressed his lips together so tight he looked like an infant refusing a spoonful of baby food... but he seemed deep in thought. More important, Remedy noticed, he wasn't ushering her from his office.

"Your overpayment piece... nominated for awards, wasn't it?" he said.

She nodded. "Pulitzer. Didn't win."

He cracked a smile. "Oh, it won. Hell, even after the legal expenses and bad PR you still probably saved the DOD several million by exposing those lousy contracts. And by the way, my buddy was an a-hole for helping arrange those deals in the first place. Just because I like his lunchroom stories doesn't mean I think he's good at his job. You, on the other hand..."

"My lunchroom stories suck," she said, with a half-smile.

"But you've got the job part nailed."

She lowered the notebook but didn't get up.

"I still have no official comment," Klase said, gesturing towards the door.

"Fine... what's your unofficial comment?" she said.

Klase took a deep breath.

"None of this gets attributed to me," he said while glancing around the office, as if to make certain the door and windows were sealed before speaking.

Remedy nodded.

"Project Upsweep ended four years ago," Klase said. "Yeah, the island's there, but the subjects... they're all gone. The place is abandoned."

Remedy shook her head. "I'm not buying it," she said. "There were at least fifteen people on Amelynd. Where'd they all go?"

"The project file says they're dead."

"Come on. Give me some credit here."

Her phone vibrated, then flashed another text message from Carl Sharp, the same sheriff who had left her four voicemail messages since Sunday afternoon.

"That's the truth, Ms. Conover, whether you want to believe it or not," Klase said, over the vibration sounds. "Look, you're right: the DOD was involved. Hell, we secured the damn thing. But we backed out after a white squall decimated the island."

"White squall?"

"A sudden, violent windstorm," he said. "White squalls roar up out of the sea in a matter of minutes. No dark, threatening clouds, no warning at all, except for some white-capped waves and light-colored cloud bands. This thing made landfall too, very rare. Wind gusts hit 175, sustained speeds never dropped below 140. That's the equivalent of a category five hurricane. Those Upsweep people—and there were twenty-three of them, not fifteen—they had no chance."

"You couldn't pull them out before it hit?"

Klase shook his head. "Wasn't for lack of trying. Let's just say the squall created some unusual conditions, and the politics too. Project organizers insisted we maintain the isolation protocol, same way NASA maintains their Mars biospheres."

Remedy's gut told her Klase was genuinely trying to help, so the only question was whether she could believe her gut. She thanked him for leveling with her, used her broom to push herself to her feet, then half-walked, half-staggered towards the door. The tingling sensation in her hands and arms told her to focus on what she was doing, but as she reached the door she couldn't resist one last glimpse at the sand mobius. Somehow, she thought, it now seemed to be counting the cover-up's remaining time rather than hers.

"One more thing, Ms. Conover."

Klase stepped away from his desk. "You've got some big stones," he said. "Coming in here like this, in your condition. Cornering me in a field office while I'm away from D.C. What newspaper did you say you're with again?"

"The *Sirretta Valley Mountaineer*."

He flashed a grin. "That a blog? Or one of those free throwaways that show up in my driveway?"

"Paid circulation of twelve hundred," she said.

"Jesus Christ," Klase said, between laughs. "How long you been working this story?"

She shrugged. "Couple years, off and on."

He nodded. "But not as a career move. I mean sure, it might get some attention, but it's not page-one material, certainly not something that someone who used to be a rising star with the *Dallas Morning News* would go after. No, I think you're inside on this. Some sort of axe you're grinding, am I right? Care to let me in on what set you down this path?"

"Not really."

He laughed again. Remedy didn't have anything to say, so she kept quiet.

"Then at least tell me this: why the broom? Why not use a cane?"

She shrugged. "A broom's more stable."

"And more unsettling, which I'm sure you don't mind. Function over fashion?"

"Whatever gets me from Point A to Point B," she said.

Klase ran his tongue over his bottom lip, as if weighing what she'd said. "Off-the-record... there's a civilian who might have some insights into what happened on that island. You might have heard of him, he's a pro baseball player. Razor Castillo."

She didn't follow baseball, so the name meant nothing. "He was on the island?" she said.

"No... not directly. Track him down, you'll see what I mean."

It wasn't much, but Remedy was glad to come away with something.

"One more thing," Klase said. "I have it on good authority the Project Upsweep file was doctored."

"Doctored? Wait, you don't mean...?"

"One of the subjects made it home," he said.

"And they're still alive?"

He nodded. "Didn't remember much. Babbled on about a memory gap, accused us of a deliberate wipe."

"Was it?"

"You shitting me? Outside of movies, the only guaranteed memory wipe is a kill. I just told you: the subject survived."

Klase looked away. "I can't say anything more," he said. "But he did make it home."

Remedy let the moment ripen before pushing for a name.

"Wanamaker," Klase said. "The guy's name was Jon Wanamaker."

FOUR

Five minutes after leaving Klase's office, Remedy's heart was still pounding. *I knew it*, she thought as her elevator descended from the DOD field office's sixth floor. *Jon was holding out on me. All that time, he covered it up. That bastard! How could he keep that from me? Why would he keep it from me?*

Her chest felt compressed and her mind reeled as she digested the real meaning behind what she had finally confirmed.

My husband was on Amelynd.

She shut her eyes, suppressing the bitterness, strangling unwelcome memories. *Ex-husband*, she corrected herself, reopening her eyes. Whatever his reasons, she figured they no longer mattered. This was now a national news story with a local angle. The fact she knew Jon personally was inconsequential... she hoped.

The strangers around her squeezed out of the car as soon as it reached the ground floor, but she waited until the doors attained a full yawn before she let go of the side rail. Walking was a recipe: plant broom, slide one leg forward, pull the other leg to catch up, repeat. Her broom bore evidence of the strain, its bristles curved and its blue paint flecked, a stain patch on the handle from the oils in her hand.

"No way you're a witch," a gray suited, balloon of a man said as she left the elevator. "So, maybe you have MS, like my sister."

She smiled. "Both, according to my boss."

The broom was embarrassing but the bristles generated a steadying, upward force against the downward push of her arm, a big advantage over the knob on a cane and much better than using Hearse—her disability scooter—or a wheelchair. Gray Suit gave her an encouraging smile as the elevator's mirrored doors shut. She watched the two halves of her reflection join together, convinced the image staring back looked mismatched. Up top, she saw a youthful face with endearing cheeks and ginger hair; down below, the atrophied shoulders and marionette-thin arms and legs. Her hands looked scrawny too, clinging to the worn-out broom. A turquoise blouse and dark pants masked some of her ordeal... but not enough of it.

She spotted Sarah out front, still wearing her lab coat from work. Scurrying workers at the DOD's unmarked Sirretta County facility formed a kaleidoscope of black suits, red dresses, blue jeans and delivery browns. Most of them stared as Remedy slide-staggered across the lobby, toward Sarah. One whispered "look at the drunk woman" to a colleague.

"I wish you'd use a cane, like everyone else," Sarah said, helping her walk from the building to the parking lot.

Remedy looked at the people watching her and shrugged. "Give me a cane, you may as well trip me," she said, then filled her in on what she'd learned from Klase.

"Jon was on Amelynd and he didn't say anything?" Sarah said. "We need to tell Sharp. Did he call you yet? I gave him your contacts."

"Yeah, and about that—"

"I know, I blew it," Sarah said. "But the chance to see Jon squirm..."

"Fine, but now I'll need to hurry up and touch base with Jon before the sheriffs figure out he's part of this and he clams up," Remedy said.

Sarah shook her head, reciting reason after reason they should contact Sharp right away, all of them legitimate.

"No," Remedy insisted. "I'm so close now, Sare. This story... the experiments, the cover-ups, and now maybe some famous baseball pitcher's involved... it's big."

"Meaning you've got what you wanted: the big career finale," Sarah said, shrugging off her lab coat, exposing an equally bland turtleneck. "And now you're in way over your head and you're not in the condition to handle it."

Typical Sarah, Remedy thought. Haughty attitude, never mincing words, and most irritating of all, on the mark.

"Hey, this finale's no more my choice than any of my other finales."

Sarah scoffed. "I'm not sure turning your ex into a career break is the best way to move on."

"I didn't plan on him being my career break... I just noticed he wasn't acting like himself when he left so I started doing a little research, you know?" she said, her broom's bristles straining as she slid her right foot forward.

"All I know is you're borderline progressive," Sarah said, then launched into a clinical diatribe on multiple sclerosis that Remedy relegated to background noise.

She felt like a voodoo doll, invisible pins and needles jabbing at her entire body. Tree trunks seemed to have replaced her arms and legs, all sluggish and numbed of most tactile sensation. Her hands acted as if everything she touched was slicked in butter. Worse, it was only noon but she already felt so wiped out she knew she needed to lie down for the rest of the day.

And yet here was Sarah, telling *her* about MS.

She swiveled herself into Sarah's silver sedan, not so much sitting down as falling onto the waiting seat, then slipped her shoes off. She only wore shoes for work and social events; the soles muted what was left of her tactility and balance. Clothes used to be fun, but these days her first-pressing Billie Holiday and the rest of its vinyl companions were her only leisure activity. Her wardrobe was all about comfort. Anything more form-fitting than her baggy silk blouse and knit pants meant friction against a stiff, aching body.

Sarah appeared behind the wheel a few seconds later, put on a pair of roadrunner earrings from the glove compartment, and started the car. Half an hour later, they approached the Sirretta Canyon's sleeping maw. The highway transformed into a tight, two-lane road bracketed by sheer rock on one side and the Sirretta River on the other. A sign at the entry blared death tolls and legal warnings, cautioning visitors not to swim in the dangerous river. Left unstated were the dozens killed by rockslides, animal encounters, or head-on collisions while maneuvering the serpentine roadway.

Sarah tackled the curves like a NASCAR driver, to Remedy's chagrin. Speckled granite, saffron grasses, and wandering livestock covered the steep slopes opposite the river gorge. The Sirretta churned and bubbled to the left of the road, gathering in deceptively calm pools before transforming to foaming rapids. Thrill-seekers inner-tubed the currents, Darwinism in action, then dropped out of sight as the gorge deepened. Soon road and river sat separated by a 200-foot drop, and the sheer rock walls receded into pine-speckled mountains.

Forty-five minutes and a four-thousand-foot elevation change later, they sped over a final hill and entered the Sirretta River Valley.

"Three hours from L.A., and a world apart," Remedy said.

"You got *that* right," Sarah said, with a more emphasis than Remedy expected.

Majestic, boulder-strewn peaks loomed over rolling hills. Turkey vultures rode thermals, ground squirrels dashed from hole to hole, and a scrawny coyote stared at passing cars from a nearby hill. Even during a week soured by the wildfire, which continued to redden the sun and pump black smoke above several mountains to the southeast, the valley's beauty seemed too extensive to shroud. Ahead, Remedy saw the pebble-piled twin dams—main and auxiliary—shouldering Lake Isadora. Once a set of gold rush communities, the Sirretta Valley now housed a different sort of gold: water, so precious in the drought-stricken west that Porterfield farmers often let fields lie fallow so they could sell their water shares to thirsty municipalities.

Sarah exited the highway near the valley's only traffic lights—two of them—and turned the car up a mountain incline toward Quail Point, the ski resort and rafting town at the northwest end of the lake. In the distance they saw whitecaps on Isadora, its waters languishing from the ashen sky and years of drought. Spindly tree branches reached out of the reservoir like the ribs of a fossilized giant, bones of contention between fishermen who insisted they attracted trout and businessmen fed up with unsightly trunks.

The winding highway begged slow traffic, and soon Sarah's sedan was fourth in a chain of cars, all trailing a hand-painted monstrosity of a camper truck that looked as if it had been rescued from a wrecking yard. Turnouts and angry horns failed to sway the driver, so everyone fumed until Wofford Notch, the next town along the road, provided a four-lane road for passing.

Remedy anticipated the satisfaction of eyeing the oblivious driver as they roared past, then noticed the camper's tinted window moving downwards.

"Sarah, wait! Look!"

The window opened just far enough for a hairy arm to reach out.

"There's a sign in his hand," Sarah said. "Can you read it?"

Remedy tried, but it had been a long day and her double-vision was setting in—another MS symptom.

"I can't tell. But he definitely wants us to see it."

Sarah slowed the sedan, to pull up even with the truck.

"It's just one word, Rem, in big, dark letters. It's..."

She gasped. Remedy strained, but couldn't make out the word.

"It's 'Upsweep,' Rem. The sign says 'Upsweep.' "

They looked at each other, startled.

"Pull over, up ahead," Remedy said. "There's a parking lot out front of the post office."

"I'm not sure that's a good idea."

Remedy bit her lip. "Maybe not, but whoever this guy is, he must have information for the story...and I need it."

"I don't know..."

"Just pull over!"

Sarah looked unhappy but moved them into the right lane, ahead of the truck, and signaled she was turning into the post office driveway. The hairy arm pulled back inside the truck, which then followed them into the lot.

Parking wasn't a problem; mail reached the valley around 11 a.m., so the "rush"—sometimes reaching five people inside the post office—was long over. Remedy could see Virginia Hanafin through the glass windows, twisting her dishwater blonde hair into a braid behind the front counter. A few yards away, a set of carved wood doors fronting the tiny Wofford Notch library looked sealed as well, no great surprise to Remedy since it was only open two days a week. A vacant field next to the post office was covered in overgrown weeds and yellowed grasses, the glass shards from broken bottles gleaming in the afternoon sun.

"Oh I don't know, Rem, this doesn't look very good," Sarah said. "I'm getting us out of here."

"No, wait, the guy from the truck's walking over."

The man approaching the car looked as if he planned to tear it apart with his bare hands. He wore a camouflage flak jacket and jeans caked with mud. A sheathed knife with an odd, concave shape hung from his belt, and a handgun peeked out from where it was strapped around his ankle. His shoulder-length hair and shaggy, matching beard looked soggy and matted. He smelled so bad, even at a distance, that Remedy found herself wrinkling her nose.

"Uh-uh... I'm leaving," Sarah said, putting the car in drive.

The man seemed to read her intent, breaking into a run as Sarah pulled away. Before Remedy had time to shout a warning something smashed through a side passenger window. The sedan surged forward as Sarah stepped hard on the gas, but it was too late. The man hung on the side of the car, one hand shoved through the window while the other gripped the curve of the roof.

Remedy forced her body into a half-turn and gave her broom handle a weak thrust in his direction, trying to push him from the car. His glass-covered hand hit the door lock, and a warning bell chimed from the dashboard as the passenger door swung open.

"Hey dirtbag, get off my car!" Sarah said. "Now!"

He swung himself inside. Remedy whacked at him with the broom handle, but didn't have the strength to deliver much more than a few pokes at his face and shoulder. He didn't seem to notice. Instead, he pulled the concave knife from his belt sheath, mumbled something she couldn't hear... and took dead aim at Sarah's head.

FIVE

Hands shaking, Erich Bonnicksen grabbed an FMR printout, accidentally dropped it, then picked it up again and confirmed the name at the top of the brain scan was that of Razor Castillo. He steadied himself enough to read the data, already aware of what he was about to find. Mouse models were one thing, but for this to be happening in a human, twice in two months...

"Hurry up, I ain't got time for this," Razor said.

The pitcher fingered his mustache as he reclined on a desk, feet propped up atop a filing cabinet, designer shirt unbuttoned to mid-chest. He seemed obsessed with clean teeth, checking them in a hand-mirror like a fixated model. At six-foot-seven, he literally sat *across* the room, his lanky physique defying media accusations that he once took performance-enhancing drugs. The bronzed, leathery skin on his hands and face spoke more about a childhood tending sugarcane fields than did the sports reports, which preferred focusing on the seven suspensions levied against him for fighting teammates, umpires, even spectators. If baseball legend held that Dominican ballplayers never drew walks because they had to hit their way off the island, Razor had warped the fable to fit his tempestuous personality.

"One moment, Mr. Castillo," Bonnicksen said.

He stared at the scan results, saw what he expected, and felt as if he might have a bowel movement. *This is going to put me with Newton, Einstein, and Darwin,* he thought. *It also just might kill me.* Everything in the results looked familiar—same as the scans he found on mice brains two years ago, and last month's scans on Percipient 7X, a middle-aged male assigned to identify thoughts or actions initiated by an isolated young woman tagged Exhibit C. He still couldn't stomach what had happened in those cases. *Wait until I.K. Emily hears about this,* he thought. He noticed his right hand covering his mouth and couldn't remember having moved it there.

"You say the image of the man falling into a river happened on Sunday," he said. "How come you waited three days to have me take a look? Our post-study terms are very clear: report issues within twenty-four hours."

"Hey, this is time out of my life," Razor said, while spitting a wad of chew at an office trash can—and missing. "My lady's waiting downstairs, and my other lady's waiting across town, know what I mean? I got a photo shoot in two hours, a signing in three, and then the clubbin' heats up at midnight. You think I want to spend what's left of my minutes hangin' with some school geek?"

Bonnicksen wondered when an elite think-tank like Cambridge's Sidney Institute had last been referred to as "some school," and its dean of applied science as a 'geek.' Maybe not so long ago on the geek part, he decided. He saw Razor staring at the floor, disinterested. Another balding, doughy man wearing glasses and a tie—why would a pro athlete care? Hadn't he himself just told friends the only thing his dark-suited wardrobe was missing was a pocket protector? Hadn't they told him, in return, that he wasn't trendy enough to wear a pocket protector anyway?

He double-checked his files on Exhibit C's most frequent test partner... her *percipient*... against Razor's file. Comparing files was always tricky business, but the basic brain activity mapped by the Functional Magnetic Imager wasn't all that different: think about food, a dedicated segment of the brain becomes active; focus on a color, another segment becomes active; and so on.

So... think about what another individual is seeing in an unknown location... was it possible the FMR results would also match? Bonnicksen looked at the paperwork and felt his stomach ice over. Sure enough: Razor's FMR patterns matched those he saw in Percipient 7X, who had worked with Exhibit C. He pulled paperwork on his earlier work with mouse models, preliminary trials that demonstrated certain mice had attempted to climb, run, or tunnel whenever a single, isolated companion mouse was doing so at the same time.

The canary mice, Bonnicksen later called them. Those mice weren't the issue, any more than Percipient

7X was an issue; none of the percipients were, which was the good news where Razor was concerned. The isolated companion, on the other hand... the *agent*... whether mouse or human, the agent was always the dangerous one, the one with back-channel brain processes so strong that other randomly chosen individuals were able to gauge their actions and experiences from afar. The agents were the test subjects Bonnicksen couldn't stop thinking about, especially Exhibit C... the woman who nearly killed everyone in the lab, using only her brain.

Oh God, he thought.

Exhibit C and her percipient were part of an active research program; Razor wasn't. His program, Project Upsweep, had ended four years earlier. If Razor was suddenly picking up impressions from his agent without even trying, it meant that agent's backchannel brain processes were even stronger than Exhibit C's.

"I, uh... I won't lie to you, Mr. Castillo, I think there's a chance what I'm seeing is a problem. Have you had any other experiences like the one Sunday afternoon? Any other time you felt as if... how did you put it... as if you were looking through someone else's eyes?"

Razor pushed back the sleeves on his shiny, silver shirt, which smelled of engineered fabrics.

"No, and I don't want it happening no more," he said. "Winning games is big-time stuff, and I got enough stress as it is. Just give me something to get rid of this mental crap, got it?"

Bonnicksen felt fear clamping his stomach like a ghostly hand, and found himself wishing Razor would somehow revert to the cash-starved minor leaguer of four years ago rather than the hot-headed pitching icon he'd become. At least that would make it easier to do what would have to be done.

"You spent three months in my program, and you still don't have a clue how important this is, do you," he said. "How dangerous it is."

Razor hopped off the desk and walked over to Bonnicksen. "Only one thing dangerous here, that's you mouthin' off to my face," he said. "Your program was nothing to me, just a few bucks for a kid trying to keep a baseball dream alive, that's it. Four years later, I'm still trying to forget everything about those twelve weeks of my life, including you and your useless project."

"Well it wasn't so useless. I checked my records. You gave us some of the most convincing data we've had."

"Yeah, well I'm good at more than games, you know."

"In this case, you were apparently better than most. You gave us a location lock four times, and you had seventeen pattern locks, nine climate locks, even one scent lock. I mean, a scent lock—you knew someone was smelling rosemary, in real time, even though they were isolated on the other side of the world. That was a first for us, Mr. Castillo. Are you sure you haven't had anything unusual happen since the project ended?"

Razor grinned, flashing his straight, white teeth. "Struck out twelve one night against Seattle."

The pitcher seemed to notice Bonnicksen's blank, uncaring expression.

"Fine, geek-man, so you don't like baseball," he said. "No, I've never had this happen until now, not since your experiments anyway. Just tell me what the problem is and solve it before I knock you through the wall, *comprende*? I can't do my job with freak-show images inside my head."

Bonnicksen answered with a jittery laugh he didn't recognize, something an animated creature might use while watching a mallet head toward its face.

"What you saw on the mound," he said, "was the result of an anomalous mind-matter interaction."

Razor held a curled palm near his genitals and mock-stroked. "*Inglés* or *Español*, man. None of that geek-talk."

Bonnicksen put the files on his desk. "Look: our brains have processes for acquiring information from other people without any direct contact. You helped demonstrate as much in our study four years ago."

"Yeah, then why you so freaked?" Razor said.

Bonnicksen wasn't sure how to answer, so he asked a question instead.

"Who was your agent?"

"I got the best, man, dude got me a signing bonus worth—"

"Not your sports agent. In the experiments four years ago you were the percipient, the guy trying to sense the composition and character of the place where another person, the 'agent,' was stationed. Who was your agent?"

"Bro, I don't remember—some Eskimo, I think. You can look it up in your records, right? All I know was you guys handed me a check and times were different for me then. That's all I was here for, the dough."

Bonnicksen nodded. He knew they never had an Eskimo in the program, but 'some Eskimo' told him exactly who the agent in question would have been... and the answer didn't come as a surprise, either.

"I have to make a call," he said, wondering whether I.K. Emily might solve the problem... unless she *was* the problem, he realized. In the month since Exhibit C, it was clear they had divergent views on how to handle people like Razor's agent. He wanted containment; she wanted results. That probably meant a mixed message for the... personnel... assigned to manage the situation.

"Forget your call, man, how 'bout we get to helping me, now?" Razor said. "You made my mess, you solve it."

Bonnicksen frowned. The pitcher had an inadvertent point: why rely on I.K. Emily's personnel when he had his own in-house solution?

"Go pack a bag, and hurry—and tell anyone who tries to stop you to get lost," he said. "We're booking a plane to California."

"Plane, hell. I've got games all week, and a life."

Bonnicksen felt a chill run down his spine, thinking about what had happened with Exhibit C.

"We don't get to your agent, you're not going to have either. None of us will."

"You jerkin' me, man?"

Bonnicksen felt like he might lose his lunch.

"This is an incredibly dangerous situation," he said. "We wait, people die... a lot of people. Maybe even all people."

Razor rolled his eyes, but looked more concerned than the eye-roll suggested. "So... what, then? You just expect me to drop everything? I'm way too big-time for that, geek-man."

Bonnicksen took a deep breath, then exhaled it slowly.

"We've got maybe a week left, Mr. Castillo," he said. "Seven days until everything we understand about reality and the laws of physics gets ripped to shreds."

SIX

Remedy trembled, convinced she was about to see her friend stabbed to death, but their assailant kept the knife an inch from Sarah's head. The serrated, concave blade looked hand-forged, its sides covered in scratches and nodules—more of a dagger than a knife, Remedy realized. The polished, cedar pommel sticking out from the bottom end of the man's fist looked like an animal carving, though Remedy couldn't tell what animal. It had a bulbous head with round, white eyes, a pronounced snout, and a toothy, open jaw. Like the blade, the pommel looked hand-made... but less function, more form.

"Go," he said, in a voice so low they had trouble hearing the word.

"Go where?" Sarah said, her eyes staring at the steering wheel, as if determined to make certain she couldn't see the blade. Remedy noticed sweat running down her friend's forehead, and her nose wrinkling from the man's putrid stench.

Several seconds after a long look out the rear window, staring at the wildfire-scorched hills south of town, he finally answered.

"Just go. Highway, toward Quail Point."

Sarah hit the gas hard, clearly as irritated as she was afraid. Air rushed through the smashed window, dribbling glass shards onto the rear passenger seat, but their assailant didn't act like he cared. Remedy angled her body toward the back seat as they pulled out of the post office lot, to get a better look at him. He exuded a sickening, sulfurous stench and was barely recognizable as a man. His face was mostly matted hair and mud, coated so thick there was little sign of lip movement when he spoke. His nose was missing a gouge of flesh, an open wound leaking some sort of clear fluid. A horizontal scar over his left eye was as red as his acne-scarred cheeks. Even his beard looked unkempt, a haphazard blend of whiskers, mud, and leaves. His opened flak jacket exposed a leather undershirt fronted by narrow cedar slats that looked hinged and lashed together. An I.D. tag on the jacket bore some sort of insignia, but Remedy's vision was too blurry to figure out whether it indicated a corporate brand or a nondescript military program. On his best day, he might have resembled a Hell's Angel in a rainstorm... but, Remedy decided, today certainly wasn't his best day. She stared at the twisted countenance, part Rambo, part Bogeyman, and couldn't help wondering whether it reflected the man's career or his psyche.

"Lay it out for me," he said to Remedy, lowering the dagger.

It was hard to hear him over the sound of the air coming through the shattered window. It was even harder to answer. Remedy's jaw trembled in terror, her throat felt like sandpaper, and her hands shook. She found herself hoping the man didn't notice her fear, not wanting to give him any more advantage than he already had.

"What are you talking about?" she managed.

He glanced at the hands of a muddied plastic watch that hadn't seen a drugstore shelf for twenty years.

"I said, lay it out," he repeated to Remedy, who suddenly realized she might have heard his guttural voice elsewhere, a few days earlier.

She waited, hoping to hear him speak again, to see whether she really did recognize his voice. Instead, he cocked his head and stared at her.

"Oh... Upsweep," she said, her jaw still shuddering. "The story. You want to know what I've got."

He didn't break the stare.

"I... I can't do that," she said, wondering whether those would be her last words ever.

He maintained the stare for another moment, then sent his head into a slow, deliberate rotation until he could see outside. His jaw wiggled as he jostled something between his teeth, then spat. A small, silver object shot through the smashed window, and it didn't look like candy.

Remedy recoiled. *Was it a bullet?*

"You're the guy who made those threats," she said, risking a guess. "The guy who left voice messages."

Sarah cursed, and Remedy knew she would take hell for not mentioning the threats earlier.

The man didn't say anything. In front of them, the highway widened into four lanes, transforming into Mulberry Boulevard. If Quail Point was the valley's penthouse then Wofford Notch was the basement, its road split by a weed-filled median and surrounded by auto repair shops, mobile homes, tattoo parlors, and several hole-in-the-wall restaurants. There was no town center, although most of the businesses clustered near a tiny, one-screen theater. Homes sprinkled the mountains looming above the boulevard.

"Who do you work for?" Remedy said. "Why are you in the Sirretta Valley?"

She had assumed the threats were from some government lunkhead hired to help the DOD save face by scaring her off, preserving the cover-up. This guy, on the other hand, looked and acted far too crazy for government work.

"Why is *anyone* in this valley?" the man said, in response to her question. "Just give me your source."

Hearing him say that emboldened her, easing her terror. In her mind, this was no longer about defending herself. It was about defending her profession.

"I don't give up sources," she said.

Sarah whipped the car around a corner, onto a lakeside street lined with trees and run-down mobile homes.

"Uh-uh—no small streets. Circle back to the highway," the man said, flashing the dagger. "Now."

Sarah lifted her hands in frustration, but did as instructed.

"Look, enough of this," Remedy said. "You know about Project Upsweep, so do I. You want to know my source, I want to know yours, and neither of us are going to budge, knife or no knife. Now, are we done here?"

No reaction. She started to wonder whether she'd just shown her hand too soon.

"A name," he said.

"I'm not giving you any names."

Another blank expression, another unsettling gap before answering.

"A name I'm giving you," he finally said. "Erich Bonnicksen."

"Yeah, fine, we both know who he is: the remote perception guy at the Sidney Institute. But he's not my source, so what about him?"

This time he didn't answer at all, even after Remedy waited in uncertainty for several seconds. The broken passenger window gulped wind as they traveled down the highway, mimicking the sound of a helicopter.

"He's on target," the man said. "That's why your story can't go public."

"I don't get it. So what if he demonstrated remote perception? Two human beings sensing the same thing over long distances doesn't mean the end of the world."

Again, he stared for several seconds before answering.

"Don't dumb it down. Glottochronology and the end of the secular analytical paradigm changes everything," he said.

Remedy wasn't sure what to say; she wasn't sure what *he* had just said, or that she believed him capable of speaking such words. A thought popped into her mind: this certainly wasn't some government lunkhead. He not only had weapons, he had knowledge... maybe the knowledge she needed for her story.

Still... the words just didn't seem to match the man she was seeing. Her gut told her he was mimicking terms someone else had taught him. If so, then that someone probably had information she needed.

An uncomfortable, silent minute passed. Even with the airflow through the smashed window, Remedy felt her stomach turning from their passenger's trash-dumpster fragrance. They drove through the outskirts of town, where the four-lane boulevard re-funneled itself into a two-lane highway. The road paralleled the lakeshore before directing them through undeveloped, scrub-covered hills that seemed especially dry amid the smoke and embers from the fire. Sarah gave the steering wheel several nervous taps, but seemed more inconvenienced than terrified, even though there was a crazy man with a knife to her head. Remedy wished she had her disposition.

"So... where do we stand?" she finally asked.

He looked at her but still didn't say anything. Remedy couldn't tell whether he hadn't quite heard the question or was deep within his own world. All she knew was it was damned unsettling.

"I need more," he finally said. "Tell me what you know about Project Upsweep."

"I've already told you—"

He held the dagger closer to Sarah's head. "Tell me the rest."

Remedy's heart skipped a beat. She saw Sarah flinch, catching sight of the blade.

"Fine," Remedy said, fumbling for her notebook. "All I know is that it's a defunct research project designed to test the theory of remote perception," she said, skimming her notes. "Apparently, if you station someone at a randomly selected location, a second person with no information about the location is still able to describe the location with pretty amazing accuracy. Bonnicksen and his team suspected what they call 'an anomalous channel of information acquisition.' In other words, some unknown element of human consciousness that links our thoughts and lets us channel information to one another."

The man motioned her to keep talking.

"Project Upsweep was supposed to be Bonnicksen's attempt to document that undefined element of human consciousness," she said. "That's how he came up with the project name. Upsweep is an underwater sound that's so difficult to isolate it can only be only heard using special equipment."

The man nodded, as if she hadn't told him anything he didn't already know. "Yeah, yeah, the Navy funded the research, stuck a bunch of people on Amelynd Island for the initial phase, then pulled out after the squall," he said. "Get to the linguistics. The aftermath."

"What aftermath?" she said. "Bonnicksen never returned my calls, and I couldn't find Amelynd listed anywhere until I borrowed one of Jon's... until I borrowed some maritime maps."

She stroked her naked ring finger. Even now, with someone threatening her, she felt the pain of their split.

"But today Klase probably told you the Navy went in and rescued one participant," the man said, staring out the window.

"It was, uh... a linguist, right?" She hoped "my ex-husband" wasn't visible on her face.

This time the silence lasted for nearly three minutes. Remedy tried asking a couple of questions, but he didn't answer or make any indication he'd even heard what she'd said.

"You think maybe he can't hear me?" she whispered to Sarah.

Their assailant's head whipped their direction.

"Not likely," he said.

Remedy swallowed, nervous. The man returned his attention to the window, and this time Remedy didn't bother trying to interrupt. She looked out at the same scenery that seemed to engross him so thoroughly and was surprised to discover they had already reached the grasslands near Quail Point.

"Pull over," the man said to Sarah.

"There's no turnoff until the golf course in—"

"No, here, along the side of the road. Now! Pull over here!"

Sarah did as she was told, to the sound of a horn blaring behind her, from the only other car on the lonely two-lane roadway. Remedy watched a truck with no paint, just primer, pass by. She hoped the old woman driving the truck would look over and notice someone was holding a knife to Sarah's head, but no such luck. The man seemed amused by the horn, erupting into a throaty, maniacal laugh that spooked them even more than his silence.

"Your story—you'll keep it narrow," he told Remedy, his green eyes glinting.

"That's what this is about?" she said. "Keeping things quiet?"

"Bonnicksen only," he said, ignoring her. "No Navy, no DOD. Place all the focus on Bonnicksen and his remote perception research. You'll censor the rest."

She nearly laughed. This guy sure doesn't know who he's talking to, she thought.

"What's your interest in calling attention to Bonnicksen?" she said.

Again, no direct answer. "The glottochronology, the paradigm, the linguistics, none of that comes out," he said. "And don't expect any sympathy just because you're a crip."

She feigned amusement. "A 'crip,' huh?" she said. "What makes you think I'm not already on my way to talk with the man who was rescued from the island?"

He broke into a wild grin, revealing yellowed teeth that complemented his worn exterior. "Because... I shot him at the river, same day I set the fire."

Sarah rolled her eyes, and Remedy could tell her friend's annoyance had just tilted the scales away from her terror.

"You're as bad at lying as you are at showering," Sarah said. "I saw the island survivor that day too. Not a single hole in him."

Remedy grimaced, expecting the worst, but he lowered the dagger and spat at the inside of Sarah's windshield, leaving yellowed, mucus-scented saliva dripping toward the dashboard in streaks.

"Oh, there's holes in him alright, just like there's holes in me," he said, holding up his forearm. An open lesion, split like rotted tomato, glistened with bubbling, clear fluid. "Doesn't really matter whether I'm the one that takes him. He's good as done either way."

Remedy's mouth hung open as the man opened the door, jumped from the car, and bounded into the dry grasslands next to the roadway. After four leaping steps he threw himself to the ground, rolled, and disappeared beyond a modest rise. Only his words lingered, hovering inside the car like the stale, smoky air.

SEVEN

Ten minutes after their assailant's unconventional departure, Sarah pulled her now-battered car up the steep driveway of Remedy's Quail Point home. The wood-sided A-frame had bay windows, an elaborate front deck, and a weathervane that made a small, bearded lumberjack figure chop wood whenever a wind kicked up.

"I'm telling you, Rem, the scuzzbag lied," Sarah said while working the gas pedal, trying to ease the car up the hill. "Jon was with Carl Sharp when I examined the brain. He was fine."

But that didn't clinch it for Remedy, since that had been three days ago. Uneasy, she tried shifting her body; her right leg barely moved and her arms felt numb, like android limbs. The silk blouse, though baggy, seemed as constricting as a straitjacket.

Her relapsing-remitting MS was fairly textbook: debilitating numbness, tingling, and weakness which went into brief, partial remission every few weeks. The cycles meant she was lucky; half of the 500,000 people with the neurological disorder never went into remission. Medications shortened the episodes, but as the medical pamphlets put it, "no treatment predictably halts progression of the disease."

Remedy translated it more simply: there was no cure.

Sarah inched the car up to the garage door, a refurbished wooden roll-up at the apex of the incline, and shut the engine off. Setting the parking brake seemed like an exclamation point, signaling that the long, awful trip from Porterfield was finally done. The car's interior was a disaster: glass shards everywhere, side window smashed, yellow saliva streaks on the front windshield, remnants of their assailant's stench still lingering.

"So... how much do I owe you for gas?" Remedy said.

Sarah burst out laughing. Remedy too.

"I wonder if insurance covers nutjobs busting windows," Sarah said.

"Well, your car's sure got the spit and stink to prove it."

They laughed again. With no looming danger, the carjacking seemed absurd, even surreal... and their nervous, relieved laughter felt good. When they finally stopped, the moment felt awkward.

"Look, I'll pay for everything... somehow," Remedy said.

"That's what I'm worried about," Sarah said.

Sensing an imminent scolding, Remedy attempted a distraction. "I finally found a Sam Cooke last week," she said, while using her phone to check email.

"What about Joni Mitchell?"

"Haven't landed the Joni or the Otis Redding yet," Remedy said, her pointer finger scrolling through messages. "Their first-release albums are crazy rare, so... wait... the preliminary report on the bottled brain is in."

"Already? The county crime lab is that fast?"

"No... which means they must have found something as soon as they started," Remedy said. "I'm downloading the report now."

"Why would they send it to *you*?"

"They wouldn't. My source at the lab, on the other hand... here we go. It's short, but... wait, look at this. Are they serious?"

Sarah glanced skyward. "Now what?"

Remedy took a moment to read through all the material, making certain she hadn't misunderstood. She hadn't. "The brain had an embedded ID tag, it's registered in a Navy research database. That doesn't make sense. Who registers a brain?"

Sarah shrugged. "Certain federal programs require registration as a control against black market organs, especially if there's government funding involved," she said. "Who's it registered to?"

"Good question," Remedy said. "Let's see if the report says... oh, wow. Just... wow."

"Well don't leave me in the dark. Who's it belong to?"

Remedy looked up from the report. "The Sidney Institute," she said, astonished.

Sarah wore a blank look. "What's Sidney?"

"It's a think tank in Massachusetts."

"The same lab that did Project Upsweep?"

"Yeah. How could a brain from a study finished four years ago show up on the opposite side of the continent, floating in Blackmule Gulch?"

Sarah's eyes flared. "That crazy guy probably knows," she said. "He seemed to know everything else you've been looking into. Sounds like you'll need to get in touch with the people at Sidney."

"I've already been trying to reach Erich Bonnicksen, the project director. He hasn't exactly rushed to return my messages."

"You're thinking he's hiding something," Sarah said.

"Sure smells that way to me. Look at this—whoever compiled this report did an Internet search on the brain registration tag numbers. Turns out it's from one of the victims the Navy retrieved from Amelynd, an active participant in Bonnicksen's project. Apparently the brain from each victim was surgically removed and kept for study, to document any physical changes related to remote perception."

"Wait—someone was dumb enough to sign a consent form allowing *that*?" Sarah said.

Remedy cocked her head. "Everyone in the study was dumb enough, including my hus... *ex*-husband, apparently."

Sarah nodded. "Good point. So then, whose brain was it?"

"Doesn't say, but the cops are just getting this too so I suppose they'll be calling Bonnicksen to find out," Remedy said, glancing over the report again. "Apparently the brains were stored at the Sidney Institute after

Project Upsweep ended in disaster. Maybe that explains the reference to Upsweep on the note inside the bottle."

Sarah slid her hands from the steering wheel, onto her lap. "So, someone stole the brain and dumped it in the lake—which is exactly what I told Sharp, by the way. Why would anyone do that?"

Remedy shrugged. "The report says there's no indication that the brain's different from any other human brain. Pretty weird that Jon was the one to find it though. A little too weird."

"It's not weird whatsoever," Sarah said. "Remember how he was acting before you two ended things? The blank stares, the disconnected comments... like he wasn't in the same room. You filing for divorce was the right move. Nothing's too weird for that guy. Your only mistake was waiting so long to file the papers after he cleared out."

"You only saw him a few times," Remedy said. "He wasn't usually like that."

"He was whenever I was there. And now you know he was part of the Upsweep project, so think about it: him finding a brain from the same project can't be a coincidence. Maybe he's the one who tossed it into Blackmule Gulch in the first place."

The hollow feeling Remedy felt in her stomach told her how much she hoped it wasn't true. "I mean, my gut says no, but after bailing on our marriage the way he did, with no explanation..." she said, leaving the rest of her uncertainty unspoken.

The two women sat in their seats, staring at Remedy's home through the assailant's dried saliva streaks, listening to the click-click-click of the lumberjack weathervane. The looming A-frame needed new sealant but still looked on par with the elegant, neighboring homes, which dated to a fading decade when developers bet their fortunes on the Sirretta-adjacent hillsides.

"I'll ask Sharp to have his people check the car for prints and maybe DNA from the saliva," Sarah said, "but you'd better back off your reporting until they I.D. the guy."

Remedy took a breath and held it for a moment before releasing. "I might be able to track that dagger he had—it looked ceremonial, right?" she said. "If I can find out what it's for, I can get a lead on who this guy is and then—"

"Rem..."

"He mentioned 'glottochronology' too... whatever that is. And a paradigm. 'Secular-analytical,' was that it? I'll check into those, that should—"

"Rem! I'm sorry, but you're in no shape for a story of this magnitude."

Remedy felt her temper rising. "So what, I should back off?" she said. "I have a public responsibility."

"Oh, please."

"Sare, this is my last week on staff. There's no second chance for me. Besides, switching from full-time to freelancer is concession enough. It's not as if my body's going to get any better."

And it's actually getting worse, she thought. MS induced the body's immune system into attacking the coating around nerves in the brain and spinal cord. Doctors likened the nerves to an electrical cord; without the coating, the signals are forever distorted. Physical challenges aside, she knew it was only a matter of time before she'd be dealing with forgetfulness and other cognitive impairments.

She grabbed her broom and used it to swivel herself out of the car.

"Do you need this bad enough to risk your life?" Sarah called.

"Yeah," she said. "Maybe I do."

She remembered the high of daily deadlines and the vibrant feeling that her work actually contributed to society. That was a whopping six years ago, before the MS. Before doctors recommended a less-stressful job in a quiet location. Before Jon.

"Look, I get the lure," Sarah said. "Secret island experiment, government cover-up, it's a good story. I just think it's dangerous for someone who's in no condition to defend herself... or run away."

Remedy flecked blue paint from the broom's wooden handle. She recalled seeing a baseball player put his bat over one knee and snap it in half, and wondered how satisfying it would feel to do the same with the broom.

"I can get it done," she said.

"You probably can," Sarah said. "But you're not considering your limitations. And don't give me that crap about one last, glorious story, or closure on your marriage, or proving that an MS patient can handle tough assignments. That's only part of this, and you know it."

"Thank you, Dr. Freud."

"I'm serious. You're still ticked off about the way the headline-hawkers sensationalized your stories when you were in Dallas."

Remedy didn't answer. Her thoughts wandered to the years she spent arguing with her editors, ripping their personality-driven, horserace-style coverage. Most of all, she remembered the long showers after finishing work, usually around midnight. The dirt and sweat from a day's toil went down the drain, but the stain of having a hand in it all never left.

"You have an issue with me doing things the way Reporting 101 says it's supposed to be done?" Remedy said.

Sarah laughed. "The journalist who hates journalism."

"I don't hate journalism," Remedy said. "I hate its present iteration."

"That doesn't change the reality that your health's declined since you were in Dallas, and this is a very dangerous story. Much as I want to keep helping you out... I've already told Stanford I can't start the lab appointment until next month. I really can't stall them any longer. Maybe you hand this one off."

Remedy took a deep breath. As usual, Sarah was right. The disease was already forcing her to give up her staff job. No one at the *Mountaineer* would question her for passing the story to someone else.

"That's not me," she said. "I have to see it through."

Sarah's expression said otherwise. Remedy watched her drive off, regretting that they had wrapped on a sour note. She slide-staggered to a small, wrought-iron entry gate at the property's border. The three wooden steps leading to her deck felt like six, but the front door, buttressed next to the garage, never looked so inviting. The deck looked inviting too, coated in dark stain, bracketed by cypress trees, and topped with bistro furnishings. A set of French doors offered direct entry to the living room but Remedy, preferring to keep a steadying hand on the home's exterior wall, opted for the longer route.

Inside, Hank Williams, Stevie Wonder, and Sly Stone welcomed her home; Buddy Holly, the Ronettes, and a few other vintage pressings were framed and mounted a few steps away. Her Top 100 playlist auto-activated as she shut the door, today's digital downloads given gravitas amid yesterday's vinyl.

She glanced twice at an empty alcove near the hall, certain it was just begging for the new Sam Cooke. A few paces away, the living room furnishings were worn but comfortable: once-white carpet, leather sofa, matching chairs. Watercolor prints beamed cheery mountainscapes. So did the bay windows and the French doors, which faced the front deck and its mountain view—her favorite feature of the house.

Hearse, her least favorite, sat in the far corner of the room. The disability scooter was coated in dust, its apple-red paint job blunted. The yellowed headlight, embedded into a vertical yoke, stared like a one-eyed serpent. Sarah and a few other friends had meant well when they pooled their money to buy it... but they didn't understand the deal it demanded in return for a ride.

"I won again, Hearse," she said, while lowering the playlist volume. "Another day, and you still didn't get me. And let me tell you, this day was tougher than most of them."

With now being the toughest part, she realized. Texting a source out of the blue was awkward, but when the source was your ex-husband... She wrote the message, deleted it, tried another version. Finally, she settled on simple.

    Jon it's Rem. I need to talk with you
    for an important story I'm writing. Are
    you around?

Her heart pounded as her finger hovered over the phone's "Send" button. Finally, she let the hammer fall. The message lingered, then shot into the "Sent" screen with a gentle hoot. She re-read it then waited, chest hollow, fingers chilled.

No immediate answer.

Step two, a quick computer search for "Razor Castillo," took her to the Boston Red Sox website, where she filed a phone interview request with the team's media relations office. Removing her shoes, she slide-stepped to the kitchen for a snack then returned to her computer and began dictating to the voice-recognition software. Two hours later, her back felt like a cement slab and her vision mimicked a Rorschach impression, but her story draft was finished—and it included the island, the linguistics, and everything Muddy Guy didn't want mentioned. She still needed quotes and information from Bonnicksen, Castillo, and Jon, but the initial story could run without them.

In the corner, the scooter stared.

"Not a chance, Hearse," she said, grabbing her broom. "I'd sooner let that psycho back in the car than let *you* come get me."

Her body felt bad, but her emotions soared. If Muddy Guy wants to take me on, she thought, he's going to have to do it in my arena.

EIGHT

That same afternoon, Jon stepped out of his blue pickup, thrilled to hear the whine of an approaching aircraft. He checked his phone's calendar: the tiny plane was arriving only forty-five minutes later than planned, not bad considering it was midweek and the local airport, situated just east of Isadora, was usually open only on weekends. He certainly didn't have the clout to open a closed airport, but Virginia Hanafin did... another debt he owed Ernie.

The school day was over, but his job wasn't—for another two days, anyway. Earlier in the week the district had postponed its layoffs, exactly as Carl Sharp said it would... and Virginia supposedly had a hand in *that*, too. After Friday... well, eleventh-hour funding was usually reserved for valley natives, not valley Natives, which was why seeing the approaching plane boosted his spirits. Just knowing that Francis Hanlon was aboard that aircraft... the pending arrival of his longtime friend and linguistic mentor seemed a perfect antidote to what felt like the longest week of his life.

Words had danced through his head every hour since returning from the fire. On top of that, Carl Sharp had now phoned him three days in a row, usually with thinly veiled accusations presented as follow-up questions to the investigation. Then there was the sniper, who hadn't been caught and who, at least in Jon's mind, was aiming at him from every shadow. If he'd ever had a more stressful week since moving to the valley, he couldn't think of it—not even the week he'd left Remedy, which had been pure agony.

He walked across the unstriped dirt parking lot, where several small aircraft were tied to posts like horses out front of a saloon. Sirretta Valley Airport was more air than port, its concrete runway leading to a triple-wide mobile home that served as an office. The place was too small for the fire-fighting aircraft to use; even the helicopters were refueling elsewhere. There were no hangars, just the dirt lot. Jon counted seven planes tied down, with plenty of room for the one Francis was coming in on.

His emotions soared as the plane landed. He didn't know a thing about planes, only that this one was about the size of a sofa with wings, but so long as Francis was aboard he didn't care. He followed it as the pilot taxied into the dirt lot, kicking up a dust cloud.

"You call this place remote?" he heard a gruff voice saying as the aircraft's passenger door cracked open. "Where I'm from they call this a city."

Jon felt a huge grin spread across his face as he saw the pilot and two other passengers, all middle-aged men, hand Francis his cane and help him out of the plane. He wobbled, took a moment to regain his land legs, then spotted Jon.

"I lied to these boys, told them the bass fishing at Isadora's the best anywhere, just so I could hitch a ride," he said, loud enough for them to hear.

"Tell them about the Alaskan sockeyes," Jon said, also loud enough for them to hear. "You'll need a ride back too."

The three men laughed and waved. Jon waved back, then gave Francis a warm embrace. His friend looked the same as always: like he worked the night shift for Father Time. His curmudgeonly expression and messy white hair instilled charm to a face that otherwise resembled a crushed rubber squeeze ball, full of ripples, cracks, and creases.

"Wish we could just go fishing and forget the rest," Francis said. "How're the trout bitin' around here?"

"Good enough that I've got some poles in the truck," Jon said. "You know... if you're up to it at your age."

"Whoop your butt at fishing at any age," he said. "Let's go."

They walked to Jon's truck. Francis was a little shorter than Jon, but only because his years had given him a modest bend. His "uniform" was a checkered shirt and blue cotton pants that had been washed so many times they no longer reached his ankles. Today he'd gone fashionista, topping off his outfit with a tattered, pea green sweater that didn't quite obscure his bulging belly.

"I owe you for doing this," Jon said.

"Nah," Francis said, throwing his cane on the truck's seat and hoisting himself up, arms and legs quaking from the strain. "I owe you for keeping my broken promise to your grandmother all these years. Now let's catch some fish."

They left the airport and had lines in the water fifteen minutes later. The dinnertime sky was still dirty orange and the air smelled like burned marshmallows, but none of that mattered to Jon. Even his ribbons eased up; Francis was there, they were fishing together, and everything was good.

Hearing the older man's news from Rowock—strong salmon runs had tourism booming, more turnouts had been added along the roads, and the population had nearly hit nine hundred—was as pleasant as the fishing. Jon's memories flashed to snow-capped Sitka spruce and glistening rivers. Totems too—dozens of them, their maniacal caricatures and forgotten tales unfolding vertically into the bald eagle-filled skies. Trails in the picturesque Sierras were nice, but hiking the Alaskan wilderness to find towering likenesses of white-feathered *Kolus*, a supernatural bird with a curved beak, or *Sisiutl*, the shape-shifting serpent and a god of warrior invincibility, was another experience altogether. For all the trouble he'd had in his hometown, and on Prince of Hollis island overall, Jon couldn't deny how much he missed it.

Francis was ahead, two trout to two crappie, when Jon addressed the elephant fishing alongside them. "The sniper implied we could win The Race, Francis," he said. "That's how big this is."

Jon felt butterflies as he said it. No one had a better handle on The Race than the ninety-three-year-old Francis. Though long retired, his career as a linguist with the University of Alaska had taken him to sixteen states and seven countries, and resulted in native language preservation efforts lauded by the Navajo, Ojibwe, and Zuni tribes. Even now, in his tenth decade, he spent his free time consulting with U.S. senators in an effort to further amend the Native American Languages Act.

Just as important to Jon, Francis was born and raised Tlingit. He knew firsthand how desperate the situation was on Prince of Hollis island, and throughout southwestern Alaska and British Columbia where Tlingits still made up significant portions of the local population. Though Francis wasn't born on the island, like Jon was, he spent more than a few of his working years in Rowock, encouraging their people to pass what little was left of their native tongue on to their children.

But mentor and role model were really the least important elements of his connection with Francis, Jon knew... especially now that the elderly linguist was one of the few people from Rowock who would still speak with him. He had told Francis about the words streaming through his head during their weekly phone conversations. So far, he seemed to be reserving judgment.

"I didn't spend the last two days traveling all the way from Alaska to talk about The Race," said Francis, who was attaching the second trout to their stringer. "We could do that by phone. Uh-uh... I know what seeing that buoy must have done to you. I'm here to make sure you're okay."

Jon swallowed the emotion he felt welling in his chest. "I live near a lake," he said. "See buoys every day."

"Don't be an ass. You know what I mean."

"Yeah, I do, but I can't bring the girl back, right?" he said. "The Race, that's something I have a shot at. Maybe."

Hearing *the girl* spoken from his own mouth made him shudder. It sounded so heartless, and he hadn't meant it that way. *Emma*, he told himself, invoking her name like it might forgive him. *Emma Kitchtoo.*

He kicked at the dirt. They were fishing on Franklin's Point, an elevated finger of land situated between Isadora's half-century-old twin dams. It featured a two-lane roadway, an outhouse, and not much else. Normally it had a view, too, but the smoldering wildfire on the hillsides some twenty miles south had become an air-quality nightmare, reducing an unobstructed lake vista to a game of find-the-landmarks.

"What happened with the little girl wasn't your fault," Francis said.

"They might disagree with you in Rowock."

"Doesn't mean they're right. She fell through the ice. You had nothing to do with it."

No, I didn't. But Jon understood there were times when perception, accurate or not, formed people's reality. In the grief-stricken Kitchtoo family's retelling, young Emma would have understood a warning sign scripted in Tlingit if the Wanamaker family hadn't helped U.S. government troops stamp out native languages decades earlier.

Jon pulled his book satchel from the pickup's cab and fanned it in front of his nose while they fished, telling himself it would clear the smoky air.

"It's like we talked about before I left Prince of Hollis," he said. "There's only one road back to Rowock for me."

Francis turned away from the haze, leaning his elbows on the truck hood, his head angled down. "That's a near-impossible road, Jon," he said. "Resurrecting a language... yeah, it'll buy you respect, make people realize they ostracized a good man. But trust me... there are easier ways."

Jon saw the tip of his pole bend and tried to hook whatever was nibbling, but didn't get it. "What if the sniper saying he'd steal my chance to win The Race meant he thinks a new opportunity's opened up?" he said.

Francis looked skeptical, something Jon didn't want to see—not from Francis, of all people.

"Wishful thinking," Francis said, pushing his face up to Jon's and staring into his eyes as if he thought he might spot something. "Those words of yours, the ribbons—can you see them now, even while we're talking?"

"They come and go, but yeah, they're there. Translucent, sort of. Streaming past like... I don't know, computer code or something. Except they're sentences."

"Yeah? In what language?"

Jon felt his stress easing, just from sharing.

"That's the thing: it's in a bunch of languages," he said.

"How can you read the ribbons if the words are a mix of languages?" Francis said.

"My head's processing them as English, but the words themselves are in multiple languages, including some I don't even know. The only obscure one I can actually read looks like a variation on Tlingit, but... there's something different about it. Maybe it's an older form, or an extinct dialect?"

Francis seemed to find the idea interesting. "You saw them during your marriage too?"

Jon nodded. "Not in heavy swarms like this, but yeah. They're normally mild, like my eyes have an astigmatism, only the shadowed edges are sentences. Right now, it's more like the sentences are out front and real world's being pushed into the shadowed edges."

Francis gave a puzzled look.

"I know, it's bizarre," Jon admitted.

"Tell me how it first happened," Francis said, moving even closer to Jon's face, eyeball to eyeball.

Jon tensed, knowing this was a detail he'd never discussed... and preferred not to. "Same as last weekend: I just started seeing words... sentences, really," he said, deliberately leaving out the specifics about when and where. "Streaming past, right in front of my face. Swarming, like now."

He didn't like keeping it so vague, and he definitely didn't like keeping Francis in the dark about the aftermath of that first time... but he was mostly in the dark about that aftermath himself, and Francis hadn't seemed to notice anyway.

"I'm assuming you were still married at the time... was your wife with you when you saw the ribbons?"

"Not the first time, but later, yeah," Jon said.

"Could she see the words too?"

"If she could, she never mentioned it."

"She'd have mentioned seeing words flying past your face," Francis said.

Jon's stomach tightened; he knew he needed to come clean, at least in part. Stalling, he reeled in his line, checking the bait for nibble marks before recasting.

"Look Francis," he finally said, "I should probably tell you... I never told Rem about the ribbons... or about Upsweep, for that matter. Or... Emma."

"You hid all of that from *your wife*?"

"Yeah, yeah, I know it was wrong," Jon said. "It's complicated... but that's why I left, to protect her from my insane situation. Trust me, I'm not as much of an ass as it sounds."

Francis gave him a look. "If you say so," he muttered, shaking his head. "So then, is this is the first time the ribbons have hit you with this kind of intensity since the divorce?"

Jon nodded. "They get heavy sometimes, but never the swarms, not until this week."

Francis stared into Jon's eyes a few seconds longer, cocked his head to either side as if looking in his ears too, then waggled a white, scraggly eyebrow. "I don't see nothing in there."

"Very funny," Jon said, tracking '*a mountain incline towards Quail Point*' as the phrase passed, right to left. "The docs say I'm fit as a fiddle—really, that's what they say around here. They told me I'm imagining the whole thing."

"But you're not."

"No."

"How 'bout that. Of the two of us, turns out it's you everyone thinks is senile."

Francis laughed at his own joke, grabbed his pole, and reeled in a third trout as if he'd known it was waiting for him all along. "These words, can you just ignore them?"

"Yeah, sort of. But it's like trying to watch Closed Captioned television without reading the captions... only in this case the words fill the entire picture, even with my eyes closed."

Francis strung the fish, recast his line, then tugged at his sweater, stretching it to his pants pockets. "Any chance the sniper was just part of the ribbons?"

"No, Ernie saw him too."

"Ernie? He's the friend from the hike, right?"

"Yeah, he drives the local bus."

Jon reeled in a trout, his first, as Francis signaled their score with three fingers, then one. Apparently the two crappie didn't count.

Francis scrunched his nose. "Okay, so both you and the bus driver saw the sniper, and you say he knew your Tlingit name."

"Yep: Onatay. Even you didn't know that until just now."

"Uh-huh. But I'll bet he knows other things about you too."

"What makes you say that?" Jon said.

"Because a few minutes later you were looking at the red buoy, and I don't think that's a coincidence. Either the sniper or someone he's connected with knows your history in Rowock. If so, that's a solid lead."

Jon was thinking the same thing. Virtually no one outside of Alaska or British Columbia had ever heard of Rowock, a town of just eight hundred residents on a spruce-covered island—Prince of Hollis—that was accessible only by ferry or float plane.

"So, the sniper knew about my—" he started, then stopped. Words burst before his eyes, darker than before, spraying then coalescing.

"Again?" Francis said, seeing Jon's expression go wooden.

"It's crazy, there are so many words, in so many languages... like a museum for human speech."

"Tell me how many languages you see."

The individual words moved fast that Jon had to wait until they coalesced into sentences. "Seven... no ten," he said. "Francis, these sentences are a mishmash, I don't know whether—"

The lake, the fishing poles, the mountains... all of it flickered.

Francis too, he realized, stunned.

More flickering ensued... and then everything vanished altogether.

NINE

Three times zones away, Erich Bonnicksen fast-forwarded through the Project Upsweep footage on his tablet as his limo carried him through Boston's Wednesday afternoon traffic, toward a hastily scheduled warehouse meeting with I.K. Emily. *Or at least, with her audio-only computer monitor*, he thought, remembering the way a similar emergency meeting had played out when the Exhibit C crisis arose. Face-to-face interaction wasn't part of the deal when you worked with I.K. Emily, but that was a minor inconvenience in exchange for the guaranteed funding and extensive connections.

The limo turned a corner, forcing Bonnicksen to angle his tablet screen away from a sunbeam. Fast-forwarding through footage of a younger-looking Razor Castillo seated inside the Sidney Institute's lab, he watched the pitcher sniffing the armpits of his workout clothes and bickering with technicians as they outfitted him with cerebral sensor nodes. Then Bonnicksen spotted the section he was looking for and hit "play" on his tablet.

"There's a lot of noise," Razor told an unseen technician. "Wind, maybe? And everything's wet—flooded, I guess. Changing though, and fast, like the whole damn world's disappearing. Aren't you going to help this guy?"

"Just stay with your agent," came the technician's off-camera voice. "Tell me what he's doing."

Razor gestured with his middle finger. "Bite me, lab jockey. There's nothing but white space and words, and... wait... people are dying, man! Lots of them. The dude did something, and now people are dead!"

He ripped the sensor nodes from his head. A heated, off-camera argument ensued, followed by a loud grunt from the technician—from a punch to the jaw, as it later turned out. The video went dark.

Bonnicksen loosened his tie, feeling warm from nerves. Upsweep and his subsequent work had produced bar-moving results: thirty-five of his last forty-two percipients had identified at least some portion of their agent's hidden location or emotional state, even when separated by thousands of miles. The remote perception back-channel hypothesis certainly appeared valid.

Whatever. He knew the public wouldn't care. His corollary experiments on the agents, on the other hand... like the test Razor had inadvertently picked up on... those were the potential fame-makers. Whereas most people used back-channels to change their environment without realizing it—making clocks issue one less tick per minute or delaying traffic lights an extra split-second—Wanamaker and a handful of others could often do so at will... and that was before they had isolated them, before they'd genuinely needed the skill to survive. *Now the door's open for these people to try all sorts of unimaginable mind-over-matter interactions,* Bonnicksen knew... including the disaster with Exhibit C that appeared to be repeating with Wanamaker.

Worried, Bonnicksen opened up his phone's address book, found Wanamaker's contact information, and left a call-me-back message with the added nugget that he was heading to the Sirretta Valley soon and that it was vital they meet. He ended the call then glanced out the limo's window, at Boston's late-afternoon morass. The Big Dig finished years ago, but the Big Traffic never went away. His email didn't either. Checking, he found a message from his lab technician, which linked to a news report from that morning. The headline, *Message In a Bottle—Alongside a Brain*, said enough, but the article contained a frightening detail: the message itself.

Sidney, Upsweep, Amelynd. Because Bonnicksen lies.

"You've got to be kidding me," Bonnicksen muttered.

He suspected the timing, so close to Razor's sudden link with Jon Wanamaker, couldn't be a coincidence. Taking a closer read, he discovered details about Wanamaker evading a sniper, then a wildfire, before finding the bottle alongside a distinctive buoy. *No wonder he didn't answer the phone. But who was the sniper?*

"Emily's man," he guessed aloud.

If so, it meant she had gone behind his back. He looked away from the screen, annoyed. Had I.K. Emily gotten cold feet after the Exhibit C massacre and ordered a hit on their former research subject... without telling *him*? She'd always claimed Russ Kitchtoo, a former special-ops dirtbag, was stationed in Wanamaker's vicinity for emergencies only... but in this case, it seemed he'd *created* the emergency by botching an assassination. Razor Castillo hadn't sensed Wanamaker's thoughts for four years until Kitchtoo went on his arson-sniping attack. Had that played some role in boosting Wanamaker's capabilities?

More importantly, what was Kitchtoo thinking, staging a harebrained assassination attempt without getting approval from *him*, the brains behind Upsweep? If he had simply left Wanamaker alone there wouldn't be any need to haul the dumb baseball jock cross-country.

Irritated, Bonnicksen pulled out his phone and dialed a number he was never supposed to call... four times, to no avail. The calls directed into a greeting-less voicemail box. He hung up without leaving a message. To his surprise, an incoming call from the same number hit his phone seconds later.

"Talk," he heard.

Bonnicksen recognized Kitchtoo's guttural voice, but also heard something in the background... a distant, anguished groaning. Someone in pain, perhaps? He shifted in his seat, uneasy. Why I.K. Emily continued to employ this terrifying ape, he'd never understand.

"You screwed everything up," Bonnicksen said.

Dead air.

"Did you hear me?" he said. "All I needed from you was post-island monitoring. Now, thanks to you,

Wanamaker's officially dangerous—and what's with the bottled note? I don't want you playing games."

He expected yet more dead air. Instead, he heard an irritated, single-word reply.

"Orders," Kitchtoo said.

Orders? Bonnicksen's thoughts swirled. *So, it was I.K. Emily's doing.* He'd specifically reported in to her and the entire Upsweep panel not ten minutes after Razor Castillo had left the lab... and not one of them had mentioned any such orders.

"Are you saying I.K Emily gave you an extermination code?"

This time the pause didn't last so long.

"No code, not yet," Kitchtoo said. "Timeline's changed, that's all."

"Changed how?"

The distant, anguished groans grew in intensity before Kitchtoo answered.

"People are tired of waiting."

It took Bonnicksen a moment to figure out what he was hearing. If there was no extermination code, it meant Kitchtoo was claiming that wasn't the motivation for his actions.

"So what, someone's got you... *provoking* Wanamaker?" Bonnicksen said. "Trying to stimulate results?"

Furious, he swore into the phone without waiting for an answer. I.K. Emily and the brute had trampled all over acceptable scientific procedure... *again*... so now the only question was how badly they had screwed everything up. Given the way Razor Castillo could suddenly pick up Wanamaker's thoughts from across the country, it sure seemed like things were leading up to a replay of the Exhibit C scenario. *God forbid,* he thought. Seven people, massacred; an eighteen-day cleanup; fabricated, whitewashed explanations to families and Sidney administrators... why would anyone override protocol after dealing with *that* mess?

"Do you have any idea what Wanamaker will do to you if he figures this out?" Bonnicksen said. "And what's with adding *my* name to the note? Don't you understand you're leading the police straight to the Institute's lab, and to the Upsweep project?"

And to me, he thought.

Kitchtoo erupted in a brief, wheezing laugh, suggesting the amusement had to scrape its way out of his throat.

He does understand, Bonnicksen realized, his chest tightening. I.K. Emily was practically a shadow, the DOD would keep quiet, and the small-time reporter who kept leaving him phone messages could be ignored. But now, because of the note, it wouldn't be long before police investigated whether the bottled brain was from his lab... and from the island project, four years ago.

That was a definitely a problem. Upsweep may have been covert, but at least it was quasi-legal, operated in conjunction with the DOD, and many of the more intense aspects were easily masked. The subsequent studies, on the other hand... illicit trials focused on influencing events... or *people*... if authorities got wind of those, or discovered last month's Exhibit C massacre...

Bonnicksen slammed his fist against the leather seat. *Just as I figured. I'll have to take care of this myself, and right away.*

Kitchtoo breathed heavily into the phone. "We're done," he said, and disconnected.

"Yeah, we're done alright," Bonnicksen said, even though no one was on the other end. He wondered whether the bottled note was I.K. Emily's way of throwing him under the bus. Otherwise, Kitchtoo's actions made no sense. Why would he leave the brain in a lake where it might never be found? *Because he knew he could steer Wanamaker straight to it,* Bonnicksen decided. From the get-go, I.K. Emily had made it clear that the reason she wanted Kitchtoo for the monitoring job was because he had some long-running dispute with Wanamaker. Deploying that extra psychology seemed part of her strategy.

Bonnicksen could only guess that somehow, maybe by setting the fire to maneuver Jon toward the lake, Kitchtoo made certain the brain would be found. Did he mark it in some way that would trigger an emotional response from Jon? Probably. That way Jon would not only connect the cryptic message to his time on Amelynd, he would understand that Kitchtoo was involved—whether he discovered the brain personally or heard about it later.

Bonnicksen felt the limo accelerate, finally escaping traffic just as his cell phone rang once again. His hackles rose, thinking it was Kitchtoo calling back, but "I.K. Emily" flashed on the I.D. screen instead.

"I'm ten minutes away," Bonnicksen said, answering.

"You phoned the burner number four times," I.K. Emily said, her smoker's voice firm.

"It's an emergency number and this is an emergency," he said.

"Emergency my ass, Mr. Bonnicksen. Our very promising research subject is doing exactly what I'd hoped when I instructed Mr. Kitchtoo to provoke him. The pitcher's new back-channel evidence proves it."

Bonnicksen fumed. He'd never met Emily face-to-face and he wasn't even convinced it was her real name, but as donors went she was usually easy to deal with—until now, anyway.

"You must've missed the end-of-the-world part," he said.

"Oh, I didn't miss a thing," she said, indignant. "Yes, the subjects using that back-channel are going to go hog-wild with it sometimes. Yes, there was a massacre. And yes, you had to put the Exhibit C woman down. We both knew that was a risk."

"It wasn't just the one woman. There were two other people showing signs so I put them down too, as a precaution. Now there's Wanamaker. I thought his back-channeling ended awhile back, but apparently it didn't, and now you're provoking him. Because of you, we need Wanamaker taken out, fast."

"And he will be... soon," she said, lowering her voice. "But let's not forget the objective here. If we can isolate exactly what Wanamaker's doing *before* we exterminate him, we'll be very close to duplicating it. We've monitored long enough, Mr. Bonnicksen. It's time to generate clear results."

That's your objective, not mine, he thought. Here he was, on the verge of becoming the Einstein of cognitive neuroscience, engaged in groundbreaking work that would completely redefine human capability, and all I.K. Emily could think about was using her head to manage insurgents. Showing the public they could change the world using only their mind... well, that was the real payoff, the one that would transform society—and assure his scientific beatification.

"Tell Kitchtoo to stop trying to provoke him," he said. "I'll take care of things personally."

An ominous silence ensued.

"That wouldn't be wise," I.K. Emily finally said, her consonants crisp.

Bonnicksen ignored her. "I'll use the same method I used to handle Exhibit C," he said. "We'll lose Wanamaker, but after a few more subjects, with additional controls, we'll isolate what he's doing regardless."

Bonnicksen knew she wasn't happy but didn't care. This was *his* research and *his* rules, not hers. "One more thing: between last month's cover-up and now this Wanamaker mess, we're going to have cost overruns," he said, but she interrupted before he could go any further.

"Just give me a number and it's done."

He doubled the usual number. Several seconds later, an email appeared on his phone, indicating a new deposit into the lab's bank account. *Wonder where she gets it*, he thought, then decided he'd rather not know.

"I'm one block away from the warehouse, so let's reconvene this meeting in five min—"

"Our discussion's done. And do not *ever* call the burner number again."

She ended the call. *Yeah, screw you too*, Bonnicksen thought, satisfied that he would be handling things firsthand... with a little help, since dealing with Wanamaker meant using the dumb jock.

His cell phone rang yet again—a call from the lab technician. Bonnicksen hadn't bothered to learn his name.

"Erich, bad news," a prim, Middle Eastern voice blurted. "Inventory records confirm we're missing one Upsweep brain specimen... and some sheriff already called about it, asking for you."

"He can ask all he wants, understand?" Bonnicksen said. "Once I get Razor out to Wanamaker, we're good."

"Yeah, about that..."

"The neural mine isn't responding?"

"Everything on the mine's nominal, it'll work as soon as you're within thirty feet," the technician said. "The problem's with your ballplayer buddy. The police just put out a warrant on him."

Aw, Christ, Bonnicksen thought. "How bad is it?"

"Assault charge. Soon as he closes out the Yankees, they're taking him in."

TEN

Jon gasped as Francis, the lake, the lingering odor of smoke, and everything else disappeared. Only the words remained, streaming and vibrant, more visible than ever. For a moment everything seemed blank, and silent, then Jon noticed a sound... no, a voice... Francis's voice, calling him.

"Jon, snap out of it!" Francis said. "Jon!"

His surroundings returned... sights, sounds, everything.

"It's okay... *I'm* okay," Jon stammered.

Francis had a hand on Jon's chin, something Jon hadn't even noticed until now. "Don't give me 'okay,' you went nonresponsive on me," Francis said. "That's how strong of a connection you have with those words. It's an extreme example of the research first presented in—"

"Yeah, yeah, I know the linguistic theories," Jon said. He closed his eyes and shook his head, not wanting to believe. "How do I stop this?" he said. "What am I going to do?"

He already knew the stakes. The ribbons had cost him his marriage, but until now that had been in the past. Just the thought that things were again spiraling out of control...

The tip of Francis's fishing pole was bobbing, but they ignored the nibbles. Instead, Francis tilted Jon's head by the chin and peered up from underneath, as if he were trying to pinpoint the gender of his eyelashes.

"First off, you're not crazy," he said. "Your mind is attuned to languages, particularly lost languages, and I'm convinced something's boosted that talent. This is a linguistics issue, not a mental health issue."

Jon shook his head, frustrated. "What does it matter? Either way I need help. I have to do *something*."

The older man nodded. "You said the sniper implied that he knew you were seeing the ribbons, right?"

Jon kicked at the dirt as he had earlier, creating a small hole with his toes. "More than implied. He said he'd blast the words from my head and steal my final shot at The Race."

Francis thought about it. "So, he knows how much saving the Tlingit language means to you."

"Maybe. My work on The Race is no secret."

"But your Tlingit name is, right? And the ribbons. Who else knows about those?"

"Just you... and now Ernie, since he heard the sniper say it. Erich Bonnicksen too—the guy who headed the Upsweep project. I mentioned it to him after I first saw the ribbons."

"I know his work," Francis said. "Thinks we have unused back-channels in our heads. What does he have to say about what's happening to you?"

Jon picked up his fishing pole, which he'd dropped when the ribbons hit. "He doesn't. I've only talked to the guy a couple times since Upsweep, and I don't plan on changing that now. But... guess who left me a message a little while ago, for the first time in ages?"

"Bonnicksen? That can't be a coincidence. Probably worth calling him back."

Jon cracked a half-smile. "Don't need to. He says he's on his way."

"Here? From across the country? Why?"

"Don't know, and I don't plan on meeting him. I know I'm being stubborn, but the guy's an arrogant jerk, Francis. One of those people who thinks his degrees separate him from the rest of us mere apes."

"That may be," Francis said, "but given what's happening, I'm starting to wonder whether your involvement in his research project somehow affected those linguistic talents of yours. What exactly happened out there, anyway?"

"Not much, until we got hit by a squall," Jon said. "Before that, a bunch of esoteric tests... like checking to see whether scents, Yoga, or underwater submersion had any effect on whether we could use our thoughts to keep a pile of green leaves from turning yellow. Far as I could tell, it didn't. Then the storm slammed us. After that, everything's a blur until the Navy pulled me out."

"A blur."

Jon knew Francis could smell a half-ass answer. But what else did he have? That all these years later, visions of sheeting, blood-misted rain still sent him bolting awake at night? That a scream-scored fog descended between his ears every 4 a.m.? That ever since Amelynd, the sight of an incoming storm front terrified him more than anything?

"All I know is, something's missing," he said. "It's like some animal took a bite out of my brain, and whatever frayed tidbits it left tell me to run like hell if anything bigger than a puffy cloud rolls in."

They watched a sailboarder glide several hundred yards across Isadora's surface before wiping out.

"Bonnicksen did tell me the ribbons might be a by-product of me using the remote perception back-channels, kind of like you just said," Jon suddenly remembered. "But it was just a guess, and he never mentioned it until whenever we last spoke... so probably about two years ago, long after Upsweep was over."

"That's a big bomb for him to drop without offering more details," Francis said. "But it means he probably has data to back it up. You need to talk with him, Jon. Whether you like him or not."

The sailboarder wiped out again, this time right after mounting the board. The lake-top saga continued while Jon spent several minutes describing details of his escape from the fire, the sniper's tightrope-like walk across McCullough Crossing, and the bottled brain.

"Red buoy... same way you found the little girl," Francis said. "Whoever did it didn't just want you to see the brain, they wanted you to *feel* it."

"Maybe. All I know is..."

He hesitated.

"What is it?" Francis said.

"Nothing. It's just... their plan worked, okay? It got to me, seeing that buoy. It got to me pretty hard."

Francis placed an arm around Jon. They stared at the lake, or what little they could see of it through the hazy air, for several silent moments.

"You tell the police about the connection?" Francis said.

"No."

"I wouldn't have either. They ever find the gunman?" Francis said.

"Not so far as I know."

"It's been three days. You'd know."

Jon shrugged. "I'm not convinced they even believed me," he said. "The cop looking into it seemed more interested in my past than the actual case. Even after four years and a couple thousand miles, I can't get away from Rowock."

They saw the sailboarder fall into the water several more times, then paddle ashore and call it quits, just as a U.S. Forest Service helicopter arrived to fill up the water bucket swaying from a line beneath its belly. The helicopter's fill-up took less time than it took the sailboarder to get the board into his SUV.

"So, ribbons aside, the question here is, who is this sniper and how does he know your deepest secrets," Francis said. "Unless maybe the ribbons are somehow connected too."

"I don't see how," Jon said.

"Yeah, well, I don't either. All I'm saying is your subconscious, perusing all that scrolling text... maybe you're not so isolated as you think. Maybe after a couple prior bouts of experience you've advanced into some sort of linguistic MMO, except it's not the internet, it's the universe."

Jon did a face-palm. "What in the world are you talking about?" he said, surprised Francis even knew that massively multiplayer online environments were a thing.

"Just thinking aloud, about what you said before," Francis said. "About the ribbon words being an older form of Tlingit."

The old man didn't clarify what he had in mind. He removed his sweater, placed it on the hood of Jon's truck, and changed the subject.

"Why am I here, Jon?"

Jon felt uneasy, hearing the question. "You already said it yourself. You traveled here to see whether I'm okay. Remember?"

Francis shot him an insulted look. "I'm old, not senile like you! What I asked is, why am I talking to you *here*, in the California Sierras? Why aren't you living in Juneau, or Atlin, or anywhere in Alaska or Canada where we might actually be able to teach our language to our own people?"

Jon looked at the rocky ground beneath his feet, then shrugged. "People back home still think that girl drowned because of me, right?"

He heard a sigh. "Not all of them," Francis said.

"No, not all of them, but enough of them. Let's not forget they practically ran me out of town. Here I am, trying to help those people..."

"*Those* people? You mean *your* people, right? *Our* people!"

"Fine," Jon said. "Point is, they still think the little girl couldn't read the warning sign because of my family. Right?

"They needed someone to blame," Francis said, "but that was a few years ago. These days it's different."

Jon scoffed.

"I'm serious," Francis said. "I've spent some time setting people straight, okay? Your family's cooperation with the government, the way they went along with the English-only restrictions as a façade... people get it. They know the Wanamakers were teaching the language behind closed doors."

Jon wasn't buying it, not when the girl's family was Rowock's answer to the Hanafins.

"Bottom line is, if I can't work on saving the language in Rowock, or in any of the places where Tlingits live, I'll save it from here instead—and *that's* why you're here," he said. "You of all people should respect that."

He immediately regretted saying it, since he suddenly wasn't sure whether Francis truly did respect him... and if not, Jon didn't want to know. They stood in silence once again, watching the firefighting helicopters arrive and depart.

Then Francis's lips inched into a slender, satisfied smile. "Your grandmother, she'd have been proud of you, turning her pet project into your white whale," he said. "But I've told you before, there are other whales out there too."

"Is this your way of saying there are other fish in the sea?"

"You know what I mean," Francis said. "Irene would have understood you going in your own direction."

A plume of pink fire retardant plummeted from a bomber plane flying south of the lake, snuffing flames across three distant hillsides.

"I know," Jon said, as they watched the plane ascend. "I also know she could have steered clear rather than letting me move in with her when Mom took the rest of the family to Portland."

"Eh, so you know how to carve a *Sisiutl*, big deal," Francis said.

Jon grinned. "That's what my brother and sister tell me every Thanksgiving," he said, "but they have so little concept of their ancestry. Thanks to Grandmother, I do."

He paused, lost in fond memories.

"She's not gone, you know," he added. "I mean, she is, but when I'm running The Race, she's still with me. Mother's told me she feels the same way."

"Yeah," Francis said, "Irene's still with me, too. But just because I promised her I'd win The Race doesn't mean you have to carry the baton now that I've hit old age. The obligation doesn't transfer."

"No, it doesn't," Jon said. "It's something I *want* to do. Losing languages the way we are... we're leaching cultures, knowledge, perspective. It has to stop."

Francis laughed, a hybrid of a cough and an extended hiccup.

"Tell an old man something new," he said. "You can't dictate how the world should run, Jon. Not even when you're right. And you made a mistake letting all this ruin your marriage. You should never have hid this stuff from Remedy."

"I know," Jon said. "There's not a day that—"

He hesitated, startled as hundreds of words burst before his eyes, swarming like bees. "They're coming in stronger."

Francis stood up from leaning against the pickup, transferring his weight to the handle of his cane. "So don't let them. Fight."

Jon whipped his head back and forth, frustrated. "That's what I've been doing for days, but this is different. I don't think—"

The ghostly words charged before his eyes, streaming past like TV news bulletins, only multiplied several hundred-fold. Francis and Engineer's Point disappeared, supplanted by phrases, all nonsensical: "...*for undisclosed operations... blue jeans and delivery browns... warning bell chimed...*"

"*Ku'cta-qa*," he cried aloud. "Francis, if you can hear me, they're too strong, I can't break away!"

If Francis answered, he couldn't hear it. He shut his eyes but the words remained, now changing direction, hurtling past his head, looming up before him until the letters seemed so large he might fall between them. He screamed as he felt his body tumbling. Pain rippled his left arm. He shook himself, opening his eyes as he reached out and felt... rocks. The lake extended to the horizon before him, Francis knelt nearby. Something red covered his arm—blood?

"It's okay Jon, you scraped yourself when you collapsed," he heard Francis say. "Relax, you're still here."

"Did I disappear? Did you see the words?"

The old man wore a look of pity. "All I saw was you yelling and throwing yourself to the ground. Nothing else."

He hesitated, then added, "What language was it, Jon?"

"What? Are you serious?"

"It's important."

Jon shook his head. "I mean... it happened so fast, it's a mix, and I was inundated. My mind was busy translating, so..."

"Forget all that, just think about your first impressions. What language did you see the instant those things started pouring across your vision?"

Jon looked skyward, thinking.

"Tlingit, maybe," he said. "But... not the words we speak. They're similar, but..."

"But different," Francis said. "Very, very different. Differing declensions, structures, assemblies, pronouns. Probably a few terms you can't even translate."

"Yeah... I think so. What are you getting at, Francis?"

"Just a guess. Not even that, really. More of an old linguist's fantasy, so forgive me, but..."

"I'll take whatever you've got, long shots included," Jon said.

"Yeah, well this is the longest shot you'll ever hear: I'm thinking root language."

Jon felt his eyes widen. "Long shot" was putting Francis' guess mildly. He couldn't quite stifle a smile.

"Setting aside the 'how?' component," he said, "you're talking about a language that hasn't been spoken in what, three thousand years?"

"Four. Maybe more."

Jon let the smile ripen to a doubting laugh. "There wouldn't even *be* a written version for me to see, everything was passed on through speech alone. I mean, I guess if we're embracing the wildest linguistic theories then I'll roll with it, but..."

"I've published research on root languages for decades, so yeah, maybe seeing one of them expressed in this manner is just an old man's wishful thinking. But if it isn't, then we're looking at a completely different linguistic framework. That's the incredible opportunity here. It's also the danger."

"What danger? Other than me scraping myself up, looking like an idiot?"

Francis banged the foot of his cane against a small boulder, for no apparent reason.

"I'm not entirely sure," he admitted. "But I can tell you this: language determines how we perceive objects, colors, time, everything. What's important right now is that this alternate linguistic framework probably poses risks."

"Like?"

"Like, it could change the way you interact with the world, because you'd be interpreting reality through a completely different framework. Now, that could theoretically expose some latent human talents, which is certainly an unprecedented, groundbreaking opportunity. But shifting to a new linguistic framework after a lifetime under the first one might also cause... issues."

Francis didn't elaborate, and Jon was suddenly glad he didn't.

"We need to get in touch with Bonnicksen, Jon. Soon as he gets here."

Only as a last resort, Jon thought.

"Don't give me that look," Francis said. "That man knows something we don't, and if I'm right it's crucial we find out what it is."

"And if you're wrong?"

"Then..."

Francis seemed to stop himself from saying anything more, but Jon recognized how his ribbon "attack" must have looked to Francis.

"I'm not crazy," Jon said, a plea rather than an affirmation. "These ribbons, this whole mess... I know you can't see them, but they're real."

The Tlingit elder gave a wheezy sigh, then pushed himself to his feet with such deliberate effort there might have been a 100-pound weight strapped to each of his aging thighs. He put a curled forefinger to his mouth, deep in thought, before speaking.

"How many of me left?" he said, a strained rasp to his voice.

"What do you mean?"

"You've got the young, fresh mind! How many Tlingit elders are there?"

Jon shrugged, trying to calm himself enough to do the math. "A few dozen. But elders fluent in the language? Ron Nokes died a couple months back. That leaves four of you."

Francis nodded. "And none of us speak it daily. Two of them don't care whether the language stays or goes. And we're all at death's door."

Jon shook his head, trying to soften the reality, but Francis brushed him off with the wave of a hand.

"No, it's true and you know it," he said. "We're all in our nineties. Your aptly named race against time is just about over. The kids are more interested in video games than learning what's left of their language, and we'd be no different if we were their age."

He ran a hand across his forehead, his mood sobered, and Jon followed suit. He knew Francis was thinking about the English-only school curriculums from the

1900s, and the whippings doled out to Tlingit children who used their native language.

"We lose The Race, our people become totems," Francis said. "Tlingit, but silent. Unable to tell our stories the only way they can be told."

He turned to look at Jon. "You ask me to believe you're not crazy, but the truth is, I have no choice. That sniper thinks these ribbons of yours give us a chance to save the language? Maybe so, maybe not. What I know is, the language is dying and so am I. If I decide you're crazy, then Tlingit has no chance and I lose everything I've worked for. If I decide you're not crazy..."

Jon cracked a grim smile. "Then we still have hope."

Francis winked. "Let's tilt at some windmills, Quixote."

ELEVEN

George Klase took a sip from his coffee cup, wondering when things had reached the point where he could hear some nameless, blasé voice recommend killing twenty thousand people and consider it a routine day at work. He looked at his watch with a sour face, more so when he saw *6:05 a.m. Thursday* on the display. Applying new research to national security was his career dream, realized; the early-morning Jump briefings were the tradeoff.

"Fine," he heard, a deep voice from table's end. "On to Topic 38."

Despite the early hour, Klase's elbows bumped against those of his DOD colleagues and he didn't see an empty chair anywhere in the room. He held a seat two-thirds of the way along a stretch limo of a conference table. The hulking, burnished mahogany slab was destined to become a museum piece, supporting some of the nation's most influential elbows as they outlined socio-political machinations that would never reach public eyes or ears.

Or maybe it's just a goddamn table, Klase thought, sleepy eyed. But no, the field office in Porterfield hosted some of the DOD's most important strategy briefings every year, and why not? No one suspected an armpit city like Porterfield held national security importance.

No one but the broomstick reporter, he thought with a smile. He had little use for news media, but couldn't help admiring the way she didn't give a damn that she was falling apart. *A reporter with a soldier's mentality*, he realized. *Now there's a first.*

He took a sip of his coffee—black, no sugar, certainly nothing from the latte family—listening as several strategists discussed covert tech tactics for weakening a despot's hold over a small island country.

"Nanotech," he heard.

"Climate manip."

"Phantom sound."

The latter suggestion caught several ears. Klase looked over and saw a goateed male, probably of Middle-Eastern descent, dressed in formal U.S. military attire. He didn't recognize him, but in a room filled with nameless participants that wasn't such a surprise. At Jump meetings, named for the early-hour start times intended to give strategists a jump on their day, attendee faces changed week to week, sometimes day to day. Researchers, even those of the high-clearance variety, were expendable... used, abused, then tossed. Only their tech, and their outcomes, mattered.

The deep voice at table's end spoke again. *Clockhand*, Klase remembered. The man's conference tag was

Clockhand. The rest of the attendees, himself included, weren't important enough to be assigned a tag.

"Phantom sound?" Clockhand said, skeptical.

"Shrill sound," the goateed man said. "Delivered and directed in short bursts, at pinpoint locations."

"Feeding my mother-in-law's voice into this a-hole's palace is supposed to drive him out?" Clockhand said, drawing a few chuckles.

"Not a voice, a sonic mystery," Goatee said, ignoring the snickers. "Maddening, undecipherable, untraceable. After awhile patience and judgment break down, opportunities arise. This thing's already tested: Forest Grove, Windsor, Coventry, Taos, and more."

Eyeballs roamed up and down the table as participants measured their colleagues' reactions against their own. Opinions gathered, judgments cast, the matter settled, quick as that. "Worth studying," Clockhand said in a noncommittal voice, as Goatee's face sagged. "On to Topic 39."

Klase perked up, recognizing one of the fourteen agenda items that fell into his bailiwick.

"I recommend full containment on 39," someone said.

"Agreed—extermination," another voice added.

Klase shook his head. "No, isolation and study."

Muffled chatter broke out along the conference table. *They aren't accustomed to hearing someone argue an approach that isn't a sure thing,* Klase knew.

"The situation's already out of control, correct?" Clockhand asked.

"Two incidents," Klase said.

"Two that you know of."

"Correct. But we still have our operative in the region."

"The unstable Eskimo?"

More snickers.

"He wants the Upsweep agent dead, only reason he's held back is because of orders," Klase said.

"So instead, he's playing with his food," Clockhand said.

"It's a decent ace in the hole. Plus Bonnicksen's en route."

If anyone thought that news was a positive, they didn't speak up.

"The Sidney guy?" Clockhand said. "We've already cleaned up his island mess and his lab mess. This time it's real-world—right near a ski resort town for God's sake. We can't take the chance at an exposure. No, this matter's settled. Full containment. On to Topic—"

A deafening electronic crackle filled the room, from the conference table's center. "Isolation and study," a grainy voice boomed, from a tiny, black video screen.

Startled silence filled the room, Klase's included. In seventeen years of Jump meetings, the faceless black screen had sounded only three, maybe four times, and I.K. Emily, an alias for the DOD's head of covert scientific intelligence operations, was always on the other end. She had a smoker's voice and a bit too much enunciation. What she didn't have was patience.

"Okay... we now have an additional recommendation of isolation and study for—" Clockhand started.

"Not a recommendation," the woman said.

Klase listened to the exchange, stunned. *I.K. Emily is Bonnicksen's government funding angel*, he thought, his mind reeling. *I.K. Emily!* If anything involved unethical science, conducted under-radar using money-laundered federal funds, I.K. Emily was somewhere in the picture. Fetal stem cells, human cloning, electronic torture, horrific implants... maybe the stories were real, maybe fabricated, but nothing seemed too outlandish when I.K. Emily was involved. If *she* wants Jon Wanamaker left alone, Klase realized, she must think there's real power in whatever resulted from Bonnicksen's remote perception research.

"That's, uh... well, there are of course countless risks if we go that route," Clockhand said, hesitant.

"More like countless rewards, most of which the lot of you are incapable of seeing," I.K. Emily said, her tone as unwelcoming as the video screen's static. "The linguistic back-channels stimulated in this man's brain offer us control... over individuals, over nations, over situations. *Complete* control, I might add... the kind that only remote manipulation conducted via a human neuronal back channel can offer."

Clockhand cleared his throat. "With respect... it only offers the Upsweep agent that control. Not us."

Klase noticed they didn't refer to Jon Wanamaker by name. *They probably don't even know his name. Just another expendable research subject.* He thought again about the broomstick reporter. *Bet she'd love to be a fly on the wall in here.*

Ripping sounds erupted from the video screen, as if someone had torn a phone book in half. "Forget your respect," I.K. Emily's voice returned. "Your obedience is all that matters. Am I clear?"

"Yes ma'am. But we do have intelligence that Bonnicksen intends immediate eradication—"

"Bonnicksen's a fool, and no threat to us whatsoever. I will reiterate: the Upsweep research subject will be allowed to develop unhindered, exactly as he has since the Sidney Institute's project concluded. In just a few days, when the fruit is ripe, I will harvest personally. Understood?"

"Yes ma'am."

Klase thought his head might explode. I.K. Emily was handling matters personally? Did that mean she was already on site in the Sirretta Valley?

"Should we at least station cleanup crews in the Porterfield region for rapid deployment and containment if the incidents from the island or the lab repeat?" Clockhand said. "I mean, given that this is now a real-world situation, with multiple lives and witnesses?"

More static, more ripping.

"Station your crews," I.K. Emily said. "If this matter doesn't conclude to our satisfaction we will indeed contain the entire region, meaning no witnesses, no survivors, no regrets, and that includes the researcher and his team as well. I'll want a clean slate, Croatoan Protocols: nothing left, nothing traceable."

"Understood," Clockhand said.

"Understand this as well: this is an all or nothing matter. We'll have control, or we won't. I feel confident that we will... and when we do, your bombs and phantom sounds will be obsolete."

She spoke one last sentence, then the crackling video screen went silent. So did the room. Again, eyeballs roamed up and down the table, gauging reactions, but this time participants understood their opinions were irrelevant.

"Topic forty," Clockhand announced, relieved sighs filling the room as they moved on.

Klase couldn't move on, not just yet. He took a third sip from his coffee cup, marveling that the prospect of killing twenty thousand people had barely flagged his attention but the situation with Jon Wanamaker struck him as wrong. A man harboring so much potential, yet so unaware. Risking everything, too—himself, his friends, his family, and now his community too, yet all of them kept completely in the dark.

Unless that ballsy broomstick reporter were to find out.

He shook his head, scolding himself, knowing it wasn't his kind of move. He was no snitch, and he'd hold his patriotism against that of any man. Then again, this wasn't a typical situation. Big picture, this was fate-of-the-world type stuff... only the world had no clue.

No, he told himself. *It won't be me. I'm no media snitch.*

Then he thought about I.K. Emily's final sentence, possibly the last words he'd hear bursting from that tabletop video screen for years. Words that made his throat catch. *Like a noose*, he thought. I.K. Emily's final words grabbed at his throat like a big, nasty noose.

"We're about to rewrite history," she said. "And when it happens, I alone will be the one who decides who lives... and who dies."

That didn't sound like someone with the nation's best interest in mind. It sounded, he thought, like a power grab. And maybe... just maybe... it sounded like a reason for sharing some knowledge.

TWELVE

That evening, Erich Bonnicksen walked along a street in suburban Cambridge, checking addresses. *Where is this guy*, he thought, annoyed.

The police had released Razor Castillo a day earlier, just a few hours after arresting him. The pitcher plowed straight into the news media mob waiting out front of the police station, away from Bonnicksen and into a waiting limousine. Bonnicksen wouldn't forget watching Razor give him the finger through a side window as the limo drove off.

Now, one night and many promised favors later, he had the pitcher's location. Dense tree canopies filtered the streetlights, shrouding an already darkened block, but he'd spotted a stocky security guard leaning against a black town car across the street, his face illuminated by a phone screen, oblivious. Bonnicksen double-checked the address of the brownstone he was looking for, then took its front steps two-by-two. The stoop didn't have a video doorbell or any other visible camera system, which surprised him, but more surprising was when Razor himself answered the door.

"Aw, get wrecked," the pitcher said, pushing it shut again.

Bonnicksen shoved himself against the door before the lock snapped, then pushed it open, into Razor's leg.

"You—out here, now!" Bonnicksen said, grabbing Razor by his designer shirt and pulling him onto the stoop. "I tell you we have a chance to save lives and you go out and get yourself arrested for—what was it? Oh yeah, assault and public indecency. Nice work."

Razor pushed Bonnicksen's hands from his shirt, which shined under the neighborhood's streetlights, then clocked him with a hard right. Bonnicksen couldn't believe how brain-numbing the hit felt. His vision blurred, his eyes watered, and his knees buckled from the pain radiating across his left cheek. Next thing he knew, he was sprawled across the stoop and Razor was following up with a hard kick to the gut.

"Look man, I don't know how you found me but you may as well get back in your ride, because I'm not gettin' on no plane," Razor said. "I'm the closer in this town, *comprende*? Two weeks to play and we're one game up on New York. How you think that's gonna play if I don't show up for games?"

Games, Bonnicksen thought, through the pain. The simpleton's worried about *games*.

"You gonna have to wait until the season's over," Razor said, giving Bonnicksen one last, rib-jarring kick. "You can tell that reporter the same thing, the one who keeps dropping your name when she leaves messages.

No media, no plane, no you, *comprende*? Right now, I'm going back to my lady."

Even dazed, Bonnicksen was surprised to hear a reporter was leaving Razor messages mentioning his name. *Must be the same reporter who keeps leaving messages at the Institute*, he decided. But how did she find out about Castillo?

The security guard had finally noticed the commotion and was walking over, his arms spread wide because they were too thick to hang straight. Razor waved him back, went up the steps, and slammed the door behind him.

Bonnicksen slowly pushed himself to his feet, head ringing. This is ridiculous, he thought. Eleven-something at night and he still hadn't managed to get the dumb jock to—

A gut-wrenching yell from behind the door sent the guard racing inside the brownstone. Bonnicksen, though woozy, managed to slip in at the same time. Everyone pulled up short as they spotted Razor on his knees, hands clasped to his head, an elderly Dominican woman kneeling at his side.

"I wiped out again," Razor said, mumbling. "Saw some old Eskimo dude... really old. And water... a big lake maybe. Then everything smeared, all whiteness and words." He tilted his head up at Bonnicksen, looking frail. "What the hell you do to my head, man? Why is this happening to me?"

Bonnicksen rubbed his swelling cheek. "I'm not sure, but I think you're still tapped into your agent. Somehow we opened up the part of your mind that handles remote perception, and you're still picking things up."

"That was four years ago! Why is it back now?"

Bonnicksen shrugged. "Maybe the guy's getting better at what he does."

"You know what, I don't even care—just make it stop," Razor said.

Bonnicksen wished it were so easy. "That white space you saw?" he said. "That's going to be the entire world by this time next week if you don't get on that plane to California with me."

Razor grimaced. "I can't, bro. I go AWOL, I sell out my teammates and all the people who follow the team. Not to mention, it'll be a breach of contract—and that's a very big contract."

"It's a contract you'll never get to fulfill if you don't get on that plane."

"So what, I'm just supposed to not show up to work? I go missing, my face'll be all over the news. The media, they'll have the whole world looking for me, man. That California reporter's just the first of dozens."

Bonnicksen scowled, realizing he hadn't considered the possibility someone might actually recognize Razor.

"You let *me* handle the reporters," he said. "Just phone your manager, tell him you'll be away for personal reasons, and leave it at that. This is a hushed situation and you signed a confidentiality clause when you joined Upsweep."

"Doesn't seem right," Razor said. "*You* don't seem right."

Bonnicksen suddenly realized he was listening to a different person; Razor's macho-super-jock façade seemed to have followed the athlete to the floor. That's when he noticed the elderly woman he had seen while running inside didn't seem to jibe with Razor's macho speech out front.

"Yeah, that's right, 'my lady' is my mom," Razor said. "You got a problem with that?"

The security guard wore a sardonic smile; apparently Razor had strung him along too.

"That dough from your project, and my big contract, it's all for family," Razor said. "Here, and in San Pedro. I can't bail on it. Too many people need me throwing that baseball, collecting appearance fees, endorsing products, raking it in any way I can. You want me to leave it behind, it better be something big."

"Believe me, this is big," Bonnicksen said. "Remember all that terrible stuff you sensed when you linked with your agent during our project? If we don't find him, that terrible stuff's going to happen again... only this time, it'll happen to everyone. You and I, we're the only people who can stop him."

"Why? You haven't told me one single damn reason why you need *me* with you for this."

Bonnicksen knew he needed to make the mop-up work sound heroic.

"Because you're the only one who can tell me what your agent's doing, where he's doing it, what he's thinking... and the closer you are to him, the more accurate you'll be," Bonnicksen said. "If you can do that for me, at close range, I'll be able to solve this problem for both of you.

"That's the other thing to consider here, Mr. Castillo: it's not just you having trouble. Your agent, a man named Jon Wanamaker, he's having similar issues with visions. He needs to be free of this problem just as badly as you do."

Razor cursed, then pulled himself up from the floor. His mother nodded, trying to direct his choice.

"Then let's hurry this up," the pitcher said. "The team's got me on the inactive list while they look into the assault. That'll buy me a couple days."

Bonnicksen cringed. He liked things better when he thought the pitcher was just some dumb, playboy jock who didn't know the meaning of responsibility. Now he was actually going to feel bad, ushering Razor away to die... though his swollen, throbbing cheek and aching gut diminished the guilt.

He looked at his watch: nearly midnight. Assuming they left the following morning, they wouldn't get to Los Angeles until mid-day Friday... and then they had a three-hour drive to reach the Sirretta Valley. Frustrated, he pulled out his phone, booked a flight, then left another message for Jon.

That's when he noticed a voice message—one of many—from the reporter digging into Wanamaker's past. He wondered whether he could use her interest to his advantage and decided he could. Moments later, he reached her voicemail.

"Ms. Conover, this is Erich Bonnicksen from the Sidney Institute, returning your call—several calls, I guess," he said. "You've been asking for details on Project Upsweep, and whether Jon Wanamaker, the sole survivor, poses any danger. In fact, he does. If for any reason you encounter him, you need to know he's extremely dangerous, not just to people but to our entire way of life.

"The good news is, I have a way to stop the threat in its tracks and I should be in your area by tomorrow night. Razor Castillo, who I'm told you've also been trying to reach, will be with me as well. This problem's about to be solved, Ms. Conover. We'll call you with more details when we arrive."

He ended the call.

"This threat-stopper you're talking about—that's me, right?" Razor said.

Bonnicksen patted him on the back. "You're used to saving ball games? This week you're going to save the whole damn planet."

THIRTEEN

The following morning didn't seem like morning, at least not to Jon. His ribbons were getting worse, pulling at his mind with such force he had a feeling he couldn't hold them off much longer. He watched a set of words scroll past, in sentence format: *Not for me. My dad says I'm dropping out.*

Doesn't even make sense, he thought as the sentence vaporized. He hoped Francis would have more information by day's end.

"They're just words, Mr. Wanamaker. Not sticks or stones."

Jon barely heard Arturo Morales, one of the fifth-graders in his Friday morning language immersion class, but he certainly noticed the irony, The boy's take on Native American versions of the Sticks and Stones idiom didn't convey Jon's growing fear that the adage was a lie. *Words can hurt you,* his subconscious seemed to warn. *They've been hurting you for a very long time.*

"Mr. Wanamaker? Are you okay?" he heard.

He sensed his students anticipating one of the infrequent, mice-will-play moments when he stepped away from the classroom for a breath of fresh air, waiting for the straggler ribbons to fade.

"Just distracted by the fire smell," he told Riley Allison, a freckle-faced honor student. He'd seated her in the last row because she excelled at paying close attention. *Maybe I'm the one who can't pay attention*, he thought.

He paced before the class, looking his usual teacher self—button-down shirt, blue jeans, a book satchel slung on his shoulder—and yet not, his eyes bloodshot and his chest heaving as if a ventilator forced the air.

Forget the ribbons, he scolded himself. Thousands of languages are on the brink of extinction! Another twenty gone every year! Focus!

He launched into a vocabulary lesson, hoping to keep his mind together long enough to finish. The students appeared intimidated as he explained the difference between 'shah' and 'shaah,'—the abrupt version a mountain, the latter a woman—but caught on quickly as he outlined the difference between *"waknaus"* ("eagle-eye") and a subtle hand gesture that makes the same word mean "intestine."

He explained how the Tlingit version of "star" is a five-syllable word, taught them to pronounce "wolf" as *"gooch,"* and to avoid saying the word with a more guttural emphasis, which transforms the word to "hill."

"That's the key: most native languages rely as much upon gesturing as speaking," he said. "'*Haganah*' means 'mighty men of valor,' but say it with wide eyes and gesture to the head, and the word indicates someone more powerful than others."

Sensing an opportunity, he had his students create their own personalized versions of what they thought the wide eyes and head gestures would look like, a fun, rowdy break that soon had everyone in stitches. The laughter-filled chatter was so loud it took an unusual three-ring bell pattern for Jon to realize the classroom intercom had crackled to life. He signaled for everyone to lower their voices.

"—your attention: this school is now on lockdown," they heard. "This is not a drill. All classes to immediate lockdown."

The classroom chatter faded to disbelieving silence. The school's bells resumed their three-ring alert pattern, which was different from the fire drill alarm. The unfamiliarity was unnerving. Thirty startled pairs of eyes looked at Jon for direction.

"Under the tables," he ordered, feeling as stunned as his students. He grabbed for his classroom keys as the lockdown message repeated. *This can't be real*, he thought. *A lockdown at a tiny elementary school, in an upscale ski resort town? Is this a hoax?* But no, he recognized Larry Holochwost's voice on the intercom—the dusty, septuagenarian principal himself was announcing the lockdown. This had to be real.

Jon switched off the lights and locked the classroom's two doors, one interior and one exterior, then ran to the floor-to-ceiling windows and began lowering the blinds, one by one—all the while trying to remember lockdown procedures he hadn't thought about for ages. They basically boiled down to, 'go dark and go silent.'

The bells paused their three-ring alert as the lockdown announcement repeated. Jon tugged the release cord for the final set of blinds then stopped short. The blinds were stuck. Additional tugs didn't help—a potential disaster since the objective was to keep an intruder from looking inside classrooms for targets.

"Just stay out of sight and keep calm," he told them, seeing fearful eyes peering out from beneath the classroom tables. "If there's any danger, the sheriffs will handle it. Everything's going to be fine."

The bells resumed. Jon felt his phone vibrate, lifted it, and saw a group text message to all school staff, sent from Holochwost.

```
Armed male on campus. 911 contacted.
Maintain lockdown.
```

He climbed onto an adjacent bookcase, leaned one foot between several potted windowsill plants, then reached up and batted at the jammed wad of aluminum strips, hoping the blinds would release. They lowered an inch, squeaking from years of disuse, but wouldn't drop.

Glancing outside, he saw what he always saw: the exterior walkway encircling his classroom, which was part of the school's main building. A vending machine on the walkway stood ignored, just as it had ever since the school started using it to sell fruit rather than candy. Just beyond the machine, the school's middle-aged, pony-tailed janitor, Butch Kinbacher, was jogging up a set of playground stairs with a walkie-talkie in hand, acting as if he'd just been deputized. Behind him, a boulder-sprinkled mountain nuzzled the school against its sprawling torso.

Otherwise, nothing. No sign of an intruder, police, anyone. Jon hopped off the bookcase, scooted beneath the tables alongside his students, then tried group-texting several of the school's teachers; no one knew details about what was happening. The three-ring bells continued, sounding more ominous with each passing moment.

Then they stopped.

Jon's students looked at him, their eyes pleading for an explanation. Silence, it turned out, was more ominous than the nerve-wracking bells. He again reassured them that the sheriffs would solve any problem.

"Mr. Wanamaker—footsteps," Riley whispered.

Jon stuck his head out from the beneath the table, listening to the footfalls heading down the school's cement walkway, just outside their locked door. The sound wasn't crisp like the high-budget footstep effects inserted into movies. Instead, it had a gritty quality, like sandpaper smashing rice cereal.

Or trail dirt stuck to boot soles, Jon suddenly thought.

But the armed man on campus couldn't possibly be the sniper from the trail... could he?

A diffused silhouette passed the closed blinds, man-shaped... if the man were dressed in rags and leaves. The shadow's edges clarified as the person walked past the window with the open blinds. Suddenly the silhouette became less diffused, more of a darkened head with long, tumbling hair. Jon strained to see details but looking up from the floor, with bright daylight behind whoever was walking past, he couldn't make out anything more.

"The sheriffs are probably checking the hallway, making sure it's safe," he whispered to his students as the footsteps faded, wishing it was true, knowing in his heart that it wasn't. "Whatever the problem, they'll take care of it soon."

He felt his heart pounding, and couldn't imagine how terrifying this must be for the kids. The footsteps drew further away, then returned along with the diffused silhouette before fading yet again... because of the school's layout, Jon decided. Quail Elementary's circular building arranged its classrooms and offices like slices of pizza around a central cafeteria. Inner doors fed into the cafeteria, outer doors accessed an exterior walkway that encircled the building... which might explain why footsteps would arrive, fade, and then return. The intruder was circling the school.

Circling because... why? Were they searching for some particular classroom? Some particular *person*? Jon's thoughts again flashed to the sniper at the Sirretta River Trail. Was it possible this school gunman was the same guy? That this entire school lockdown was because *he* happened to teach here?

The footfalls returned, loud and then soft. *Circling,* Jon thought. *They're still circling.* Then he considered the window with the stuck blinds.

"I'm moving over for a quick look," he told Arturo, Riley, and the others. "Stay down, and stay calm. Don't move. The police will be here soon."

Arturo looked pale. "Don't, Mr. Wanamaker," he said. "You stick your head up there, it might get blasted off."

The other kids agreed, and he appreciated their fear and concern.

"I won't stick my head up, that's a promise," he said. "I don't want to give this guy any reason to come in here. I have another idea, but I need the rest of you to stay put. I don't want the intruder to have any reason to think this isn't just a dark, empty room."

He waited until the footsteps were at their faintest then made his way over to the bookcase adjacent to the window. Hopping onto it, he laid himself across the top, well below the window. Removing his phone from his pocket, he double-checked it was set to silent mode, opened the camera app, then held the phone between the plants along the window sill and waited.

The footsteps approached again. Jon listened until the passing shadow seemed darkest, hit the camera button, then waited for the footsteps to fade before lowering the phone and rejoining his students.

"Let's see it!" Riley whispered, as everyone clambered toward the phone.

Jon tapped his photo app, eager as his students.

A single gunshot interrupted. Several students gasped; one let out a short scream. Everyone hit the floor, scrambling to get back under the tables, out of sight. Jon scrambled too, shielding the kids as best as he could, stunned that the gunman could have spotted his phone. He felt terrified, but not just because of the gunman. Mostly he was terrified that his decision to get a look at the gunman might lead to a student's injury... or death.

But the more he thought about the gunshot he'd just heard, the more he realized something no one had noticed amid their terrified chaos.

"It's okay, it's not here!" Jon said, hurrying to quiet them, and his own nerves. "The shot was from somewhere on the other side of the building. Stay down, keep calm!"

Sure enough, none of the students were hit, or hurt in any way. He heaved a relieved sign, then checked his phone again. No new messages. *Come on, where are the sheriffs?*

He heard footsteps again, but this time they were clear and frantic—approaching fast, no grittiness whatsoever.

"Come on you bastard, come and get me!" they heard Mr. Kinbacher shout, and saw the janitor's shadow—very different from the earlier shadow—race past.

His footsteps faded but another set approached... the gritty footsteps, walking at a faster pace this time. They pulled to a stop, and the diffused, man-beast shadow came into view once again... but this time it raised its arms, and the hands were holding some dark, blurry item.

A gunshot blast rocked the classroom. The students screamed. Several burst into terrified tears. At least one of them yelled Jon's name. He felt his heart leap into his throat as he looked at each and every one of his students, praying none were bleeding or dead. So far as he could tell, they weren't.

A second blast; more screams, but this time one of them came from outside. *Kinbacher*, Jon thought, his heart pounding. It was hard to tell for certain... but no, it was Kinbacher. It had to be.

In an instant, the classroom went from chaos to silence... a deep silence Jon had never heard at the school before, so quiet he could hear wind rustling shrubs on the mountain behind them, and a raven's faint call from some distant perch. He angled his head upward, looking at his students. Again, no one appeared to be bleeding, or hurt. Most had their eyes closed or their heads ducked between their crouched legs, too afraid to look up, to see what might happen next.

Then he realized what he'd never heard: the intruder's departure footsteps. Maybe they'd been lost to the chaos following the gunshots, certainly a possibility given the three or four seconds of cries and screams that followed the blast. Maybe the gunman had fired his shot then took off for cover.

Or maybe he was still standing just outside the classroom.

Jon felt his shuddering hands turn icy. He lifted his head, slow as he could, determined to stifle the sound of his movement. Once he had enough angle to get a look at the windows, he paused. Swallowing hard, he glanced up.

Ku'cta-qa, his mind screamed, seeing the bulging, leafy, man-monster silhouette standing there, just beyond the blind-less window. Backlit by daylight, he was more shadow than man. Still, the longer Jon looked the more his eyes adjusted enough to make out a few details... matted, shoulder-length hair, shaggy beard, military-style jacket.

The silhouette moved. *Outward*, Jon thought, relieved. The silhouette was growing smaller, meaning the man was walking away from the window. *Fine, let him wander the campus, away from the students and staff.* The way Jon figured it, the more the gunman wandered, the more time it bought for the sheriffs to arrive. *What was taking them so long, anyway?* He glanced at the classroom clock, saw that only six minutes had passed since the lockdown started.

Only six minutes? It seemed like hours.

In the mountains, with only a handful of cops and long distances between towns, response times took a lot longer than six minutes. His eyes darted back to the window, expecting to see that the silhouette was now out of sight. Instead, it had stopped moving... but remained visible. *Meaning the guy didn't go very far*, Jon knew. But why? What was so important about this side of the building? Unless...

He remembered the sound of the second gunshot... the screams that followed... the tears. But now, much more than before, he also remembered how one of his students had cried out in terror, shouting two words in a moment of pure panic... a call for help, really, directed at the only person nearby who might be in a position to assist. He could practically see the two words streaming before his eyes, along with the rest of the sentences stalking him.

"Mr. Wanamaker!"

The words were shouted, just after the gun blast. Were they loud enough for someone outside the classroom to hear? Jon told himself to stop being paranoid, that one attack along a hiking trail did not mean today's situation was connected whatsoever. Still...

Words can hurt you, his subconscious told him again.

The silhouette moved. It was ballooning in size, becoming larger at such a fast rate that the guy must be running straight toward—

"He's coming through!" Jon shouted to his students, just as the ear-jarring, spine-rattling sound of smashed glass erupted throughout the classroom. The kids screamed as they skittered across the floor on hands and knees, as far away from the window area as they could. Jon felt debris hitting the back of his head and shoulders, and his nose wrinkled as a horrific stench filled the room. Shaking himself, he saw dozens of tempered glass particles raining down, crackling and popping into even smaller pieces as they smacked against the tile floor.

He looked up. A man's head was sticking through what was left of the window... or at least, he assumed it was a man. The bearded face was so thick with matted hair and mud that he looked like something a sorcerer might conjure from Earth's bowels... and he smelled like it too, exuding a sickening, sulfurous stench.

At first Jon thought maybe someone had shoved the man's head through the window. Then a pair of muddy eyelashes fluttered, and firefly-like sparkles flashed as daylight caught the tiny shards of glass sprinkled across the man's filthy cheeks. His eyes popped open, green and hardened. Several students screamed. A blood streak dribbled forehead-to-eyebrow, but the man didn't seem to notice. He didn't move, didn't chip at whatever glass that was still intact around his head, didn't even seem to care that he was staring at more than thirty people. All he did was inhale.

That single, loud inhale, pulled through his gashed nose, sounded like air pumping through a heating duct. The exhale that followed was even louder. The man's eyes glanced left, then right, but he still didn't move his head, as if he preferred it looking like it had been lopped off and mounted onto the broken window.

Again the ribbons fought for Jon's attention, pulling hard, insisting he look. He did, spotted *"the ear-jarring, spine-rattling sound of smashed glass,"* and considered giving in. Their narrative offered relief, he told himself. Two dimensions, much less terrifying than three.

But no, he scolded himself, there were lives at stake. He gritted his teeth and pushed with his mind, shoving the sentences away.

"Unlock the inside door," he told his students, tossing his classroom keys to Riley. "Get into the cafeteria. All of you."

He stood up, positioning himself between them and the creepy head, in case the man decided to continue coming through. Shuddering and feeling as if he might throw up from fright, he suddenly wasn't sure whether to beat the man over the head in self-defense or ask whether he was all right. The kids seemed just as frozen, but as soon as they heard Riley unbolt the inner door they hustled out of the classroom.

Jon, keeping his eyes locked on the man's face, told Riley to close the door behind her once everyone was out.

"And re-lock it," he added.

"But—" Riley started.

"Lock it up. Now."

He heard the deadbolt slide into place. The man's eyes weren't looking left or right anymore. They were looking straight into Jon's. The stench was so putrid a drag from a sewer pipe might have felt refreshing.

The man finally moved... but only his jaw, which began chewing like a cow, slow and sideways. Jon heard an odd sucking sound, and something jostling inside the man's mouth, like marbles clinking together. Then the man puckered his lips and spat.

Something bloody and metallic flew through the air, hit the floor, and rolled to a stop near Jon's toes. He jumped, startled. The man grinned, flashing a set of yellowed, decaying teeth. Then he sucked, puckered, and spat a second time. Again, something small and metallic hit the floor, mixed with saliva and blood.

Bullets, Jon saw. The man was sucking on bloody bullets as if they were breath mints.

He looked at the hideous face, searching for anything that might ID him, seeing nothing. Only...

The gashed nose, he thought, wondering. He'd once known someone with a similar gash, someone who certainly knew all about the red buoy with the wolf logo, and the lifeless, nine-year-old girl floating next to it. But this hideous... *thing* sticking through the window looked completely different. It couldn't be the same man... could it?

Could it really be Emma Kitchtoo's father?

Sheriff sirens sounded. *Finally*, Jon thought. He saw more words stream past: *Backlit by daylight, he was more shadow than man.*

The man moved his mouth again. The cow-chew led to another spit, slightly bloody but this time bullet-free.

"Soon," the man said, his voice low, rough, difficult to hear. "I'll blast those words of yours, very soon."

He broke into another wild grin, then pulled his head out of the window. What was left of the tempered glass showered onto the window sill. A silhouette once again, the man backed away, let out a throaty, maniacal laugh... and vanished.

FOURTEEN

Remedy was skimming web articles about Razor Castillo, trying to figure out what possible connection a professional baseball player could have with Upsweep, when her phone's text tone—the Ronettes' *Breakin' Up*—diverted her attention. She assumed the incoming message had something to do with her article, which had just posted to the *Sirretta Valley Mountaineer*'s website an hour earlier. Instead, the screen displayed a text message from Julie Henderson, her editor at the *Mountaineer*. She read it, gasped, and read it a second time to make certain she hadn't misunderstood.

Quail Elementary on lockdown, suspect at large. Get here asap.

In her *Morning News* days, a Friday afternoon summons to the office would have meant an hour in traffic. In Quail Point it meant a five-minute ride... in this case from Chris Casey, the paper's photographer.

"Forget the office," Remedy told him when he pulled into her driveway, dropping herself onto the cracked, dusty front seat of his aging compact. "Let's get to the school. They're only a mile apart, and this is the biggest news story up here in years."

Casey, who was in his mid-twenties but had a sun-baked face that made him look ten years older, didn't seem surprised. "Pretty sure Julie's already sending Ron Wahl," he said, swiveling the car into a three-point turn. "They might not be happy if you show up too, since... well... you know."

Yeah, I know, Remedy thought. *They're worried if I hobble up the school will think the paper's hiring cheap help, the parents will feel the media didn't treat the matter seriously, the sheriffs will blow us off, and some able-bodied reporter from Porterfield will waltz in and scoop us on everything. Fat chance.*

She studied the text message and found her loophole.

"Oh, did the message say 'get here asap?' Because I thought it said 'get *there* asap.' My bad. I must have read it too fast."

Casey laughed. "Good luck selling that."

"Good luck to whoever doesn't buy it. It's only two o'clock, I'll have this thing covered and filed by four."

"You do know your ex still works at this school, right?" Casey said as he sped toward the center of town. "You two might end up crossing paths."

"I'm counting on it."

She suddenly realized the oddity, having two significant stories in the same week—Upsweep, and now this—

that both had ties to Jon. Just a coincidence, she assumed... unless it wasn't. She grabbed her phone and replayed Erich Bonnicksen's voice message from the night before, wishing she'd noticed his incoming call. "If for any reason you encounter him, you need to know he's extremely dangerous..." she heard, listening for the umpteenth time.

She wondered whether it was true. It certainly didn't fit the personality of the man she married... but neither had the way he'd bailed on their marriage without any explanation, nor the fact he hadn't returned her messages. *Maybe Muddy Guy's the least of my worries.* If nothing else, the message confirmed something important: Bonnicksen and Castillo knew one another, which explained why Klase thought the baseball pitcher might have information. She wondered whether Castillo also had a connection with Jon. With both sources on their way to the valley, she figured she'd have answers soon.

"If you see my ex at the school," she said to Casey, "get a few shots of him."

"You're that convinced he's in the middle of this?"

"I'm convinced he's in the middle of *something.*"

They pulled to a stop, behind three other cars and a sheriff blockade of Sierra Way, the street adjacent to the school. Casey U-turned to a side street, but it was also closed.

"End of the line," he said, shrugging.

"Go—get up there on foot," she said. "I'll be right behind you."

"Sure... or else, you know, Ron's probably on his way so—"

"I'll be there. Just go."

Casey slung his camera around his neck, opened the car door, and was gone. For a split-second Remedy imagined Sarah telling her that Hearse, in full-throttle, could have gotten her up the hill right away. *Yeah, damned if I'm letting that happen.*

She pulled herself from the car, grabbed her broom, and made her way up the hill one steep, wobbly step at a time... but rather than remaining on the sidewalk she veered right, onto a narrow pathway that wove between a boutique hotel and a neighboring brew house. *This never works in the city*, she knew. Metro police always checked for cut-throughs. But maybe in the mountains...?

Her back ached and her torso and legs tingled from numbness, but she kept moving. Sure enough, the uneven dirt pathway led to Sierra Way, just across the street from the school's playground... and no officer was positioned there. As she reached the top, she heard a loud and unnerving sound from the school—maybe glass being smashed?—so she ducked next to the hotel's shrubbery to avoid being spotted. Across Sierra Way, officers crouched on the school's lawn, their weapons drawn. A second set of officers had already fanned out around the school's circular building, armed with rifles and shielded by helmets and armor.

Gunshots erupted from the far side of the school; an "officer down" message boomed from the patrol car up the street; sheriffs, armored and otherwise, charged around both sides of the circular building, presumably converging around whoever was on the opposite side.

Remedy knew if she was a parent, she'd be charging in too... and right now she basically *was* a parent, since her job, as she saw it, was to represent the community. She rose up from the shrubs, planted her broom in front of her, and headed across Sierra Way's four empty lanes, feeling the asphalt's heat through her thinly soled shoes. Her MS forced her to cross the road like an ostrich, step and stop. Halfway across, she heard shouts from an officer stationed at the barricade up the road—the barricade where Casey, Ron Wahl, and several others were corralled.

The officer ran toward her. She knew she couldn't win the footrace, but she also knew she didn't need to. The closest cover was now near the school, and with an active shooter that was exactly where the officer would have to direct her.

More gunshots rang out... this time from above, she realized, looking at the school's rooftop. *No one there. So where...?* She saw movement on the mountain behind the school—just a brief scuttling between shrubs. The sheriffs must have seen it too; gunfire erupted from the schoolyard as officers aimed for the spot on the hillside.

"Get down!" the approaching sheriff yelled. 'Into the bushes!"

She did as directed, forcing her pins-and-needled legs to cooperate. The officer, a bald man with a mustache, didn't join her; he continued further onto campus and joined his colleagues, who were methodically converging on the gunman's position.

Another gunshot sounded. Remedy saw someone rise from shrubbery that was nowhere close to where she'd seen movement just moments ago—several hundred yards away, well north of the officers' current positions. The suspect took three steps, dropped, then rolled over the edge of a deep, shrub-filled gully separating one mountain from the next. His body plummeted out of sight... though the jiggling shrubs suggested he was still on the move, headed up the gully.

Remedy's breath caught. She'd only gotten a quick look, but still...

That was him, she thought. *That was Muddy Guy.*

Just thinking about him sent a chill running neck-to-ankles. *Muddy Guy is the school's armed intruder.* That meant there might truly be a connection between Upsweep and the lockdown. Was Muddy Guy at the school to assassinate Jon? If so, why would he pick such a public place? Did Sarah calling his bluff about killing Jon somehow make him decide to get the job done right away? Did it mean Muddy Guy might now come after her again too? Or Sarah? She suddenly remembered the earlier gunshots and wondered whether Jon was okay.

The sheriffs scrambled across the mountainside, converging on the gully, but Remedy knew it wouldn't matter. The shrubs had gone motionless; Muddy Guy was gone. Even if he wasn't, he seemed very comfortable in hostile, outdoor surroundings. The sheriffs, she figured, had very little chance of finding him, let alone capturing him.

Tapping her phone's dictation app, she messaged an overview of everything she'd seen to the *Mountaineer*. Standing up, she used the broom to steady herself then headed toward the school's exterior walkway. Her story checklist was simple: she needed to talk with the principal, the teachers, the students. She also needed to touch base with the sheriffs, so she could find out the condition of the officer who'd been shot.

But mostly, she thought as an uneasy lump formed in her throat, *I need to talk with Jon.*

FIFTEEN

Peering through the scrub of his own hair, Russ Kitchtoo watched the cadre of sheriff's officers inching their way into the hillsides, whirling and aiming their weapons at every fluttering cicada that skittered across the trail.

Kitchtoo sheathed his dagger-like *quoth-lar*, knowing they wouldn't nab him. First off, they had already passed the spot where he had wedged himself into the tiny daylight space between leaning boulders, meaning he had an open exit off the hill if that's what he wanted. Second, the cops were having too much trouble keeping their footing in the loose scree—all while climbing an unfamiliar hillside without lowering their heavy, cityscape-designed weapons. Their only chance, he knew, was to spot him from afar so they could establish a firing position with cover and no need for movement. But they weren't going to spot him. He was like a mountain lion; no one saw him unless he let them.

Which he would, in just a few minutes. Some mercs kept sharp by honing their skills at shooting ranges and backwoods camps; Kitchtoo preferred the wrong end of a live manhunt.

Wanamaker's one lucky SOB, he thought, *having a pro like me assigned to take him out.*

He felt like an animal, exactly the way he liked to feel when working a job. His matted hair reeked, and dirt seemed to sprinkle onto him like iron filings to a magnet. His body sores didn't hurt but they smelled, and refused to heal. Primal voices tugged at his brain from within, voices which usually turned work into pleasure.

Jostling his tongue, he shifted four bullet heads from one cheek to the other as if they were candies. Their metallic flavor had an earthy aftertaste that had something to do with modern casings and manufacturers finding a cheaper way to produce the rounds. The changes spoiled the natural lead flavor from years past, but that's the way it was. Sometimes he ordered vintage rounds over the Internet, because they were such a delicacy, but not while he was on a job. Vintage rounds were for relaxing at home with his feet up and the flat screen tuned to a cooking channel.

Reaching into his pocket, he fingered two more slugs and popped them into his mouth with the others. Kitchtoo liked the intimacy, that feeling of control as he manipulated them with his tongue or clamped them between his teeth Seriously, did people really suck on mints? *Mints?* Bullets were bite-sized grenades... and he liked the idea that if anyone managed to pump him full of lead, he was already one step ahead of them.

Doesn't hurt that they seem to freak people out, either, he thought.

He spit a round into his right hand and threw it like a stone, watching it sail a good sixty yards. As a child in Rowock, he could peg a leaping salmon seventy yards out. Today's target was much easier. He watched as the slug hit a jagged, granite hunk embedded near the trail. Three sheriffs jerked sideways; one fired his weapon. The shot ricocheted off the granite, adding to the echoes already reverberating off the nearby peaks.

If the slug hits in front of you, that means I'm behind you, Kitchtoo thought, frustrated. This team was too easy.

Moreover, this wasn't how he wanted to be spending his days. The initial assignment had him taking Wanamaker down within three days, which sounded good. Now, those three days had stretched into a week with no clear end in sight. I.K. Emily had taken over Bonnicksen's show—the DOD's too, not that any of them actually realized it—and though Emily assured Kitchtoo that Wanamaker's time was short, she insisted they could both benefit by holding off until matters developed further.

For Emily, the objective was squeezing as much information as possible from an unknowing research subject. Kitchtoo had a very different goal. But both plans dovetailed with a desire to see Wanamaker end up dead. Delayed timeframe aside, that was fine with Kitchtoo.

He unsheathed the *quoth-lar* with his left hand while unholstering a pistol with his right, then stepped out from where he was wedged and fired off several shots, hitting one cop square in the hand. *Damn*, he thought, annoyed since he'd aimed for the fingers. The officers ducked for cover, time Kitchtoo was already using to his own advantage. If he'd wanted, he could have overtaken them, possibly even contained them. Instead, he scrambled for a lateral position, to extend his live training exercise. Tossing brush and other debris to his left, he dropped himself just below the sloping sandy edge of a runoff gully—practically in plain sight if not for his filthy, camouflaged appearance and the fact the tossed debris was rolling and splattering twenty yards away. The cops aimed for the moving splatters and fired, none the wiser.

Kitchtoo sighed. *How many more days of finding ways to entertain myself can I stand?* At least the buoy and creating a stir at the school seemed to set a match under Wanamaker; with any luck that sellout would sink further into the words he was seeing, just as I.K. Emily predicted. If so, it would bring Kitchtoo a step closer to the only reason he'd left Wanamaker alive for the past four years: to force the man to use those sentences in a way Kitchtoo didn't realize they could be used until I.K. Emily brought him up to speed. Once that happened, then he could go ahead and snuff Wanamaker.

He wondered whether I.K. Emily appreciated the irony, her hiring him to off a man he wanted dead anyway. Not only that, she was part of the same government that once tried to crush Tlingit culture. Charging her triple, as retribution, and then leaving the extra money to

Rowock's community center wasn't good enough... but it was a start, and he loved that his merc-rep was so solid that I.K. Emily continued turning to him for help with her most unpalatable situations, such as the one with Wanamaker. He especially loved it because she was fully aware he didn't always follow her orders, yet she kept coming back anyway. Sometimes the mess you made was still better than the one that needed cleaning up in the first place.

Still... having to play games with the sheriffs while waiting for Wanamaker's skills to develop... he might need to charge higher than usual. He wondered whether he'd feel that way if the local cops knew how to stage a better manhunt.

"Perp smells like a landfill took a dump on him," Kitchtoo heard one of the sheriffs whisper. Sound traveled in the great outdoors.

"By design," came the curt response.

"What do you mean?"

"Some of those merc-types get as filthy as they can, thinking it disorients opponents. Pretty sure he could've broken free of us, but for some reason he hasn't."

"Proves he's a pro, then."

"Proves he's a nutcase."

I *am* a nutcase, Kitchtoo thought. He wasn't himself, not anymore. He'd known that from the moment he'd seen little Emma in the water, drowned at only eleven years old. That was the moment home and happiness became words, and feelings ballooned into the only adversary he couldn't overcome.

Emma was all he had, all he wanted. She was his world.

And she'd still be alive if not for the Wanamaker family.

There was no moving on. *Nutcase. Lunatic. Unstable.* He'd heard them all in the years since and found the irony amusing. The true nutcases, he knew, were the people who gave up when things turned south, the ones who took the easy paths. Was it crazy to think that a Tlingit family choosing to cooperate with the federal authorities' early 1900s language ban destroyed their culture? That the Wanamakers' claim it was just a cover to keep private language lessons alive was irrelevant? That a united, forceful "no!" from the Tlingits wouldn't have saved their language, their community, their identity, their culture?

Was it crazy to think that the warning sign posted ten yards from where the ice patch gave way would have saved his wonderful Emma... if only she were able to read it? Was it too outlandish to expect the Wanamaker family should pay for that crime with an eye-for-an-eye exchange: Jon Wanamaker, the family's last living member, dies as punishment for Emma Kitchtoo's death?

So what if it is, he thought. He preferred a world full of him to a world full of them. Let crazy be the new normal. Wanamaker's family had to pay, meaning Jon had to pay. But Emily, the quintessential, tragic face for the price of losing a language, would come first. Sure, he wanted revenge... but where Emily was concerned, he wanted so much more.

Several sheriffs drew close to his position, probably without even realizing it. He climbed up from the gully, exposing his position to three of them, shooting two before they could react. The third fired four shots, all aimed at Kitchtoo's chest.

Taking the easy path, Kitchtoo thought, disgusted.

Life's so-called crazy paths were always more difficult—wresting his torso a full ninety degrees to one side while firing, which shrunk three-fourths of an opponent's target, had taken him years to master—but they usually worked. He heard the third sheriff's bullets cutting the air to either side of his body, followed by a startled grunt as Kitchtoo's dagger-like *quoth-lar* stabbed clear through the cop's left shoulder.

The rifle cluttered to the ground. Kitchtoo yanked backward on the *quoth-lar*, jerking it free from the cop, then kicked him. The cop staggered and fell, clutching his bloody shoulder. Kitchtoo looked at the other two sheriffs, the ones who he'd shot without warning. They were down, and probably had broken ribs, but their vests had saved them. *Damn cops would probably give me more of a challenge if I offed one of them*, Kitchtoo chided himself.

He used their pant legs to wipe the blood from his blade, spat three of the bullets he'd been sucking on straight into their faces, then hesitated.

What the hell, he decided... then sliced off his right earlobe with the *quoth-lar*. He studied it for a moment, admiring the lobe's supple shape, then glanced at the stunned officer with the bloody shoulder and tossed it onto his chin.

"Souvenir from Crazy," he told the cop, his guttural voice rasping from hours of swallowing—and applying—trail dust.

The earlobe hit the sheriff's chin and rolled down the side of his cheek, a slender blood trail left in its wake... plenty of DNA that crime databases would tie to someone else, thanks to I.K. Emily.

No, Kitchtoo thought, *I'm certainly not myself anymore.* That, mingled with what he'd learned about Jon Wanamaker's mysterious sentences, was why his daughter, against all odds, might still have a chance at life.

And, he thought with a vindictive sneer, *why Jon doesn't.*

SIXTEEN

J on stared blankly at his smashed window, still able to hear the muddy gunman's gritty, fleeing footsteps, still seeing ribbons... still a mess. He shook his head, trying to come to grips with what had just happened.

Correction: with what was still happening. He watched sheriffs race past, heard them shouting at the intruder from somewhere across campus, winced as gunfire exchanges erupted. Now that his students were separated from that maniac and the sheriffs were on-scene, everything felt different... as if he'd passed the baton and his portion of the insanity was done. He watched more officers run past his window, listening as their radios gave a play-by-play of the chaos outside. It all seemed so surreal, as if someone had installed a television into the side of his classroom and he was watching the latest cop show.

Eventually the sheriffs were at his window, and his door, assuring him the campus was now safe. Old man Holochwost was on the intercom, instructing students to remain indoors until their families could be contacted. There was no way school would continue—not today, probably not for several days. That was fine with Jon, who wasn't so certain he could continue right away either. It wasn't so much the trauma of surviving an active shooter on campus, though that was certainly part of it. What he really couldn't get out of his mind was having thirty children all looking for him to keep them safe... and not being able to ensure that he could. He already knew that helpless feeling would stay with him forever.

His knees buckled and he rocked backward, falling onto his butt just as Carl Sharp arrived. The ribbons arrived as well... not that they had ever really left. *"Even now, with someone threatening her, she felt the pain of their split,"* rolled before his eyes. Private stuff... the kind of stuff he felt he had no right to see. Answering Sharp's questions while watching the ribbons wasn't easy, but he managed to give a basic rundown of the glass-smashing incident.

"Why would the guy do that?" Sharp said, helping Jon to his feet.

Jon shrugged. "Nutcase?"

"Maybe. I'm not so sure. This guy managed to sharp-shoot your school janitor from two hundred yards, then downed one of our officers and evaded capture in some pretty rough terrain. Wasn't just the local unit either. Three of our guys are SWAT, up here on rotation. He dodged some pros and made it look easy. I'm thinking that makes him a pro too."

"Is Kinbacher okay?"

"No… but he'll live," Sharp said. "The perp shot him in the hands. That's not chance, it's a defensive firing tactic that's so rare it's damn near urban legend. The merc aims for the weapon rather than aiming to kill. In this case, the hands were the only weapon so that's where our perp shot Kinbacher—once to each hand, on the run, at distance. I've never run across anything like it."

"And your officer?"

"Vest saved him," Sharp said. "You got a good look at the shooter, right? Ever see him before?"

Jon thought about it. "No idea—he was covered in mud and leaves, like he thought he was part of a military raid. I could barely see his eyes."

"But there was something familiar about him," Sharp said, leaving the statement open-ended.

Fishing, Jon thought. *He still thinks I'm involved somehow. If Kitchtoo's the gunman, then he's right.* But now wasn't the time to reveal a possible connection with the Rowock buoy incident, not without any evidence… and it didn't matter since he knew he could answer Sharp's question honestly without bringing it up.

"If you're asking whether he was the guy Ernie and I saw by the lake, I really don't know," he said. "But yeah, it's possible."

"What'd he say when he shoved his head through your window?" Sharp said.

"He said, 'soon,'" Jon said, feeling his fingers chill and his stomach twist at the memory of that one, frightening word. "But why threaten me when he could have just killed me? What does that mean?"

Sharp put a hand on Jon's shoulder. "It means he's a nutjob, like you said. I'll arrange for extra patrols near your home. We can keep you safe."

Jon gave a dubious smile, recognizing the same sort of false promise he'd given his students. "I don't suppose you've got any leads?"

Sharp shook his head. "He took out the school's video cams—again, a pro. Can't be too many guys out there sucking on bloody bullets though. With all that saliva and blood, the lab will get something concrete."

"Wait," Jon said, suddenly remembering his phone. "I might have a picture of him."

He told Sharp what he'd done.

"Jesus Christ," Sharp said as the photo popped onto the screen.

The image wasn't perfect, but it did show a close-up profile view of the silhouette man in all his muddy, leafy glory. Sharp had Jon message a copy to a sheriff's department email address.

"Where'd he get the bullets he spit?" Jon said.

Sharp started to walk away without answering, then seemed to change his mind.

"Kinbacher," he said. "The guy dug them out of Kinbacher's hands."

Jon nodded, but muted any further discussion since he saw his students filing into the classroom to collect their belongings. Several were in tears. Others thanked him. A few hugged him.

"I'm proud of every one of you," he told his class, and he meant it.

The students filed out of the classroom, many of their families already waiting out front, sheriff's officers on hand for security. Only Arturo remained. Jon nearly asked why, then remembered this was his day to give the boy a ride home.

His phone vibrated with a new message from Holochwost.

```
Mountaineer's here, TV crews en route.
Can you talk with them?
```

That'd be a no, he thought, replying with the more polite suggestion that he was too frazzled and needed some peace and quiet. He knew Holochwost wouldn't be happy but was willing to risk it. News media, he didn't mind; the very likely chance it meant running into Remedy, on the other hand... he couldn't bear it, at least not today. Besides, he figured, Kinbacher deserved the media's attention. The janitor was a hero.

Outside his classroom, students hugged, parents embraced their kids, and Sharp answered tough questions. Jon saw it, yet didn't. Words licked at his thoughts then dropped back, like leashed animals. He forced them away, tucked his lecture materials into his satchel, then beckoned Arturo, who was waiting for him near the shattered window. The two of them headed for Jon's pickup... through the interior door, where no one would notice them leaving.

Jon made a left turn out of the school parking lot, onto the only portion of southbound Sierra Way that the sheriffs had reopened. Even with a head full of chaos he thought Quail Elementary looked like a postcard, its circular building set against the towering mountain. *Though maybe not today,* he decided, seeing sheriffs posted throughout the school's playground.

"Never been so happy to go home," Arturo said, pushing his backpack toward the floor near the front passenger seat, until it hit the tops of his feet. The boy's shoes had holes, his blue shirt had the faded look of a hand-me-down, and there was a chip missing from his right front tooth.

"Me too," Jon said. "You okay?"

"I thought we were gonna die."

Jon could tell from Arturo's voice that he was still shaken.

"He was a scary guy," Jon said, looking beyond a new set of ghostly, streaming sentences as he drove. "But the sheriffs are on him. He won't ever show up at the school again."

The boy kept running his fingers through his dark, tousled hair, beads of sweat running down his pronounced forehead.

"What about you, Mr. Wanamaker? Are you okay?"

"He didn't hurt me. I'll be fine too."

Jon glanced at Arturo, appreciating the concern. The boy looked like a rookie hitchhiker, eyeing Jon as if he half-expected him to dump him along the route even though the two had been commuting together for weeks.

Jon suddenly remembered how scattered he had been acting at the start of class. His students were probably already scared before the gunman even showed up.

"The important thing," Jon said. "is that everyone's safe. Another week or so, everything will be back to normal."

"Not for me. My dad says I'm dropping out."

Jon nearly gasped, his mind flashing back to the spectral sentence that had scrolled before his eyes during class. The same words, he realized—the exact same words about dropping out.

"Is this a joke? Did someone tell you to say that to me?" he said, his voice strained.

He scrutinized the boy's face but saw only bewilderment. Of course it wasn't a joke, Jon understood. He felt guilty; Arturo was one of his favorites, a dedicated student mired in a constant struggle to stay in school. Without a teacher showing up at his door every morning, the Morales family—hard-working immigrants with six kids and low-paying jobs—would have pulled their son from school months earlier. Instead, Jon used his informal ride service as a stay-in-school incentive, an approach that would never fly in a metropolitan school district.

"I'm sorry—you're right, I'm not myself," Jon said, forcing a smile. "It's just... I know your parents need you to work, but I keep hoping there's another way. If not, I get it. Sometimes you have to put family first."

He wondered how much of that was him grinding an axe; Jon's father had left the family before Jon was born. *Doesn't mean it's not good advice*, he decided.

They took the transition lane onto Paulton Road, crossing over the Sirretta River and into a charming nest of posh boutiques, restaurants, and upscale hotels. One block later, Jon reached Hanafin Park, Quail Point's Old West centerpiece. Cars inched behind a stalled SUV near the park; car-sized ribbons inched across Jon's vision, obscuring his view of the road.

"*Of course it wasn't a joke*," formed before his eyes.

He slammed on the brakes.

"The same words," he mumbled, stunned, as the pickup skidded to a halt.

People in the park pointed and stared. Arturo was staring as well. "Mr. Wanamaker, what's going on? We're in the middle of the road!"

Jon caressed his head and his temples, again trying to contain the ribbons as he stepped on the gas. "Sorry... not feeling well, I guess."

Maybe Francis was right, he thought. If his mind was truly shifting to an alternate linguistic framework after a lifetime with to the first one, it might be causing mental issues.

They reached the edge of town, where four-lane Paulton Road funneled itself into a two-lane highway. The road then paralleled the river before directing them through six miles of scrub-covered hills and a local economy that flatlined where the upper Sirretta met Isadora. As they arrived at the aging motels, churches, and mobile homes near the edge of Wofford Notch, they could see the lake and its sun-baked edges off to their left, cracked and shriveled as a triathlete's lips.

"Doesn't mean it's not good advice," Jon saw.

"Ku'cta-qa," he said, his hands at his head once again. "How do I stop it?"

"Stop what, Mr. Wanamaker? What's happening?"

Jon didn't answer. The words streamed before his eyes, screaming for attention. So did the highway, which again widened into four lanes as they entered Wofford Notch. They raced along the two-mile boulevard, past the diner, the one-room market, the tattoo shop, the hitchhiker.

A familiar-looking hitchhiker, Jon thought as a chill rose along his spine. He looked in his rear-view mirror and saw someone large, hairy, and muddy.

"Oh my God—Mr. Wanamaker, that's the crazy guy!" Arturo shouted, looking back. "He's taking off... heading behind the market!"

Jon's heart pounded. He hit the emergency button on his phone; the 911 operator said she was sending sheriffs to the location right away. Jon's word-clouded mind reeled, picturing the man he'd seen, comparing it to the man who shoved though the classroom window and his faded memories of Russ Kitchtoo. *Could it really be the same person? Several years and several thousand miles later?* The intruder's face was covered in mud, hair and leaves, so he couldn't be certain. He wondered whether he was so bothered by the red buoy, and the ribbons, that he was seeing connections that didn't exist. Still, if there was any chance... he needed to tell Francis, tell Sharp, tell the school, tell everyone.

The ribbons came at him again, this time with force, drawing closer than before, pounding his head like a migraine. Panicked, he whipped the pickup onto a lakeside street lined with trees and run-down mobile homes. Laundry hung between trees, old cars sat on repair blocks, dusty dogs wandered unleashed.

"You've got to get out," Jon blurted, to Arturo. "You're only a block from your place, so you'll be fine. And I'm sorry—we'll definitely talk about your schooling when I'm feeling better."

He looked at the words again. "*The ribbons came at him again, this time with force,*" it read. He suddenly remembered experiencing something this extreme once before... four years ago, on the island.

"Mr. Wanamaker...?"

"Go, Arturo. Please... go now."

Arturo hopped out of the truck and started walking down the road, but slowed and turned to look back. Jon stepped out, hoping to wave him away, but by now he was too lost in the hundreds of words scrolling past his eyes. The sentences gained speed and clarity, and appeared to describe what he was doing, seeing, even what he was feeling. He felt a twitching sensation inside his head, as if an unused muscle were coming to life.

For a moment he saw words describing things he didn't recognize: a baseball pitcher, a big guy in a government office. Then fear for his life consumed him. He pulled away with his mind but the sentences followed. Jon felt his legs moving backwards, trying to run from something they couldn't escape: his own head.

Arturo watched his teacher, uncertain what to do. Ever since first grade, his neighbors in Wofford Notch had warned him to be on the lookout for people who took part in Satanic practices. Halloween costumes, playing Dungeons and Dragons, back-spinning records (whatever those were)—all works of the Devil, they claimed, especially for non-English speakers. Telltale signs of Satanism also included irrational behavior, nervous sweats, and muttering in unknown tongues... and here was Mr. Wanamaker, doing it all.

As a first grader, Arturo might have actually believed his teacher was possessed. Now that he was twelve, he knew the adults in his town had some weird ideas. Still, his favorite teacher was in the middle of the street, walking in circles, acting crazy. Arturo watched Mr. Wanamaker panting like an exhausted runner, eyes moving left to right, sweat dribbling down his forehead.

Then he remembered Mr. Wanamaker telling the class that a friend of his was marrying someone they all knew. Just like that, an idea formed. Dashing to the closest home, he pounded on the door until a bald, elderly man answered.

"Hey Mister, my teacher needs help!" Arturo said, pointing.

"I'll call 9-1-1," the man said.

"No," Arturo said. "Call the lady at the post office."

SEVENTEEN

Jon squeezed his head between the palms of his hands, feeling as if it might help contain something inside. He knew he was in the middle of the road, heard cars swerving to avoid him, understood that the people watching from their front yards probably thought he was crazy. None of it mattered to him, not with the ribbons taking over.

Kaleidoscopic lights burst inside his head, then receded, the recesses of his mind rubbing against layers of thought and existence as if they were tangible, pliable substances. This time Jon didn't resist. He let the sensations carry him forward, delving deeper into his psyche. Reality—his Tlingit heritage, the muddy sniper, the Sirretta Valley—seemed secondary. Wispy words continued scrolling horizontally before his eyes, stringing together in sentences describing what he was doing, seeing, even what he was feeling. They streamed through his mind, slowing in speed and gaining clarity as they went. A sentence formed before his eyes: "*He knew he was in the middle of the road...*"

The words, he realized, were drawing closer to the point where they would meld with what was actually happening. The twitching sensation inside his head returned. A twinge of fear pulsed through him as he wondered what would happen when the sentences melded with reality.

He looked at the words again. "*The twitching sensation inside his head returned,*" streamed past. He stared at the description of his actions, his independence metamorphosing to... he couldn't tell what. His world became two-dimensional, the events involving himself and everyone he knew reduced to text as his life and the words describing it *came together as one.*

He was out... here... somewhere. It felt so strange, so impossible.

So good.

The words no longer floated in front of him, they were around him, somehow a part of him, or maybe he was a part of them... and yet separate. He felt a sense of mastery, control, comfort. Complete peace. He wondered: could this be Paradise? Could he be dead?

No, he decided. This was different. He felt alive, more so than ever before. His mind felt fifty times its original size, and he had the sense his hands and feet could reach clear across the universe. What was happening? Were other people going through the same experience? Maybe Erich Bonnicksen would know, or his family in Rowock... but no, he couldn't go to them. That just wasn't an option.

I'm here. Above the world and yet part of it. Ernie, are you okay? Where are you? Where's Arturo, the people in their yards, the cars? There's no one here, just...my words. So dark, so isolated... where am I? How can this be, my thoughts are... words! No... they're more, they're... what, reality?

What is this?

What am I supposed to do?

When I don't think, nothing appears. So, if I do think... if I compose something... what? And what about Arturo? Is he still nearby, watching me act crazy the way Francis watched me?

The boy knew more Tlingit than Jon knew Spanish. Maybe Tlingit seems exotic to him, Jon thought. No matter—the boy loved the language and Jon loved teaching it, regardless of a student's ethnic background. Anything that keeps Tlingit alive is a step in the right direction, he figured.

And now I'm losing my best student.

Arturo's parents were about to put him on a lifetime treadmill of dead-end, low-paying jobs. Jon saw it all the time: families with so little money their circumstances undermined their children's future. Some of the kids couldn't study because they were hungry. Others didn't have a quiet place to study—too many siblings and only one room. Most weren't encouraged to do their schoolwork anyway; college was a dream for the financially secure. Arturo deserved better... they all did. No different from—

Anything that keeps Tlingit alive is a step in the right direction.

Maybe I can—?

No. No, probably not.

Could I? They're just words. It's not as if they actually do anything. What if...

How about something simple, like...

Arturo placed a hand to his ear as a sentence formed within his head, then repeated, and kept repeating until it, and its meaning, became clear.

Jon pulled away with his mind, returning his psyche to a normal state of consciousness. The words before his eyes vanished, and everything became three-dimensional again. He heard scrub jays chirping, and the sound of wind rustling the pines alongside the road... but what he really heard was the silence. The people watching from their yards said nothing. A lady he didn't know, slender with auburn curls and a stuffed grocery bag at her side, held his arm, talking.

No, Jon realized, someone else was speaking. Several feet away, on what was left of a cracked, root-lifted sidewalk, his twelve-year-old student repeated a sentence once, twice, a third time.

"*Gunalchéesh ax x'éit yisa.aaxí,*" Arturo said, looking bewildered.

"*Gunalchéesh ax x'éit yisa.aaxí?*" Jon mimicked, then translated, "Thank you for listening to me."

Arturo placed his hands atop his head, frightened. He shrugged his backpack onto the street, pulled out the homework sheets from Jon's class and tossed them in the air, stepping away as they scattered, as if they might infect him.

Jon stood up, nudging the woman with the auburn curls away. "Arturo, are you okay?" he said, his voice quaking, his thoughts traumatized by the possibility that he had done something dreadful to a great kid. "Arturo?"

The boy shook his head violently, as if a spider was wandering his scalp. "*Gunalchéesh ax x'éit yisa.aaxí,*" he said again. "What is that? Where did it come from?"

Jon heaved a sigh, relieved to hear Arturo speaking English again. Still, the ramifications... tears rolled down his cheeks and he dropped to one knee, overwhelmed. One sentence, he thought. Just one simple sentence. What if I'd done more? He realized his legs were shaking, and he felt so scared he thought he might throw up. He held a hand over his mouth, then dragged it across his face, trying to reassure himself that he was still... himself.

Arturo, standing a few paces away, wore a confused expression, as if someone had pulled the rug out from under his entire concept of normalcy.

"What just happened?" Arturo said.

Jon couldn't say anything, couldn't bring himself to utter words for fear of the consequences. Seeing ribbons was hard enough; discovering they described important events, as the sentences had done by showing him he would find a bottle in Blackmule Gulch and revealing Arturo's father wanted his son to drop out of school, was even more astounding. But this... this was overwhelming.

The kid stared at him, waiting for any kind of explanation, but Jon had none to give. Instead, he listened to a voice from his past resonate within his head.

—*You're a monster* —

Monster, hell, Jon thought. I'm a miracle.

EIGHTEEN

Leaning against a school drinking fountain, Remedy listened as Quail Elementary Principal Larry Holochwost praised Jon, and Butch Kinbacher, for risking their lives to protect students from the gunman. Holochwost's chest-length beard and baggy clothes made him look like the proverbial mountaintop guru—*fitting, since he's four thousand feet above sea level*, Remedy thought—but he seemed clueless when she asked to speak with the men he was praising.

"I'm not sure if that's possible," he said. "Mr. Kinbacher is being treated by paramedics and Mr. Wanamaker left to drive one of his students home. He was in the classroom that was... breached. I think maybe he needed to clear his head."

Remedy nodded, but she had a feeling that wasn't Jon's only reason. *He left because he knew I'd be here*, her gut told her. Not that she blamed him. Their conversation, whenever it finally happened, wasn't going to be an easy one.

She heard objects jiggling and saw Carl Sharp walking up, his flashlight and holster jostling with every step. The deputy looked unhappy.

"You're really going to push me on a day like this?" Sharp said to her, and she knew right away that someone had told him her explanation for crossing the barricaded road during the incident.

"The trail near the hotel was open," she said with an apologetic shrug. "Anyone could have wandered across just like I did."

He gave her a sarcastic look. "And I'm sure you just happened to be visiting the hotel at the time."

"Something like that. I did make a point of waiting for your people to move forward, so there was no interference with any law enforcement activity. And my media ID—"

"Yeah, spare me," he said. "Your press badge doesn't get you behind barricade lines and you know it. Lucky for you I've got bigger fish right now."

Sharp glanced at Holochwost, who was still standing there, listening.

"This'd be the part where I badger the hell out of the reporter, who then tells me stuff no one but me can know," Sharp told him.

Holochwost got the hint and excused himself. The school's entry still bustled with officers, and TV crews from Porterfield, but the students, parents and faculty had already left. Sharp pulled Remedy to one side without any regard for how it might affect her balance, which she appreciated since it meant he didn't give a whit about her MS.

"Your story today mentions a dirtbag who might be connected to some defunct research project," Sharp said. "I can't help notice he fits the description of the school gunman... not to mention the carjacker Sarah Ushida reported, and the sniper who might have started our wildfire."

"Yeah, I caught a quick look at him on the hillside," she said. "No guarantees but I think it's the same guy."

"One of my officers said the same thing. You have anything that'll help me figure out who he is?"

Only Jon, she thought.

"No," she said. "But tomorrow I'll be talking with the researcher who headed the Upsweep project."

"The guy from back east? I've been trying to reach him all week. When you talk with him, tell him to touch base with me asap."

"Done. Just keep Muddy Guy away from me, will you? Away from everyone."

"'*Muddy Guy*?' Aw, please tell me you media people aren't turning him into some psycho celebrity. That's the last thing we need."

"That *is* the last thing we need," she said, wishing more of her colleagues felt the same way. "Tell you what: if you catch him, I'll keep the sensational stuff to myself and just report the story."

"Oh, I'll catch him," Sharp said, walking away. "The guy attacked a school. This is now a full-on manhunt—and *that* you can quote me on."

She watched him conferring with his officers and took it as her opportunity to duck back inside the building. The central cafeteria was empty so she took a moment to file her reporting to the *Mountaineer*, with a CC to Chris Casey and Ron Wahl since they were working the same article.

`Not even 3:15, you beat your own 4 pm estimate`, Casey wrote back, along with his location.

She went outside and found him taking shots of the investigation.

"Ron's already back at the office, Julie's got him adding his stuff to yours," Casey said, aiming his camera at the shattered classroom window. "Guess this'll be your transition story, huh?"

"Transition?" she said, then remembered: next week she'd switch from full-time to freelancer, with Ron taking over her daily reporting duties. She wondered how well she'd take to working an abbreviated schedule from home. *Not well*, she already knew. *Damn MS.*

"Just a heads-up," Casey said later, as they drove toward the *Mountaineer's* Hanafin Park office. "There might be a little ceremony in your immediate future."

She looked at him like he'd just said the car's engine was about to die.

"Are you serious?" she said. "Because I specifically told everyone not to—"

"You didn't actually think they'd let your last Friday afternoon on the job go without a sendoff?"

She let out a frustrated sigh. "I'm not leaving. Just... changing how I work."

He grinned. "I get it, I really do. But you know... people need the closure."

"Yeah, well, I'm not closing anything."

She felt bad jumping on Chris, who probably had nothing to do with it.

"Look, just show up, have some champagne, and they'll be happy," he said, pulling the car up to the *Mountaineer* and it's western, saloon-like exterior. "Consider it a celebration for the biggest story we've had around here since that cow swam across the lake."

Fine, Remedy thought, irritated. *I'll imagine it's for the story*. But when cheers erupted as she slide-stepped through the newsroom doorway, it was clear there was no pretending the party wasn't for her. She forced a smile as her co-workers—all eight of them, miraculous considering half were still assigned to fire coverage—hoisted champagne glasses. Julie Henderson, their bee-hived, fifty-something editor, gave a heartfelt toast, and despite lingering misgivings Remedy appreciated the sentiment. For thirty minutes she sipped champagne and chatted with everyone as if she was happy and the invisible needles stabbing her arms, waist and feet weren't forcing her to give up her job. But their poignant appreciation sharpened her regret. She felt like Wile E. Coyote, immersed in laughter even as the edge of a cliff crumbled beneath her feet.

Henderson, who wore an outdated plaid suit and bragged she needed a man about as much as she needed a new hair stylist (and she thought she didn't), put an arm around Remedy. "Carjackers, conspiracies, slipping police lines at a shooting... I see you're still pushing to go out in a blaze of glory," she said.

Remedy flexed her hands, testing the intensity of the pins and needles. "Any better way to go out?"

She watched Henderson light a cigarette, smell it, admire it, then snub it out. "Wouldn't know," she said. "Never plan to go out."

Henderson placed the snubbed cigarette back in an ashtray advertising "Bourbon Flat Days," a weekend of frog-jumping competitions and whisker contests.

"Know what I don't understand?" Henderson said. "Some 1800s guy sets up a tent with a plank across two barrels by the river, sells booze to miners, forms Bourbon Flat, which later becomes Quail Point... and it affects how I personally will spend my weekend more than two centuries later. You ever think about that?"

"Not sure I follow."

"People from another time, affecting your daily life."

"So maybe somewhere in my family tree," Remedy said, "are two people who, if they didn't get together, wouldn't have passed on the crappy genetics that have me leaving my job today."

Henderson held up a finger. "But maybe they also passed you the talent that's kept you in this business," she said. "This party isn't the end, you know. You'll freelance stories to me every few days, weeks, whatever. Doesn't have to be now."

Remedy grabbed her broom. "No," she said, "it has to be now."

"So you can go out on your own terms."

"Yeah. Except I'm not going out."

Henderson nodded. "Any meds you can try?"

"Nothing without side effects. They trim the relapse totals, if you don't mind the kidney damage. Better to tough it out than be someone's guinea pig."

Henderson reached for a filing cabinet, opened the top drawer, and produced a lighter and another cigarette. This time she didn't snuff it out.

"You know, six years ago I figured you and your *Morning News* resume would blow outta this pea-speck town in a week," Henderson said. "Turns out you're a helluva reporter, and a helluva woman too. Your family's eaten some serious Ohio crow, that's for damn sure."

"Not sure they'd agree with you on that."

Henderson took a deep drag then blew smoke into the newsroom, daring her staff to complain. "Media haters never do," she said. "But you don't turn your stories into blogs. You're a fact-conduit, old school. Hell, I'm going to miss having you in here every day. As far as I'm concerned, the shift to freelance doesn't change a thing. This paper will always run your work. *Always.*"

Remedy was so surprised by the compliments—possibly the first Henderson had ever offered—she wasn't certain how to react. A text chime interrupted before she could.

"Front desk says some old guy's in the lobby, asking for you," Henderson said. "One of your sources?"

Remedy couldn't think of anyone who fit the description. She gave Henderson an appreciative pat on the shoulder then slide-staggered to the lobby—the only other room at the paper's office. A man who seemed to have more trouble standing than she did waited by the reception desk, rocking leg to cane, cane to leg, amid the scuffed desks and ten-year-old computers.

"Remedy Conover?" he said, through squinting eyes.

If he wasn't so old, she might have worried about answering. As it was, she found herself wondering whether the man might be connected to Muddy Guy.

"Yes...?" she said, without moving close enough to shake his hand.

"We need to talk, right away," he said.

"Okay..."

"I'm sorry to drop in unannounced, but I'm a friend of Jon's, and a linguist, and..."

"Jon?" Remedy said. "You mean Jon Wanamaker?"

"Yeah," the man said. "I'm here to talk with you about your husband."

NINETEEN

As soon as the old man mentioned Jon, Remedy knew two things: hearing him described as her "husband" still cleaved her insides... and she had seen this person before. She was certain they'd never met, but he looked familiar, enough so that the fact she couldn't remember his name was driving her nuts.

Then it hit her.

"You're in Jon's old photos," she said. "Mr. Hanlon, right?"

"Francis," he said, holding up her story in the newspaper's print edition. "I see we're both looking in on the same person."

Remedy felt abrasive fingertips against her palm as they shook hands. She was uncomfortable meeting him now, without Jon. When they were married they'd invited him to visit several times, but he hadn't wanted to leave his home on Prince of Hollis island... which made her wonder what had finally convinced him to leave now.

He motioned her outside and the two of them exited the *Mountaineer* office at a snail's pace, one clinging to a cane, the other a broom. Smoke-diffused daylight diluted the paint jobs on the western-themed buildings lining Big Red Road, but Hanafin Park, a few paces away, looked a vibrant green. Just beyond the park, several Forest Service trucks loaded with men and equipment chugged out of Quail Point, fire-fighting crews headed for long shifts.

"I hear it's still not contained," Francis said.

"It's up to forty-five thousand acres," Remedy said. "No homes though. Not yet, anyway."

He nodded. "Again, I apologize for coming during such a busy time but your husband got your text messages and asked me to stop by."

"Ex-husband," she said, smoothing the sleeve on her blouse. It didn't need smoothing, but she needed busywork whenever she thought about Jon.

Francis nodded. "Yeah, shame about that. He doesn't know what's good for him, that's for sure. Nice of you to wait so many months before filing for divorce."

She gave a courtesy smile. "Jon always talked about introducing us, but everything went so fast," she said. "Dating for a year, then married for less than a year before... well, before it ended."

She didn't mean to create an awkward moment, but she knew she had. "Are you still with the university in Anchorage?"

"Ketchikan," he said. "Emeritus. I'd do more but the body says no."

"I know what you mean."

Francis looked at her broom. "Why not a cane?" he said, gesturing to his own.

"Not as stable. Try it."

She passed him the broom then watched as he tested its angles, felt its upward spring.

"Not bad," he said, passing it back. "Anyway... Jon keeps telling me he plans on talking with you, but I'm expediting. Today okay? Five-thirty?"

She felt exhausted but accepted the offer anyway. "You do know about what happened at the school, right?" she said. "Is Jon really up for this?"

"He texted me earlier, said he's fine. I'm not driving these days but Jon's friend, Ernie, is the local bus driver. You know him, right?"

She did. She also knew when someone was pushing for something just a bit too hard, the way Francis was, but if this was her avenue to an interview, she wasn't going to question it.

"Good," Francis said. "Ernie's been taking me around when there's no one else on the bus, which seems to be about half the time. If it's not too much of an imposition, I'd appreciate it if you'd ride over to Jon's place with us. We'd both like to talk with you while we head over."

Remedy agreed, then went inside the *Mountaineer* lobby for her notebook and recorder while he phoned Ernie. When she came back, Francis was seated on a bench facing the park, watching two children play tag between sycamores.

"Ernie says ten minutes," Francis said.

She forced a smile. "Mr. Hanlon—"

"Francis."

"Francis... I've messaged Jon several times this week. Why didn't he send a reply, or call?"

His answer seemed measured.

"Tell you what, he stared at your message, on and off, for hours," Francis said, looking deep in thought as he spoke. "Lot of emotions in play here. I guess you don't need me to tell you that."

"No," she said, her tongue suddenly dry. "But I do need you to tell me what's going on, because I'll be honest with you, the Sidney Institute researcher who ran Project Upsweep says Jon's extremely dangerous."

"Erich Bonnicksen said that?"

So... he's familiar with Bonnicksen and Upsweep, she thought.

"He did," she said. "Which makes me wonder if maybe the sniper who went after him, and the gunman at the school today, think he's dangerous too. Is he?"

Francis coughed, the cracks and bags on his face contorting in multiple directions with each wheeze. "Jon is a good friend of mine, practically family... but right now he's messed up in the head. Losing it... acting nuts."

"He seeing a doctor?"

"He's seeing words, Ms. Conover. Loads of 'em, streaming before his eyes. Calls them ribbons. They're coming at him in dozens of languages but one of them stands out: an old version of Tlingit. Really old. He says he's reading the words in English... but that's because he's used to reading English and his mind's translating best it can."

"That's... bizarre. What caused it?"

"No idea. But the bigger issue is, what's it leading to?"

So this is why he wanted to talk with me, Remedy thought. She moved herself next to Hanlon and followed his lead, leaning against the apparel shop as he explained how Jon's ribbon swarms had hit along the Sirretta River Trail.

"They're just words," she said. "Doesn't sound very dangerous to me."

Francis scrunched his wrinkly face. "Might depend on where the words are coming from."

"I don't follow."

"Not sure I do either. But I think he's tapped into something significant... maybe the part of human physiology that's responsible for language development, old and new."

"New?" she said. "The world's languages have been around for ages. There aren't any new ones."

Hanlon issued a cough... or was it a laugh? Remedy wasn't sure.

"You think the words you speak aren't new?" he said. "Try reading anything from the 1900s—a blip in time, big picture. You'll notice the difference right away."

Good point, she realized.

"Every year we invent new ways of saying old things," he said. "In the process, words go extinct. Zits were once *murfles*; *flesh-spades* became fingernails; to *chantpleure* was to sing and weep at the same time.

Language is fluid, always adapting. Lot of it gets lost along the way. Back when humans were still in the hunter-gatherer stage there were about twelve thousand languages; today there are about six thousand."

"We've lost *six thousand* languages?"

"Six thousand, and counting."

Remedy shook her head. "Does it really matter? I'm sure some of those lost languages were pretty primitive."

Francis wrinkled his face again. "There's no such thing as a language that's more primitive or more complex. The minute you try learning some obscure jungle language, you discover the nouns may not be as big but the verbs may be bigger."

Remedy flexed her shoulders; the pins and needles in her back were killing her. "Okay, so we're hemorrhaging languages and now Jon's seeing some of the old words that we've lost."

"Special words," he said. "Words from a mother language that probably hasn't been used in four thousand years, maybe longer."

"Mother language?"

Francis nodded. "A root language spoken by the people who created an entire culture. There were a number of so-called Mother Tongues, one of them probably launched the entire Semitic language family."

"And Jon's seeing the Tlingit mother tongue?"

"Again, it's just a guess. But yeah."

Remedy shifted her shoulders and legs, to keep them from stiffening.

"I'll grant you it's weird, but you said Jon can translate the words," she said, giving him her polite, time-to-deliver-the-goods smile. "So, what does it matter?"

Francis swirled his tongue over his lips, thinking. "It matters," he said, "because language shapes the way we see reality."

"Huh? You just lost me."

He smiled. "Yeah, my apologies. I'm trying not to be too professorial, but run with me on this: language is what provides the framework that the mind uses to interpret reality."

"Okay..."

"Given Erich Bonnicksen's research, and Jon's involvement—as you've outlined in your article—I'm thinking Jon's tapped a back-channel within himself, something linguists call a language module."

"Meaning... what?"

"Meaning that back-channel gave Jon use of the Tlingit mother tongue... a language that presents a such a different framework of reality that he now sees something you and I can't even imagine: the ribbons."

She resisted a condescending smile. "So? They're just words."

Francis waggled his cane at her in a nuk-nuk-nuk motion.

"But words form our reality," he said. "Easiest example: people lacking words for a color usually can't see the color. In rainforest cultures, which have dozens of words to describe the color green, native people can look at a shrub and see multiple shades. You and I would only see two or three of them."

The skeptical smile she'd resisted until now broke through. "You're really going to stand here and claim language defines the way we see things?" she said.

"Me and an entire field of researchers spanning decades would stand here," he said, pointedly. "And yes, language is *absolutely* what gives you the framework for understanding your experiences. Without that framework you're blind to what's right in front of you."

She shook her head. "Sorry. No disrespect, but I'm not buying it."

He smooshed his lips into a scowl. "No one believed a woman in a gorilla suit could trot through a video of three people playing basketball, thump her chest, then walk off, all without being noticed," he said, "but half the people who watch the 'Invisible Gorilla' video created by two cognitive psychologists don't see the gorilla, which is why it was an Internet sensation."

She remembered hearing about the video, but had never watched. "That's not linguistics," she said, "it's lack of focus."

"No, it's linguistics," Francis said, "because everything you see, or fail to see, is a linguistic construct. Did you know that until 1802 people thought clouds were all one puffy, identical thing? Then someone with a different frame of reference realized clouds had several basic forms, and he named them—cirrus, cumulus, and stratus. Suddenly everyone awoke to the differences, and modern meteorology was born."

Remedy gestured for him to continue while she opened a notebook and activated her phone's voice recording app.

"Time, that's a linguistic construct too," Francis said, waiting as she scribbled notes. "Cultures perceive time differently depending upon whether their language frames it as a past-present-future sequence or a single process... or whether it conceptualizes the future as behind them."

She thought it over, unconvinced but fascinated.

"So, what does all of this mean for Jon?" Remedy said. "I get that he's now seeing sentences we can't see. But other than it being a confusing nuisance for him, it doesn't seem like too big of a deal."

Francis took a deep breath, and held it in long enough that Remedy worried his cracked, doughy face might pop.

"Maybe it isn't," he said. "But two things worry me: first, the sniper on the Sirretta River Trail knew about the words and seemed to think they mattered. More importantly, Erich Bonnicksen's apparently coming here, all the way from Boston, even though he and Jon don't get along and haven't spoken since Upsweep. That means Bonnicksen knows something we don't... and from what Jon's told me about him, it's probably something significant."

He hesitated, then added, "I'm worried, Ms. Conover. Jon thinks he may have stumbled into a way to preserve the Tlingit language, but..."

She waited. "But...?"

"I have a nasty feeling," he said, "that whatever he's messing with could get himself, and the rest of us, killed."

TWENTY

emedy felt uneasy as she and Francis watched the Sirretta Valley Transportation bus approach Hanafin Park. Much of what he had just told her seemed outlandish, and yet he had a valid point: both the sniper and Erich Bonnicksen seemed unusually preoccupied with Jon.

"Did you tell Jon you're worried?" she said.

"I did, but he's more focused on whether it might give him a way to save the Tlingit language, like the sniper implied. Maybe too focused."

Remedy sighed. "He's still obsessed with *that*."

"I take it you remember his commitment to The Race," Francis said.

She smiled. "He talked about it more than he talked about you— and he talked about you a lot. Yeah, I know about The Race."

The bus—a white, heavily windowed, overgrown camper that looked like a cousin to the shuttles circling airports—turned the corner at Hanafin Park and pulled up in front of them. Remedy felt a few butterflies as the accordion doors opened; post-marriage friend fallout meant she and Ernie hadn't spoken with each other for a couple years.

Then she saw Ernie leaving the driver's seat to greet them, a devilish expression on his face. "Jon's gonna kill me for doing this without him," he said to Remedy, crinkling his nose to shift a set of wire-framed glasses. "But hell... the idiot should'na ever screwed things up with you in the first place."

Remedy couldn't help but break into a grin. "Talk like that will result in a big tip for the driver," she said. "Or at least a big hug."

"Deal," he said, stepping off the bus so they could embrace. He looked the same as she remembered, except for one thing.

"You're smiling," she said.

His one-sided grin, something of a rarity, stretched further left. "I'm engaged," he said. "Just this week, actually."

He told them about Virginia Hanafin as he helped Francis, and then Remedy, onto the bus. The interior was default public transport motif: beige plastic siding, aluminum handrails, worn bench seats.

"Matter of fact I just got a text from Virginia as I drove up," Ernie said, swinging himself into the driver's seat. "There's something going down near Hanafin Road, she says Jon's name was mentioned. I think we need to get over there, fast... just in case, you know... trouble."

Remedy exchanged concerned looks with Francis. She felt the engine vibrate her seat as she leaned her broom and shoulder bag against her leg. As they pulled away the bus doors closed, reopened, then closed again.

"Still scatterbrained after being shot at," Ernie said, releasing the door lever.

Remedy ears perked. "You were with Jon? That wasn't in the report."

Ernie's narrow eyes, peering from the wide-angle mirror above the windshield, paralleled his eyebrows. "Yeah, Carl Sharp knows I'm seeing Virginia, so he did me a little favor and left me out of the whole thing."

He saw Remedy's stunned expression and added, "Not until after he made sure I wasn't involved, of course."

"Of course," Remedy said, making her sarcasm obvious.

Once Ernie had the bumpy, rattling shuttle bus underway she pulled her notebook from the shoulder bag and had him tell her about the sniper and the bottled brain. The bus shuddered as it hit fifty miles per hour; between that and her shaky hand, her jotted notes looked like stick figures.

"I won't pretend to understand most of this, but I do know this much: Jon needs help," Ernie said, angling himself as he steered the bus around a tight, mountain curve. "He's always acted like a man carrying a lot of weight, not that he ever said why. But before, there was the sense that he had things under control. Now... it's like he's overwhelmed, for no apparent reason."

Given the circumstances, Remedy didn't find that particularly abnormal. "He's been sniped, and today he was attacked at his job," she said. "Don't you think 'over-whelmed' is a pretty reasonable reaction?"

Ernie shrugged. "I got shot at too," he said. "But for him it wasn't so much the sniper, it was the buoy. Something about finding that bottle next to the red buoy really got to him... like it reminded him of something."

Remedy saw Francis shift in his seat, but couldn't tell whether it was from secrecy or discomfort.

"So why come to me?" she said. "The marriage is long done. I'm just a reporter on a story, probably the last person he wants to see right now."

Ernie scoffed. "I think we all know you're far more to him than a reporter on a story."

"If that were true, he wouldn't have walked out on the marriage."

Francis lifted his cane like a pointer. "Unless something forced the issue," he said, a not-so-subtle reference to their earlier discussion. "There's nothing but regret in that man's voice when he talks about leaving you, Ms. Conover. That, and a whole lot of sorrow. I think—and Ernie agrees—that you're the one person who might be able to ground him. Pull him back from whatever demons are after him."

She studied the sickening, gray smoke plume towering over half the valley's sky, then closed her notebook with an audible snap. "That's not why I'm here, gentlemen," she said. "Right now, I have a job to do."

"And we get that," Ernie said, his eyes darting between road and mirror as they drew closer to the weed-filled median and mobile homes at the Wofford Notch outskirts. "We also get that you'd be pissed after what he did. I sure as hell would be. All we're hoping is that somehow, in the course of you two interacting for the first time in ages, maybe it helps stabilize him somehow. No other obligation. Okay?"

He slowed, made a left turn onto Hanafin Road, then stopped abruptly. A small group of people blocked the roadway, waving the bus to go back. Just beyond them, a blue pickup was in the middle of the road, at the end of a long set of skid marks.

"That's Jon's truck," Ernie said, then added, "I'll help you off, but I can't leave the bus so... wait, there's Jon."

Even at a distance, maybe three houses away, they could tell something was wrong. Jon was wobbling, and moving in strange patterns, while a boy standing nearby seemed shell-shocked.

"So much for not leaving the bus," Ernie said, pulling the shuttle to the side and the keys from the ignition. "I'll be right back—and don't you dare mention this in your newspaper."

He leaped down the bus stairs, headed in Jon's direction. A burned-rubber smell, possibly from Jon's tires, wafted through the open bus door.

Francis looked at Remedy. "Hell if I'm staying," he said.

"Exactly what I was thinking."

She grabbed her broom and slowly followed Francis off the bus. Even parked, the shuttle floor jiggled enough that she had to focus on keeping her balance, especially on the high, shuttle-to-ground step.

"Jon's coming this way," she said, feeling her chest and stomach grow cold. Until today, her arduous research and the physical challenges of reporting her story had kept her personal feelings at bay. Now, looking at her husband... *no, ex-husband...* everything seemed different.

"We don't have to do this together," Francis said. "I'll tell him you're—"

"No, I'm fine. Let's go."

She walked forward, his forearm in one hand, her broom in the other. Ernie had already reached Jon, who was in the middle of the street. His dark hair appeared mussed, his buttoned-down shirt was drenched with sweat, and he seemed to be having as much trouble walking as she and Francis did, leaning heavily upon Ernie's arm. The boy stood on the nearby sidewalk, next to a slender woman with auburn curls.

"I think Jon and the kid are both in shock," Ernie said as Remedy and Francis approached, "but I can't figure out why. The lady helping the kid says she's already called for help. The kid's speaking gibberish and Jon hasn't said anything."

"That's not gibberish," Francis said, listening. "It's Tlingit. The boy's thanking us for listening to him."

"No," Jon suddenly muttered. "No... not Arturo thanking. I'm the one thanking, Francis. I used the ribbons, I placed the sentence in his head. The sentence stuck."

He lifted his head, focused his eyes on Francis. "It stuck, Francis. The Tlingit stuck: *gunalchéesh ax x'éit yisa.aaxí.* You see how huge this is? Arturo didn't know the words. Now he does. The ribbon words actually stuck."

Francis's eyes widened enough that his crow's feet momentarily smoothed. Remedy gave him a questioning look, but he didn't elaborate.

"Why's your truck in the middle of the road?" Francis said.

Jon didn't answer, and again looked lost in his thoughts.

"His engine's still running, and with those skid marks he must have hit the brakes pretty hard," Ernie said, "but there's no sign of an accident."

Remedy saw the woman with the auburn curls comforting the boy—Arturo, Jon had called him. Other people were milling about, neighbors from the looks of the opened gates along the street, many of them typing on their phones. *Guess that's how Virginia hears stuff so fast*, Remedy thought. She had Ernie ease Jon toward her.

"Jon... what happened?" she said. "Are you okay?"

They locked eyes. His pupils looked dilated, his stare vacant, as if the windows to his soul had ballooned. He blinked, and for a moment he seemed to register her face and her reason for being with Francis. His expression changed, projecting a trace of the confident masculine facade men unconsciously present when trying to look strong in a difficult spot.

"You're here, I'm so glad you're... oh that's right, for the story, your messages," Jon said, half talk, half mumble. "I'd be glad to help you out... I might need some time first, but I'm glad to help you out."

She put a hand on his shoulder.

"Not just for the story, okay?" she said. "You first, story later. Deal?"

He nodded, let go of Ernie, and stumbled over to Francis. "Everything's changed," Jon said in an exhausted voice. "Everything."

"What happened, Jon?" Francis said. "What's changed?"

He shook his head, suddenly grinning like a poker player setting four aces on the table. "Everything," he repeated.

"Jon, I know this is awkward but I've told Remedy what's been going on," Francis said. "She's investigating Bonnicksen's work. I think she can help us."

Remedy noticed Jon was breathing heavily, almost a pant.

"When I was a child, I would always say, `tell me my name' to my grandmother," he said, his voice stilted. "She didn't speak much English, so she would say the word '*Onatay*,' point to the moon in the sky, and make the soft howl of a wolf. All these years, I thought I'd never know what she meant."

Remedy sensed his point: with so few people left who understood the language, he didn't know the meaning of his own name.

"But now," he said, "maybe..."

He disappeared into his own thoughts. Remedy pulled out her phone and hit the emergency button, but he shook his head before the call connected.

"I need to be alone," he said, turning away. "I need to think things through."

He stepped away from Remedy and walked down Hanafin Road, toward the distant lake. Ernie raced forward and grabbed an arm, slowing him, but Jon shrugged it off. Two strangers from the crowd chased after him as well, urging him to wait until the ambulance arrived, but he kept moving.

"Mr. Wanamaker... wait!"

Everyone, Jon included, turned upon hearing the loud, young voice.

"This is messed up," Arturo called, taking a few hesitant steps in Jon's direction. "You gotta tell me how you put those words in my head."

Jon bowed his head and shook it, as if fighting cobwebs. "Soon as I figure it out myself, you hear me? I'll get you some answers. I promise."

Arturo nodded. He still looked shaken, but his body language had calmed.

"Jon, give me a chance to help," Remedy said. "I know about the ribbons, remote perception, the island—and I've heard from Erich Bonnicksen. He's on the way here right now. Something's going on, bigger than all of us. We can figure this out together."

He looked up at the sky for several seconds this time, then tossed his truck keys to Ernie. "I look around," he said, "and I see Arturo, and Ernie... Francis... and you...

Rem. I brought you so much heartbreak and never wanted to, maybe never needed to, and..."

He hesitated, looked skyward, then back.

"My whole life is standing in front of me like I'm on some kind of TV show. My job, my heritage, my wife, everything that I value. It's all here. But in my head... in my head there's so much more that's not here. It's... out there somewhere. Or inside... I'm not really sure. But there's so much more, miracles and nightmares and an entire universe, more than all of you can even..."

His voice trailed off. Remedy moved forward but Jon raised a hand, waving her off. "I'll put it together," he said, lips quivering as he wandered away. "I'll be myself again. Soon. I promise." He turned and jogged off, away from the street, away from the crowd, away from the pressure.

And away from the only people who might be able to help him, Remedy thought, saddened.

TWENTY-ONE

Turbulence rumbled Erich Bonnicksen's plane as he glanced at the seat next to him. Razor snored like a percolating coffee maker, but at least they were finally on their way to the west coast.

Once we land, he told himself, everything becomes simple: a three-hour drive to Isadora—*oh God, three hours in a car with Razor*—followed by a short time tracking Jon down in that hole-in-the-wall town where he lived. From the look of the online maps, the Sirretta Valley was so small he probably couldn't avoid bumping into Wanamaker if he tried.

We'll find him by tomorrow night, he decided. With any luck the hired help—*I guess I'd better call him Kitchtoo*—would be somewhere nearby. Cliché be damned; two birds, one stone was a perfectly fine way to operate.

Turbulence hit again, a notch more violent this time. Bonnicksen caressed his left cheek, which was still bruised, swollen and sore from the pitcher slugging him earlier in the week. *At least the jerk's asleep,* he thought.

No reason for Razor to see the video he was loading on his tablet.

He muted the tablet's volume and hit "play." A darkened room appeared on the screen: his lab from five weeks ago, or at least what was left of it. Piles of wire lay strewn across the floor, the shattered remains of what once formed cages. The walls seemed curved, misshapen into crevices and tunnels. Seed mounds, chewed up newspaper, and cheese chunks littered the corners.

A human silhouette stepped in front of the camera, beckoning others to follow. Bonnicksen saw three of them move inside, all armed with assault rifles. The video jiggled, the sign of a shoulder-mounted camera. Someone in the midst of the team carried it, Bonnicksen remembered—the eight-man strike team.

More silhouettes fanned into the room, blocking much of the onscreen view. Something moved along the right-side wall; the silhouettes whirled, their rifles discharging, sparks and smoke blurring the video until everything quieted. The lead silhouette held up a hand, signaling the others to wait, then stepped toward the area where they had seen the movement.

Three seconds later, the silhouette split into five vertical segments that fanned apart and collapsed to the ground, as if sliced by massive, unseen claws. Rifle flashes erupted again, but this time the ammunition dropped to the floor as soon as it ejected from the barrels. The room swayed; walls changed color, from green to blue to yellow. Silhouettes flew towards the wall like leaves to a tornado, some disappearing into thin air, others bursting into pulpy, goopy clouds that showered onto the floor.

Thank God I muted the sound, Bonnicksen thought. The screaming was bad enough, but the sound of the bodies ripping apart was the worst part of all. No, he corrected himself... paying *beaucoup* bucks for the cleanup, and more importantly the cover-up, was the worst part of all.

The lab image undulated, warping as if someone had grabbed the entire building and treated it like a wet rag, twisting out the water with both hands. Linoleum transformed to soil; ivy started growing across the room. Then Bonnicksen saw what he was looking for, the split-second frame that had haunted him for the past month.

A female silhouette sat amid the ivy, her eyes two tiny spots of light, bleached, assured, unforgiving. Exhibit C, Bonnicksen knew. The person responsible. *The muzzled animal inside every one of us.* Only this particular woman had minimal education and devoted very little time to introspective, philosophical thought—her background screenings, conducted prior to bringing her into the lab, made it very clear that she wasn't exactly a deep thinker. That suggested Exhibit C was prone to knee-jerk, emotion-fueled responses with only limited means of shaping, or controlling, her wishes compared with, say... Jon Wanamaker.

Yet look what she managed to do. Now imagine the same thing in Wanamaker, a man with extensive linguistic capabilities and focused intent. If Wanamaker was now capable of using his mind the same way Exhibit C had, then yes, it made him a deadly threat, but it also made him an outstanding road map. Killing and lobotomizing him was the next big opportunity. From there things were easy: study Wanamaker's brain then rinse and repeat, duplicating Upsweep and the work with Exhibit C while adding further controls. The payoff—exposing a means of utilizing the same back-channel skills without producing the same threat—wasn't very far off. Which meant safely manipulating environments from afar, using only the mind, wasn't far off either... nor was the moment he would join the scientific pantheon.

Too bad the neural mine's my only option, he thought. The vicious device would rupture Wanamaker's cerebral cortex, meaning some forty percent of his brain tissue would be damaged upon detonation... at least if Exhibit C was the guideline. Still, that was better than the nearly sixty-percent obliteration rates with Exhibits A and B, and left more than enough pertinent tissue to study post-mortem. Discovering that a simultaneous detonation in both the percipient and the agent preserved additional brain tissue, for reasons he still didn't understand... that was a major leap, even if it only worked when the two individuals were within short range of one another.

Tomorrow night, they will be, he told himself. The Wanamaker threat's just about over.

He looked at Razor. The jock had no idea what they had injected into his head four years earlier, just like Exhibit C's percipient in the more recent trials never had an idea. But just as that latest neural mine succeeded when the strike team did not, so too would the mine sitting inside Razor's skull. The micro-mechanical disk was a human brain's worst nightmare, capable of wirelessly transmitting electric current so strong it shattered neurons at their atomic level.

That's why Razor's intense perceptive link with his agent, Jon Wanamaker, was crucial: it meant their minds were linked. Get Razor into reasonably close proximity to Wanamaker, detonate the neural devices, and the resulting neurological trauma would blow through Wanamaker's mind.

Bonnicksen only regretted it meant imploding Razor's head in the process.

TWENTY-TWO

Jon ambled toward the lake, awash in sentences and unable to stop thinking about the one he himself had crafted.

"*Gunalchéesh ax x'éit yisa.aaxí*," he said aloud. Basic Tlingit words... except one moment Arturo didn't know them and the next, he did. Even as the shock and confusion eased, the miracle seemed just as astounding.

This was a true game-changer for The Race, he knew. No, the sentence he had thrust into Arturo's head wasn't perfect; it couldn't be, not when all that remained of the Tlingit language was so fragmented, pockmarked with unknown words and missing speech segments. Still... what he had accomplished was light years beyond simply viewing the ribbons. He had interacted with them, producing a real-world change, with no apparent side effects to Arturo or himself.

"Abracadabra," he said, brainstorming. The clichéd "magic word" had unknown origins, but armchair linguists claimed it was derived from ancient Hebrew and translated to "It came to pass as it was spoken." Others favored a dubious, Aramaic origin that nonetheless reaffirmed linguistic power: "I create like the word." Did incantational words, though fantasy for anyone speaking modern languages, have a historical basis in fact? Did some languages... root languages, mother tongues unspoken for millennia... did they have genuine ability to influence, or even shape, existence? Were they the remote perception mechanism within the human brain that Erich Bonnicksen was attempting to isolate with his island experiment?

Is that what Project Upsweep opened up inside of me?

He lost track of time, meandering near the lake until he turned toward a U.S. Forest Service campground that served as the community's perimeter. He knew his house was the first place people would come looking for him... but he also knew he was thirsty, famished, and exhausted. It was time to get home.

Ten minutes later he was there. The residences along his dirt road conveyed rustic charm, huddled beneath the looming Sierras. He approached cautiously and spotted Enid Schulien, one of those retired widows who stationed themselves in the front window as if it was a job, pretending she and her two schnauzers weren't watching from the double-wide across the street.

His house, a stucco cottage nestled between mulberry trees, was Ernie's former home and looked it; the place had paneled walls, speckled indoor-outdoor carpet with no padding, and windows that rattled whenever a breeze kicked up. It wasn't much but Jon was there by design, having transferred all claim to the Quail Point A-frame he'd co-owned with Remedy over to her. *The least I could do after leaving without an explanation*, he figured.

Inside, his DVR was recording and his answering machine indicated new messages, but everything else looked the same as always. After seeing a gunman's head burst through a window and then watching his own words embed language into a student's mind, it felt reassuring to see his home looking exactly as it should.

He heard a knock at the door and found Carl Sharp out front. Questions followed, mostly about what had happened with Arturo, but Jon kept things simple, telling Sharp he had grown dizzy and stopped the car in the middle of the road. Truthful, to a point, he knew. He also knew Sharp was more concerned with finding the school gunman.

"But trust me, I'm far from finished looking into things," the deputy said while driving off.

Jon's head swirled; more words streamed past. Francis was right; he needed to talk with Erich Bonnicksen. But that would mean digging up horrible, buried memories from Project Upsweep... from Amelynd. There had to be a better solution.

His front doorknob twisted. Ernie let himself inside, no knock, no warning. Jon wasn't thrilled to have another guest, but didn't necessarily mind either.

"Drink?" he offered, opening the refrigerator.

He shuffled a plate of shriveled roast beef to reach a smattering of sodas. Ernie spotted a beer and took that instead.

"I parked your truck along the side of the house," he said, slapping the keys on the kitchen counter. "I see you're doing better."

"Where's Rem?"

Jon's bottle opener kept sliding on Ernie, but he managed to pop the beer cap. "Having an early dinner with Francis," Ernie said. "I wasn't sure you were ready to have her in your face, asking questions."

"I'm not. Tell Rem she can come over tomorrow morning."

"You sure?" Ernie said.

Jon took a seat on an adjacent barstool. "I owe her a lot more than that, don't you think?"

Ernie swallowed some beer. "Don't know what to think. I mean, leaving your wife with no explanation, in the shape she was in... you've always admitted that was a shit move, Jon, but you've never explained it."

Another swallow, probably for the tension rather than the beer.

"Pretty crappy being stuck with someone in such bad shape, so I get it," Ernie said. "Even all skin and bones, she still looks good, but I suppose after awhile..."

"Up yours. I didn't bail because of the illness. If anything, I fell for her even harder after I saw how well she handled it."

"Yeah? Then why'd you leave?"

Jon wanted to tell Ernie about the ribbons, about how they gave him access to information and events that he had no right knowing. He wanted to tell *everyone*, if for no other reason than to get it off his chest. But he understood the fear it would create if he did. He felt that same fear with every ribbon.

"Look Ernie, it's not that I don't trust you—"

"Not sayin' it is," he said, studying the beer label. "I am saying Remedy isn't doing that story for her career, no matter what she claims. She's out there giving you a chance to reconnect. So don't be an idiot."

He took another swig of his beer, sauntered up the hallway, then hesitated at the front door.

"Virginia said yes," Ernie said. "Thought you should know. The way I see it, you're either my best man or you're not invited. All depends on whether you decide to get some help for whatever's swirling in your head."

He shut the door behind him. Jon watched his hunched silhouette pass by the front curtains, wondering whether this was another lost friendship. Ernie was right, though; Jon knew it in his heart. But give up The Race? It was like he'd told Francis: *when I'm running The Race, my grandmother's still with me.* Giving up was not an option... especially now.

Frustrated, he went outside for some air. His patio was a cracked, concrete rectangle, and the dirt road out front needed weeding. An old pickup bed needed weeding too, even though it was on cinder blocks. Jon looked down the road, at the shimmering lake patches peeking at him between the campground oaks. He knew he could always—

He fell against the wall of the house, scraping his hand on the stucco. The ribbons were back, blurred but tugging, begging, pleading.

"No," he said, muttering at the wispy outlines as they streamed past his eyes. "It's too much... no more..."

He fell to his knees. The streaming sentences felt like a raging current, pulling his mind along with them until everything *came together as one.*

Uncertain, he waited. When nothing happened, he experimented:

Tlingit words, phrases, and stories tore free from the past, resurfacing after decades. People in his neighborhood found the language embedded into their minds, and whether educated by school or by street they understood every word.

Other words emerged as well, words unspoken since the beginning of—

Push harder, his subconscious prodded. Push boundaries.

Everything in sight spun out of control. Trees bobbed up and down, plants enlarged and shrank. Lake water leapt from its border and danced to the tune of a bracing rock beat. A quicksand pit formed on the underside of a passing cloud and sucked Enid's two schnauzers away.

Jon heard a spark and felt a body-jarring jolt hammer the inside of his head. He staggered backward, stunned, trying to figure out what happened, but there wasn't time—not with tree-and-quicksand chaos everywhere he looked. The same crazy, impossible stuff he had first seen during the storm on Amelynd Island, Jon suddenly remembered. Desperate, he refocused on the streaming sentences, beckoning the ribbons toward him. He saw them curving like a diverted stream, edging closer.

I'm in. But how do I regain control?

There was no sound, no motion, only Jon alone with his blank mind. Then he remembered: abracadabra. *He found the Tlingit words, translated them, reoriented them... and wrote.*

The trees stopped moving, the plants returned to normal size. Lake water and passing clouds regained standard properties. The missing schnauzers plummeted from the sky, slowing to a soft, safe landing. The neighbors, though frightened, would recover, especially Enid Schulien, who didn't even... didn't even...

Jon felt the ribbons slipping away. Panicked, he stretched his weary mind, desperate to grab on, to fix the remaining damage, to make things right. But the ribbons seemed to snap away from his head, like a rubber band. As they soared off, he fell out of contact... then passed out.

TWENTY-THREE

Waning sunlight formed horizontal fingers that shone between the Sierra peaks, straight into Jon's eyes. Dazed, he shook off his cobwebs and peered around. The house and the neighboring mobile homes were pockmarked. Trees were aflame, fencing torn asunder, sections of earth missing. The lake had receded, and the remaining terrain was a black-scorched checkerboard littered with debris.

Just like Amelynd, he thought. *Only there, the disaster was triggered by that god-awful squall.*

For a split-second, he could picture the terrifying cloud wall, the eerie, supernatural glow, and the downed, wind-whipped palm fronds impaling colonists. Then, the subsequent, existential threats... *so much worse.*

But no, there was more. *What was it? Why can't I remember? What the hell happened?*

He screamed.

His torn-up neighborhood, bad as it was, wasn't the level of what he'd seen on the island. He tried to stand up but couldn't, dizzied and stunned. The fact there was still sunlight meant he hadn't been out for long, but still... Sirens sounded in the distance. He heard Enid Schulien talking, saw a gathering crowd looking his direction.

It's time, he knew. *Time to call Bonnicksen.* He took a deep breath, held it in, then let the air out slowly as he dialed Bonnicksen on his cell phone.

"Jon—thank God," Bonnicksen answered. "Where have you been, I've been leaving messages for two days. Listen, we've got an emergency and it involves you. I'm on a plane to California right now, so just stay where you are, okay?"

"No, it's not okay. What's happening to me? What haven't you told me?"

Jon heard someone barking orders on Bonnicksen's end, ordering him to shut down his phone during landing.

"I can't talk now, the flight attendants are all over me for answering the phone. Idiots! As if this call isn't a billion times more important to their safety than the stupid regs, huh Jon?"

"Why is it so much more important? What do I need to know?"

"Listen, you remember what I said to you after Amelynd?" Bonnicksen said. "About how I'd need to check back with you as the research gave me new results?"

Painfully so, Jon thought.

"Well, this is one of those times, and it's crucial I see you right away. I'll be in the Sirretta Valley in a few hours and I've got your percipient with me. Are you at home? We can meet you there as soon as we get to your area."

Jon looked at the madness around him and wasn't sure what he should say.

"I'm home but the streets are... closed off," he chose, uncertain.

"Doesn't matter, I'll get in," Bonnicksen said. "Just stay where you are, okay? My plane gets into L.A. in a few minutes, I'll drive to your place from there. Got it?"

Jon lifted his eyes. It wasn't the first time someone had acted like the drive from Los Angeles to Wofford Notch was no different from hopping on the freeway.

"This can't wait, Erich. I'm seeing words... Tlingit words, but they're different, and if I ...

"Yeah, yeah, I know, things probably seem crazy but I can solve everything when I get there."

That'll take hours, Jon thought, factoring in how slow the winding, two-lane Sirretta Canyon road could be on Friday evenings. "I need answers now. Not later."

Bonnicksen sighed, and sounded put-out. "Whatever's happening, don't do anything," he said. "Just stay put and wait for me. Once I'm—"

The connection ended with a click and, Jon imagined, a minor scuffle with the flight attendants. Another typical conversation with Bonnicksen, he thought: heavy on the foreboding, but with little useful detail.

He heard a crunching sound on the debris-laden street and returned his attention to the frightened, confused neighbors. More than two dozen of them were there, standing motionless, staring at him as if they'd come face to face with the epitome of evil. Little by little the details registered in Jon's mind, telling him all he needed to know: the Bible in Enid's hands, the fear in their eyes. He saw it all, and understood.

"I've just called for help," he said, his voice strained. "Someone's on the way... someone with answers."

No one responded. Many of them seemed afraid to speak.

"I know the new words in your head are scary, but they're just Tlingit words," Jon said, backing away. "Nothing threatening, just a set of words. They're not complete... not even close... but you people are helping me save an entire culture's language."

The crowd exchanged terrified glances. Owen Gleason, who Jon didn't know but recognized as a neighbor from two streets away, stepped forward. He was NFL-wide, wearing a jacket with a holster-shaped bulge.

"So... you're admitting it was you, then," Owen said, his eyes trained on Jon, unwavering. "Wrecking everything... shoving un-American words into our heads... that was you?"

Tlingit's a lot more American than English, Jon thought, but remained silent.

"How?" the man said. "I don't see how that's even possible... how *anything* I just saw is possible."

"It's... hard to explain," Jon said.

Owen shook his head. "It's not hard to explain at all. What I just saw, with the trees, the water, the dogs? That's Devil's work, no two ways about it."

Jon didn't like where this was headed. "Owen, I promise you there's no Devil involved."

"Your promise doesn't mean a thing," Owen said. "I've heard how you teach that ape language to the kids at the school, how you messed that kid up with it this afternoon. That's what you're saying you've put in our heads, right? The ape language?"

"It's an American Indian language," Jon said, softly. He could tell there was no reasoning with such a frightened, angry, rural group. Scanning the crowd, he spotted Enid near the back, her arms folded, her judgment final.

Owen motioned to the group. They surged toward Jon, approaching from all angles. Jon told himself to run away, call Carl Sharp, wait for the sheriffs to arrive... anything non-confrontational. The last thing he wanted, especially given all that he had just done, was anyone getting hurt on his account... himself included.

But in that moment he also recognized an unsettling truth: calling the sheriffs might not help. His guttural language had made people suspicious to begin with. The way he'd left Remedy, who was well-known around town because of her job, didn't exactly add to his popularity. Now, he knew, things would be even worse. Sharp was already skeptical, and Ernie wouldn't be there to ease tensions.

Streaming sentences appeared before his eyes again. He pushed them back, conscious of the risk, not wanting to lose control like he had the last time.

But as people climbed through the rubble, intent on cornering him, he had nowhere to go. Sentences loomed, the neighbors advanced, desperation mounted. Worse, his wondrous linguistic tools beckoned. Jon closed his eyes, locked onto the wispy words. Sentences started forming...*and his solutions took hold.*

Weapons fell from hands, neighbors fell to their knees, and Jon fell from grace... or at least, that's the thought that popped into his mind, anguished at having to use his new-found ability as a means of control. Desperate to defuse matters quickly, he used the neighborhood's demographics to his advantage, releasing an airborne anesthesia from a local survivalist's basement stash. Doziness hit them fast. Jon, immune from the effects, watched his neighbors gently collapse into the weeds along Maple Lane, fully asleep.

He took a deep breath. This time, using the words felt comfortable. He had no sense he might lose control.

Don't fall into the trap, he told himself. Don't be one of those guys who sips power and goes nuts. Stay true to who you are. Win The Race.

Even as Jon formed his thoughts, he could see the sentences describing them pass before his eyes. In only a few moments he'd grown accustomed to it, his initial fear supplanted by curiosity and a desire to explore his limitations. Already he sensed that it didn't matter whether he crafted detailed paragraphs or a single sentence, so long as he specified the result. But there was so much more to learn.

Curious, he studied the paragraphs imprinted in the firmament. They seemed endless, remaining in the ether like computer text, the older sentences absent but accessible if he scrolled his way into the past. Jon did just that, finding portions focused on a baseball pitcher, some DOD guy, and

Bonnicksen. Moreover, he discovered that Russ Kitchtoo was indeed the sniper-carjacker-school gunman... and was apparently working for both Bonnicksen and the mysterious I.K. Emily. Reading through the text, he began to understand how their lives intertwined with his actions, his circumstances.

He paused, stunned. All of the sentences, whether they documented his own thoughts and actions or those of others, somehow connected to him.

It's a narcissist's dream, wasted, Jon thought. He had no interest in reading about himself. His culture? Sure. Himself? Why bother? He already knew about himself.

Still, he now knew for certain that Bonnicksen and I.K. Emily were right: the ribbons were useful for much more than saving a lost language. They offered power... and control. He knew he needed to make certain neither of them ever attained it.

He looked over the sections describing his school day, his dazed exploits out front of his home, his encounter with the neighbors. What struck him wasn't the text itself, but the fact things had happened between then and now that weren't documented. That was important; it meant the ribbons, and his text-review ability, were not all-encompassing. Events could still happen beyond the realm of the specific text, and that was something he would have to keep in mind.

He eased his mind into a normal state of consciousness, exhilarated, but his thrill faded as the significance of what he could do, and what he had learned, hit home.

"Ku'cta-qa," he uttered, overwhelmed.

His neighbors were still asleep near the road but someone else had arrived, moving past them, into Jon's driveway. "What the hell, Jon?" Francis said, looking stunned. "Seriously, what the hell?"

Jon couldn't muster much of an explanation. "I know... this wasn't the plan, Francis," he said. "This was *never* the plan."

Francis surveyed the broken asphalt chunks, toppled trees, and lopsided mobile homes lining the street. "Are these people dead?" he said.

"No, asleep. Another half hour or so, they'll be fine."

"Christ, Jon, you can't do this kind of stuff to people without—"

"I know, but things got out of hand and I needed to contain it fast. Wait, did Rem see this?"

Francis scrunched his lips, sending bags of skin bulging across his face. "Ernie was already driving her back to Quail Point right before you launched into this... *whatever* this is."

Jon took a breath, relieved Remedy hadn't been nearby. "He didn't give you a ride too?"

"The restaurant's only three blocks up, I felt like walking. Probably lucky I don't have a tree sticking out of my ass after what I saw happening."

The thought that Francis could have been hurt sent shivers up Jon's spine. He told him how he had used the ribbons to add Tlingit vocabulary to the local lexicon. "Just like I did with Arturo," he said, "but more extensive this time."

"From the look of things, you embedded a lot more than words into this neighborhood," Francis said, and there was no mistaking the fear in his voice.

Jon couldn't deny it, so he didn't.

"Between this, what happened with the kid, and the school gunman," Francis said, "not to mention you being connected to the wildfire and Remedy's story about your involvement in Bonnicksen's project... Jon, the sheriffs are going to take you in for questioning and hold you for a good long time. Probably until they can explain what you've done... and we both know they're never going to be able to explain what you've done. Hell, *we* can barely explain what you've done."

Jon knew Francis was right. The Arturo incident alone was bad enough: an emotionally traumatized young boy claiming his teacher had done something odd was a good way to get a cop's attention. Add in the rest of it...

"So...?" he started.

"So, we need to go," Francis said. "Once your neighbors are awake they'll be calling the cops, assuming they hadn't already called before you hit 'em with your voodoo. We don't have much time."

"Maybe even less than you think," Jon said, and brought Francis up to date on what he had learned from the ribbons about Russ Kitchtoo and Erich Bonnicksen planning to assassinate him.

"Go pack a bag," Francis said. "We're getting out of here, fast as we can."

"Are you serious? You really want me to run away with that madman on the loose?"

Francis tightened his lips, then pointed his cane at Jon.

"You are now, by far, the most dangerous man in this valley," he said. "That's the only thing the cops, Kitchtoo and Bonnicksen are going to care about. The only way to solve things is to get you into hiding, fast."

His eyes narrowed.

"Like it or not," Francis said, "you're about to become a fugitive."

TWENTY-FOUR

Remedy's deadbolt made a racket as she twisted it to lock the French doors. *Of course it did*, she realized. No one in the Sirretta Valley ever used their door locks. She heard Ernie's bus drive off as she slide-stepped to the living room, her stomach churning from the chicken-fried steak he had recommended for dinner.

Her computer, an aging desktop, still displayed her research from earlier in the day. She sat down and skimmed it. The web documents indicated aboriginal cultures had so few words for water that many of them couldn't see ripples unless someone pointed them out. Fishermen, on the other hand—with their extensive oceanic vocabularies—could identify specific confluences of tides, winds, and temperatures rather than seeing the ocean as a single, homogenous water body.

It seemed to support what Francis had told her about linguistic frameworks. Curious, she searched 'glotto-chronology' and found Muddy Guy had been referring to a method for tracing human languages back to a handful of mother tongues. The 'secular analytical paradigm' described standard scientific operating procedure: leave everything out but the facts. Under earlier paradigms, subjective information was considered acceptable for science studies.

She leaned back in her chair. Was Muddy Guy suggesting that Jon's ability marked the start of a new scientific paradigm?

One more search, she decided. By the time she was finished the sunset was too, but she had found the information she wanted.

"The dagger our attacker used, it's called a quoth-lar," she told Sarah's voice mail, wishing her friend had picked up. "It's a hand-made hunting weapon used for centuries by Indian tribes in the coastal northwest. The carved pommel's some kind of bear head."

Remedy paused, thought about what she wanted to say, then continued. "Sare, the Tlingits are from the coastal northwest. There's probably some connection between Muddy Guy and Jon."

Tears formed as she ended the call. *Dammit.* Treating Jon like another generic source wasn't working. All this time she'd held her feelings in check, but now, having seen him for the first time in two years...

Why do I still care about the guy?

She hated herself for giving a damn.

Her cell phone beeped. Two voice messages awaited, even though the phone had never rung. *Crappy mountain cell coverage*, she thought. She heard Carl Sharp asking whether she knew Jon's whereabouts and deleted it without returning his call. The second message was from Erich Bonnicksen.

"Change of plans—can we meet tomorrow afternoon?" his message said. "Razor Castillo and I are in Los Angeles, but TSA's detained me for questioning because I used my phone during landing, of all things. It looks like we'll have to make the drive to your area in the morning instead. I've already left a message for Jon Wanamaker, but I want to be sure you have the information you need to write... an appropriate story."

Meaning a puff piece that makes you look good, Remedy thought.

"Please remember, Wanamaker is quite possibly unstable, and very, very dangerous," the messaged finished. "I'll take care of this matter and provide all the details tomorrow."

Remedy texted him that a Saturday meeting was fine, then left her desk, ready to collapse onto her bed after a long day. Halfway to the bedroom, she noticed Hearse's unblinking eye. "I'll bet you're on Sarah's side," she said to the scooter. "After all, if I risk my life for this story you might never get me."

No one answered but the house itself, which came alive with creaky voices and the distant click-click-click of the lumberjack weathervane as the wind rose and fell. Windows rustled, and a dog scampered up the street. Periodic taps upon the roof told her the autumn leaves were starting to fall.

She suddenly felt very alone. Jon, gone for two years now; the nearby homes vacant, their owners now weekend visitors from distant cities; Sarah on the verge of relocating; her estranged Ohio family, disgusted with their "dishonest media" daughter. Even Pippin, her collie, had been gone for a year... and now her job at the paper was just about over. She felt as much an island as Amelynd.

Island... something about the word stood out in her mind. Why, of all places, did Bonnicksen pick such an isolated, difficult-to-reach place as the site of his remote-perception experiment? Had he known someone with an island? Even if he did, how did he score what amounted to a Naval blockade for such a low-level research project?

She wondered whether she could convince George Klase to help her. He had been brusque, but more or less open with her by the end of their interview... and he was a senior project coordinator for the DOD, meaning he probably knew the sordid backstories behind a good many programs.

Inspired, she left a message for Klase, inviting him to brunch in the Sierras before he returned home to the east coast. A few minutes later she had a simple, texted reply: `Tomorrow`.

Perfect, she thought. Rest time would have to wait. Returning to her computer, she scoured university archives, government documents, anything that might offer clues. A hint eventually materialized, in the form of an attendance roster for a linguistics conference held six years ago. Three names stood out: Erich Bonnicksen, George Klase… and Jon Wanamaker.

Coincidence? No way, she decided. Sure, there were a couple hundred attendees, and there was always a chance the three men never crossed paths… but no way. She clicked the website's homepage, and several other buttons, seeing plenty of nondescript banners but no conference sponsor information. *Who held this thing?*

Another round of web surfing served up an answer. "I.K. Emily?" she uttered aloud. "Who's that?"

Whoever it was had zero web presence with the exception of a real estate holding that listed an interesting entry: "Amel., South Pacific." Her gut told her Klase would have answers.

A guitar riff erupted from both phone and computer, signaling an incoming call.

"You sure about the quoth-lar?" Sarah's voice said.

Remedy smiled. "It's one of the few things I am sure of."

She heard a flush and cringed, realizing Sarah had been calling from a restroom.

"Yeah, well here's some news for you," Sarah said, over the sound of a squealing door hinge. "Virginia Hanafin's over here visiting a patient, she told me the sheriffs just put out a warrant on Jon. Some sort of vandalism to his street in Wofford Notch."

"Vandalism? Jon?"

"Yeah, he's a piece of work but it seems weird to me too. Let me mention the quoth-lar to Carl Sharp."

"Sure. At least now I know why he left me a message looking for Jon."

"Yeah, well Virginia also claims Carl already ran some checks on the guy who headed Upsweep."

"Erich Bonnicksen?"

"That's him," Sarah said. "Seems Bonnicksen has a lot of ties to the Department of Defense. Carl thinks DOD brought our stinky friend into this, and that they specifically wanted someone familiar with Jon. Pretty sure Carl's going to find it real interesting that the guy who busted up my car was carrying a Tlingit weapon."

"Muddy Guy knows Jon personally," Remedy said.

"Seems that way. Have you talked to Jon yet?"

Remedy wasn't sure whether the answer was yes or no. "Almost—it's a long story," she said. "Listen to this, though."

She told Sarah what she'd learned about aborigines, fishermen, and I.K. Emily. "The only thing I can't figure out is why Erich Bonnicksen would go to the time and expense of using an island," she said.

"Bonnicksen's trying to detect an extremely subtle, back-channel connection between people, right?" Sarah said.

"Yeah."

"Well if it's that hard to detect, he probably needs some serious distance between people for anyone to actually believe he's found it," she said. "Using an island doesn't raise any red flags, not to me. It might be a tad unusual, but it makes academic sense."

Remedy felt an idea germinating. "Sare, let me send Jon to you after I've talked with him," she said. "Give him a medical once-over, see if there's any evidence of what we've discussed so I have it for the story."

"He'd have to consent."

"He will."

"What if he's already under arrest?"

"Then convince Sharp the exam might help his investigation."

She could hear Sarah's hesitation. "Five minutes, no more."

Their connection cut out, leaving the click-click-click of the lumberjack weathervane. She heard other sounds too: her refrigerator, her creaky deck, a passing car. This must why some people leave their TV on all the time, she thought. Background noise soothes the nerves.

Something about what she had just noticed struck her as unusual. She thought about it and clued in: the deck was creaking. That either meant there was a heavy wind, which there wasn't, or...

Her shoulders tightened, and her chest went cold.

"Or," she said to herself, "Muddy Guy's outside."

TWENTY-FIVE

Remedy grabbed her phone to call 911, convinced Muddy Guy was spying on her through the bay window, ready to smash his way inside.

She took a brief look at Hearse as a possible escape tool but instantly ruled it out. Death, she thought, was preferable to letting the one-eyed beast win. *Drama queen*, she scolded herself. Slide-stepping away from her desk, toward the outer wall, she made a point of not looking toward the windows, pretending she didn't know someone was outside. Once she reached the outer wall, she flipped a light switch and stepped backward.

Light flooded the deck, beaming from spotlights mounted around her yard. Looking out, everything looked the same as always: rusting, iron café table and chairs, ornamental cypress trees to either side, her late collie's weathered, plastic den on the deck's opposite end. Then she spotted a male figure crouched behind the dog den. He had a hand above his eyes, shielding them from the light... and covering his face. When he finally lowered the hand again, she realized it wasn't Muddy Guy after all.

"Jon?" she called through the window, suspicious.

"Yeah, it's me," he said, standing up. "Can I come in? I don't have too much time."

"No kidding, there's a warrant out on you," she said. "You need to turn yourself in, get things cleared up."

She studied him, trying to gauge whether he was acting any different from that afternoon, when he'd looked like he was in shock. He noticed and assured her he was fine, but she kept hearing Bonnicksen's warning screaming from her subconscious. *I should keep the doors locked and call 911*, she thought, but she already knew she wouldn't. Jon meant too much... to her story, she told herself. Just her story. Nothing more.

A lie, she knew, but a reassuring lie. She swallowed hard. The next few minutes wouldn't be easy.

Jon, peering through the glass, looked just as troubled. His face was flushed, and his collared shirt was buttoned to the neck as if he thought he needed to cinch it up like battle armor.

"Seriously," she said. "Why are you lurking around if you don't have much time?"

He wore a sheepish expression. "Cold feet?" he offered. "I started wondering whether I could go through with this."

"Well, you're here," she said, "so we may as well get this done."

She invited him inside, the formality of it feeling odd. *He used to just walk in.* She pieced their time frame together: Jon had moved from Rowock to the Sirretta Valley four years ago, not long—she knew now—after Upsweep ended. The two of them met in the valley and married a year later; he left without explanation, she filed for divorce a year after that. *Two years*, she thought. *I haven't met one-on-one with him in two years.*

Their small talk seemed exactly that: small. He complimented her blouse. She voiced surprise that he was using the canvas book satchel she'd given him.

"Where's Francis?" she said.

"Up the road, hiding the truck. With the sheriffs looking for me, we didn't want to leave it out front."

So much for having a buffer to get the conversation started, Remedy thought.

"You should turn yourself in," she repeated. "Or at the very least get yourself to Sarah so we can find out what was going on with you this afternoon. She's willing to give you a quick medical exam. We could bring the Sheriffs in on things from there."

"Francis mentioned an exam too. I'll try."

He lifted up a bookcase photo of her as a child, running with her first collie. "I heard you lost Pippin last year," he said. "I'll miss that dog."

She felt her patience waning.

"Jon, that's not why we're here."

He held up a hand. "I know... believe me, I know. It's just... I want to talk about us first, something I couldn't do on Hanafin Road. Know what I mean?"

She sighed, stepped in front of the sofa, then angled her broom to pivot herself backward, onto the cushion.

"Not really," she said. "You left—*you*, not me. Without so much as a word. Just gone. Did you really think I wouldn't eventually file divorce papers? So hey, good for you, the marriage is done. Now why aren't we talking about the Upsweep cover-up?"

His head seemed to hang, rather than rise, from his shoulders. *Or maybe that's just my mind presenting what I want to see,* Remedy thought.

"Because I'm hoping maybe you'll understand that my leaving wasn't about you, it was... okay, this sounds cliché, but it was me," he said, his voice trailing off. He sat on the sofa, careful to keep several inches between them.

She gave a brief, sarcastic laugh. "Whatever. Right now, I just need to do my job. Then we never have to put ourselves through this again. Right?"

"Rem..."

"No," she said. "My job. Nothing else."

"Fine," he said, leaving the sofa, "but I need you to know, for what little it's worth, I understand I was an ass. I'll beat myself up over the choice I made, and the way I handled it, for the rest of my life."

She watched him walk, sofa to bay window, the canvas satchel sagging from one shoulder. His legs looked as shaky as hers, his face ashen.

Good, she thought.

"Let's just get to work," she said, needing to hear herself speak, stilling her heartstrings. "I have questions, a lot of them. And Jon, someone came after me and Sarah.

Big guy, dirty, smelly, might be the same guy who fired shots at the school. Sometimes uses a *quoth-lar*."

The word seemed to crack Jon's angst. Remedy knew he was surprised to hear her say *quoth-lar*.

"Russ Kitchtoo," he said. "Special ops, originally from Rowock. He was the reason I left. He blames me for his daughter's death."

"Is he right?"

Jon seemed crushed.

"You know me better than that," he said, his voice weak.

"Oh... do I?"

She didn't bother hiding her bitterness. Another uneasy moment passed.

"Yeah," Jon said, "you do. But I get why you might think otherwise. So no, I didn't hurt his daughter. She was walking across thin ice, it gave way, she drowned. It was an accident, Rem—a tragic one. But nothing more. I wasn't even there."

"So why does Kitchtoo blame you?"

Jon shook his head. "It's not so much me as my family... and it's complicated. When government troops took control of Native American regions of southern Alaska—this is decades ago, obviously, in the early 1900s—they created English-only schools and punished any students who spoke Tlingit. My great-grandfather sided with them... but it was a cover so he could turn down the heat, to keep his underground lessons under wraps. He tried to keep the language alive, Rem—the only way he could when he was surrounded by dozens of soldiers beating the pulp out of anyone who dared speak one word of Tlingit."

"What does any of that have to do with Kitchtoo's daughter?"

Jon told her how the girl couldn't read an old warning sign near the pond because it was written in Tlingit. "Russ claims that if my great-grandfather hadn't helped the government troops, then years later his daughter would have understood the sign."

"Seriously?"

"Yeah, the guy's nuts," Jon said, still pacing between the sofa and the window. "Don't get me wrong, it's terrible that he lost his daughter. And I hear he's well respected in the private ops world, whatever that means. But he's had this wild vendetta against me for years.

Remedy lowered her notebook. "You never mentioned any of this to me before," she said. "Not once. Two years together, you never brought it up."

He looked down. "Yeah... I thought it was done when I moved. But now here he is again, two thousand miles from where it started, still coming for me. As soon as I saw the red buoy in Blackmule Gulch I knew he was the sniper."

"Because...?"

"Because after his daughter died he anchored the same kind of buoy in Rowock, at the spot where she drowned, as a tribute. Far as I know it's still there to this day."

"So, you're saying that buoy and the brain you found were meant specifically for you? As what, a threat? A message?"

"Who knows, the guy's a nutjob. Kitchtoo set the fire to herd Ernie and I to the boat dock. From there, there was only one direction to go, and the buoy was easy to spot."

"Wait, how could he know you'd be out hiking?"

"We go almost every weekend, and Ernie's fiancée talks to everyone in the valley. If someone wanted to know where I'd be, it'd be easy to find out."

Remedy's gut told her there was more to the story than simple revenge. She lifted her notebook and began jotting the new information.

"Here's what doesn't make sense: Kitchtoo knows you were involved with Upsweep," she said. "That's not an easy find. In fact, how did he know I was reporting a story on it?"

Jon scowled.

"Erich Bonnicksen," he said. "Turns out Kitchtoo's working for him. Your appointment with Klase probably tipped Bonnicksen to your story. Bonnicksen, in turn, is working with some sort of shadowy government figure who funds his research."

"You mean I.K. Emily."

Again he looked surprised. "Yeah, that's the name. I.K. Emily thinks Bonnicksen's Upsweep research triggered my ability to see the words streaming through my head. They each want that for themselves, and the more I connect with the ribbons, the more I understand why.

That's probably why Bonnicksen decided I was too dangerous and told Kitchtoo to kill me."

"Bonnicksen's trying to kill you?" she said, stunned.

"Yeah, but I.K. Emily ordered Kitchtoo to wait until whatever's happening to me develops further," Jon said. "So instead, he decided to provoke me, thinking it might speed the process."

He hesitated, then added, "The sheriffs don't know about any of this, Rem. I couldn't tell them without exposing Upsweep, and I signed a million non-disclosures with the DOD, the Sidney Institute, and the Navy."

So Kitchtoo learned about glottochronology and the ribbons from Bonnicksen or I.K. Emily, Remedy realized as she assembled the pieces. "Bonnicksen's coming here tomorrow. What are you going to do?"

"Still working on that. Stay away from him, probably."

"He could have come after you any time after Upsweep. Why now?"

"Upsweep wasn't his only work experimenting with back-channels. Someone he calls Exhibit C got out of hand. He thinks I will too."

Remedy hesitated a beat. "Will you?" she said.

He shrugged. "Not the way Exhibit C did, that's for sure. That ended in a massacre."

Remedy again flashed to Bonnicksen's warning messages. "So did the island," she said.

He flinched.

"You were the only one who survived," she continued.

His face stiffened, and for a moment Remedy wasn't sure he was going to answer. "Barely," he finally said, but seemed lost in his thoughts.

"Tell me how. Tell me the whole thing."

He shook his head. *From frustration*, she recognized. *He's not refusing. He really doesn't know.*

"There was... this wall of clouds, but it felt like so much more, like some sort of demon in atmospheric disguise, and..."

He looked into her eyes. "I know this isn't making any sense. But that storm... the Navy called it a white squall, and it took something from me, Rem. I'm missing a piece of myself, some part of my head that could explain everything, and I don't know how the hell I can get it back."

He shook his head a second time. "If that thing ever comes back, promise me you'll run. Get as far away from it as you can."

He let silence punctuate his horror.

"You went home to Rowock..." she prompted.

"Yeah," he said, but still sounded lost in bad memories. "That's when Emma Kitchtoo drowned. So I went for the massive life-shift, moving here to teach the language preservation program. Then I met you... and you know the rest."

Remedy shook her head. "You're leaving something out, Jon—the ribbons. Suddenly seeing tons of words... there must have been a trigger."

"Rem..."

"Maybe stress, maybe the white squall... but the squall ended Upsweep two years earlier. We were already married when you first saw them, that's what you told Francis."

"Rem, listen!"

His sharp tone startled her. In their admittedly short marriage, Jon had never raised his voice.

"What I'm trying to tell you is... I hid some things from you. From Francis too."

"Okay..."

"You already know I didn't tell you about Upsweep, or Emma Kitchtoo. But there's something else... something even more important."

She could see him shaking, struggling for the words.

"I've been saying we were married the first time I saw the ribbons, but that's not true," he said. "It happened long before that... two years before we even met."

He turned away.

"I first saw the ribbons on Amelynd," he said.

Remedy put a hand to her mouth. "After the Upsweep tragedy?" she said.

"No... during it," he said. "I'm pretty sure this whole ribbon ordeal started right smack in the middle of that white squall."

TWENTY-SIX

Remedy lowered her notepad, trying to keep her cool.

"So... you've seen ribbons for *four years*?" she said, glaring.

Jon took a breath. "Not in swarms.... that's only happened three times: on the island, during our marriage, and now. But here and there... yeah. I was seeing them the whole time we were dating, and during our marriage."

Remedy felt as if she'd just taken a punch. "Okay, that's... well, that's news. How come you never mentioned *this* the whole time we were together?"

He turned again, facing her. "I knew how crazy it sounded," he said, "and you were already dealing with health problems of your own. Plus, I thought I'd gotten it under control. Sometimes I'd go a couple weeks without seeing them. But eventually another swarm came, and I started seeing..."

She saw him struggling for the right words.

"I'd see stuff about *you*," he said. "Personal stuff, you know? Past and present, no limits. It was messed up. I started worrying that maybe the words were somehow dangerous to you. That *I* was dangerous to you."

Remedy knew she should give herself time to process this information... but she didn't. "So instead of trusting me, of working through it with me, you decided... what? To leave me without so much as an explanation?"

Her tone, she knew, had reverted to bitter ex-wife... and she didn't care.

"Yeah, but... it was about saving *me* too," he said, sitting on the sofa again. "I couldn't live with the idea that you'd think I'd gone insane. So... I just left."

A dozen alternatives to Jon's solution ran through Remedy's mind. She felt like screaming them out; instead she gritted her teeth, waiting for him to finish.

"Anyway," he said, his voice barely a murmur, "you deserve to know."

They sat there: just them, Hearse's Cyclops eye, and the sound of the lumberjack weathervane. Remedy felt drained, and devastated.

"Okay... if you first saw the streaming words when you were on Amelynd, is that how you survived?" she said, her voice stilted. "Did you use the sentences to reach the rescuers?"

He shook his head. "If I'd known I could do that, I would have," he said. "I don't remember much about the squall—everything happened fast, so it's all a blur. But I do know I was helpless, and desperate. Stuck in the rubble, dehydrated, delirious, I kept projecting my thoughts the way Bonnicksen instructed us, imagining I could get a message to my percipient back at the Sidney Institute."

"And it worked?" Remedy said.

Jon looked pale. "You'll have to ask Bonnicksen, I could never get a straight answer. But I do know there was a point where I started seeing words, right in front of my face. After that, all I remember is the Navy pulling me out from under rubble, loading me onto a chopper."

He paused a beat before continuing. "Turns out my percipient was some baseball player. I've never met him, but I plan on checking the ribbons for more details."

Remedy felt her story instincts ignite. *Razor Castillo might be the man who received Jon's SOS? No wonder Klase suggested I get in touch with him.*

"No one else made it off Amelynd?" she said.

Jon glanced away, and appeared shaken. "No. Twenty-two others... gone."

Remedy took a breath. "Did you kill them?"

His face went pale. "No! You really think I'm a murderer?"

"I honestly don't know what to think," she said. "I do know you attended a conference with Bonnicksen and George Klase prior to Upsweep. Did they tell you anything about I.K. Emily's interest in all of this?"

Jon stood up, still looking shaken. "That was several years ago," he said. "All I remember is Bonnicksen claiming I.K. Emily would fund The Race—which never happened, by the way. If not for him saying that, I wouldn't have signed up for Upsweep... and there's not a day that I don't regret that I did."

"Jon, this is important," she said. "Anything you remember could help us pinpoint who I.K. Emily is."

He walked across the living room, opened the French doors, then hesitated.

"I'll tell you what's important," he said. "Tonight I embedded Tlingit into my neighbors' heads... and I'm pretty sure I can do a lot more."

She forced her wobbly hands to grab her broom, then stood up.

"Like?" she said.

"Like... I don't know, impossible stuff, okay? Wishes-granted kinds of stuff. Because of the ribbons I'm seeing."

She waited. Emotional exhaustion was setting in, probably for both of them. She knew it would exacerbate her MS, especially if she dwelled on everything... and she definitely sensed some dwelling in her future.

"My point is," Jon said, "I owe you so much... let me see if I can give you a break from what you're dealing with. I mean, I can't make any promises, but I could try..."

No! God, no!

"The last thing I need," she said, "is some wild, roll-of-the-dice treatment. And honestly, at this point I'd rather not feel indebted to—"

"Oh... no, no, no," he interjected. "I'm the one who owes you here, and I know it. Like I said, I screwed up. I'm sure all that grief didn't do much for your health, right?"

There's an understatement, she thought. She remembered the months following his abrupt departure, when her MS flared so severely she was left bedridden and near-helpless, wondering whether she was stuck with a life of caregivers and misery.

"I overcame your damage," she told him. "I don't need your help."

"But Rem—" he started.

"Don't," she said. "Just... don't."

"Okay... okay, I won't touch you, I promise," he said. "But at least let me show you why it's on my mind."

He concentrated *and her living room blurred, only Remedy understood that it was them blurring, not their setting. Edges turned crisp; a massive, metallic edifice loomed before them, breathtaking in a fashion that puddling iron rarely achieved. This wasn't in Quail Point, or anywhere in the Sirretta Valley, Remedy realized. It was...*

La Tour Eiffel.

They were standing near the base of the Eiffel Tower.

But how could...?

More blurring. They were back, inside Remedy's home.

"Oh my God," she said, and felt herself falling.

Jon grabbed her before she collapsed and helped her into a chair. Her broom clattered to the floor, banging against Hearse on the way down. Everything was familiar: her furniture, her album display, her home. But it didn't *feel* familiar. It felt more like a giant eraser had wiped it away, swapped it out for a fantasy, then put it all back... yet the eraser's aroma still lingered, meaning everything was now different.

Jon pulled up a chair and placed it next to hers so they could sit close. "It's okay," he said. "This is your living room. It's real."

She wanted to believe him; she *needed* real. Needed it bad, after what he'd just shown her. "What did you just do?"

"Imagined it, wrote it, took us there. It's crazy, right?"

Beyond crazy, she thought. *It's thrilling, terrifying, captivating... so many strong emotions, all at once.* Talking about it was one thing, but actually experiencing it... the whole thing was, ironically, beyond words.

"Oh my God," she repeated.

Jon nodded. "Now do you understand why I can't just leave it alone... but at the same time, why it scares me so much? Why I thought I needed to get clear of you, or anyone else who might get hurt?"

She shook her head. "Yes, but... no, we still could have dealt with this together. You should have trusted me."

"I know. I was wrong. The whole thing was just so insane."

That, at least, she now understood. "This is beyond insane," she said.

He put a hand on her shoulder. "Not anymore," he said. "Taking you to the Eiffel Tower, that was just a dream of mine. Now let me try giving you *your* dream."

She shook her head, uncertain.

"I hate seeing you like this," Jon said, eyeballing her broom, her bare feet. "You didn't deserve this. No one does, but especially you."

She leaned back, stunned and exhausted. Her vision was so blurred that she couldn't see Jon's face clearly. Her legs felt numb and wobbly. Her arms barely moved, and her fingers had been frozen in place for at least an hour. Worse, her back was killing her and she felt robbed of her energy, as if she were capable of breathing but not much else.

She remembered the way she'd brushed off the significance of her final healthy moment—could it really be six years ago? Numbness in her face, that's all it was. Sure, a week later it was spreading throughout her body, but doctors assured her it was no big deal, probably just an allergic reaction.

"Take a precautionary month off?" Remedy had protested to her *Morning News* editor. "Why would I need a whole month?"

Why, indeed. The MS diagnosis came three months later.

She felt her jaw shudder. Jon had caused her so much pain... what if he could now ease it? Tears begged her to let them roll, but she refused. Sure, she thought, maybe he could heal me...but maybe not. What if he changed something that altered her in other, unknown ways? What if the trade-off was losing herself?

"Rem, I can help you," Jon said. "I know this can work."

She stood up from her chair, wobbling. Most people didn't realize there was a *feeling* to good health. She had not only missed it, she had given it a funeral and grieved for its passing.

"Please," Jon said. "Please, let me try."

"Okay," begged to break free from her mouth. Then she remembered:

"Doesn't have to be now."

"No, it has to be now."

"So you can go out on your own terms."

"Yeah... better to tough it out than be someone's guinea pig."

The words echoed inside her head. *Her own terms. Better to tough it out.* Just a simple conversation with Julie Henderson, but so much more. She dropped her face into her hands.

"MS is hell," she said, "but it's a blessing too. People never appreciate how precious the little things can be. On those days when I beat it back long enough to walk, or fix a meal, or type a story, I'm on top of the world."

She took a deep breath as she raised her head.

"Count me out," she said, the words barely a murmur. "God help me, but count me out. I don't need your maybe-cure. I beat MS without you."

She was surprised by how good it felt to say the words. For years she had fought to prove MS didn't make her any different from everyone else. Now she knew that it did... and that, horrible as it was, she could take enough satisfaction from her victories to keep the temptation of a high-risk cure at bay.

Jon's head slumped once again.

"Look," he said. "If the idea that it's coming from me is bothering you..."

"No," she said right away. "That's not it at all."

"Then why? You'll always know you beat MS on your own for years, regardless of my cure. Why put yourself through more?"

She closed her eyes, wishing she had a good answer, then gave him the only thing she could come up with.

"Because I'm human?" she said.

He studied her, looking heartbroken, rejected, dismissed.

"Okay," he said.

He stepped through the French doors, took one more look back.

"Okay," he repeated.

Tears streamed down his cheeks as he left. Remedy felt matching streaks on her own face. *Liquid sadness*, she thought. But a few of them were liquid pride.

Quite a few.

TWENTY-SEVEN

eadlights off, dashboard dark, Jon sat in his truck feeling numb. Ribbons notwithstanding, his mind was blank—an improvement from the past ten minutes, when his only thought centered on marching the three blocks back to Remedy's house for another go at curing her.

The truck shuddered; it did that whenever he left the engine idling for too long. He went ahead and let it idle anyway.

"You're in no shape to drive," Francis said, from the passenger seat.

"I'll manage."

The two didn't look at one another. *Another reason I like Francis so much,* Jon thought. *He knows when to give me a minute.*

The minute ended up a full fifteen.

"You know someplace we can we hole up until we figure things out?" Francis finally said.

"The school has a cabin for summer programs," Jon said. "It's empty now that we're in September."

He switched on the headlights and pulled the truck onto the road, away from Remedy's riverside neighborhood. Turning at Hanafin Park, he and Francis crossed the river, eventually passing the school and the ski resort as they traveled through Quail Point and beyond—all familiar sights, yet Jon couldn't stop thinking everything looked different. The valley itself seemed different too, and not just because the wildfire's orange cast was bleeding into a deepening dusk.

No, he thought, everything seemed smaller. He knew the town hadn't changed. Was it the ribbons, changing his perspective?

"You know the irony?" he said, his eyes tracking a possum as it made a gung-ho leap into the brush beyond the opposite lane. "I could *make* Rem accept a cure. I could make her do anything. All I'd have to do is write it into the ribbons, and she'd be healthy."

Francis nodded. "And then you'd be exactly what Bonnicksen thinks you are."

Jon cursed. He whipped the truck into a turnout then slammed his hands on the steering wheel, swearing again.

"Cuss all you want, you know I'm right," Francis said.

"I'm trying to help her!"

"I know you are. Doesn't matter. It's her choice. You don't get to force it on her."

Jon swore again.

"I'm not Exhibit C, okay?" he said. "If I do something with these ribbons, forced or otherwise, it'll be for a good reason!"

Francis angled his head. "Who gets to define 'good,' Jon?"

"Oh, please!"

"I'm serious," Francis said.

"Fine, but you're missing my point," Jon said. "Imagine giving every Tlingit descendant—or everyone, period—a grasp of basic Tlingit. A language on the brink of extinction would suddenly flourish. How is that such a bad thing?"

"It isn't... unless it's forced."

Jon sighed, frustrated. "Francis, I can see and interact with the world in a completely new fashion," he said. "It's Whorf's concept, only with a much bigger scope. Am I supposed to ignore that?"

The old man uttered his cough-laugh. "Benjamin Lee Whorf wrote a good many things from that research desk of his at Yale," Francis said, "but he never once said you could use language to tear up a neighborhood."

"Yeah, yeah, I'll give you that," Jon said, "but you get what I'm saying."

Francis started to answer, then stopped when they noticed flashing police lights approaching from the opposite direction.

"Probably for us," he said, but the patrol car blew past them at high speed. "I hope this cabin we're headed to has another truck we can use, because it won't be long before they're going to be looking for this one."

"What a mess," Jon said, pulling back onto the road. "The cops want me, Kitchtoo's got his vendetta, and now Bonnicksen will be gunning for me tomorrow. What am I going to do?"

Francis thought about it.

"You'll remember *Ku'cta-qa*," he said.

Jon gave him a puzzled look.

"In your grandmother's stories there wasn't anything that the land otter people couldn't save you from," Francis said, double-clutching his cane. "Drowning, stuck in a blizzard, lost, starving... *Ku'cta-qa* was your best hope. But Irene always left one thing out: those people ended up turning into *Ku'cta-qas* themselves."

Jon changed lanes, passing an old VW. "Better than dying," he said.

"That's the point, it wasn't better," Francis said. "In Tlingit legend, how you die means *everything*. With ceremonial preparation a dead person's spirit got reincarnated back into the clan. As a *Ku'cta-qa*... well, that's why we say people missing and presumed dead have gone to the otter people, right? Because their soul is forever lost. What could be worse than that?"

He paused a beat, then added, "I don't care how much good the ribbons can do, Onatay. Don't let them cost you your soul."

He liked hearing Francis use his Tlingit name. He liked Francis, period. *Bonnicksen's neural mine and Kitchtoo's manhunt don't stand a chance with him in my corner.*

They saw glowing reflectors, indicating a highway-adjacent driveway. Jon pulled into it and spotted the school's cabin nudged between ponderosa groves. *Finally*, he thought. The prospect of a good night's sleep was sounding good.

"No need to worry," he told Francis. "I won't use the ribbons to change people."

Unless, he thought, *they leave me with no other choice.*

TWENTY-EIGHT

Oblivious to her Saturday morning schedule, Sarah Ushida set her most cherished memory free. Automotive rumbles ceased, and an unpaved hospital parking lot dissipated into Miamoto Yoshiko's clasped, wiry forefinger and thumb.

"My roadrunners," Miamoto's aging, raspy voice said, raising the small, dangling objects to eye level. "Your grandfather carved and painted these earrings for me at Manzanar."

Sarah held out her seventeen-year-old hand and watched her grandmother drop them into her palm. The sakura earrings were so well polished they looked like stone. Glistening red-and-white dabs delineated the feathers, with a hint of green for depth and a natural wood finish on the feet. Even the earring pins looked brand new.

Miamoto grinned, creasing the wrinkles on her face. Her white hair seemed equally brittle and her pink muumuu, swarming with an impressionist lily pattern, had seen more than its share of wash cycles.

"They're yours now," Miamoto said. "Whenever I see you raising yourself above the pack, I see my camp dream come to fruition."

Miamoto wiped tears from her eyes, and Sarah did the same. A blaring car horn cleared the haze, restored the automotive rumble, and returned Sarah to the Sirretta Valley Hospital parking lot, which was just a Frisbee toss from the auxiliary dam. Removing her earrings, she wondered why she had thought of her late grandmother. Maybe, she thought, because so much of her life and career could be traced to that gesture. She knew others considered her arrogant, and wasn't proud of it, but she wasn't ashamed of it either.

She stared at the passing traffic then stood up, remembering her unfinished lab report, the scheduling for Monday's sessions, and the procedures outline for—

She jumped. Remedy's ex was standing right next to her.

"Jon? What the—?"

"Sorry, no one was at the front desk, so..."

Yeah, right, she thought. Rem was lucky to be rid of this loser.

"The sheriffs are looking for you," she said. "You ever go talk with Remedy?"

"Last night," he said. "That's why I'm here. She wants me to have a medical exam, for her story. Says you're open to it."

Sarah scowled. She could never shake the feeling Jon was hiding something. "That was before I realized I could be arrested for doing it," she said.

"Please Sarah," Jon said. "I'm serious about this."

"And I'm serious about you turning yourself in."

"Just listen to what's happening to me first, okay?" He gave her a brief rundown about the ribbons.

"Pretty far-fetched," Sarah said. "Claiming *words* can make real-world changes? Really?"

"I know how it sounds," he said, "but craftsmen use the same parts of their brain when they think about words as when they're making complex tools."

Sarah raised her eyebrows. "Meaning there's a known link between language and the physical world."

"Absolutely."

She listened as he gave an overview of language's role in defining reality, wondering whether there was even a chance Remedy had stumbled into a much bigger story than anyone had given her credit for.

Mostly, though, she began considering the merits of becoming the first researcher to publicly document his ability.

"Maybe I can make this exam happen for you after all," she said, gesturing for him to follow her inside.

"Okay, based on what you told me about the craftsmen I'm assuming you're familiar with functional magnetic resonance imaging," Sarah said.

Jon was lying down, his body tucked inside a tunnel-shaped MRI machine. Sarah stood at a computer workstation several feet away, double-checking the aging machine's parameters.

"Yeah, in linguistics we use FMR imaging to map which brain regions are in use during speech and language comprehension," Jon said.

"Good... so you understand that when a particular brain region is engaged in a cognitive task, say, identifying a piece of fruit, it requires extra energy to do its job," she said. "That energy arrives as glucose—sugar that's carried to the fruit-naming location via increased blood flow."

"Sure," Jon said. "The magnet in the MRI detects the increase in blood flow, then depicts it on screen as a splotch of light inside my brain."

"Exactly," she said. "The goal here is to map the precise brain locations related to this new cognitive skill of yours."

She typed the exam parameters, and a ghostly physiognomy of Jon's brain appeared on the screen. The three-dimensional, black-and-white image rotated at several angles, allowing her to examine the entire brain.

"Basics first," she said. "State your name."

The MRI hummed to life as he responded, and the computer software began processing information. Several seconds later, a portion of the brain outline turned bright blue on her screen. Satisfied, she had him perform a series of physical actions, from clenching his fist to flicking his toes. As he did so, more blue flashes appeared, often in different regions.

"Now tell me about the process you use to change reality," she said.

Jon thought about it. "I'm not sure... I write it with my mind, and it happens," he said, and the entire brain image lit up, each pixel flickering at different rates. A moment later, the screen went dark.

"Whoa," Sarah said.

"What?"

"Just... results. Think about something else you did using the same method. You mentioned implanting phrases."

He told her about Arturo speaking a Tlingit sentence. Interesting, she thought, watching the screen—no burst of light when Jon thought about the result rather than the process. Perplexed, she ran a brief diagnostic on the MRI equipment. Everything checked out.

"I'd like you to use the ribbons right now, while I have you monitored," she said.

"It's... an unsettling experience. There must be another—"

"I think it's the only way we can do this accurately."

He looked reluctant. "Okay..."

She stared at the monitor; everything looked the same. Then the entire brain image lit up again, each pixel flickering at its own, frenzied pace. Sarah was overcome with dizziness as *Jon connected with the streaming sentences.*

The neuro-imaging lab vanished, supplanted by text. He scanned the content, curious. Miamoto Yoshiko's wiry forefinger and thumb scrolled into view, as did the wooden roadrunners.

And then, Manzanar.

The World War II internment camp loomed beyond its barbed-wire perimeter, a stark, historical blemish in the California desert. Wartime paranoia sentenced Miamoto and another ten thousand Japanese-Americans to more than two years there, shivering through 30-degree winter nights in the unheated barracks, laboring amid 100-degree summer days, hunkering down from the heavy winds that dusted detainees, with only cloth partitions separating one family's living space from the next.

Today the suffering often seemed forgotten... sometimes even by Asians, in part because the Japanese language outside of Japan was fading. The Japanese-American culture's unique perspectives were endangered, and Sarah was as much to blame as anyone. Sure, she could read some Japanese, but she couldn't speak the language.

Until now, Jon decided.

Now, in addition to ubiquitous English, Sarah Ushida could read, write and converse in fluent Japanese.

Jon returned his attention to the MRI tunnel. Readings continued pouring into the computer as if he had never left, blue light still illuminating the brain outline on the monitor. Jon returned his world to three dimensions.

———————

Sarah shook the cobwebs from her head, and the momentary dizziness passed. The monitor image of Jon's brain was dark.

"*Hai, daijoubu deshou,*" Sarah started, then hesitated.

"Did you..." she said. "This... this Japanese in my head, it's your doing?"

"Yeah."

She knew she should be amazed, maybe even thrilled, but instead found herself shuddering. *This guy was just... in my brain,* she realized. *He made something happen, something significant, and I had no say in the matter— none.* She wondered what more he could have done. Could he make her say something she didn't want to say? Change her opinions? Alter her personality?

Could he have killed her?

She helped Jon out from the machine then returned to her computer and pulled up the images from the session.

"Anything?" Jon said, seating himself in one of the exam room's two plastic chairs.

She hoped her fear wasn't showing. "The brain activity's routine until you did your mojo. Then look at what happened."

She shifted to a video replay showing the dizzying flickers that had appeared throughout his brain. "An overwhelming number of your neurons fired," she said, "but each in their own pattern and in some cases in multiple patterns within the same neuron, as if something specific was happening on a microscopic level."

"Meaning... what?"

"Well for one thing, it's pretty clear your entire neural system activates when you start writing things."

Stop thinking about the way he was in your head, with unlimited control and no restriction, she told herself. *Focus on the science!* She wished her emotions—especially an innate fear of losing control—were doing a better job of listening to her mind.

"Your brain exhibits blood flow patterns throughout both hemispheres when you use the ribbons," she said. "Now, everyone uses their entire brain, but not all at once... so that means there's an unknown mechanism at work here."

She folded her arms against her chest, realizing she had only scratched the surface of the information she needed.

"Let's cut to the chase," Jon said, standing up. "Is my use of the ribbons risking my health?"

Your health, Sarah thought. What about the risk to *my* health... or to the world's health?

"I honestly don't know if there's a risk," she admitted, suddenly wondering whether her information might be needed as a first step toward finding a way to block him. "But with more tests we should be able to get a much better idea of what we're dealing with."

She saw him thinking it over.

"Unfortunately," Jon said, "there are people who will use the test information to try recreating the ribbons in themselves."

She sensed he already had someone in mind.

"Would that matter?" she said.

"Yeah," he said. "It would matter a lot. Go ahead and give Rem the verbal rundown so she knows what we found, but that's it. No physical or digital copies of the FMR imaging, and no written report."

Sarah looked up from her keyboard, taken aback.

"Are you seriously so dumb that you're going to leave before we have complete answers?" she said, copying the test files onto a flash drive. "I mean, really? Given what you can do?"

Jon gave a polite smile. "I'm not interested in rewriting the science books, Sarah," he said. "All I want to do is save a dying language."

What a simpleton, she thought, pocketing the flash drive.

"I hope you'll forgive me," Jon said, "but I need to make sure you don't share those FMR images."

She didn't like the sound of that.

"Make... sure...?" she said, uncertain.

"You have my word that you won't be hurt."

Sarah didn't need to hear any more. She turned and walked out of the lab, her stomach in knots. The hall leading to the second-floor elevator was empty, and to her surprise the car was waiting. Stepping inside, she punched the button for the first floor and watched the doors close, relieved Jon hadn't followed.

Then she again felt overcome with dizziness. *As her head cleared, she pulled the flash drive from her pocket, tossed it to the floor, and crushed it with her foot.*

When the elevator reached the first floor, she didn't get out but instead punched the button to go back up to the lab.

Jon was still inside, but didn't say a word as she opened up a cabinet, pulled out a fire extinguisher, and used it to bludgeon the MRI workstation. When the computer's case finally cracked apart, she removed the hard drive and destroyed it as well, until the floor of the lab was covered in smashed electronic components.

Satisfied that all documentation of Jon's secrets were destroyed, she returned the fire extinguisher to the cabinet. Then she...

Jon froze the scene. He hated doing this. Besides, he had promised Francis—and himself—that he wouldn't use the ribbons to mess with people without their permission.

But he had no choice, not if he wanted to be sure Bonnicksen could never obtain the images. Having them end up in Bonnicksen's hands meant they also ended up with I.K. Emily... and Jon wasn't willing to give a power-hungry shadow figure any more clues to accessing the ribbons than they already had.

No—the Miamoto Yoshiko text, *he told himself*. Look at the Miamoto Yoshiko text!

As expected, the sentences about Sarah's grandmother stirred unpleasant feelings. He felt them whenever he discussed the political circumstances that eroded native languages with people from other cultures. The Tlingits' experience with racism and ignorant government officials was very different from what 1940s-era Japanese Americans experienced, he knew... and yet, it was also similar. Miamoto and his grandmother would have understood each other's plight.

Would they have understood what he just did to Sarah?

Jon double-checked both the flash drive and the hard drive, making certain they were destroyed, then left the lab.

Sarah watched him leave, initially stoic, then broke into sobs. She remained there, crumpled on the floor, for nearly half an hour before finally rising to look at herself in a mirror. Her nose looked puffed from the sobs, but it wasn't her nose that she was concerned with, it was her eyes. She moved as close as she could to the mirror, looking straight into her own eyes.

"It's me," she said as tears flowed. "Just me. No one else."

She removed her hummingbird earrings, clutching them within the palms of her hands as her body slid back down, all the way to the floor.

"Just me," she repeated, again and again. "Please... let it just be me..."

TWENTY-NINE

Three miles from the hospital, Remedy sat in a booth between her broom and the side wall of Cassie's Diner, unable to imagine a man with position and power like George Klase actually showing up for a Saturday brunch meeting as they'd agreed.

But five minutes later, he did.

"There's a line to get in?" Klase said, studying the dozen retirees waiting outside as he slid into the booth.

"Place is a local institution," Remedy said.

He shook his head. With faded vinyl tablecloths and dead flies suspended in withered corner webbing, Cassie's was clearly one of those places that remained in business because it had survived, not because it was good.

"Long as they can poach me some eggs," Klase said.

He didn't seem in the best of moods but otherwise looked the same as she remembered: flat-top, bright green eyes, and that square jaw. His Hawaiian shirt, on the other hand, was difficult to process.

"Look, if you'd rather talk someplace more discreet..." she said.

"This is fine," Klase said, sounding crabby. "Let's just get to it: your husband sees words in his head, he's started using them for his own purposes, and no one knows what's going to happen when he does."

So he knows everything, she thought.

"Ex-husband," she muttered.

She gave him credit; he now had her on the defensive from the get-go. *I can live with that*, she decided. If he was willing to go full-disclosure, she was too. She took a breath, to give each of them a tension-tamping moment and a chance for her to regroup.

"How dangerous is he?" she said, lowering her voice.

Klase looked directly at her, for the first time. "You tell me," he said. "From what I'm told, he can pretty much do anything he wants. Am I right?"

"Maybe. But he says all he wants to do is save his native language."

Klase scowled. "You heard about his neighborhood, right? Things will only escalate."

She wished she could deny it, but something told her she couldn't.

A pair of menus dropped between them, left by an aproned waitress rushing toward another table. Remedy wasn't sure which had more dirt, the yellowed menu laminate or the diner's filmy windows.

"I saw the attendance roster for the International Linguistics Association conference six years ago," she said. "You, Jon, and Erich Bonnicksen were all there."

Klase sighed. "Yeah, for a handshake, finalizing a pre-arranged deal."

"The deal for Bonnicksen to use Amelynd."

"Yeah," he said. "People with higher pay grades than my own gave him permission to use the island. I arranged for the Navy to provide supplies and transportation. At that point they were to vacate and secure the region."

"Secure it? How?"

"Like I told you, isolation was the prerequisite. We stationed an asset fifteen nautical miles out and established a no-fly zone over the area."

"Asset? You mean a ship?"

He nodded as napkin-wrapped sporks landed between them, another aerial drop from the waitress. They glanced at their laminated menus, then ordered.

"So what did you and my ex discuss at this conference?" she said.

Klase shrugged. "Not much. I'm no linguist, and he didn't seem to know much about football. Bonnicksen insisted on having a linguist involved in the project and Wanamaker was the guy he brought in. At the time it seemed insignificant."

"Then everything changed with the squall."

"Yeah."

Remedy heard something odd in his voice.

"You think there was something else in play?" she said.

He took a deep breath.

"I think our assets have been through a squall or two. Cat-fives included."

She waited, uncertain what he was getting at.

"Even though isolation was the prerequisite, there was a point when our people decided 'screw Bonnicksen, we're going in anyway,' " he said. "With sustained speeds at 150 and nothing but huts on Amelynd, they knew Bonnicksen's people were good as dead without an extraction... and they're good at their jobs. They knew they could still save a bunch of those people."

"So how did Jon end up the only survivor?'" Remedy said.

"That's what I've been asking for four years."

The waitress brought their coffee. Remedy stifled a smile as she caught Klase glancing into it, checking for flies.

"I've talked with everyone involved in that rescue attempt," Klase said. "More than two dozen people, plus the CO, helmsman, and navigator. And I've found two things."

Remedy found herself leaning forward.

"One," Klase said, "This white squall that hit them was dense, compact, and it came out of nowhere."

"How far out of nowhere?"

He shrugged. "They detected it less than seven minutes prior to landfall on Amelynd. That's how far."

Remedy sat back in her chair, shaking her head. "That doesn't sound right," she said. "Are you sure the Navy people weren't trying to come up with excuses for not making the rescue?"

"No, as a matter of fact I'm *not* sure," he said, irritated. "I'm not sure about anything with this entire situation. All I'm telling you is what I found out from the inside. And I agree, the whole thing is damn unusual... including the second thing I found."

"Which is?"

He fiddled with his menu, as if trying to figure out how to explain his next point. "To a man," he said, "the rescuers claim they were kept from the island."

"Kept?" Remedy said, her voice skeptical. "Kept how?"

"Severe headwinds from nowhere. Mammoth waves. At one point an entire school of fish was swept up out of the sea, onto the deck. This was an experienced crew, I should add. They'd never seen any one of these things happening, much less all of them in such a short period of time."

"So what, they're claiming witchcraft? Maybe a cloudy face with puffed-up cheeks blowing them back?"

Klase waited a beat. "You done?"

She didn't apologize.

"I had the same reaction," he said. "My bullshit meter was screaming at me. You want to know what? It still is. Maybe you're right. Maybe those guys blew the rescue, it cost twenty-two people their lives, and they're pulling excuses out of their asses to explain why."

He shrugged.

"Thing is," he said, "they sure could have come up with much more plausible excuses."

Remedy saw his point. The craziness of their stories added suspicion and invited investigation, which seemed an unusual tactic for a cover-up.

"You want to hear the oddest part of it all?" Klase said.

He paused the conversation as their food arrived. Remedy forked her scrambled eggs around the plate, checking whether they were tender or dry, deciding they were a bit of both. Klase seemed pleased with his cholesterol haul: two poached eggs, four sausages, and a side plate of hash browns.

"The craziest part of the whole thing," he said, resuming where he had left off, "is that the ship's XO claims his people saw the first indications of emergencies on Amelynd *before* the squall made landfall."

Remedy took a moment to let the information settle in.

"Before? Are you sure?" she finally said.

"I told you, I'm not sure of anything. But it's what they said."

"What sort of emergencies?"

Klase downed a forkful of hash browns before answering.

"Possible landslide," he said. "A collapsed structure. Isolated dust clouds. Brief indications of a structure fire."

Remedy forced herself to take a bite of her eggs, mostly for appearances since she still didn't feel like eating. "The Navy saw all of that? How?"

Klase shrugged.

"Satellite, and other monitoring methods I can't discuss. Not that Bonnicksen was aware of it."

"Didn't that break the isolation protocol?"

Klase cracked a mild smile. "Sure, but not in any way that the study's participants were aware of. You think the DOD's going to invest without oversight?"

Remedy thought about it. "How long before the squall did they notice the emergencies?"

"At least an hour."

"So for whatever reason all this chaos broke out, and then the squall comes out of nowhere."

He tapped a finger to his head.

"Now, if the initial damage wasn't an act of God... and I seriously doubt it was," he said, "then that means someone caused it—maybe even the kind of someone Bonnicksen likes studying, the kind who can manipulate events with their mind. What if that same someone caused the squall?"

Jon, Remedy knew.

She looked away, first at the other tables, then out the window, anywhere she could avoid Klase's probing eyes. *But if he knows about Jon's ribbons, it means he has a source with information specific to...*

"Tell me about I.K. Emily," she said, shifting her gaze back to Klase.

He raised his eyebrows and looked surprised, but didn't answer.

"He—or is it a she?—sponsored the conference you attended," Remedy said. "They also gave Bonnicksen use of the island. Who is this person?"

For the first time since she'd met Klase, he looked uncomfortable.

"We promised each other full disclosure," she said, when he didn't answer right away.

"Yeah, well... some things are so classified that I don't know enough to disclose anything. Nor do I want to."

Got him, Remedy thought.

"So I.K. Emily *is* behind everything," she said. "Bonnicksen's just a pawn, whether he knows it or not. Isn't that what you're saying?"

He speared his fork into the hash brown pile and pushed his plate away, suddenly ignoring the heaping food that had so engrossed him.

"I think there's a very good chance that she's... interested... in Jon Wanamaker's skills," he said. "And trust me when I tell you, that's not a good thing."

"Why? Who is this woman?"

"Woman?" he said, rubbing his napkin across his lips. "Sure, maybe she's a woman. Or maybe it's a job title rather than a person, and there's a succession of I.K. Emilys. All I know is she's a voice on a blank video screen that's only set up at the highest-level meetings. Military actions, chemical warfare, torture, foreign espionage, terrorism... I.K. Emily never said a peep on any one of them. But when the name Jon Wanamaker came up, she spoke up, and spoke up clearly, insisting the DOD back away. So yeah... I think it's fair to say I.K. Emily's *very* interested in Jon's capabilities."

Remedy leaned back from the table as the wait staff collected their plates, an implied mandate to finish so the diner could usher in the next round of people waiting outside.

"So I.K. Emily suspected a link between remote perception and linguistics, and used Bonnicksen to prove it," she said, once the table was bussed. "Now Jon is that proof."

Klase didn't answer, but his expression suggested he agreed.

"I still don't understand why she cares. What good is all of this to her?"

Klase looked at her like she was an idiot. "What good is using your mind to do just about anything imaginable, unhindered?" he said. "Are you seriously asking that? Can you imagine the level of control someone could attain if they figure out how to harness that? Look, Bonnicksen's just some narcissist who wants to become his generation's Einstein. I.K. Emily, she's out for world domination."

"So, you think she's cultivating Jon as her latest pawn?"

"What I think," he said, "is that Wanamaker's a lab rat. As soon as Emily finds out everything she needs to know, she'll get rid of that rat and use the knowledge for herself. She already has an operative tailing him."

"Russ Kitchtoo," Remedy said, under her breath.

"Yeah, a real wild card as far my office is concerned but he's ready to carry out her orders. That's why I'm here, Ms. Conover. It isn't for you, or for the eggs, or for my undying love of the slanted news media. It damn well isn't because I enjoy selling out my belief in the good work my agency does. This is about love of country—love of world, even."

He glanced out the filthy windows, looking irritated with himself.

"If I.K. Emily finds a way to get the same level of skill that your ex has, we lose our democracy," he said. "Hell, with the geopolitical agenda she'd have, it'd be the end of everything. And I mean everything."

Klase looked her in the eyes again. "You get the word out about this," he said, "we might have a chance to stop it."

Remedy leaned back in her chair, overwhelmed. From the outset, she'd suspected her Upsweep story involved some sort of cover-up, perhaps even a conspiracy. But this... this was so far beyond anything she'd anticipated she wasn't even certain how best to proceed, especially since so much of the information was from an off-record source.

"I can slip you the minutes from the meeting where I.K. Emily spoke," Klase said, apparently sensing her concern. "That, and a few requisition reports with the I.K. Emily name authorizing. But there's not much else. For the most part you'll have to report everything from the outside."

"Do you have any idea how impossible that is?" she said.

He looked surprised. "No more impossible than working a job in your condition, and still doing it better than most."

Barely doing it, she thought.

Her phone vibrated. Klase's too, at the same time. He gestured for her to go ahead and take a look at her message while he checked his. When she did, she found a text from Julie Henderson.

    911 regarding Jon, call me asap.

"I have a feeling," she said, "that I.K. Emily just got closer to her goal."

"That's the gist of my message too," he said, standing up. "I suggest you finish your story, pack your things, and take some time away from this valley."

"Because...?"

"I'm sorry, Ms. Conover... but based on the intel DOD's receiving, I'm requisitioning emergency air and ground support to the Sirretta Valley," he said. "They'll be locking this place down within twenty-four hours."

THIRTY

Remedy heard what Julie Henderson was saying to her over the phone but couldn't believe it, so she repeated it to make the words sink in. "Jon took out three sheriffs and a SWAT team? Are you sure?"

She heard Julie exhaling cigarette smoke. "Yeah, one minute they had him cornered near the hospital, the next they were piled up in a heap, disarmed," Julie said. "Of course there's no proof, it's not like anyone actually saw him doing anything. He was just standing there, same as with the school kid, same as with his neighbors."

And the same as he did with me last night, Remedy thought. She was already back on her sofa at home, having wrapped up with Klase an hour earlier.

"I want to run with the allegations," Henderson said. "Tell me you've finished interviewing him."

"I have, and he confirmed several things, but—"

"Forget 'but,' just get me what you've got and we'll run it. There's more than enough circumstantial evidence for a story questioning Jon's role in the events happening around here lately. If he wants to deny it, we'll print that too."

Remedy cringed. There was no way she would write a story based on allegations alone.

Her doorbell rang, derailing the conversation. She saw Sarah on the front deck and told Henderson she would call her back.

"I take it back," Sarah said, rushing through the French doors. "I take it all back—everything I said when I tried to get you to ditch your stories. You've got to get everything in print, Rem, as soon as you can! It's our only chance."

"Sare, calm down. What's going on?"

"I wish I knew," Sarah said, then told her what happened at the hospital lab.

"He actually *became* you?" Remedy said.

"I'm telling you, for those few minutes he was right there, in my head, controlling my thoughts, my actions... it was terrifying, Rem. Jon forced himself into my mind. My mind!"

Sarah looked so worked up Remedy worried she was having a seizure.

"You might be misinterpreting what Jon did," Remedy said. "He did the same thing to me, and yes, I suppose it felt like he entered my mind to do it, but there was nothing malicious about it whatsoever."

Sarah made a face. "That's because with you it was voluntary."

Thinking back, Remedy wasn't so certain it was. She suddenly realized she'd let the issue drop after Jon had blown her mind with the Eiffel Tower. But he hadn't waited for permission—in fact she had just rejected his offer to use his ability on her when he went ahead and used it.

"Okay, you may have a point," Remedy said. "But I still find it hard to believe he's acting out of malice."

"Hey, you want to defend that jackass, fine, but you know I'm right," Sarah said. "Even under ideal circumstances he needs to have permission to do what he's doing. If he doesn't, he's guilty."

Remedy took a breath. Sarah *was* right, she knew. "Jon's a first-class jerk sometimes," she said, "but I've never seen him hurt a fly and he's always trying to do the right thing. To hear him tell it that's what he was doing by leaving me—which is horse crap, but you get what I'm saying. He's not the kind of guy who would hurt people."

"Unless," Sarah said, "just like with your marriage, he thinks he's doing the right thing... even when he isn't."

Remedy cocked her head, doubtful.

"Don't you get it?" Sarah said. "The guy can make us do whatever he pleases, and we have no way to keep him out. You do see that's a problem, right?"

She did. If that's what Jon was doing then he was wrong, regardless of his intent.

"This is all I've got," Sarah said, pointing to her own head. "It's the only thing that separates me from everyone else—and I mean, it *really* separates me—yet this guy waltzed in and took it away from me! Just like that, I couldn't do anything to stop it!"

"Okay, okay, I get it. You're certain about the results of that FMR test you conducted?"

Sarah exhaled in exaggerated fashion, puffing out her cheeks. "Hey, you see who you're talking to here? You think I'm going to screw up the exam?"

"I mean it, Sare, I need to know that you're certain about everything you just told me. There's no evidence anymore, remember?"

"No, there's no evidence thanks to that idiot ex of yours!" Sarah threw herself onto the couch, her facial muscles rippling from stress. "Okay, fine, I'm not certain of anything anymore... but yes, I looked at the FMR results a dozen times before he made me destroy them. They definitely indicated that when he plugs into these words he sees, all of the neurons in his brain are firing simultaneously."

"Which means... what?"

"No idea," Sarah said, removing one of her roadrunner earrings for no apparent reason other than to keep it clutched in the palm of her hand. "Look, during childhood our brains experience periods of explosive growth, and on rare occasions adult brains undergo the same kind of growth. That's when we're most capable of learning new skills, or new ways of thinking."

"You think that's what's happened with Jon?"

"All I know is, there has to be a physical explanation for why he can see ribbons while the rest of us can't,"

Sarah said. "Maybe the neural growth spurts occurring in his brain simply never stopped."

"Or maybe the remote perception experiment promoted the growth spurts," Remedy said. "He told me he first saw the words when he was on Amelynd for Bonnicksen's project. That can't be a coincidence."

"Yeah... whatever. Either way, you've got to get this in print. Let people know what this idiot is capable of. Get him locked up or contained somehow, before he does this again—and he *will* try it again, you can bet on it."

Remedy looked out the window, ignoring the jabs shooting up her spine. Intense, midday sun had transformed the mountains into devil droppings, crusted, twisted, and blurred from the rising heat waves. By evening, those same dark hillsides would look like blankets kicked away by the town's spread-eagle feet.

"I'd love to get this in print," she said, "but I don't write things I can't back up. All we've got are allegations, and some pretty wild ones at that."

"Aw Christ, Rem, don't give me your soapbox, just nail this guy!"

Remedy noticed Sarah's hands were shaking. "Sare, what's going on?"

"What's going on is, I can barely tell what's real and what's not anymore," she said, looking terrified. "Sometimes I don't even know if what I'm thinking comes from myself or from... *him.*"

Remedy remembered how shaken she was after Jon brought them back from Paris, and how difficult it was to tell what was or wasn't real. At least she'd had a minor advantage: she knew Jon, meaning she had some small baseline of trust despite their turbulent history. For anyone who didn't have that same baseline, the experience would be much more frightening. *If level-headed Sarah is this traumatized*, she realized, *this community could be facing psychological disaster.*

"I won't be the only one, Rem," Sarah said, guessing her friend's thoughts. "People need definition to their reality. Without it... it's just too big of an adjustment."

Remedy twirled a finger through her hair. "You want me to do my job? Give me evidence. Right now, all I've got is Jon's crazy ribbon claims and a whole lot of allegations. I'm hoping Bonnicksen confirms everything on the record, but until he does very little of this is provable."

Sarah swore several times. "Fine," she said, "do what you have to do, but don't let that bastard off."

She stalked toward the French doors.

"You're leaving?" Remedy said.

Sarah pushed the doors open without answering.

"Sare, don't go... you're still too worked up and besides, Kitchtoo's still out there. It's not safe. Stay here today, we'll talk this through. It'll help both of us."

Hinges squeaked as Sarah swung the first of the two doors closed.

"I'll be fine," she said, without looking back. "Right now I just need to get out."

"Out where?"

"Anywhere that'll get me past this," she said. "Maybe home, maybe work, maybe another country. I don't know where, and I don't know when I'm coming back. All I know is I need to make sure he's not in my head. To be certain I'm still myself."

Remedy started to object, then stopped. The two women looked at one another.

"Do you hear something?" Sarah said.

Remedy nodded. She heard it too—a deep rumble, distant but pervasive, as if generated from all directions. Definitely not an earthquake, or thunder, or a jet... but whatever it was, she had a feeling it couldn't be good.

THIRTY-ONE

Carl Sharp was admiring the way Search & Rescue's new sport utility handled the Sirretta River Canyon's tight curves when a refrigerator-sized boulder smashed onto the hood.

The truck's forward momentum rocked the boulder backward, striating the windshield. Heart pounding, Sharp rammed his foot against the brake pedal. The SUV, already slowed by the boulder, skidded across the two-lane road then collided with the towering granite that formed the canyon wall. Sharp saw something explode in front of his face, then felt his nose throbbing. It took a few seconds before he was coherent enough to understand that the vehicle's airbags had deployed.

Shaking glass shards from his head, he looked in the cracked rearview mirror. His hair and mustache were streaked with blood, the crest of his nose had turned blue, and multiple cuts crisscrossed his face and arms. The nose pounded; probably broken, he decided.

All this, just to submit the annual weapon certifications, he groused.

He heard another boulder drop onto the road, just beyond the driver's side window. A third hit above the SUV's rear passenger seats, caving the roof just behind his head. Bursting out of the truck, he saw more boulders, some of them rolling, a few tumbling over the edge of the road, plummeting toward the Sirretta river.

Then a baritone rumble sounded from above.

"Son of a bitch," Sharp said, realizing he had only survived the warm-up act. Racing across the road, he jumped the mangled guardrail and tossed himself over the canyon's edge. *Better to die from a 200-foot fall than be buried under a rockslide,* he thought. As it turned out, he hit an embankment and rolled only a short distance before his hands found enough of a hold to stop the descent. His fingers stung and his nails split as he forced them into shrubs, indentations, and any physical feature that would keep him from dropping any further. Below, a graveyard for rock lined both sides of a pronounced bend in the river, as if the canyon was grinning at him with a mouth full of dilapidated teeth.

The mild rumble of boulders falling onto the highway intensified into a roar, and Sharp felt the earth vibrating his hands as tons of granite poured off the Sirretta Canyon's sheer walls. Most of the debris hit the two-lane road and lost momentum, burgeoning into a massive pile, but a few of the smaller rocks continued over the side, their speed hurtling them well over his head. Below, the river resembled a dish-washing basin, gurgling with bubbles and foam from the splash of the falling rocks.

By the time the canyon calmed, Sharp was covered in dust and lined with blood streaks, but alive. His uniform had so many blood-stained holes it looked like a Halloween costume, and his badge was missing, apparently torn from the shirt during the fall. He took a moment to calm himself, then studied the vertical terrain to either side and spent the next half hour climbing back up to the road.

It wasn't until he reached the top that he realized there *was* no road; the asphalt was now covered in mounds of dirt and granite. Several of the boulders looked the size of a house, and most of the others were larger than Sharp's buried SUV. He hoped no one else had been driving in the canyon when the slide hit, but knew that wouldn't be the case.

Looking up, he saw more overhanging boulders, seemingly reaching over the gaping holes left by all the fallen rock. In a few hours, or minutes... *or seconds, the way my day's going so far*, he thought... they would come crashing down too. Scrambling over the debris, he headed away from the slide, down the fifteen-mile gorge that served as the main thoroughfare between the Sirretta Valley and Porterfield. After he had walked nearly an hour, the debris piles thinned and he spotted red lights flickering in the canyon's shadows. He rounded a curve and nearly stumbled against a sheriff's car parked in the middle of the highway. Mark Dancy, a rookie with a Howdy-Doody hairstyle, was motioning a long line of traffic to U-turn back down the canyon when he spotted Sharp.

"Carl!" he said. "Sirretta dispatch's been trying to raise you. You okay?"

"Maybe after a few hot showers. What's the word?"

"Wish I could tell you. Dispatch can't raise anyone up at the station either."

Sharp caressed his swollen, throbbing nose.

"This has got to be the worst slide this canyon has ever had," he said, brushing at the dirt on his face. "Cal-Trans is going to have months of bulldozing before this thing opens up again."

Car horns blared as a man wearing a cowboy hat tried to make a three-point-turn with his pickup and failed. He ended up blocking both lanes of the road at the exact spot where the other cars were trying to U-turn.

"You don't understand, Carl," Dancy said, moving to direct traffic. "None of the radio or phone calls going into the Sirretta Valley are being answered. Business, government, civilian, none of them. All those fire crews, silent."

Sharp was so surprised he stopped caressing the nose.

"What about cell phones, or short wave... hell, what about CB?"

Dancy motioned at the pickup driver, directing him out of the turn.

"No response on any of them," he said. "Even texts and emails aren't getting replies."

"Hmm," Sharp said. "There's more than just a slide at play... an earthquake, maybe?"

Dancy shook his head. "Both Caltech and the Geological Survey recorded no tremors other than the slide vibrations."

Sharp folded his arms, ignoring the blood smears.

"Then we'd damn well better send some units up one of the other roads to see what's going on up there."

"That's just it, Carl, we can't. This wasn't the only rock slide. The other roads are as clogged as this one."

"What about 155, over Bluehorn?"

"Blocked. Another massive slide, plus some sort of problem with fallen trees. Walkett Pass is out too. Big ol' sinkhole near the summit."

"A sinkhole at the top of a four-thousand-foot mountain pass?" Sharp said with more than a hint of skepticism. "Okay fine, let's use Lion's Trail. The road's a bitch, but it'll get us into Brodfish—"

"Listen to me. They've already checked it, we're shut out. It's up to the air support units."

Sharp used his hands to brush the dust and debris from his hair. "Are you saying the entire Sirretta Valley—two communities, probably 15,000 people—has been cut off from the rest of civilization?"

Dancy nodded. "The guy in the pickup thinks it's the Commies. Command's thinking it's terrorism."

Sharp snorted. "Terrorism? Who'd want to take out a Podunk valley in the Sierras? Sure, the resort's up there, but they could bomb the whole place to hell and no one in Washington would think twice."

Dancy shrugged.

Sharp took a breath as fatigue and the gravity of the situation hit home. Something very unusual was going on, and he couldn't help but think that if they didn't hurry up and figure it out, Sirretta Valley residents were going to end up dead.

THIRTY-TWO

"Something's happening," Razor said, grasping at his face, looking like he was about to claw at the skin. "The guy's doing his voodoo. Rocks are moving, trucks crashing, all kinds of weird shit. What am I supposed to do?"

Bonnicksen slowed their rental car, a burgundy, BMW knock-off from one of the new overseas companies. First the TSA delay, because he'd answered Wanamaker's call on the plane, now this. Somehow, a plan made early in the week had turned into a Saturday arrival... and on top of it all, his swollen left cheek still hurt something fierce.

"Don't do anything—not yet," he said, frustrated. "We'll get our chance once we get you into the Sirretta Valley. At that point you'll be close enough to take care of the problem."

"How am I supposed to do that?"

By letting me push the little red button, Bonnicksen thought. "Don't worry, it'll be easy. We're almost to the Sirretta Canyon, from there it's only—aw, what now?"

He hit the brakes as the two-lane highway dropped them past a rise, straight into a traffic jam at the canyon's entry. Off to their right, an electronic traffic board flashed messages indicating a rock slide had closed the road indefinitely.

"Great," Bonnicksen said. "Stay here, I'm going to make sure the cops understand this is an emergency."

He pulled over, walked to the front of the traffic, then buttoned his suit jacket and introduced himself to a sheriff's deputy with a disheveled uniform and a bloodied nose.

"This is life or death," he told the deputy, hoping there was an alternate road. "I've got to get up to the Sirretta Valley ASAP."

The cop stared at him like he'd heard the same thing from forty other people. "Sir, we have a landslide. All roads into the valley are closed."

"Wanamaker," Bonnicksen muttered, staring at the canyon wall. "It's got to be."

The deputy, who had been walking toward another officer, stopped.

"You mean Jon Wanamaker?" he said. "The guy who fished the bottled brain out of the lake?"

Bonnicksen hesitated. For the first time he saw the officer's brass nameplate and realized there might be trouble. All those unanswered voicemails... he was going to need to play this carefully. "Officer Sharp... are you telling me these road closures aren't the first of the unusual events around here?" he said.

"Never mind what I'm telling you," Sharp said. "Tell me why you think Wanamaker's involved with these roads."

"Yes... okay.... see, that's not going to be easy without giving you some cognitive and behavioral neuroscience first," he said. "But I'm betting Wanamaker's responsible for all this, and if I don't get up to that valley and stop him it's only going to get worse—a lot worse."

Sharp squinted. "Who are you?"

Bonnicksen gave him his title with the Sidney Research Institute.

"You're the man I've been trying to reach," Sharp said. "The one from the Upsweep project... your project."

"Yes... well, exactly... I decided to come answer your questions in person," Bonnicksen stammered.

"Uh-huh... sure you did," Sharp said, motioning for additional officers to join him. "I'm going to need you to come with me for questioning, but right now I'm trying to figure out why every roadway into the Sirretta Valley is suddenly sealed off... and I'm getting the idea that you might know something about it. Does this have something to do with a brain from your lab ending up in my lake?"

Bonnicksen clenched his teeth, hoping he wasn't showing his anger. Russ Kitchtoo's handiwork had certainly thrown a monkey wrench into things.

"I can only guess someone stole it," Bonnicksen told Sharp, hoping a small truth could cover a large lie.

Sharp wasn't biting. "I think maybe you and I should sit down and talk about—"

"You're that cop!" Razor shouted, running up. "The one whose truck got smashed by the boulder. I saw you, just a few minutes ago."

Sharp looked confused enough to detain them, so Bonnicksen decided to head off the problem.

"Look officer, I've been trying to tell you we can help," he said. "But we've got to get into Quail Point to do it. If you're trying to find Jon Wanamaker, then we're the people who can do that for you."

The deputy stared at them for a few seconds, then nodded. "You fill me in on what all this is about and how you can solve it," he said, "and I'll have the two of you riding with me on the first chopper headed into that valley."

Forty minutes later they were en route, the Sheriff's helicopter accelerating over the yellowed chaparral that gave California its "golden" nickname. Bonnicksen breathed a relieved sigh. For the moment, it seemed the need to stop Jon Wanamaker's hijinks outweighed Sharp's concerns about the bottled brain... or his purple, clearly broken, nose.

Bonnicksen liked the deputy's approach plan: rather than a typical flight pattern into the valley, something Wanamaker might expect, they would loop around the north side of Isadora, following the upper Sirretta River Canyon until it fed them into Quail Point.

The flight went quickly. From high up, the river's slender course glinted in the sun like a ribbon tied around the fir-cloaked mountains. Sharp's pilot, a middle-aged man with a clean-shaven head and the ample cheeks of an oversized baby, lowered the chopper into the river's broad gorge and took it to full speed, following the contour of the mountains.

Bonnicksen's head suddenly lurched; the pilot had throttled down, and looking out the cockpit window he could see why: two black specks, zooming over the mountain peaks to their left. Sharp leaned against the glass.

"Military fighters," Bonnicksen heard him say through their headsets.

The deputy glanced at the pilot. "This isolated valley crisis is moving up the chain of command faster than I imagined," Sharp said. "Takes DOD authorization to get emergency air support. Toole, lift us up a little, will you?"

Toole brought the chopper up, out of the canyon. Ahead, the jets roared towards the valley, passing a two-lane highway that crossed over the river.

"Jansendale Bridge," Sharp said, gesturing at an unspectacular structure devoid of trusses. "We're at the northern edge of the valley, between—"

He stopped as one of the jets pulled into a drastic, vertical climb. Sparks showered from its fuselage, something shot from the cockpit, then a fiery explosion burst in the sky ahead.

"What the—" Sharp said.

"Parachute!" Razor said, pointing to a distant, billowing comma veering away from the fiery debris. "The pilot made it."

They watched the descent, stunned.

"Look, the next one's pulling up too," Razor said.

The second jet veered upwards at a near-ninety-degree angle but its fuselage seemed to scrape against an unseen object, showering sparks and wobbling the plane until the aircraft managed to escape into open airspace.

"There's some kind of barrier out there... see it?" Bonnicksen said. "It's barely visible but every now and then the sunlight's reflecting off it." He loosened his tie, suddenly feeling warm. The sheer impossibility of what he was watching reminded him of the Exhibit C video. Exchanging looks with Razor, he wondered how the pitcher could remain so calm.

"Turn this thing around, man," Razor ordered Sharp, as if he were in charge. "We're almost up to the same spot."

Sharp took an extended look at the plummeting aircraft debris then nodded at Toole. Bonnicksen's stomach leapt into his throat as Toole rammed the cyclic hard left and pumped the RPMs, sheet metal screeching against bolts, rotors vibrating so hard he thought they would crack apart. They came about on a downward angle, and the straining sounds diminished, replaced by the roar of the engine.

"Look out—more of them!" Sharp said as Toole leveled the chopper, straight into the path of several oncoming fighters.

Razor swore in Spanish as the jets parted and flew past, two on either side of the chopper. The sound was deafening; Bonnicksen felt the aircraft engines vibrating his chest as they passed. They heard more explosions, thought it was the fighters, then looked back to see they had opened fire against the barrier with no apparent results.

"He's actually done it," Bonnicksen muttered. "Wanamaker has taken it all the way."

Sharp spun around. "All the way to what?"

Bonnicksen moistened his dry lips. "You remember I told you human consciousness could control parts of the physical world?"

Sharp nodded.

"Well, Jon Wanamaker is showing us it's true. I'd say this guy can pretty much do anything he wants."

Bonnicksen felt his nerves drain what little color was left in his face. He needed to urge Sharp and Toole to get him away from here, now, before Jon killed every one of them. The words were right there, atop his tongue, waiting... no, *pleading*... to be vocalized. But no, he realized. He couldn't. Not with the lingering possibility that he could duplicate Jon's remote manipulation.

He wanted to tamper with reality, like Jon. He wanted the world to understand what they were capable of... but most of all, he wanted to be the one to show them.

I.K. Emily, Wanamaker, Razor, Klase, Kitchtoo, the DOD, the Sidney people, now Sharp... they were all just means to his legendary end. The imminent danger didn't matter, not with his life's work at stake. The possibility he might document, then experience, even a moment of what Jon could do... just a single moment... far outweighed the chance of death.

He glanced out the window as Toole slowed the chopper to a hover. Smoke and flaming debris were dissipating near the barrier, which looked intact.

"What do you mean, saying Wanamaker can do *anything*?" Sharp said.

Bonnicksen saw the officer's face reflecting disbelief, doubt... fear. "Exactly what it sounds like I mean," he said, "and yeah, it's a problem. But you know what?"

The others looked at him, waiting.

He gave a nervous chuckle. "I've still got a plan."

THIRTY-THREE

Remedy was outside, wishing she hadn't let Sarah drive off so soon after the mysterious rumbling, when everything flickered. The deck, the mountains, and the world itself seemed to blink away, then reappear.

The tingling in Remedy's arms lobbied her mind, trying to convince her nothing had changed, but some small nuance of what she was seeing said otherwise. Then she realized what it was: the sky was clear. There was no lingering wildfire smoke, no smell of cinders.

Jon put the fire out.

It sounded ludicrous, but if he was using the ribbons then she knew there was a chance she was right. She could only imagine how stunned the firefighter battalions must be feeling, and made a note to contact them for her story.

Her phone alerted her to an incoming text message from Chris Casey, relaying news that the *Mountaineer*'s phones and computers—and his own—had stopped connecting beyond the valley. His follow-up texts blinked in one after another, painting the larger picture:

```
Bunch of stuff happening: Quail Point FD
reports a massive landslide in the canyon.
    FD, FS, and SO have lost external comms.
    Phones, sat, wifi, shortwave, CB, & Ham
are local-only.
    Social media posts bouncing.
    SV airport says radar nonfunctional,
grounding flights.
    Crap… I think we're isolated.
```

Remedy limped to a deck chair and sat down. *Maybe none of it's Jon's doing*, she thought.

Her intuition—or was it common sense?—disagreed.

"I can't sit on this any longer," she decided, calling Julie Henderson's number at the *Mountaineer*... then reconsidered, disconnecting the call before Henderson answered. "Except there's no way to tell people. No one would ever believe it."

Her phone rang. She saw Henderson's name on the display, returning the disconnected call. *Just send it to voicemail*, she thought. But she didn't. She couldn't.

"Yeah, Julie? I might... well, I might have something for you," she said, knowing she sounded tentative, uncertain. "You looked outside lately?"

"Just cut to it, already," Henderson said. "If you've got news on how a fifty-thousand-acre wildfire and a sky full of smoke just vanished, hit me with it."

In the face of everything else, the hard-assed Henderson didn't seem so difficult.

"Look, I know what's going on," Remedy said. "But I honestly have no idea how to explain it, and no one is going to believe it anyway."

She sighed, realizing how idiotic she sounded, expecting Henderson to respond accordingly.

"How wild is it?" she heard instead. "Second Coming? Elvis?"

"You wish," Remedy said, with a slight smile. "That'd be simple. This... it isn't simple."

"Tell me."

She did. The condensed version still took several minutes.

"Aw, hell," Henderson said when she finished.

"Yeah," Remedy said. "I know."

She heard Henderson take a deep breath, and maybe a drag on a cigarette.

"Any evidence?" Henderson finally said. "I mean, anything documented? Something that isn't divorcee insights, off-the-record tips, or the blatherings of a dusty old Eskimo?"

"Not really," Remedy said.

Henderson sighed. "Of course there isn't. Look, I'll run what you've just given me as a follow-up story, like we already discussed—one that raises questions about Jon's post-Upsweep abilities and whether he might be using them here in the valley without presenting it as fact. At least then people will have some conjecture to help them begin to explain what they're seeing. I mean, for Chrissake... the sheer impossibility of actually printing this as news, that's a hurdle you're not going to clear without evidence."

Fair enough, Remedy thought, having said much the same thing to Sarah. Hearing Henderson reaffirm their belief in the old-school approach felt good.

"Can you find Jon again?" Henderson said. "Somehow talk him into giving you something we can use?"

"I have no idea where he..." she started, then she saw Jon and Francis climbing onto the deck from the front steps. Her chest froze, even as her temper boiled.

"Let me call you back," she told Henderson.

Francis remained near the steps; his sweater had caught on the wrought iron fence, maybe a bit conveniently. As Jon approached, Remedy decided she wouldn't hold back, no matter how dangerous he might be.

"What the hell are you thinking?" she said, standing up so she could match his eye-level. "Are you out of your mind?"

"Rem, I promise you, it's all for—"

Remedy slide-stepped to him. "You know what, right now I don't even care," she said. "Don't you get it, Jon? You're scaring the crap out of me—out of everyone. I mean sure, the Eiffel Tower was breathtaking, and now the wildfire's gone and everything's shiny, and yes, I'm blown away by it, but... this community, we're seeing things we can't explain, experiencing things that... that shouldn't be happening, and yet they are."

"Yeah, but—"

"But what? You ripped up your neighborhood!" she said. "You've boxed us in, and put your neighbors' lives at risk. Sarah, she's such a mess I'm not even sure she'll ever be the same. And you—*manipulating* her? Turning her into your puppet? Turning this whole valley into your puppet? Is this who you are?"

Francis looked at Jon like this was a topic they'd discussed as well.

"Who's next?" she said. "Me? Do I have free will anymore? Do any of us?"

"Rem, please..."

"Don't give me 'please,' answer me! How am I supposed to know you won't puppet me like you did Sarah?"

Jon inched away from her. "Because I've learned... from her, from Arturo, from Francis, and especially from you," he said. "What you're seeing right now, I don't have to be in anyone's head to make it happen... and I'll restore everything in a day or so, once I have a handle on exactly what I can do. At that point I'll go to the sheriffs and clear up the warrant—and you can quote me on that in your next article."

Remedy shook her head. "How am I supposed to know you're telling the truth?"

He shut his eyes. "Because you know me," he said. "You know that as lousy as I've been, all I care about is winning The Race. That's it."

She felt a knot in her throat and hoped it was boiling anger, even though she knew it wasn't. "Really?" she said. "That's it?"

He looked at her the way he did before their marriage. "I guess it's complicated. Right?"

She glanced away again, upset with herself. People were having their lives treated like rubber bands, flung to and fro, all because her husb—*ex-husband*, couldn't stop messing with things... and here she was being civil with him.

Jon sighed. "Look, I'm adjusting to this on the fly too. You think it's easy having a billion words clouding your thoughts? Seeing everything you know suddenly change into something... malleable? Not knowing whether one poorly constructed sentence derived from a language I don't fully understand might hurt the people I love?"

"So then why are you messing with it at all?"

She knew it was a dumb question.

"Are you really going to tell me you wouldn't mess with it if this happened to you?" he said. "It's a mind-blowing rush—and for the record, it's not like I'm robbing, raping, and conquering, which I'm pretty sure I could do, by the way. So stop acting like I don't have a conscience. This wild stuff you see, it's all temporary, me figuring out how to use this thing. That's it."

Francis freed his sweater, mounted the three deck steps, then placed a hand on their shoulders. "You both have very valid points, but we don't have time to debate this now," he said, slow and deliberate. "Bonnicksen arrives in Quail Point today. For all we know he's already here—and he plans on killing Jon."

Remedy wished she could pace away her anger and anxiety, but her legs weren't up for pacing. "You're certain he wants you dead?" she said, to Jon. "I mean, he could be coming here to help, like he said in his messages."

Jon shook his head. "Saw it in the ribbons," he said.

"Ribbons which you could still manipulate, to make sure Bonnicksen fails?" she said.

"Sure, but only if I 'puppet him,' as you put it," he said. "I'm trying to do this another way."

"So then why are you in Quail Point?" she said. "Get yourself someplace where he can't find you—another state, another country, whatever it takes."

Jon walked to the deck rail, looking at the mountains. "Because he has my percipient with him—the man from Upsweep who can see what I'm doing, where I'm doing it, anytime he wants. There's no hiding from that."

Remedy fingered the bottom edge of her blouse, twisting it as she thought things over. "Then he'll know you're here, at my place," she said. "Maybe he already does."

"That's what I'm counting on. Let's just make it easy and bring him here, Rem. You'll get your story, and then I'll take care of things."

She didn't hide her suspicion. "Take care of things how?"

Jon turned his back to the rail, facing them.

"As quickly and as peacefully as possible," he said. "I've put a lot of thought into this, and if things go right I'll settle things with Bonnicksen, Kitchtoo, even I.K. Emily."

"Meaning what?" she said.

"Meaning I'll finally have answers," he said. "We all will."

An old adage flashed through Remedy's mind, and she found herself hoping this was one instance where it didn't apply. Still, try as she might she couldn't stifle the cautionary wisdom behind it: *be careful what you ask for.*

THIRTY-FOUR

Bonnicksen plummeted through warm autumn air, the deafening roar from Toole's chopper quickly muted by a deluge of bubbles. His body shuddered, the icy Sirretta River jarring his focus. He waited for his descent to slow, then kicked toward the bright sky above.

The pull of his flotation vest lifted him fast, but *fast* was relative when submerged beneath frigid, racing water. Just when he thought his lungs would burst, he surfaced, sucking air in short, violent gulps as the churning water pushed him downstream.

Razor Castillo breached the surface a few yards away, his soggy Red Sox cap popping up alongside. The current grabbed both men, tugging them past jagged boulders, through webs of face-slashing reeds. Flailing, Bonnicksen looked skyward in time to see Carl Sharp toss a gray, buoy-sized can from the chopper. The object exploded into an inflating raft as it hit the river, prompting Sharp to toss himself into the water near the raft. A quick hand-signal later and Toole had the chopper raised up, headed back towards Porterfield.

Bonnicksen chopped and splashed against the current. His dog-paddling was more like cow-paddling and swimming in his boxers felt weird, but he managed to reach the raft. Sharp was already aboard, using an oar to hold position near a foxtail thicket at the edge of the river. One at a time, he grabbed Bonnicksen and Razor by the armpits and pulled them inside.

"Alive?" Sharp said.

Bonnicksen nodded, trying to catch his breath. His swollen cheek throbbed, but not like it had in the chopper. *Score one for icy water*, he thought. Around them, the riverbanks were cluttered with weathered boulders that gave way to scrub oaks and spiky ceonothus bushes.

"Toole will be back after refueling," Sharp said, holding a hand to his broken nose as if it might ease the throbbing. "I managed to pull the supply bag out of the water and get it tied onto the raft, so you'll get your clothes and phones when we get to Quail Point. Meantime we've got some class three rapids and maybe a class four coming up. The river's low this time of year, so the rapids aren't as bad as in the spring, but still..."

"They'll be bad enough," Bonnicksen said.

They each grabbed a paddle as the current yanked the boat through a gullet of narrow, rock-strewn channels. The accompanying roar amplified a sense of doom, and existence soon boiled down to three things: raft, water, and holding on.

"Lean forward and paddle hard!" Sharp said.

Razor pumped a fist in the air as the little raft plunged over a huge rapid, hit the water pooled at the bottom, then spun, sending them backward toward a second rapid. With no time to turn the boat, Sharp swiveled on his knees and directed the boat straight into the next rapid. They shot through, the raft flipping over as if someone had turned it with a spatula.

Bonnicksen grabbed onto the boat's rubbery edge, holding tight as they plunged beneath the icy water, then felt himself—and the raft—flipping upright. He gasped for air, blinking his waterlogged eyelashes enough to see they were heading through yet another channel.

After multiple rapids and a splash that could have doubled as an ocean wave, the river calmed. Bonnicksen wiped his eyes and collapsed onto one of the inflated rubber supports, his heart pounding. Razor gave a thumbs-up.

"Baby stuff," the pitcher said, reclining against the raft's inflated bench.

They didn't see Sharp for several moments, then finally spotted him up ahead, waiting for the raft to catch up. He pulled himself aboard.

"Crash site's a few yards away," Sharp said, pointing to a rocky hillside east of the river.

Chunks of smoking, metallic debris littered the area, and a sickening, acrid smell filled the air. Blackened swatches of brush collared the debris, small tongues of flame still licking at what was left of the vegetation.

"Think the guy made it?" Razor said.

Bonnicksen was thinking no, but Sharp disagreed. "We saw a chute so I'd say yes, but he probably would have angled away from the river basin since there are so many trees here," the deputy said, studying the wreckage. "Whatever the aircraft hit, it was right by this bend in the river."

"Yes, but look—the river's still flowing normally," Bonnicksen said. "It's not backed up, meaning whatever blocked the jets isn't blocking the water."

Sharp was about to respond when they all lurched forward. The front of the raft appeared smooshed, as if shoved against a wall by the river's current, but there was no wall in sight. Sharp and Razor scurried to the raft's back end as the boat spun sideways, to throw extra weight upon the rushing water.

"Feels like flowers," Bonnicksen said, resembling a mime as he ran his fingers across the unseen surface before him. "Very little give though."

Reaching down, underneath the raft, he broke into a smile. "And guess what? It only extends a few inches below the water's surface."

He whipped his head around to face the others. "We can deflate the boat, take it underneath the barrier, then re-inflate it with the battery pump and raft right into Quail Point."

Razor shook his head. "You one lucky SOB sometimes."

An hour later, they found themselves with a sunset view of the small, upscale town... and the chaos unfolding just beyond the riverbank. Flames engulfed two cars, storefront windows were smashed, and scores of young men ran through the nearby street lugging stolen groceries, alcohol, and electronics.

"Rioting in Quail Point?" Sharp said, astonished as he steered them to shore. "People must be flipping out about the isolation... that, or taking advantage of it."

As soon as Sharp beached the raft, Bonnicksen unzipped the supply bag and grabbed his clothes and phone. "Can't call out of the valley," he confirmed while dressing, "but I wonder..."

He texted Remedy their location. She didn't immediately reply, but the message was marked "delivered." Sharp, meanwhile, was on his walkie-talkie.

"If not for the mobile communications unit that's up here for the fire, we might not have local dispatch," he said, annoyed.

Razor yanked the supply bag away from the other two men. "Makes it all the more badass we found a way inside," he said, searching for his dry clothes.

Sharp motioned for them to wait while he received a more detailed update. The longer he spoke with his substation, the more his expression hardened.

"Valleywide panic... even a possible suicide," he said, lowering the walkie. "I'll need to bring my officers up to speed about Wanamaker before we track him down. Maybe grab some painkillers for this nose of mine, too."

Bonnicksen studied Sharp, sensing an opportunity.

"Mr. Castillo can locate Wanamaker for you while you round up your men," he said, hoping Sharp wouldn't question the idea, pleased when he didn't. Instead, the deputy stared at the horizon south of them, looking troubled.

"The fire's out," Sharp said, studying the smoke-free mountain ridges. "That doesn't make any sense, this morning it was only forty percent contained."

"Got news for you," Razor said, wringing water from his cornrows. "The sundown's out too."

Bonnicksen looked at the sun straddling the horizon. "Are you nuts?" he said. "It's right there."

"Sure is," the pitcher said. "But this isn't June, it's September. By my watch, it should've been dark at least an hour ago."

Wanamaker, Bonnicksen thought, checking the time. *He's messed with the valley's daylight hours too.* He felt relieved the neural mine would soon be in range.

"Surprise, Wanamaker," he said to himself. "Get ready to have your head blasted apart."

––––––––––

Roberto "Razor" Castillo watched Bonnicksen slide a necktie through his buttoned collar, wondering what it might feel like to pop him with a 98-mile-an-hour heater. Nah, he thought. Why kill the school geek in an instant, when a bat would entertain the looters?

He buttoned his designer shirt, which was dry despite spending several hours stuffed inside the supply bag. He'd let the geek-man haul him across the country, fly him down a canyon, and nearly drown him in a river, but enough was enough. Visions and words still ate at his head—someone else's words, and all because he'd needed a few bucks several years back. It had to stop.

"Okay, so we're here," Razor said. "We're so close to this Wanamaker guy I feel like I got four eyes instead of two. Let's get your dirty work done. *Comprende*?"

Bonnicksen tossed him the condescending expression Razor had come to anticipate since scouts first showed up at his front door when he was eleven. The college geeks always acted like their computers and their money made the rest of the world their lackeys. They thrived on their imagined superiority, until it came time to grow a vegetable, patch a leaky roof, or fix a broken-down car. Then they were dumb as nails.

"Listen to me, Razor," Bonnicksen said, speaking in an exaggerated voice, as if talking to a six-year-old. "I just heard back from a local reporter, Jon's with her right now. They've texted me the contact information for someone who can drive us to their location. Soon as we get there, I need to you to do just what you did during Project Upsweep. I need you to lock onto your agent's thoughts. Be the percipient, Razor. That's all."

Razor reached for a round can in his back pants pocket. He pinched a wad of river-soaked chew from the can, wedged it behind his lower lip, then offered some to the others.

"Nah, guess you wouldn't," he said when they declined.

He took a pull on the tobacco then spit the juice at Bonnicksen's feet.

"Okay, fine, I'll tap Wanamaker's mind," he said, "long as you promise to get his words out of my head, for good."

"Easy," Bonnicksen said. "When we get to his location, into close range, we'll use this—" he pulled an oblong remote from a sealed bag in his pocket— "to neutralize the problem."

Sharp looked up from his radio. "What is that thing?" he said.

Bonnicksen admired the remote before answering. "It's kind of like a jamming device," he said. "It sends out signals that will interfere with the neural pathways transmitting images to Razor—the same pathways giving Jon the ability to mess everything up."

He indicated their surroundings. Sharp gave a suspicious look.

"And that'll put an end to whatever Wanamaker's doing?" he said.

"Absolutely."

Sharp thought it over. "Fine, but here's how we'll play this," he said. "I'll have the two of you wired, you'll join Wanamaker and the reporter. Get him talking about what he's doing to the valley. Soon as we have some solid info, I'm coming in with the SWAT team and you'll activate your device. Understood?"

"What about me?" Razor said. "You tellin' me this gizmo won't affect me when I'm plugged into the guy's head?"

Bonnicksen continued admiring the remote. "Of course it'll affect you. Tough guy like you probably won't even care, right?"

Razor scowled. Head-games were his job—pitching was primarily a mental exercise, regardless of what the broadcasters liked to say—and he could tell the school-geek was playing a game. Sharp seemed to notice the same thing.

"There's no other way, officer," Bonnicksen said. "If there were, I wouldn't have bothered bringing this busy young man all the way from Boston."

Razor wasn't sure whether 'busy young man' was sincere or mocking. *In the minors, I'd have knocked that geek-man right on his ass, no second thoughts.* Back home in the Dominican he would've done it too... and had, more than once, to a good many people.

"Don't think I don't know you're trying to play me, bro," Razor said. "Don't think I don't know this remote of yours isn't going to screw with me just as bad as it does with Wanamaker."

Bonnicksen nodded again, but Razor saw hesitancy in his eyes. Same look, he realized, as the guys who wonder if I'm going knock 'em in the head with the ball.

"So why are you going to do it?" Bonnicksen said.

Razor looked at the remote control. "Cause I can take it, school-geek. I can do the dirty work you're too much of a pussy to do. Besides, there's a chance I owe you."

His thoughts wandered to the months prior to Project Upsweep. Bonnicksen's team had spent evenings teaching percipients to clear their minds, freeing themselves of all thought outside of the task at hand. Stipends aside, those sessions had paid off for Razor, a notoriously aggressive minor leaguer continually held in check by a lack of focus while on the mound. Now, whether running to the mound in the ninth or searching for a connection with Wanamaker, he could isolate his thoughts at will.

"Got him," he said aloud, as he felt Jon Wanamaker's thoughts flickering into his head. "Everything's so vivid now that we're close. I can hear what he's saying, see what he's looking at... I can almost read his..."

Razor clutched his head, then fell silent, seeing Jon's ribbons. A smile formed on his lips, and he nodded his head in silent affirmation.

"What is it?" Bonnicksen said. "Did you find Wanamaker? Can you see what's going on?"

Razor crossed his arms, the ever-present scowl suddenly erased. "Yeah," he said, watching a shuttle bus approach, its driver waving to get their attention as more looters dashed past. "I see what's going on."

Bonnicksen looked thrilled, coddling his remote like a father with his child, but after seeing Wanamaker's ribbons Razor felt just as happy. Yeah, he thought, the remote might kill him; Wanamaker's ribbons definitely said as much. But now that he knew what Wanamaker was capable of, the payback was gonna be one for the ages.

"Go ahead, Geek Man, I can take it," he said.

It's just like a one-run game in the ninth, he told himself. Establish control, harness your skills, then blow the guy away.

THIRTY-FIVE

Vibrations rumbled, jarring Russ Kitchtoo's attention away from his cribbage board. Another pointless call, he figured, probably from someone relaying orders for him to remain in a holding pattern. He spit a bullet toward his burner phone, which he'd half-tucked into a gopher hole. The phone's screen cracked as the bullet smacked against it, but otherwise remained dark.

Not an incoming call or message, he realized; the rumbling was from something other than a vibrating phone. But the earth wasn't shaking, and he didn't hear any large trucks or loud engines nearby.

He stood up, risking a quick, unobstructed look at the riverside campground below Remedy Conover's neighborhood, where he had nestled himself after growing tired of the sheriffs. With summer over, the eucalyptus-shrouded campground was empty. Forest Service padlocks sealed the trash bins, sun-cracked roadways remained unpatched, and the outhouses had been hauled away—not that Kitchtoo would have used them when a quick-dug hole would suffice.

The odd rumbling continued but Isadora, to the south, seemed calm: no whitecaps. So too was the wind, having settled an hour or so earlier. Only the sierra peaks caught Kitchtoo's attention. They shimmered beneath a crystalline sky, as if someone had used a vacuum to clear smoke from the valley.

"About time," he said aloud, in his guttural voice.

The harassment, the buoy, the provocations... they had finally spurred Jon into action. He listened, still hearing the distant rumble, wondering what it was, knowing it was irrelevant. The only thing that mattered was that it proved Wanamaker had finally advanced his use of the words he was seeing.

The rumbling stopped, but a vibrating sound replaced it. He looked into the gopher hole. This time it *was* his phone.

He answered without speaking. The other end of the line was equally silent, save for a brief siren and what sounded like a distant train.

"It's time," a woman's grainy voice said.

I.K. Emily, Kitchtoo recognized, from their prior communication.

"Lay it out," he said. "I.D. code first."

"A-twenty-nine, gamma sixteen," I.K. Emily said. "The runoff exceeds the channel."

Kitchtoo couldn't help himself; hearing the termination order for Jon Wanamaker made him smile.

"Understood," he said.

"Proceed as *commissioned*," he heard Emily say. "No bottles, brains, buoys, or school snipes. No creativity whatsoever. As commissioned only. If it goes down clean and unseen, I double your price. Clear?"

Kitchtoo couldn't believe what he'd just heard. She was doubling his already jacked-up price? Now he knew how badly she wanted Wanamaker out... and how dangerous she considered him.

"Triple," he countered, barely able to imagine what the Rowock community center would think when *this* pile of cash appeared on their doorstep. "Wanamaker's no pushover anymore."

"Triple then. Today though. No delays."

"As commissioned," Kitchtoo said.

With a couple of crucial, pre-assassination moments that you'll never know about, he thought.

"Be advised: he's just sealed off the valley," I.K. Emily said. "No external access or communications, local only."

And yet you're on my phone right now, Kitchtoo thought. An interesting development.

"One more thing," I.K. Emily said.

He waited.

"Shovel the stable too."

Kitchtoo broke into a broad grin. Wanamaker *and* Bonnicksen? Now *that* was a payoff.

The call ended. Kitchtoo gathered his gear, satisfied. The cops were probably too busy to continue combing the valley for him, but even if they weren't they wouldn't expect to find him in the flatlands near the river.

"Okay Jonny," he said, looking skyward. "I know what you've tapped into, and I know you can read this. No more games. Let's settle things."

At first he thought maybe he'd overestimated the situation, that maybe Wanamaker's skills weren't quite as far along as he and I.K. Emily suspected. But then a sound hit his ear like a mosquito's whine, softening to a whisper before amplifying in volume and clarity.

"*Bonnicksen's in town*," Jon's voice said. "*He's planning to kill me.*"

Kitchtoo scowled; hearing Jon's voice inside his own head was a sensation he'd just as soon not experience again. He stuck a finger in his ear, hoping he could dig Wanamaker's annoying whisper away like itchy wax, but he knew the message was one he couldn't ignore. Clients were *not* allowed to finish *his* work, especially when the project, such as this one, carried a personal interest... and a personal timeframe that he wasn't about to let Bonnicksen interfere with.

"Tell me where he is," Kitchtoo said.

The mosquito whine returned. "I'd rather bring you to him."

Kitchtoo unsheathed his *quoth-lar*. Soon, he'd have it sticking out of Wanamaker's gut, but his own plan needed to happen first... which meant it was time to consider sticking it into Erich Bonnicksen instead.

THIRTY-SIX

rnie's shuttle bus roared to the top of Remedy's driveway incline and skidded to a stop, launching a dust cloud onto the front deck, where Remedy stood with Jon. She glanced at the bus windows. Two silhouettes moved past, headed to the exit door, but when the bus door opened it was Ernie who scrambled out.

"These guys you had me bring over here?" Ernie said to Jon, gesturing at the bus with a thumb. "They claim *you're* the reason we're all trapped in the valley right now. Is that true?"

"Technically," Jon said, "one of *them* is the reason."

"Jon, come on... what the hell?" Ernie said. "People are losin' it out there! I just drove past looters acting like it's the end of the world."

Remedy sensed the strain between them was about more than just the passengers. "You need to bring him in on this," she told Jon.

"Let me deal with these guys," Jon said, to Ernie, "then, yeah... I'll tell you everything."

Ernie looked irritated, but not so much that it kept him from asking whether he could help. Jon started to shake him off, then stopped.

"Actually, yes," he said, then leaned in too close for Remedy to hear him.

Ernie looked taken aback. "You're sure?"

"Yeah—but have Sarah Ushida confirm it for the boy, she saw firsthand what I can do."

"I mean, come on, he's just a kid..."

Jon placed a hand on Ernie's shoulder. "I know... believe me, I know. But the Tlingit words I placed in his mind when we were on Hanafin Road should be enough for his head to open up its own back-channel. He'll see the ribbons."

"Ribbons?"

"Later Ernie, it's gotta be later. And look, Arturo won't be able to do much, but there is one thing he can easily do."

Again, Remedy couldn't hear what Jon told him, because just as they began talking the two passengers leaped from the bus.

"Jon, thank God!" one of the two men called, racing over. "Don't do another thing, I can resolve everything right now."

Remedy recognized Erich Bonnicksen's voice from phone messages. He was shorter than he sounded, with a thick neck and a face full of rolls and clefts, and his dark suit looked far too pretentious for a remote mountain valley. Someone else must have thought so too; one of his cheeks had a swollen welt as dark as the suit. He raced up the deck's steps, one hand tugging the arm of a slender man with corn-rowed hair and a faint mustache—she assumed it was Razor Castillo—the other hand clutching some kind of remote control. The pitcher looked as out of place as Bonnicksen, wearing a nightclub shirt with trendy pants.

"I take it you're my percipient," Jon said.

"Not by choice," Razor said. The two men shook hands. As they did, Remedy noticed Razor shifting his eyes from her to Bonnicksen and then back, as if he was trying to tell her she shouldn't trust the Sidney researcher.

"Whatever you're seeing—text, maybe?—I can help you with it," Bonnicksen said to Jon.

Remedy slide-stepped into their midst. "I'll need to talk with both of you first," she told Bonnicksen and Razor, introducing herself. She noticed Ernie had already climbed back into the bus and was driving off, but Bonnicksen was in her face before she could question it.

"We can discuss things later," he said, turning his attention to the remote. "First let me—"

Francis stepped in his path. "We're gonna need more," he said.

The Sidney dean huffed. "There's no time for more."

"Make the time," Francis said.

Bonnicksen lowered the remote. "Why? You're already aware of my work, and the results. Wanamaker is my biggest hit. What more is there to say?"

"You can start by telling us about your arrangement with I.K. Emily," Remedy said.

He froze. "I don't know that name," he said.

Remedy lifted her eyes. "Mr. Bonnicksen, I have plenty of evidence that I.K. Emily is your government point person," she said, even though she didn't. "Who is this woman, and what's her interest in Jon?"

Bonnicksen's eyes narrowed. "Maybe you should ask her yourself."

"I already have," she said. "Now I need to see whether your stories match."

She hated the lie, but sometimes that was the only way to crack a source.

"Bull," he said, crushing her strategy. "You know as well as I do that no one talks with I.K. Emily."

"So then why are you so special?" she said.

He lowered his guard with a smirk that seemed to come direct from his ego. "Because I have what she wants," he said, glancing at Jon. "Control beyond anything you can imagine. Your husband already knows that... don't you, Jon."

The two men stared at each other for a moment, neither saying a word. Remedy didn't need reporter's intuition to know there was something more going on than conflicting personalities... possibly something they were keeping secret.

"Then it's all documented?" she pressed. "You have study results that explain how Jon can visualize and manipulate the ribbons?"

"Absolutely."

Francis scoffed. "If I.K. Emily wants those study results for herself, as you're suggesting," he said, "she'll never let you publish."

Bonnicksen seemed to find the comment amusing. "My goals take priority over hers," he said. "I'll be happy to provide full documentation once my papers are published in the proper journals. In fact, Mr. Castillo is part of the documentation. These two men are quintessential remote perception partners. At times, their minds are truly linked, to the point where Mr. Castillo even saw some of the sentences streaming before Wanamaker's eyes."

He gave Razor an awkward glance.

"Which is why," Bonnicksen continued, "Mr. Castillo now offers our best solution for proving the connection exists."

Razor pointed a warning finger. "Don't do it, bro," he told Bonnicksen. "Let Wanamaker handle things, he already knows more than you do."

Bonnicksen ignored the pitcher. "You wanted my help, Jon," he said, "so I brought something to clear your mind."

He tapped the remote, activating the neural mine. A piercing whine split the air, shrill enough to make Remedy feel her earwax drain. She saw Jon clench the top of his head, heard him let out a blood-curdling scream—Razor too. Suddenly she understood why Bonnicksen had dodged her calls and questions, why the pitcher had been trying to warn her not to trust him, why Jon had been so reluctant to reconnect with the man.

Above all, she understood they had made a major mistake. Bringing Bonnicksen to them was not going to give Jon a chance to clear matters up... it was going to cost him his life.

THIRTY-SEVEN

Childhood nightmares aside, Remedy couldn't remember a single moment when she'd felt so horrified that she had to stifle a scream... until now. She watched, aghast, as Razor's left shoulder exploded into a shower of flesh and blood that rained down upon her deck. The pitcher dropped to his knees, his agonized cries paired with gunshot echoes pinging off the nearby mountains.

Something sliced the air to Remedy's left. She ducked and turned her head in one motion, avoiding the sound while attempting to track it, but saw only a metallic blur.

Bonnicksen's right hand cleaved in two, palm to wrist, sending more blood and the black, plastic remains of the remote control spattering onto the wood. The shrill whine ended and Bonnicksen buckled, screaming in pain as he fell to his knees alongside Razor.

Remedy covered her mouth, horrified as she studied the blade wedged into Bonnicksen's wrist. It was dagger-length, with a carved, bear head pommel.

A quoth-lar, she recognized.

Amid the horror and chaos, it took her a second to process the meaning.

Bonnicksen's device isn't causing any of this... it's Muddy Guy. Russ Kitchtoo is here, he's already destroyed Bonnicksen's weapon and taken two of the five of us down.

She whipped her head left, then right, searching for him as she crawled for cover, seeing Francis and Jon but no one else. Francis had ducked and looked like a smooshed mattress, bunched into a ball below the deck table, but he seemed unharmed.

Razor, writhing in agony, was nonetheless convulsing with heavy, strained laughter. "He never had a chance," he exulted, through the pain. "Your ribbons said you had it covered, and you did. And I can take it till you're ready, man. Don't worry, I can take it."

Remedy did a double take. *Razor can read Jon's ribbons?* She glanced at Jon and noticed he was no longer clenching his head, nor was he in any pain. Instead, he crouched next to her, pointing toward a bougainvillea stand just across the two-lane street.

She looked, didn't see Kitchtoo, but understood he was probably there regardless.

"It's okay," Jon said, whispering. "I brought him here."

She opened her mouth, appalled.

"But why would—" she started.

Something rustled the bougainvillea. Remedy felt her legs stiffen even tighter as the man who had held her and Sarah at knifepoint stepped out from the bush, muddied and hairy. He turned and spat; something metallic clanged off her wrought iron fence. Then he retrieved his *quoth-lar*, yanking it from Bonnicksen's wrist, oblivious to the gut-wrenching scream it triggered.

"You plan on helping these men, or not?" he said to Jon, gesturing at Bonnicksen and Razor. His voice was barely audible, its rasp more distinct than Remedy remembered.

Jon wore a poker face. "Helping them how?" he said.

Kitchtoo smiled, exposing the yellowed teeth Remedy first saw in Sarah's car. Everything went dead quiet—not a single twittering bird, wind-blown leaf, or distant car. Even the lumberjack weathervane went still.

Jon seemed to realize his bluff hadn't worked. "Of course I'll help them," he said, rising up from his crouch.

"So, the only real question is whether you'll help *me*," Kitchtoo said, wiping blood from the *quoth-lar* onto his pants.

"You know I want to," Jon said. "You also know I can't."

Remedy had no idea what they were referring to but cautiously followed Jon's lead, her body screaming at her as she clutched her broom and used it to pull herself up from the deck planks.

"Sure you can, same way you can help *them*," Kitchtoo said, while looking at Bonnicksen and Razor. "Go ahead. No point in you hiding your skills, I.K.'s kept me in the loop."

Remedy froze, hearing him say those initials. Then the significance hit her: Muddy Guy was saying I.K.

Emily had told him about Jon's ribbons, just as she'd suspected.

"Thinking about stalling until the sheriff storms in, maybe?" Kitchtoo said. "The one who wired Bonnicksen? Yeah... he and the SWAT team, they're gonna need your help too."

Francis pivoted on his cane. "Jon, wait..."

"No," Kitchtoo interjected. "Enough waiting. Show me you can change things, Wanamaker. Now."

Jon looked at Bonnicksen, then Razor. Both were groaning, in agony. Bonnicksen seemed on the verge of passing out but Razor gulped at the evening air, tears rolling down his face.

"What is it you think I can do for you?" Jon said, to Kitchtoo.

Kitchtoo returned Jon's stare without answering... but then again, Remedy remembered, he always took forever to answer.

"The impossible," he finally said. "But you already know that. Your ribbons would have showed you."

Jon didn't seem surprised. "Russ... don't you think I already thought of that?" he said. "Don't you think I tried? Back on Amelynd, I tried. God knows, I tried. Went back through her sentences, read through the whole thing... every horrible detail..."

Her sentences, Remedy repeated to herself, suddenly understanding. *Emma Kitchtoo*. Even with all the facial mud and leaves, she felt as if she could now see Russ Kitchtoo, the man, versus Muddy Guy, the assassin. She saw his shuddering jaw and his vacant eyes, his mind clearly locked on to the tragedy in another place, another time. *Because under all that savagery he's a grieving parent*, Remedy remembered.

"Emma is the *only* detail that matters," Kitchtoo said, his voice as shaky as his jaw. "Just shift the language to—"

"I already changed the sign!" Jon said. "Changed it from Tlingit to English so she could understand it, okay? I changed the color, hardened the ice, chilled the weather, added life preservers... none of it worked."

"Then break her damn leg!" Kitchtoo said, as much a growl as a comment. "Just keep her off that frozen pond!"

Jon collapsed to his knees, distraught. "Anything I try... the outcome never changes, Russ! Emma's still dead—and twenty-two other people are too. No matter what I do, I can't reverse any of it!"

What? Remedy thought, stunned. She looked at Jon, then Kitchtoo. *They're seriously trying to use the ribbons to reverse... death?*

"Seeing them die, again and again... I couldn't handle it," Jon said, his voice hollow. "I still can't."

So he buried it, Remedy realized. He came home, moved to the Sirretta Valley, got married, tried to forget. But whatever Project Upsweep had triggered inside him hadn't gone away.

"You need to keep trying," Kitchtoo said. "Kill us all if you have to, but get my baby girl back."

And suddenly Remedy understood why Jon had brought Kitchtoo here: he was using him as a bodyguard, to protect himself against Bonnicksen. So long as Kitch-too thought there was any possibility Jon could use the ribbons to go back and save Emma, there was no chance he would let Bonnicksen, I.K. Emily, or anyone else kill Jon.

"Maybe you need better motivation," Kitchtoo said.

"Better than saving a girl's life?" Jon said.

"Could be."

Kitchtoo gazed at the deck-side cypress trees during his customary pause before answering. "You claim you can't help Emma, I'm thinking you just need the right incentive to work up your skills."

"Listen to what Jon's telling you," Francis said, pushing himself to his feet. "He can change just about anything, but he can't change a death. There's no way to 'motivate him' if what you want isn't possible!"

"Actually, it's real easy," Kitchtoo said... then lifted his *quoth-lar* and drove the blade straight into Francis's chest.

Sweating like a pig, Ernie hit the shuttle bus brakes and waited out front of the hospital.

The wait lasted eight minutes. It seemed more like twenty.

Finally, Sarah Ushida stepped out from the hospital's side entry, walking toward the bus like it might be filled window-to-window with gang members.

"Don't bother, I am not stepping inside this filthy thing," she said as Ernie opened the bus doors. "What's so urgent?"

"Look, I'll make this quick: Jon Wanamaker sent me."

She made a face. "Then we're done here," she said, backing away.

"Wait—he said it's for Remedy!"

Sarah stopped, checked her watch, then slowly approached the bus once again. "You've got ten seconds," she said.

"Yeah, well she and Jon don't have much more than that," Ernie said. "Jon said you and I need to get to Wofford Notch."

"That's where they are?"

"No, they're with Bonnicksen at Remedy's place right now, but it's worse than that. The sniper's up there with them too. We can help but we need to be at Hanafin Road, ASAP."

Sarah pulled out her phone, scowling. "Let me call Remedy and—"

"No calls—the sniper will hear and Jon said the sheriffs are already in the loop anyway. Now get in here, will you? We gotta go!"

"Why me?"

"I'll tell you on the way," he said, pointing to his watch. *For such a smart woman, she sure is a dumbass*, he thought.

"Fine," Sarah said, climbing up the three bus steps, cringing as her hands touched the stairwell rails. "But I'm not staying in this rickety thing with you for more than fifteen minutes."

Me either, Ernie thought, gunning the old bus's engine. *Me either.*

———————

"Francis!"

Jon eyed Kitchtoo's *quoth-lar* as he yelled, wishing he could get his hands on it, knowing he couldn't. Kitchtoo yanked it from Francis's chest, wiped the dripping blade against his pants, sheathed it, stepped back.

Francis fell to the deck. Jon, still on his knees, rushed over and bunched the Tlingit elder's sweater against the stab wound, trying to stop the bleeding as tears welled in his eyes. He saw Remedy dialing 911, but he knew what Kitchtoo would do to the paramedics if they showed up. In his peripheral vision, he saw Razor sitting up, still in obvious pain and cradling his bloodied shoulder with his other arm, but looking even more horrified by what Kitchtoo had just done to Francis.

The Tlingit elder suddenly wheezed, his chest heaving up and down as if his lung cavities were mine shafts and the air had to be lugged in and out. Jon put an arm around his shoulders, desperate to offer what little comfort he could.

"Save the old man, Jon," Kitchtoo said. "Save Bonnicksen and the pitcher too—you know you can. Then maybe you'll be ready for Emma."

"You're not listening to what I'm telling you!" Jon said. "I already tried to save her and twenty-two other people. Twenty-two people! It was too long ago, Russ! Please, please listen to me, there's nothing I can do!"

"My employer says otherwise."

"Your employer is an idiot!"

Jon took a breath, knowing he needed to calm himself if he was to have any chance at locking onto the sentences... at saving Francis and the others. Right now he could see the streaming sentences, but felt too scattered to connect.

"Look, Russ... yes I can change the sentences, I think the whole valley knows that by now," he said. "But going back to the older sentences... to sentences from years ago... it was like the ink had already dried, and there was no altering it... not for her, not for the twenty-two who died on the island."

They heard an anguished groan and saw Bonnicksen staggering toward them, blood pouring from his severed right hand.

"Twenty-three," he uttered, collapsing to the deck once again.

"He's in shock, and losing way too much blood," Remedy said, moving to Bonnicksen's side. "We need to get that arm wrapped."

"No... twenty-*three*!" Bonnicksen said again.

"Twenty-three what?" Jon said.

Bonnicksen twisted and kicked, as if his entire body was in as much agony as his hand. "Twenty-three people, lost on the island," he managed.

Jon saw Remedy flash a questioning look, but he wasn't sure what to tell her. Twenty-two people had died on Amelynd. Both Bonnicksen and the Navy filed reports confirming the number.

"The paradox, Jon—remember?" Bonnicksen mumbled. "The paradox."

Jon turned away from Bonnicksen, bothered. Something tugged at his memory, but he couldn't quite lock onto it. Suddenly, he felt worried. A crazy thought came to mind: *Is it possible I've re-woven events without realizing it?*

Bonnicksen's pain seemed to lessen as he spotted Jon's uneasiness. "Tell us, Jon: how can a person exist when they don't really exist at all?"

"How about you just stay out of this," Remedy said, waiting for 911 to pick up. "You've tried to murder two people. You're done here."

Bonnicksen reached up with his bloody hand, tried and failed to grab her by the shoulder.

"You don't want to listen?" he said. "Fine—but you'll never understand any of this until you get Wanamaker to answer a question he's never once answered for me."

Bonnicksen wheezed, gritted his teeth, then seemed to spit his words rather than speak them. "How can Jon Wanamaker exist," he said, "when Jon Wanamaker died on Amelynd Island?"

THIRTY-EIGHT

Even as Bonnicksen spoke his shocking accusation, Jon watched his words streaming past as printed sentences. The written version was identical to the spoken words, yet somehow different... more significant, Jon decided, not that it made any sense. Still, there was no denying that the written words seeped into Jon's mind in a way the spoken words could not, triggering intense thoughts, spurring emotions... jogging buried memories.

"Well?" Bonnicksen said, straining to speak, his teeth still gritted from pain. "How can you be here when you died? How?"

"There is no... I don't know," Jon said, running a hand along the flat, linear cypress leaves, wishing he could hide behind them.

"Uh-huh—the answer is what you started to say and then stopped," Bonnicksen said. "The answer is that there is no answer. It's a paradox. Now tell me, how can you not be a monster, tampering with life the way you are, literally risking everything—individuals, communities, maybe even the entire world—without knowing the answer to that paradox?"

Jon discovered he was holding his breath as he tried putting all the pieces together. He saw Remedy crouched near Bonnicksen, scribbling in her notebook, trying her best not to tell them they were all crazy. Francis, still struggling for breath, simply looked him in the eyes as if scrutinizing the person within. Razor, on the opposite end of the deck, went from the blank, bleached stare of a man going into shock to a look of momentary recognition.

"He's right," Razor mumbled. "I think... I think I saw it."

Remedy lowered the notebook. "You're not making any sense—any of you," she said. "If Jon didn't survive Amelynd then how is he here with us?"

"Exactly my point," Bonnicksen said, eyes ablaze, the adrenaline of the revelation somehow trumping his intense pain. "The lab's monitors showed your vitals flat for at least four minutes, probably more since storm conditions were affecting the readings. Flat, Jon! You were a dead man, just like all the others."

Deep inside, Jon knew it was true. He could feel that truth opening up within himself as he read Bonnicksen's words, like fresh daylight piercing a long-sealed tomb. He had already proven that he could use the ribbons to manipulate nearly anything, but using them to manipulate his own mind... to hide secrets from *himself*? That was a possibility he'd never considered... except that he apparently *had* considered it, and actually done it, while on Amelynd. But why?

Several paces away, Russ Kitchtoo looked up from cleaning his *quoth-lar*. "Zip it, Bonnicksen," he said. "Only one of us has the pipeline into Wanamaker."

They looked at Razor, wondering whether he could even talk with his left shoulder torn open. He saw them staring, seemed to take it as a challenge. Gritting his teeth, he sat up with an ungodly groan. Blood soaked his shirt and puddled below his elbow as he surveyed the injury he'd sustained. He forced a grim quarter-smile, and without him saying a word the others knew why: bad as the shoulder was, it wasn't his pitching shoulder. He laced his fingers together, shoved both hands against the wound to apply pressure, then made a point of talking louder than Bonnicksen had.

"All I know is someone saved Jon... least, that's what I saw at the time, during Upsweep, hear?" he said, every word a hurdle. "Man was dead, words swirled, man was alive. And I'm tryin' to keep his words outta my head ever since, know what I'm sayin'?"

Jon glanced at Remedy, who seemed floored. "You people are actually going to stand here claiming I married a man who died before I met him?" she said.

"Hey lady, ask him yourself," Razor said.

Remedy's eyes turned to Jon.

"Well?" she demanded.

Jon wished he could give a clear answer. "No, I... maybe, but... I'm not sure."

"What do you mean you're not sure?" she said.

"I don't know. I mean, yeah, I was hurt, starving, dehydrated… and I lost consciousness after trying to send impressions to my percipient—to Razor," he said. "But I remember flashes of consciousness in the rescue copter so…

He could still see the ship-top helipad, and feel his uncertainty upon returning to the mainland. What was he supposed to say, or do? What *can* you do when you survive a catastrophe but can't explain how? Confusion reigned: did surviving make him more of a person, less of a person, or just another example of happenstance?

"I've always thought of what happened as a near-death experience," he said. "Maybe it wasn't? I mean, what Bonnicksen's saying sounds crazy, but… it *feels* right. Which is why I'm now wondering whether I used the ribbons on myself. Wiped my own memory, for some reason that's now a mystery."

"Convenient," Kitchtoo said.

"But feasible," Bonnicksen added.

Remedy grabbed her broom, slide-stepped to Jon, then placed a hand on his shoulder. "You need to check," she said.

He was thinking the same thing. Taking a breath to calm himself, he focused, *becoming one with the ribbons. The distant past was off-limits to changes, but the immediate past didn't seem to have any such restrictions. Right away, Francis's stab wound expelled dirt and pus, coagulated, then sealed. Razor's shoulder and Bonnicksen's hand followed suit, as did injuries to Carl Sharp, the sheriffs, and the SWAT team.*

Jon probed the ribbons, scrolling backward through four years of text, searching... but the passages about Amelynd, and the white squall, didn't reveal anything he hadn't already known or expected. And yet, deep inside his mind, everything Bonnicksen and Razor had said felt on the mark.

He realized that was how he had wiped the truth from his memory: by changing the passages... meaning there wasn't any evidence. The definitive answers would have to come from elsewhere.

Shifting the ribbons, he returned to the present... to the imminent threat. Russ Kitchtoo was dangerous; he had to be contained. But looking at Kitchtoo, Jon could only think of Emma, struck cold before the prime of her life. He certainly couldn't blame Russ for trying to force a miracle. Still, it didn't change the fact Russ was an unstable, deadly mess. Jon hoped he could contain him in a humane way, and had an idea for how to do so, but he knew the man deserved better than having it happen without his knowledge, or consent.

Or, he wondered, was that just his guilt talking? Was he so desperate to make amends for treating people like words rather than individuals?

He eased his mind away from the ribbons, breaking contact. Joyful tears formed as he saw Francis, Razor, and Bonnicksen uninjured. The pitcher let out a celebratory whoop as soon as discovered he was healed, launching into high-fives with the twig-like cypress branches, the floodlight fixtures, anything he could slap. Francis did the elderly equivalent—a vigorous cane wave with a broad smile. Only Bonnicksen remained solemn, consternation overwhelming whatever relief he felt.

Kitchtoo, by contrast, looked furious.

"What about Emma?" he said.

Jon lowered his head. "It's like I told you: the ribbons won't let me change anything older than—"

"Bullshit!"

"Russ, I swear, there's nothing…"

Kitchtoo rushed forward, one hand reaching for Jon, the other a raised fist. "Get in there and change it now!" he said. "Bring my little girl back!"

Jon backed away, feeling horrible. "I'll keep trying," he said. "I need you to understand, I'll never stop looking for a way. It's not just Emma. I still can't explain the squall… or the deaths, my own included. But…"

"Goddammit Wanamaker, I'll do anything you want!" Kitchtoo said, his voice collapsing from wallops to wails. "Just bring her back. Bring…her…*back*!"

Jon didn't answer. He figured his devastated expression said it all.

Kitchtoo whisked a crumpled leaf from his matted hair, fiddled with his *quoth-lar*, spat another bullet. Then he looked at Jon.

"You know what? I believe you," Kitchtoo said, his throat cracking. "I think you'll keep trying, for Emma… and for yourself."

Jon hesitated, uncertain what that meant. A split-second later, he found out. Kitchtoo smiled, yellowed teeth gleaming as he pulled the pistol from his ankle holster and shot Jon square in the chest.

THIRTY-NINE

Russ Kitchtoo watched, satisfied, as Jon Wanamaker rocked backward and collapsed. Blood oozed from Jon's chest, and he was barely breathing. His widened eyes betrayed the shock he was trying to stifle, no doubt hoping to keep calm so he could join with the miracle sentences that were his only chance at survival.

But he won't be able to do it, at least not yet, Kitchtoo thought. Without focus, he couldn't connect, no matter how many words he saw floating past his face. That's what I.K. Emily had told him from the start.

Remedy and Francis were at Jon's side.

"Just go in and change it, like you did for the others," Remedy said, to Jon.

His desperate facial expression confirmed he couldn't do it. Razor, standing behind Francis, had a hand to his head and seemed as shaken as Jon.

"Worse than my shoulder felt," the pitcher groaned. "So many words too... everything swimming."

Kitchtoo had seen enough. He walked to the front gate, opened it, and stepped onto the deserted two-lane street, pistol still in hand. Stretching, he limbered his shoulders, arms, and legs, then stood erect. Unsheathing the *quoth-lar* with his free hand, he took several practice jabs and swings. Then he eased his way across the street, disappearing into the bougainvillea stand.

This isn't over, he knew. If I.K. Emily's information was on the mark, things were far from over. Now he could only hope that meant his daughter still had a chance.

———————————

For one brief moment, Jon felt as if the chaos was a world away. His pain and fear faded. There was only companionship, contact, appreciation, solace, life. He soaked the experience as he and Remedy shared a hug, then saw her eyes searching for more. Uncertain, he leaned in and they kissed. Memories, regrets and wishes surfaced, most of them bittersweet. His thoughts flooded with things he wanted to tell her, but he remained silent. Somehow, the kiss seemed to express everything better than words.

Nausea and weakness washed over him. His hands felt flattened and his chin droopy, like an old cartoon character awaiting the laugh track. *One last look at the Tlingit mother tongue*, he thought, eyeballing the swarming ribbons from afar. He admired their graceful patterns, thrilled. He hadn't won The Race but he had gotten to know Tlingit in an intimate fashion that most of his people would never experience.

Cliché proved true: his life flashed before him. The Race, first. Always, The Race came first. Remedy too, virtually neck-and-neck. But then he saw childhood moments with his grandmother, favorite movies, salmon fishing at the Rowock River, his first kiss, the troubles with Russ Kitchtoo, the departures sign at the dock where aircraft left Rowock. And of course, the island: Amelynd, where he first saw the Tlingit mother tongue words.

Suddenly, he spotted what he couldn't find earlier: erased passages, wiped clean from the streaming sentences but still embedded in his deathbed flashback memory. Jon's pain and fear faded away, superseded by his determination to find out what had really happened on the island. Was the connection he couldn't make a few moments earlier now within reach? He leaped outward with his mind, latching onto the streaming sentences.

His gunshot wound expelled the bullet, dirt and bacteria, then coagulated and sealed.

The erased passages hung before his eyes. He shuddered, approaching them, afraid of what he might find. Had he done something so horrible he'd erased it so no one, including himself, would know?

Scanning the passages, he found what he was searching for: his stay on Amelynd. Most of it was routine, and exactly as he recalled. Then came the squall... the delirium... the streaming sentences... the miracles. Debris lifting, wind speeds fading, wounds healing... a colleague, rescued. Then another, on and on, all of them. He saved them all!

Emma... he could save her too! Her death wasn't his fault, and her aggrieved father had tainted him and his family within the community, but none of that mattered—not now, when he could make everything right. He scrolled through the text, found the point of her death, changed it.

It worked!

But no... one sentence later, she was dead again.

What?

The twenty-two people from Upsweep were also dead. Worse, the ribbons no longer changed any of it.

That's the place, Jon knew. That's where the memory gap occurred... the point where reversible deaths became ir-reversible. But why?

The deaths weren't the only thing he could no longer re-verse. Reading through more passages, he re-experienced his attempts to dissipate the squall using ribbons... efforts which failed every time.

The squall headed straight for him. Moments later, all went dark.

Except it didn't. Someone saved him. Emma was still a memory, twenty-two others were dead, and yet here he was, alive.

Why would someone do that? Why would they want him, or anyone, to live with that on their conscience?

The erased passages offered no answer... but having read them, he understood exactly what he needed to do with Russ Kitchtoo.

———————

For all his extensive training, and his assurances to I.K. Emily, Kitchtoo knew he was pitted against a skill he had never faced... a skill *no one* had ever faced. He couldn't be sure how much of his training, if any, would apply to this fight. All he knew was that concealing himself in a bougainvillea stand was not going to slow Wanamaker down for one moment... *so he didn't flinch when, a split-second later, he found his surroundings changing, shifting him away from Quail Point.*

Paneled walls and worn furnishings materialized around him, messy and musty from having been left unattended for months. Tlingit art—hand-painted drums and sculpted representations of the animals symbolizing the four Tlingit clans—sat covered in thick dust. The pea-green sofa that doubled as a bed had an ink stain across one of the cushions, and the wood paneling was warped from too much cold weather.

Dizziness... then clarity. Kitchtoo recognized the interior of Wanamaker's vacant mobile home in Rowock, Alaska, having scouted it for personality profile information many times after Jon had moved away. Kitchtoo gave him credit for not selling it, even as he laughed at the man's misguided hope for a return that would never happen.

So, he thought, *Wanamaker wants to finish things in our home town, where they started. Okay then, bring it on.* He reached for the pistol strapped to his ankle and removed it, pulling his lips into the same half-smile he'd worn when he first leaped into the car with Remedy and

Sarah. No doubt about it: Wanamaker was a certifiable freak. He'd let go of the puppet strings, given up an easy opportunity to make the kill. Big mistake.

He looked out a window and saw the main highway through Rowock, with its National Forest backdrop of Sitka spruce and snowy hills. The serenity stood in direct contrast to his childhood experiences: fishing the local rivers when the family food money ran low; sneaking through the woods to dish out some schoolyard hazing; helping his father scrub floors at the local restaurants; and later, joining the Navy so his family would have enough income to keep their struggling contracting business. *Maybe that's why I got along so well with Wanamaker in our early years,* he thought; *because I sold out to the same white man's military that Wanamaker's family had ushered into town. The same military that stamped away the Tlingit language.*

Kitchtoo felt an uncomfortable tickle at the back of his neck... so in one motion, he raised his gun, whirled, and squeezed the trigger.

An earsplitting blast rocked Rowock as the sound of the gunshot echoed through the mobile home and out to the asphalt road, eventually reverberating against the nearby mountains. Kitchtoo felt the handgun's familiar kick against his hands as he stood face-to-face with Jon Wanamaker, waiting for him to drop. *Instead, he saw the slug appear in midair, tried to figure out why, and realized its speed was decreasing. The bullet disintegrated before hitting Jon's forehead.*

Neither man said anything for several seconds.

"I can change that for you, Russ," Wanamaker said. "The whole quiet, stoic thing. I can get rid of it, make you the life of the party."

Kitchtoo shrugged. "Already am."

He watched Wanamaker display the usual sequence of revulsion-curiosity-sympathy that people's faces expressed when they saw him.

"It's important we work something out," Jon said. "Just the two of us, face to face."

"There's only one thing important to me," Kitchtoo said.

Jon ran a finger across the dust on one of his table-mounted drums. "I keep telling you, it just doesn't work."

So I'll need to make him try again, Kitchtoo decided.

"Who is she, Russ?" Jon said. "How does I.K. Emily know so much about the ribbons, and what I'm able to do with them?"

"Look it up yourself," Kitchtoo said. "Your ribbons tell you everything."

He could tell from Wanamaker's expression that the ribbons hadn't revealed a thing. Perfect, Kitchtoo thought. Conveying a superior-to-inferior relationship was an effective psychological tactic, and Russ employed it whenever possible—such as hitting the reporter with "glottochronology."

He saw Wanamaker take a wary glance around his old home, like he was worried about being ambushed by old memories.

"How did I.K. Emily know to hire you, Russ? How did she connect the dots between your career background and your hatred for me? How did she know she'd found Bonnicksen the perfect hit-man?"

Kitchtoo lifted his pistol and fired eight shots in succession, to no avail; each disintegrated in mid-air. Sometimes he questioned the motives of the people who contracted his services, especially when the individuals tugging the strings had military and political ties, but with I.K. Emily there were no lingering doubts. Jon Wanamaker was indeed a serious threat, just as she had said. Tossing his gun aside, Kitchtoo dove at Jon's chest, knocking him flat on his back and sending two end tables skittering. Tlingit pottery smashed against the linoleum but neither the noise nor the assault seemed to faze Jon. Kitchtoo couldn't tell whether Jon didn't care, or simply had slow reactions; all he knew was that his right arm was locked in a choke-hold around Jon's neck before they hit the floor.

Kitchtoo flexed, and twisted. He'd done it at least seven other times in his career, so he knew the desired bone-snap always occurred while the neck and head were in the act of twisting, well before they finished the actual turn. When Jon's neck turned without breaking, Kitchtoo knew something was wrong. He maintained the choke hold and squeezed as hard as he could, waiting for Jon to gasp for air, but the man just waited. Kitchtoo took his left fist and cocked it square against Jon's forehead, hoping to shove the skull backwards with enough force to break it from the spine, but the head didn't move.

Frustrated, he pulled the *quoth-lar* from its sheath and stabbed, first at Jon's gut, then his chest, then his head. The blade didn't penetrate. Tossing the *quoth-lar* aside, he pointed a finger straight at Jon's left eye and shoved as hard as he could, only to have his fingertip jam up against the eyeball as if it was covered in cement. He tried the same thing with the nostrils, same result. He shoved a knee at Jon's genitals and winced; another concrete-like barrier. Through it all, Jon seemed so relaxed he reminded Kitchtoo of a parent ignoring the nagging tugs of a child.

It's over, Kitchtoo realized. Wanamaker had somehow secured himself against threats to his life. There wouldn't be another opportunity to save Emma. There wouldn't even be an opportunity to avenge her death.

"I can't bring Emma back," Jon said, reiterating his earlier comment. "But there might be another option. To make it work I'd have to get inside your head... and I made a promise never to do that anymore, not without permission. So it's your call. Are you game? Can I give it a try?"

Kitchtoo wasn't in the mood for wild ideas or twenty questions. He threw Wanamaker against the floor and did the only thing he could think of: run. It wasn't heroic, but with luck it might buy him time to regroup. *Not likely*, he decided. He didn't know the full extent of Jon's ribbons, but he knew enough to assume these were his final moments.

He crashed through the trailer door and darted into the empty street, passing the market and motels, making his way up a steep hill until he reached the Rowock Totem Park and its twenty-one caricatured monuments. Below, he could see the local cannery; beyond that, the harbor and the surrounding forest. His mind flashed over his career with the SEALS, his hostage negotiations for insurance companies, his free-lance mercenary work. He tried to remember everything, from the Alaskan landscape to the ornate totems, because he was pretty sure he never would be able to again.

The world blurred. Rowock dimmed, faded, and was gone. Kitchtoo felt himself—or was it just his mind?—being pulled through a bramble patch of hazy words, sentences, and paragraphs, each of them slicing and stinging, with distant thunder roaring as he was yanked through. This wasn't the real-time ribbons I.K. Emily told him about, he knew. It was something bigger. Something more permanent... more important.

And he wasn't making the trip alone.

It's Wanamaker, he realized. Jon Wanamaker was dragging his mind—both of their minds—through a two-dimensional, word-strewn ethos. Kitchtoo wrestled and wrenched, but couldn't break free.

For the first time in ages, he felt terrified. Torture, death, those were things he could steel his psyche against... things he was prepared to handle. But this? Kitchtoo felt completely exposed, his thoughts naked to the universe, saturating into other people's thoughts, ripping through words describing places and objects he never wanted to be near.

He pulled away, trying to break the chokehold encircling his mind, but in this arena Wanamaker was the strongman, and the linguist wouldn't budge.

Kitchtoo screamed, desperate and anguished, helpless too, for the first time since finding Emma's body. He pleaded with Wanamaker to turn back. This state of mind, this flattened, word-dominant form of existence, whatever it was... it felt worse than death. It was embalmed life, with words as the fluid, and he had to make it stop.

I'll kill myself, he decided. Body or no body, I'll find a way to end it. If I'm determined enough, I can do it. I know I can do it. You can't stop me, Wanamaker, you can't make me—

Two passing words caught his eye, passing through a nearby ribbon jumble.

Emma Kitchtoo.

He gasped.

The same words appeared again, over and over, embedded among sentences detailing her actions, her interactions, her accomplishments, her innermost thoughts.

"What... what is this?" he stammered, his thoughts audible in the ethos.

"This," Jon said, "is Emma's version of my ribbons. Even at her young age, she made millions of them—every thought she had, written across an alternate plane of consciousness without even realizing it. She couldn't see them or connect with them, of course... but in this place, she's ongoing."

"Ongoing?" Kitchtoo said, his breath bated.

He felt Jon's hopes surging along with his own.

"Ancient cultures considered written language a type of magic," Jon said. "It puts you inside the head of whoever

authored the text, rendering time and distance meaning-less."

"So... this really is Emma?"

"It's not what you wanted, and it can't be changed... but yeah, it's Emma. Odd as it sounds, you might get to know her even better than you did before."

Kitchtoo wasn't sure what to make of it. All he knew, somehow, was that Wanamaker was right... it really was Emma. In a different form, at a different place, but Emma nonetheless.

"A direct link across time," he said, his voice shaking.

He had no words to describe his growing joy. No, it wasn't perfect, not by a long shot... but this was his daughter. This was Emma!

A distant thought hit the back of his mind.

"I.K. Emily... she didn't tell me about this," he told Jon. "Somehow, she already knows about your ribbons... every detail. The back-channel behind it, the omniscience, the chance to shape events, she told me about everything. But she never mentioned the ribbons couldn't affect events from the distant past, even though she knew that's what I needed. And she damn sure never mentioned... this."

An unpleasant realization formed.

"She played me, Wanamaker. I think maybe she played me, same way she played Bonnicksen."

He looked into Emma's ribbons, feeling forgotten warmth.

"I.K. Emily, she'll know you've done this," he said. "She'll know you're alive. She always knows everything. Hurry—

get yourself back. She wants the connection for herself. She wants the power."

He felt Jon's mind receding from Emma's ribbons... and knew Wanamaker had taken the warning to heart. Kitchtoo also knew that if I.K. Emily prevailed, he might never run across Wanamaker again. That meant he'd be trapped, his consciousness forever paired with Emma's ribbons.

Exactly the end I'd have wanted, he realized.

His mind cast his *quoth-lar* away. The pistol and the bullets between his teeth, also dumped. Matted hair, dirt, odor, all of it went. He didn't need any of that now. He had what he was looking for.

Immersed in his lost daughter's eternal existence, Russ Kitchtoo absorbed, and relished... and wept.

FORTY

Jon eased his mind away from Emma's ribbons, back to his own, hoping I.K. Emily hadn't already shown up. He returned himself to Remedy's deck then broke contact. Everything looked the same, except dusk had arrived. Rem, Francis, Razor, and Bonnicksen were still there... but not really. Each wore a blank expression.

Jon rushed over to them, shouting and waving, hoping he could get them to snap out of their trance, to no avail. Then he looked around and realized that much more than the people had changed. The air smelled of smoke. Glancing south, he saw an orange glow stretching into the sky and heard the sound of military aircraft scouring the skies. The fire was back, his barrier around the valley gone.

Maybe because I was away, he thought. *Or because I didn't specify how long everything would last. Or because—*

He stopped the guessing, already knowing what had happened.

"I.K. Emily," he said aloud.

Everyone on the deck turned toward him in unison.

"Yeah," Remedy said.

"That's right," Francis said.

"I've been waiting for this," Razor said.

She's in their heads, Jon realized, horrified. I need to get her out of their heads!

"Leave them alone," he said, readying his ribbons.

To his surprise, Remedy's blank expression vanished, the others' too. Each looked confused and had questions, especially when they saw Jon's gunshot wound was healed, but he motioned them to stay silent. He returned his attention to the ribbons, which were streaming before his eyes as always. Fight fire with fire, he thought. Taking a deep breath, he reached out with his mind, to establish the link.

Nothing.

The ribbons continued streaming, so close they filled his vision, but they might as well have been on the other side of the Earth. He couldn't connect.

"And there's the proof," he understood, feeling his panic growing from within.

Remedy approached him, cautious. "Proof of what?" she said.

"I.K. Emily uses ribbons too," Jon said. "She's using them right now."

Francis looked up, as if trying to spot a hidden god. "How?"

Jon shrugged. "No idea. But I'm locked out."

Razor looked confused. "Then why is it I'm still seeing words coming at me from your head?" he said.

Jon didn't have an answer. Everyone looked worried except for Bonnicksen, who seemed satisfied. "Everything's worked out after all," he said. "I.K. Emily and I are partners in this thing... and that gives me the win."

Jon wasn't so convinced. "She'll have seen the same things I have," he said. "She'll know you were planning to publish your findings regardless of her objections."

Bonnicksen's face fell.

"I don't understand, Jon," Remedy said. "I.K. Emily's stolen your link with the ribbons?"

"No, she's linking to her own ribbons. Turns out we all have them. Somehow, Project Upsweep helped me access mine."

"And now you can't," Remedy said.

"Right."

"So how is it that she can link to hers?"

"Not sure," he said. "But Kitchtoo said she wants the control for herself, so now that she has it she's probably created sentences that block me."

The front gate squeaked. They looked and saw Razor headed out. "Sorry man... I really am, but... I can't do this crazy shit anymore," he said as he stalked off, phone glowing in his hand, then disappeared into the night.

But not as much night as usual, Jon thought. He looked up and felt his stomach turn to concrete.

A massive wall of thick, pallid clouds approached Quail Point, resembling a gleaming, raised shield shoved forth by some heavenly army. The cloud wall radiated an eerie, supernatural glow, and the treetops in its path began swaying, driven by a sudden breeze.

Jon nearly screamed, watching the focal point of his 4 a.m. nightmares approach. On Amelynd, it was a harbinger of destruction that somehow stole his memory, all while playing some unknown role in the deaths of everyone but himself. Just the thought of that happening again here, while he was with two of the people who mattered most...

His mind raced. The storm was massive, and already bearing down on them, meaning there was nowhere to run. How could he get Remedy and Francis somewhere safe without the ribbons?

"Into the house!" he told everyone. "Now!"

"That's the squall you told us about?" Francis said.

He rapid-nodded.

"In the mountains?" Remedy said. "I don't think that's possible."

"It isn't possible to have one form over an island so fast the weather instruments can't predict it, either," Jon said, "but that's what happened on Amelynd. Get inside!"

Francis and Remedy inched their way toward the French doors, but Bonnicksen pulled up a deck chair and sat down.

"I'm good," he said, even as leaves whisked off his cheek and wind whipped his hair.

"Listen, Bonnicksen," Jon started.

"No, you listen," he said. "I'm waiting right here."

"But the storm—"

Bonnicksen cracked a wicked grin. "That's no storm," he said. "That's I.K. Emily."

He raised a fist to the air, saluting the approaching cloud mass. Jon hesitated, trying to make sense of what he'd just heard. *He's lost it*, Jon thought, trying to convince himself. *Too much to process, he's over the edge.*

The wind intensified and a light rain began falling, but Jon still found himself frozen in place by Bonnicksen's words. He heard Francis urging him to come inside, and Remedy shutting her windows.

"First the white squall, then she shows up—don't you remember?" Bonnicksen said.

He didn't... which made no sense. *Even if I'd wanted to forget the tragedy on Amelynd, why would I wipe out my memory of I.K. Emily? Or was she the one who wiped it?*

The wind doubled its force, the rain too. The lumberjack weathervane spun itself into a blur. Remedy's café table and chairs were already gone, blown clear off the deck, and the plastic doghouse sat crushed against a cypress trunk. Across the street, Kitchtoo's bougainvillea stand was blown horizontal and loose newspapers bounded past like tumbleweeds.

Jon ran past Bonnicksen, forcing himself across the deck, through the ferocious wind, toward the wrought iron fence lining the property. The gale was so fierce he could barely walk, and dirt from the side of the road was blowing into his eyes, but he managed to reach the front gate and grab on. Behind him, some tiny, drowned–out portion of Francis's voice urged him back.

"Shut the doors, Francis!" Jon called out, through the driving rain.

He couldn't hear the reply, but he could guess what it was. Still, a few moments later he saw the French doors swing shut. The home's lighting flickered, then went dark, as did the entire street, leaving the thick, luminescent clouds as the only light source. Jon hoped the A-frame could withstand what was coming. He hoped he could withstand it too.

"She's had it the whole time, you know," Bonnicksen said, getting up from his chair, shouting into the wind. "That open back-channel of hers. I.K. Emily came to me years ago, when I was just starting out. Like you, she'd started seeing sentences, didn't know what was happening to her. Set me on my career path. Now we know so much more."

He made his way to Jon, fighting for every step, his eyes narrowing from the grit the storm was whipping up. "Upsweep, all of my work, it's all so she can learn," he said. "You were one of our first human guinea pigs, Jon. You showed us a lot—not the least of which being that ribbons can, in fact, resurrect the dead."

Jon cursed. He'd already established that ribbons couldn't raise the dead, having tried doing so with Emma and the others, multiple times. Why didn't anyone believe him?

Bonnicksen grabbed onto the wrought iron fencing next to Jon, holding on against the wind. The two were drenched but it was a warm rain and the wind was so forceful it was blowing the water off their cheeks. "We thought you were in the clear after she wiped your mind, sent you off the island," Bonnicksen said. "Guess your ribbons never fully went away though. Well hey, that's why you do the research, right?"

Jon couldn't fathom the absurdity of the situation: two men who never liked each other standing in the middle of a white squall, waiting for... someone. Behind them, debris smashed through two of Remedy's windows and roof tiles were ripping away in droves. Bonnicksen stared at it all, smiling, looking for all the world like the only thing he was missing was some popcorn to munch on while watching I.K. Emily's show.

Then Bonnicksen's left hand lost its grip on the rain-slicked fence. Startled, he regripped the cold metal... but then his other hand came loose. Try as he might, Bonnicksen couldn't keep more than one hand on the fence.

"What are you doing?" he shouted into the raging squall. "We've learned so much! This is our moment. We can finally put it all together!"

Thunder bellowed, and the wind whipped Bonnicksen horizontal. His body fluttered like a windsock as he clutched the wrought iron with one hand, but Jon could see that was now slipping too.

"No—don't you dare double-cross me when there's so much more to finish!" Bonnicksen said, shouting into the ethos. "I did your dirty work! I took all the risks! And now you pull this? How dare you!"

The wind lagged enough to slam Bonnicksen against the fence, then whipped him horizontal again.

"You actually think you can use the ribbons to control people without me?" he shouted. "To control events? To control reality? You don't have a chance! Do you hear me? You're a big zero without me! Zero!"

Jon inched toward him, hoping he might be able to jam a knee against the man's back or find some other way to pin him down against the wind, but the squall was too strong and they were too far apart. Before he could get to him, Bonnicksen's fingers slipped loose.

"Ku'cta-qa," Jon uttered.

Bonnicksen snagged an iron support rail with two fingers, a split-second reprieve before slipping once more. Jon gasped as he watched the Sidney researcher sail over the fence, hit the street, tumble twice, then fly up and out of sight.

Even with the squall slamming the house, Remedy wished she could keep the front doors open, to see what was happening outside—and to make sure Jon had an escape route if he needed it.

"Not yet," Francis insisted. "When it's time, I'll go help him."

"You? How can you go out in that storm any better than I can?"

"Because I'm old, which makes me more expendable," he said.

She was about to object when her phone vibrated. Startled that it was still working, she picked up.

"Tell me why we suddenly have a hurricane!" Julie Henderson shouted through the receiver, her voice barely audible over the wind. "And hurry—the phones won't last much longer."

Remedy kept things concise. When she finished, Henderson took a long pause before speaking.

"And you're okay?" Henderson said, another shout.

"Honestly? No."

"But you'll keep on it?"

"I have to! I won't let up."

Remedy thought she heard a sigh... or maybe it was the wind.

"Then neither will I," Henderson said, as something heavy smashed against the side of the A-frame. "Give me everything you have as soon as this storm passes. I'll call in my forty-two years of contacts and make sure it hits every major news outlet in the country by Thursday. And Remedy..."

She waited a beat. "You've weathered worse storms than this," Henderson said, just as the call dropped.

Wind-blown footsteps staggering across the deck kept Remedy from appreciating the encouragement. Razor appeared at the French doors, his corn-rows and clothes drenched.

"Friggin' Eskimo's thoughts are still hittin' the inside of my head," he said, wind-driven rain blowing into the living room as she let him inside. His designer shirt was sopping wet, and his trendy pants looked shredded.

"That's impossible," Remedy said. "Jon said he's locked out from the ribbons."

Razor jumped into a chair, wet clothes and all, legs crossed before his butt hit the seat. "I'm telling you, lady, he's not," the pitcher said. "I mean, he is, but... I'm still tapped into him. Words, images, the whole thing. It comes and goes, like it's from a long way off... but otherwise it's the same as before."

He leaned his head into his hands. "Man, I want to run, put some distance between me and here, get your guy's voice out of my head once and for all, know what I mean?" he said. "Want that real bad."

"So then...?"

"I gotta see this through, okay? Bein' there at the end... that's pretty much what I do. Plus your man saved me big-time. Can't just leave after that. I mean, I can... but I won't."

Remedy heard him, but was still fixated on their connection. "Wait," she said. "If you and Jon are still tethered..."

"Uh-huh, now you're feelin' me," he said. "We can sit in here and still help him out. From what I've seen, the geek man just got blown clear up the street and Jon's fighting that same crazy wind. What you want me to do?"

Good question, she thought. She imagined herself in Jon's position, helpless against the squall's power, remembering how scary it felt the first time she knew she'd lost control of her own body. If she had been in the middle of a storm when it happened...

"Razor, can you send him a thought?" she said.

He shook his head. "Maybe... but lady, no promises, okay? I wasn't always very good at it when the geek-man asked."

She nodded. "Just tell him this: 'Sometimes it's a blessing too.' Got it?"

He looked at her as if she were crazy. "No... but whatever, I'll try. I don't get it though. What's the blessing in all this?"

She gave a grim smile. "That's exactly what I'm hoping Jon will say."

Drenched and wind-whipped, Jon watched, horrified, as Erich Bonnicksen's body vanished into the night. Pain streaked through his right hand and he felt himself slipping from the wrought iron fence, but a sudden thought echoing through his mind hit him harder.

Sometimes it's a blessing too.

Why now, he wondered. Why would his mind dig up the words Remedy had used while turning down his offer to help her—to cure her? And now of all times: the moment he was on the verge of being swept to his death.

He shifted his weight, trying to keep his grip, convinced he was about to suffer the same fate as Bonnicksen. As he struggled, his mind pondered: what's the blessing in all this? Maybe that he was still alive, still had a chance? But that was in the moment only. The bigger picture, not a blessing whatsoever.

He tried to remember why Remedy considered her MS a blessing. She had mentioned that people never appreciated how rewarding the little accomplishments could be... that she was proud when she beat the MS long enough to walk, fix a meal, type a story. Achieving little things in the face of so much adversity, that was the blessing for Remedy.

"What am I supposed to do with that?" he uttered, frustrated.

Thunder rumbled, vibrating the ground, shuddering whatever windows remained on the house. Even through the squall Jon could see the ribbons, tantalizingly close. He tried linking with them. *Still locked out*, he thought. Unl*ess... unless I accomplish something little instead*? He suddenly wondered whether he didn't need full contact now that he had experience using the ribbons. Was it possible to jab rather than swing?

He reached out for the streaming sentences, confident, defiant, demanding... and punched a single word through.

Stop.

Nothing changed. The storm didn't ease up.

Please... stop.

Still no change.

I said, stop!

The rains eased, just a little. The wind backed off too, not altogether but a noticeable drop nonetheless. Jon held his breath, wanting to believe, hoping it wasn't just a lull in the storm. Uncertain, he watched, and waited.

Nothing changed. For five very long, anxious minutes, nothing changed. The squall wasn't gone, and wasn't moving, but it wasn't intensifying either. Success, Jon decided. But... now what? He still couldn't make a full connection with the ribbons.

There was really only one option: to again use a single word. The question was, what word? Sleep, retreat, surrender, even die came to mind, but in the end he chose a different direction. Maybe it would work, maybe it wouldn't, but against the mystery that was I.K. Emily, and facing such godlike power, he decided to unleash the only word in his vocabulary that no one else would ever use... the most sentimental, most powerful, most compelling word he knew.

Jon remembered telling Remedy how his grandmother pointed to the moon and made the soft howl of a wolf, while speaking that special word. Now, with his composure fading and the storm intensifying, he reached out to the streaming sentences and punctured them with that one, special word.

Onatay.

He felt stronger, feeling the air pulse from the back of his throat to the tip of his tongue as he silently pronounced the word.

Onatay.

Something surged from within, wicked and wild, primal yet intelligent. Himself, he knew. He felt as if his soul was billowing into the world, past the world. Far, far beyond the world.

"There's no ignoring this," he said, into the steadying wind. "Do you understand? Do you realize there are words that compel, that manifest power? This can't be ignored... Onatay can't be ignored."

He reached out again, attacking the ribbons, puncturing them.

Onatay.

Onatay.

Onatay!

He watched his word soar off, felt it arriving elsewhere, sensed it reaching intellect. An utterance sounded, raw and surprised... and then he noticed someone beyond the ribbons. He blinked, uncertain whether he was really seeing what he thought he was seeing: a woman in a faded blue dress, just outside of Remedy's front gate. Not just standing, but smiling. With broad, open arms and a seventy-something face wearing a welcome so warm, and so fulfilling, that Jon felt a tear welling.

The woman's smile broadened. She was about to speak... and Jon already knew what she would say.

"Onatay," his grandmother whispered.

FORTY-ONE

It wasn't really his grandmother, of course.

He wanted to believe it was, wanted it more than just about anything, but he knew it wasn't her. Irene Kwachka had died in an avalanche way back in... Jon couldn't place the year, but since he was a child at the time he figured it was at least twenty-five years ago—and she had been old back then. For all the miracles the ribbons offered, raising the dead wasn't among them.

Which meant the person standing before him, regardless of her appearance, was not his grandmother. *So, who is she?*

"Drop the games," he told the woman.

"But this is the face you want to see," she said, with a prim smile. "The one that took us down this path."

He had no idea what she was talking about. Above them, the squall continued swirling, like a militia awaiting orders.

"Just like last time," the woman said, eyeing the storm.

He looked at her. "Last time?"

Her smile vanished. "On the island."

Jon stepped back, wary. "You... you were there?"

She nodded.

"You're I.K. Emily," he said.

Another nod.

His breath caught in his throat. The shadowy figure who George Klase described as carrying tremendous influence over geopolitical decisions and events that determined the fate of thousands of people, someone so elusive that even most high-level government officials had never seen her, was standing before him.

"You're the one who's locked me out from using the ribbons?" he said.

"I am."

"And I see you know how to use the ribbons well enough to disguise yourself."

"That, and more," she said, her gritty smoker's voice supplanting the Irene impersonation.

"I'm guessing the 'more' doesn't involve saving endangered languages."

She arched an eyebrow. "It can, if that's something you want to discuss."

He shuddered, seeing the endearing face he so loved paired to an individual he despised. "Please stop using my grandmother's appearance," he said.

"But it's the perfect face. You used to dwell on her loss as much as Emma's, or The Race. Which is why, though you did in fact try tampering with Emma's ribbons on the island… you tampered with Irene Kwachka's long before that."

Oh my God, he thought, not liking where this was headed.

"Of course, you were inexperienced," she continued.

Jon's anxiety grew.

"Don't," he said. "Don't say any more."

She flashed an expression of mock sympathy.

"Naturally, it didn't work," she said. "Wording such weighty sentences can be… a tricky thing. 'Monstrous abomination,' I believe you called it. You didn't let her… maybe I should say, *it*… live for very long."

Feeling like he might be sick, Jon turned away. Could it really be true? Had he done exactly what Kitchtoo wanted… only on his own grandmother first? He wanted to believe otherwise, but deep inside he had to admit it sounded, even *felt*, like the truth. He'd always wished he could save Emma… but he would have wanted to save his grandmother even more.

Just the thought that he'd somehow *messed up the job*…

"See, that's our problem: your cold feet," I.K. Emily said. "Or, I suppose, *hers*. After seeing how badly things turned out, you decided that tampering with events in old ribbons, especially deaths, was too dangerous. You therefore used the ribbons to ensure any death dating back more than a few moments could never be reversed… a move I *strongly* disagree with."

He wanted to plug his ears. Every brain cell in his skull was telling him to get away from I.K. Emily, but he needed to hear what she had to say.

"As the man who wrote a change of such significance, only you can alter it," she said. "You refused. Back when we were on the island, you refused. All the suffering, the deaths we could have reversed... prevented by just one man: you."

He backed further away, sickened. Above, the squall descended, slow and steady, drawing closer even as the rain and wind speed remained moderate.

"Why don't I remember any of this?" he said, anguished.

"I wiped your memory—at your request," she said. "Not because I wanted to make sure you'd be clean for Bonnicksen's research, or to alleviate your guilt over twenty-two colleagues dying. No, it was because you couldn't handle the fact you personally saw to it that Emma Kitchtoo could never return."

Jon felt more lost and miserable by the moment.

"Yes, you," I.K. Emily said, pushing. "By limiting our use of the ribbons, that little girl not being alive with her father right now is entirely on you. But you can still change that. Tell me you want to, and I'll let you go in and change it."

Jon wondered whether that meant he had any shot at reconnecting with the ribbons, so he checked. Still no-go. He told himself this woman was lying, that she simply wanted control of the ribbons and didn't really know what happened on Amelynd. In his gut, however, he knew she was telling the truth.

The squall's wind speed continued growing, but the return of a light rain seemed an even bigger caution flag. If I.K Emily wasn't planning to kill him, why wasn't she using the ribbons to weaken the squall?

"You saw this same storm on the island," she said, lifting an open palm into the rain. "Erich thought maybe it formed as a side effect of major ribbon use. That man was such an idiot."

"So how *did* it form? How come I couldn't get rid of it?"

"I formed it," she said, "so fast the Navy barely knew what hit them. And I ensured you couldn't get rid of it, using my ribbons... though I hid that from Erich. Unknowns like that were how I kept him researching the back-channels. We needed to know what circumstances you could alter, and what you couldn't."

"What *I* could alter?" he said, horrified and yet defensive, worried that she might still know something he didn't. "How about all the people who have died because of *you*? Bonnicksen and the people in his experiments, for starters."

She not only didn't argue the assessment, she looked proud of it.

"You sent Russ Kitchtoo to kill me," Jon said, his anger increasing the more he thought about it. "And Bonnicksen—you knew he was coming for me with the neural mine."

She scoffed. "With your abilities? Those men could never kill you. I picked Kitchtoo specifically because I knew if I filled him in about the ribbons, he'd never let you die without making you save Emma first. You eventually realized that too. We both used the same strategy."

The rain intensified, pouring so hard it obscured Jon's view of I.K. Emily, but she didn't seem hampered by it. Instead, she began pacing, as if thinking things through.

"You're right about one thing," she said. "I'm now keeping control of the ribbons for myself. Can you imagine the two of us manipulating them at the same time? Absolute chaos. That's why I've written your connection away."

The squall lowered even further, its eerie, white glow illuminating their faces in the otherwise pitch-black night.

"What good will that do?" Jon said, testing her. "We aren't the only ones who can do this. Every human being has the same back-channels we do."

"But they're not aware of it, dear," I.K. Emily said, "and they haven't had the opportunity to hone it regardless. Even if they did, they wouldn't be using the Tlingit mother tongue to navigate it. That's a gift only you and I share. I always knew a few words, but your willingness to insert the whole lexicon into my head, back on the island, was crucial. Whatever wins The Race, right?"

"I'm supposed to believe *you*? The woman trying to kill me?"

She studied him.

"Actually," she said, "I'm the one who saved your life."

Ernie rolled the shuttle bus to a stop just outside a rusted green mobile home with cracked windows in Wofford Notch.

"This just gets better and better," Sarah said, looking at the run-down neighborhood.

They clambered off the bus.

"I don't know if I can do this," Sarah said. "Wanamaker went into my head—my head, Ernie! He violated me on a level I never thought possible. And you expect me to help him?"

"No," Ernie said. "Remedy expects you to help *her*. And because you already know what his sentence-world is like, Jon thinks this might be the only way."

She glowered, but didn't say anything. They walked past several plastic riding toys until they reached the mobile home's narrow rear window. Moments after rapping on the glass, a young boy's face appeared. His brown hair was mussed and his tooth chipped, but his lively expression told Ernie this was the boy he needed to find.

"You Arturo?" Ernie said, introducing Sarah and himself. "Your teacher, Mr. Wanamaker, sent us. There's something you need to know. Something important."

He relayed Jon's message.

"No way," Arturo said. "Are you sure?"

"It's true," Sarah said, sounding none too happy to say it. "I wouldn't trust Jon Wanamaker farther than I can throw him, but I can tell you for a fact what you just heard is probably doable."

"So, Mr. Wanamaker's really serious about this?" Arturo said.

"Kid," Ernie said, looking at the swirling wall of white clouds in the sky to the north, "you've seen what's been going on the past couple days, and yet with all of that I'm pretty sure Jon thinks what we've just told you is the most important thing happening right now."

Arturo thought it over.

"Okay... I guess," he said. "If it's for Mr. Wanamaker, then yeah, I'll do it."

Jon couldn't believe what he was hearing.

"Saved my life?" he repeated. "*You?*"

"Yes, *me*," I.K. Emily said, walking closer to him. "On the island. Your percipient was right, you were as near-dead as you could be. I stepped in, used the ribbons, saved you."

Jon shook his head, suspicious. "There's more to it. Don't even pretend otherwise."

The prim smile reappeared. "I don't lie," she said. "I do often select which facts I prefer to present."

"And which facts did you prefer to leave out?"

She reached over and used a hand to wipe the rain water that was now dripping from his chin and cheeks. "I hit you with this same squall on Amelynd," she said.

"Twenty-three times, in fact... torturing you with it... using it to kill every single person on that project, one-by-one... trying to get you to reverse the idiotic text you wrote."

Suddenly, Jon understood. "Because I'd prevented you from tampering with events in old ribbons, from reversing deaths... from the most powerful opportunities the ribbons offer," he said.

Her eyes narrowed. "You refused to change the text, each time... so on the twenty-third time, after all the others were dead, I hammered *you* with the squall too. Lucky for you Mr. Bonnicksen convinced me to reverse it while you still had some minute life signs, so he could carry out additional research. That's when you managed to use your ribbons to get a message to your percipient."

Jon placed a hand to his forehead, his mind reeling.

"And then you selectively wiped my memory," he guessed. "Leaving me with nightmares about a squall, and the Navy rescue, but little else. Bonnicksen played along with your version of what happened. I suppose you've used the ribbons to enhance your DOD legend too, securing your access and control."

He stared at her, appalled. "How could you *do* all of that?" he said. "Who *are* you?"

She looked at him like he was the most pathetic excuse for a human being she had ever met. "You say that as if you think this face I fashioned conceals someone you'd recognize," she said. "Well, here's the shock: I'm nobody to you. Just a woman with a God-given awareness of her back-channels, from an armpit of a town like this one."

"God-given? So, you've always known?"

She looked resentful. "Yeah, I've always known... known just enough to get my adolescent self into mess after mess, institution after institution. Spent most of my life burying the ribbons after that. Then Bonnicksen came along, and suddenly I knew he was serving up a way for me to learn, and emulate, without blazing down Chaos Road myself."

Jon found his preconceptions wavering.

"What about your name?" he said.

"I.K. Emily? Just a solemn reminder."

Jon didn't understand, so he waited for more.

"I.K., for 'I Killed,'" she said. "When you mess with ribbons uninformed, and before adulthood... bad things happen fast."

She spoke with sincere regret, and Jon believed her. The ribbon-wielders were a club of just two, and despite everything I.K. Emily was threatening to do Jon felt some degree of empathy. Though he might never know her real name, he had the sense he knew *her* nonetheless.

"Please stop using my grandmother's appearance," he said, for a second time.

A smug half-smile lifted her right cheek. "You've forgotten my fondness for psychological tactics," she said. "Today we take my island methods up a notch. One by one my squall will take someone's life, until you rescind the restrictive sentences you wrote on Amelynd. Only this time, it's the people you know best who are at risk.

I see the love of your life is in this house. We'll start there."

Fists clenched, she raised her arms skyward and the thick, luminescent clouds dropped so low they shrouded the A-frame's chimney. The squall's winds gusted as if freed from a bottle, knocking Jon off his feet. The same winds hit the house even harder; roof shingles flew up and away like leaves in a gutter, soaring into the cloud cover by the dozens. Several windows shattered. Aluminum gutters ripped free of the home, clanged against the structure, and blew away.

Tumbling across the deck, Jon's shoulder slammed into a hose spigot. He grabbed onto it, ignoring the sharp, throbbing shoulder pain. Rain fell in wind-driven sheets, the intensity stinging his skin and soaking his already drenched clothes, adding what felt like another hundred pounds of sagging, watery weight. Peering through waterlogged, wind-whipped eyes, he saw debris flying past at terrifying speeds. Boxes, soda bottles, and other ordinary trash from the street had turned deadly, bashing against the house's exterior, smash after frightening smash.

Beneath him, the deck groaned. Planter boxes ripped away from their foundations and rolled past, tumbleweed-style. Scalloped walkway stones dislodged from the yard, turned to projectiles. A wooden deck plank near Jon splintered, broke loose and flew through the air like a spear. He ducked as it sailed past his head, then saw it smack against the bay window, shattering it. Other planks were working loose as well, but what alarmed Jon most was seeing the same thing happening to the wood siding on the house itself. Several portions were already gone, exposing the A-frame's skeletal wooden structure. He watched the home bleed insulation and wiring, all of it billowing into the sky.

I.K. Emily's white squall was about to obliterate the house, the neighborhood, probably the entire community... just as it had wreaked complete destruction on Amelynd... and Jon had no way of stopping it.

FORTY-TWO

motionally crushed and physically spent, Jon used a drenched sleeve to wipe rain from his eyes. The silhouettes of the neighboring homes looked just as shredded as Remedy's; he assumed most of Quail Point was in equally bad shape.

The only thing *not* in bad shape was I.K. Emily herself. Even amid the chaos she was easy to spot, standing upright without a hint of wind about her, hair perfect and clothes dry. Her arms were still extended skyward, lightning shooting from the dark, swirling clouds above her fingertips as if she were a celluloid witch. And yet, what Jon noticed most wasn't the pose, or the ongoing damage. It was I.K. Emily looking at him, carefree, very much in the moment and apparently enjoying things... meaning she wasn't currently using the ribbons.

It's prearranged, Jon realized. She had used the ribbons to make the squall respond to her hand gestures, like a pet.

"Rewrite the restrictive sentences and you save Remedy," she said. "Refuse, and she joins the twenty-two dead from Amelynd."

He shook his head. "I can't give you that kind of power."

She opened a fist, wiggled several fingers. Massive lightning streaks branched across the clouds and then down, striking the house, igniting a massive spark shower. The storm's wind also intensified; the A-frame's entire roof lifted up and split in two. Half of it collapsed back down, the other half soared away, colliding with two other homes until it disappeared into the clouds.

Horrified, Jon studied what was left of the house, hoping for some sign that Remedy and Francis were okay, seeing none. With much of the roof now gone, the home's living room wall exploded away from the remaining structure and other walls were creaking and bending, threatening to do the same.

"They're not going to make it," I.K. Emily said, eyes fiery, her voice rich with conviction. "Not unless you change the ribbon restrictions for me."

Jon's jaw shuddered, his heart too. His resolve weakened, just as he knew it must have when he sat through the same torment on the island, watching, helpless, as she killed each of the other Upsweep participants. He wanted to save Remedy... to save Francis. He *needed* to. All he had to do was rewrite a few ribbon sentences.

But rewrite them for *her*? For someone who would then use them to assume complete control over the past and present? Someone who would turn the entire human race into her puppets, same as he had done with Sarah?

Not an option, he knew. Anguished, he turned his back to the house, and the chaos, glancing at I.K. Emily for some remote hint of compassion... finding none.

She shook her head, as if disappointed. Then her eyes eased left to right, several times. Jon knew what that meant: I.K. Emily was scanning the ribbons, on the verge of connecting with them.

She must not have prearranged the storm's final actions, Jon realized. *Which means...*

He leaped up and charged straight at her, hoping he could distract her enough to keep her from connecting, then pulled up short when something slender slammed onto her head from behind.

Francis stepped out from the darkness, ramming I.K. Emily with his cane, over and over. She cried out in pain while ducking, trying to get away, but he didn't let up. Jon raced forward to help Francis, knocking the woman down, knowing he had no other choice.

"Don't let her focus!" Francis shouted. "They need more time!"

The old man looked soggy and bedraggled, but it wasn't stopping him from continuing to jab with his cane. Jon pinned I.K. Emily's arms with his knee, wondering who the "they" was that needed time, and why.

I.K. Emily struggled, scratching and fighting with far more strength than he expected. Looking for a better containment option, Jon grabbed a fistful of mud from a cypress well and smashed it into her face, smearing it into her eyes, nose and mouth as she flailed.

"Another minute!" he heard Remedy shout from what was left of the doorway.

She's still alive, he thought, grateful. Then her point hit him. *Another whole minute?*

Jon knew that was an eternity against someone with I.K. Emily's ability. The cane and some mud weren't going to distract her for an entire minute. At some point she'd simply do what he would have done: ignore it, concentrate, and connect with the ribbons.

Francis seemed to be thinking the same thing. His jabs slowed, their force diminishing as he tired, and the squall's wind was still so strong he had to drop to his knees to remain upright. Jon slathered more mud but knew they'd need another solution, fast.

Then he had it.

"Back off!" he told Francis.

"We can't, she'll—"

Jon knew there was no time to explain. He pushed Francis back, then lifted I.K. Emily by the shoulders. Strong as she was, her decision to use Irene Kwachka's elderly appearance meant she didn't weigh very much. The heavy rain had already washed enough mud across her face to make her look like a female version of Russ Kitchtoo. Still, as she spat mud and shook debris from her hair, Jon could see a victorious glint in her eyes.

"Not enough, Onatay," she said. "Though you gave it—"

Jon lifted her and tossed, hard as he could, just before she finished both her sentence and her ribbon connection. I.K. Emily screamed as the squall's winds flipped her, rammed her against the wrought iron gate, then hoisted her aloft and sailed her up the street, out of sight.

It wouldn't be enough. Jon already knew it, because he knew it wouldn't have been enough if their positions were reversed. So long as I.K. Emily had a shred of consciousness left, she would still, eventually, be able to tap into the—

"Ribbons!" Remedy shouted.

Jon hesitated, confused... then he sensed the change. His ribbons, faded and distant, surged into clarity. *But how—?*

Arturo!

Ernie and Sarah must have found the boy! If so, then Arturo had managed to link with the ribbons and do the only thing possible without experience: write a simple sentence, in this case, a sentence re-establishing Jon's ability to connect with the ribbons.

That's why Francis and Remedy said "they" needed another minute, Jon understood. *"They" were Ernie, Sarah... and Arturo, who had needed more time to craft the sentence.*

Thrilled, he reached out with his mind. The ribbons felt warm, welcoming even. Still, as his mind neared the connection something seemed different.

I'm not alone this time, he realized. *It's...*

His chest felt like ice and his fingertips went numb.

It's I.K. Emily.

I.K. Emily, wherever she'd ended up, was making one last attempt to connect. Stunned, Jon sent his mind racing, knowing he needed to reach the ribbons first. If I.K. Emily managed to latch on before he did...

Then I've lost Remedy. Tlingit, the community... the world, all controlled by I.K. Emily. Life and existence as people understood it would come to an end.

No, it won't, he decided. *I won't let her do it.* Remembering the importance behind his decision to make the older ribbons unchangeable felt good. So did knowing that his grandmother's random, meaningless death wasn't so meaningless after all. Her death, and his attempt to reverse it, had meant everything.

Jon pushed closer to the ribbons but I.K. Emily did too, and he could sense she was just a tiny bit closer. Desperate, he made one final surge, tossing his consciousness forward, hoping it might snare at least a piece of a ribbon... and the words describing their lives *came together as one.*

Minds collided. Jon and I.K. Emily froze, horrified and uncertain, still unwilling to make the adjustment from a separate existence into a shared consciousness. Jon felt his mind swing wide open, exposing private dreams, muted thoughts, deep-seated horrors, and every remote essence of his individuality. The intimacy was frightening, their thoughts twisting like enraged DNA strands, their inner demons grappling to a draw.

Amid the chaos, Jon saw chilling flickers from I.K. Emily's consciousness: a ribbon-choked young woman, institutionalized; "eyes-only" research; blackened video screens; revelations trickling from pre-Upsweep disasters; dampened aging. Horrors and miracles, conjoined.

Their concurrent thoughts beckoned insanity as they struggled to merge voices. Cogent ideas became abrasive ripples, scraping Jon's neurons like cerebral sandpaper, each thought aggressively rushing for the forefront while a dozen others scrambled to stifle the charge.

She wants me out, I want her out, he knew. There's no resolution.

Then, suddenly, there was.

They sensed a third party; moments, later, a fourth one as well. The mental struggle intensified but whoever the newcomers were, they weren't looking for control.

They're pushing with me, Jon realized. Three minds pushing one, shoving it hard, forcing I.K. Emily away. She was strong, relentless even, but the others didn't give way. Determined, they gave one final, powerful heave.

I.K. Emily's mind dislodged from the ribbons, hurtling away.

The rest of them heard a voiceless scream, and felt anger burning their minds like chemicals set aflame. Equilibrium shifted and colors, both sedate and jarring, flashed nonstop. Before long an image formed, of Irene Kwachka's visage breaking off, disintegrating as if it had fallen away from the person beneath.

She was weathered. Her eyes were narrow, her nose was small. Her jaw was set, her hair unwashed. She was beautiful, she was ghastly, she was brilliant, she was a simpleton. Familiar, a little bit, but generally a stranger. More than anything, I.K. Emily was right: she was no one.

Except, Jon thought, she's also everyone.

Mental tendrils reached in their direction as I.K. Emily attempted another desperate grab at the ribbons, but no one was about to let that happen. For several moments her consciousness persisted, ghostlike threats echoing throughout the ribbonscape. Then all went quiet.

Jon's ribbons, and perhaps his life, were finally at peace.

FORTY-THREE

No time to waste, Jon decided. He made things permanent: I.K. Emily, if she survived, would have no access to the ribbons whatsoever.

He felt the other two minds recede; they weren't interested in staying. Jon probed their shared consciousness, then stopped, startled. It was Arturo and Sarah. Both had been reluctant, even terrified, but both had recognized the stakes. Shared consciousness let Jon convey his appreciation, and his certainty that he would spend the rest of his life feeling terrible for having violated their private thoughts.

They winked away, returned to conventional consciousness. *Just me and the ribbons now*, Jon thought... *and I'm nearly ready to leave too. Only a few more sentences needed:*

With I.K. Emily gone, her squall weakened and then disintegrated altogether. Despite the high winds and flooding, most of the damage to Quail Point was light and would be fully repaired in a matter of days. The canyon rockslide, the external communications blackout, and any alterations I.K. Emily hadn't already corrected were also restored to their pre-tampered conditions, with one exception: Jon extinguished the wildfire, restored the scorched lands, and cleared the smoke from the air. Maybe it was unnatural, but he wasn't about to let Russ Kitchtoo's arson run its destructive course.

He also wasn't about to mess with people's memories of the events. There was no need; Remedy's detailed news reports made certain everyone understood the science, linguistics, and human nature that was responsible for everything they had experienced. Over time, their fears would recede.

And one more thing, Jon decided.

Grinning, he unhooked sentence structures, shuffled them, then watched them reform into new sentences... Tlingit sentences, many of them unspoken for generations... right before his eyes. His mind tingled as vocabulary, perspective, and meanings sprinkled inside his head, enhancing him, augmenting the person he was just a few seconds earlier. His satisfaction only increased as he offered the same opportunity—as a choice, not a mandate—to Remedy, Francis, Razor... to the Sirretta Valley community... to the country... to the world... and nearly one of every seventy people accepted.

He broke into tears, overwhelmed by what he was seeing: the Tlingit language, resurrected. If the global community needed another common, international language, they now had one... just not one they'd expected.

Jon knew he could do more, and maybe one day, after much discussion and permission from the community, he would. But not today.

Today he had something else in mind.

Remedy... barely. Maybe.

Jon, confused, heard himself think the three words. Had anyone else heard? Was anyone else there? How much time had passed? Was he alive?

He felt shrunken, yet fulfilled. Random thoughts swirled through his head: finding the lumberjack weathervane, patching matters with Ernie, turning himself in to Sharp... finding a new career now that his old one was obsolete.

He didn't want to open his eyes. Opened eyes meant reality, which meant he might lose The Race, lose Remedy, lose everything. Then again... he might tilt a windmill or two along the way.

He lifted his eyelids, slow and deliberate, squinting from ambient light. The morning after, he guessed. Remedy, Francis, Razor... they were all with him amid the wreckage of Rem's home, staring at him like he might explode. The thought of letting out a loud sound in that tense moment, and the startled, irritated reactions it would elicit, made him burst into laughter.

"Jon...?" Remedy said, mimicking him with a cautious laugh of her own.

"Yeah... yeah, I'm okay. I mean... wait, am I okay?" He looked at his arms, his legs, his body. Everything seemed in one piece. He laughed again, a nervous laugh this time, at the irony of seeing so many streaming words yet finding himself speechless.

"You outta my head, that's okay enough for me," Razor said.

The pitcher headed for the mangled front gate, kicked it open, then stopped. "Not that I'm demandin' it, cause I ain't," he said, "but you ever feel like using those ribbons of yours to throw some riches my lady's way, she wouldn't turn it down."

"And by your lady, you mean..."

"You know who I mean," the pitcher said.

Jon smiled. "Deal. And thanks."

Razor winked, lowered his sunglasses, and left. Francis patted Jon's shoulder.

"This worldwide immersion of yours just put the two of us out of work," the Tlingit elder said with a satisfied smile. "What now?"

Jon sat up, energized. "Now," he said, "you go out and live, and experience, and be yourself, without me or anyone else in your head." He grabbed Remedy's hand, looked her in the eyes. "And maybe we make up for some past mistakes."

She rolled her eyes, but she was grinning as she did so. Jon smiled too, something he hadn't done much over the past few days, months, years.

His head swirled; wispy words scrolled. Still a mess, he knew. Maybe that was his cross. Maybe his head would always be a sentence-strewn mess. Seeing himself with Remedy, having survived everything he had just experienced and learned, he found himself questioning whether it was all truly real.

He stopped himself right there. There was no doubt it was real.

He had it all in writing.

ACKNOWLEDGMENTS

Good stories need good editors, and I'm thrilled to say *Mother Tongue* gave me an opportunity to work with one of the best. Many thanks to Betsy Mitchell for her superb insights... and for helping me tame the very daunting *Ku'cta-qa*.

Thanks also to David Bjerklie for steering me through several literary gantlets with his outstanding developmental edits, and to David Gatewood for helping me clarify some warped timeframes.

This book was inspired by remote perception studies from the Princeton Engineering Anomalies Research laboratory. Though I have certainly taken liberties in the narrative, remote perception and remote manipulation appear within the realm of human capability, and PEAR explored this topic in extensive, lively detail.

Thanks as well to the Southern California chapter of the National Multiple Sclerosis Society for their statistical insights... but moreover to my mom, Joanne Cray, truly the "remedy" for such a debilitating disease. May we all handle hardship with the cheer, grace, and determination she displayed during the thirty years she grappled with MS.

Also, my gratitude to Mary and John Nakaji, my "second parents," who met during the Manzanar atrocity. The horrific internment camp cost them nearly everything, but not the most important thing: each other.

I have a wonderful editor in my own home: Jane Augustine, who is also First Reader, document formatter, and tech support pro, but above all is my cherished wife. To her, and to our son Evan, my eternal love and appreciation.

Finally, my sincere gratitude to the residents of Klawock, Alaska, especially the Tlingit community there, whose warm hospitality and earnest resolve cannot be forgotten. This took me far too long, but I do hope I captured you well. Your language preservation effort and my time with your elders, however brief, lives on in my heart much as many of your culture's words and stories live on in yours. Oh, and you were right: totems certainly trigger the imagination.

AUTHOR'S NOTE

With sincere respect for concerns about cultural and gender appropriation, please note that I am not one of the deserving yet historically under-represented voices found in this book... or in novels as a whole.

Such voices are welcome and overdue, but not a known part of my ancestry. Family legend and a bit of genealogy tells me I'm an Irish-English-Slavic mutt, though I tend to think of myself as, well, *human*, no further qualifiers necessary.

That said, I love imaginative tales informed by empathy, creativity, research, and a heavy dash of passion for plot and characters. My guess (hope?) is that you do as well. If so, I'm looking forward to us continuing to read, write, and celebrate mind-bending stories as people of all backgrounds, together.

ABOUT THE AUTHOR

Dan Cray is the author of *The Reality Meltdown*, *Mother Tongue*, and *Piercing Maybe*, which was named to *Kirkus Reviews'* Best Books of 2018. In nonfiction, he wrote *Soaring Stones* for National Geographic Books and worked as a freelance journalist for twenty-seven years, reporting sixty *Time* magazine cover stories and sharing a National Headliner Award. He holds a UCLA English degree and lives in Los Angeles with his wife and son.

Visit him at www.dancraybooks.com

WHAT IF OBJECTS ARE MORE THAN THEY SEEM?

"Vividly imagined... an engrossing tale centered on no less a theme than humanity's place in the totality of existence, couched in a rollicking supernatural horror story."
–Kirkus Reviews